all you desire

CAN YOU TRUST YOUR HEART?

all you desire

CAN YOU TRUST YOUR HEART?

KIRSTEN MILLER

razor
bill

An Imprint of Penguin Group (USA) Inc.

All You Desire

RAZORBILL

Published by the Penguin Group
Penguin Young Readers Group
345 Hudson Street, New York, New York 10014, U.S.A.
Penguin Group (USA) Inc., 375 Hudson Street,
New York, New York 10014, U.S.A.
Penguin Group (Canada), 90 Eglinton Avenue East,
Suite 700, Toronto, Ontario, Canada M4P 2Y3
(a division of Pearson Penguin Canada Inc.)
Penguin Books Ltd, 80 Strand, London WC2R 0RL,
England
Penguin Ireland, 25 St Stephen's Green, Dublin 2,
Ireland (a division of Penguin Books Ltd)
Penguin Group (Australia), 250 Camberwell Road,
Camberwell, Victoria 3124, Australia (a division of
Pearson Australia Group Pty Ltd)
Penguin Books India Pvt Ltd, 11 Community Centre,
Panchsheel Park, New Delhi – 110 017, India
Penguin Group (NZ), 67 Apollo Drive, Mairangi Bay,
Auckland 1311, New Zealand (a division of Pearson
New Zealand Ltd)
Penguin Books (South Africa) (Pty) Ltd, 24 Sturdee
Avenue, Rosebank, Johannesburg 2196, South Africa

Penguin Books Ltd, Registered Offices: 80 Strand,
London WC2R 0RL, England

10 9 8 7 6 5 4 3 2 1

ISBN 978-1-59514-323-5

Library of Congress Cataloging-in-Publication Data
is available

Printed in the United States of America

Haven Moore checked her watch and turned back toward the city. There was plenty of time to get home before dark, yet she decided to pick up her pace. She didn't want to find herself alone with the dead when the sun finally slid behind the trees.

Haven hadn't expected to find the Appia Antica so deserted. Otherwise she might have chosen another spot for a stroll. In the summertime, the famous road on the outskirts of Rome was bustling with people visiting the ancient tombs that lined the route. But it was a cold February afternoon, and Haven had encountered only a few hardy travelers in fleece jackets and hiking boots. For three full hours she had been alone with her thoughts. That wasn't at all what she'd wanted. These days they were dangerous company to keep.

The wind picked up speed, raising Haven's black curls and setting them adrift. She captured the strands that had fallen in front of her blue-gray eyes and tucked them behind her ear. Ahead, at the crest of a hill, a familiar mausoleum stood by the side of the road.

Tall and perfectly round, it resembled a turret sticking out of the hillside. Haven liked to imagine that there might be an entire castle buried beneath it. As always, she paused and peered up at the grisly garland of carved bull skulls that decorated the structure. Below, a simple plaque identified the building as the resting place of Caecilia Metella. Caecilia's tomb was the most famous on the Appian Way, yet little was known about the woman it housed. She must have been adored to have had such a monument built in her honor. Perhaps she'd been beautiful, brilliant, or wise. Whatever her story, it was long forgotten. Two thousand years after her death, Caecilia Metella was just another soul lost in time.

Suddenly chilled, Haven zipped up her jacket and put the tomb behind her. A pristine white taxi appeared on the horizon, like the ghost of a New York City yellow cab. When it pulled over, two girls emerged from the backseat and dragged a third out behind them. As the group made their way toward the tomb, Haven could see they were sixteen or seventeen—only a couple of years younger than she. They all wore jeans and matching blue sweatshirts with the letters *HH* stitched in white. *American high school students,* Haven thought. Overprivileged delinquents sent to Rome to soak up some culture. She'd seen others like them in the piazza below her apartment, guzzling cheap wine before making fools of themselves in the fountains. At times she envied them. She knew she'd grown up a little too quickly.

Deep in conversation, the trio barely registered Haven's presence as they passed her. They weren't the carefree youths she'd imagined. The girl in the middle looked pale and miserable. She walked with her eyes on her feet, relying on her companions to guide her safely down the road.

"You shouldn't have tricked me like this," she whimpered.

"You'll thank us later," Haven heard one of the friends respond. "I still don't understand how you could visit Rome three times and never bother to see your own tomb."

Haven stopped in the street.

"I told you. I didn't know it was here," the girl in the middle replied hoarsely. "And I wouldn't have come if I had."

"But you found out about the tomb *months* ago. Why didn't you hunt down some pictures online? Weren't you curious?"

This time the girl said nothing. Haven glanced back to see her shaking her head.

"Well, you're here in person now. Look up."

The three girls came to a halt.

"Look up, Caroline!"

It took a moment before Caroline finally lifted her head. Haven couldn't see the girl's face, but she could hear her sobbing.

"Please don't cry," pleaded one of the friends. She sounded surprised by the depth of Caroline's sorrow. "Your husband must have loved you very much if he built this for you. They say it's one of the most beautiful tombs in Rome."

"You just don't get it. If he loved me, he would have found me again," Caroline tried to explain. "I've searched for him everywhere. I'm sure he's come back. He just hasn't been looking for *me*."

Haven was on the verge of approaching the girls when the third spoke. Her voice remained chipper. She didn't seem to understand what had transpired.

"Come on, Caroline. Don't you see how silly you're being? And to think you'd never have come here if Adam hadn't suggested it."

The name stole Haven's breath. Her heart pounding and face burning, she turned and stumbled back toward Rome.

CHAPTER ONE

"The train to Florence leaves in an hour." Iain was watching her from the doorway with a puzzled look on his face. "Don't you think it might be a good time to start packing?" His bags were already waiting in the foyer.

"Why would I want to bring any clothes?" Haven tried to joke. She took a slow sip of coffee and gazed down from the balcony at the Piazza Navona below. The water in the plaza's three fountains glistened in the morning light, and the outdoor cafés were starting to fill up. Once Haven had enjoyed watching the tourists ramble through the square with their maps, cameras, and unruly children. These days it often felt as if she were standing guard, keeping watch for anyone who might threaten her happiness. "I thought this was going to be a *vacation*."

"With that attitude, you'll probably be quite popular at the hotel." Iain gave her a wink. "Now stop dawdling or we're going to be late."

"What if I don't want to go anymore?" Haven tried her best to sound lighthearted, but she couldn't keep the quiver out of her voice. Iain caught her as she stepped into the living room from the balcony. When he pulled her into his arms, she could hear his heart beating, slow and steady.

"We're going to have fun," he promised, his face buried in her wild black hair. "You'll remember this trip for the rest of our lives."

HAVEN RELUCTANTLY TURNED toward the hall closet and opened its door for the first time in months. Jammed inside were all the dresses she had designed that weren't quite right. Fabric that had faded or frayed. And the suitcases she'd brought with her when she and Iain had moved to Rome, each one sprinkled with a fine layer of dust. Haven kept her hands by her side, worried that touching the cases might break the spell. The months she'd spent in Rome had been magical— that was the only word she could find to describe them. Formerly the pariah of Snope City, Tennessee, Haven finally had the life she'd craved. Barely nineteen years old, she spent her days running a successful boutique on the Via dei Condotti and returned to a sun-swept apartment that overlooked one of the loveliest piazzas in the city.

Every evening for almost a year, Haven had arrived home to an empty house. No matter what the weather was like outside, she always opened the doors to the balcony and waited for the most wonderful sound in the world. Soon, her ears would catch a note of the song that Iain whistled whenever he crossed the square. An ancient tune with no name, it was his way of telling her they would soon be together.

Minutes later, Iain would burst through the door, his arms filled with food gathered from Rome's many markets. Sometimes, he let it all fall to the floor when he discovered Haven waiting to greet him. The eggs would break, and dinner didn't make it to the table before nine. Late at night, when their hunger was finally sated, they would leave the apartment and wander hand in hand through the empty streets while Iain whispered stories of their many lives together.

*　　*　　*

HAVEN HAD LET herself hope that it would all last forever. But now she and Iain were leaving Rome, and it felt as if their golden year might be reaching its end. For more than a week, Haven had sensed something was wrong. It had started with a quick glimpse of a figure dressed in black crossing the piazza below her balcony. She hadn't gotten a good look at the man. It could have been anyone. And that was what worried her most. After that, the city seemed to be hiding secrets from her. The days grew darker, and the weather turned colder. Haven always suspected someone was watching, and every time she turned a corner, she held her breath, expecting to find the dark figure waiting for her around the bend.

At first she'd kept her suspicions to herself. But after the encounter with the three girls on the Appia Antica, Haven knew she and Iain needed to act quickly. The danger was real, not imagined. If they stayed in Rome, they risked being discovered. Iain thought she was being too cautious, but he happily suggested a trip north to Tuscany. There was something in Florence, he'd said, that Haven might like to see.

HAVEN GRABBED ONE of her dusty suitcases by the handle and lugged it out into the hall. Inside the closet, a bag of fabric scraps teetered and tumbled to the floor. Haven groaned as she stooped to gather the pieces one by one. Then her fingers brushed against a canvas at the back of the closet. She'd almost forgotten it was there. The painting had been a housewarming present from one of the few people outside her family who knew where to find them. Haven pushed a heavy coat to one side and peered between her cluttered heaps of belongings. Up close, the artwork was a swirl of color. Only when she took a step back did forms begin to emerge from the chaos.

The painting was part of a much larger series. A few others like it could be found hanging on the third floor of a run-down house not far from the Brooklyn Bridge. The remaining works—several hundred of them—were slowly rotting away in a warehouse in Queens. Not even the most morbid art collector would have chosen to display them. Each showed some tragic scene from the past—and together they formed a catalog of disasters large and small. Shipwrecks and fires, betrayals and heartbreaks, all set in motion by the same mysterious figure who could be found lurking somewhere in each image. But only if you knew where to look for him.

The day the painting had been delivered to the apartment, Haven had ripped away its wrapping, eager to see what lay beneath. The artist, Marta Vega, was an old friend of Iain's. For years Marta's work had been inspired by terrible visions of the past. The visions had stopped once she'd escaped New York and settled in Paris. There she'd started a series of paintings that reflected her newfound hopes for the future. Haven had been expecting to find such a work beneath the brown paper. Instead, she found a sinister image with a bright yellow Post-it attached.

This was the last one I painted, the note read. *I know it was meant for you.* After a single glance, Iain had whisked the painting away and stashed it behind the coats and dresses inside the hall closet. Later Haven had overheard him on the phone with Marta, his voice an angry whisper. He told the girl she should never have sent him the painting. It was the last thing Haven needed to see, and he hoped she hadn't had a good look. The time would come for them to face their demons. For now, he didn't want Haven to worry.

But Haven had seen the image, and it had left an indelible impression. For days afterward, she thought of little else. The painting showed two people—a young man and woman—surrounded by an angry mob. The faces weren't clear. But Haven recognized the girl's unruly thatch of black hair as her own. And she knew it was the only painting Marta Vega had ever created that showed not the past but the future.

Now Haven studied the painting for the first time since its arrival, looking for the minuscule figure in black that Marta inserted into each of her works. This time, he was nowhere to be found. And yet his absence wasn't a comfort. It felt as though he had stepped off the canvas and into Haven's life again. He was out there somewhere. If not in Rome, then not far away. The man in the picture—the figure in black—had been following Haven for centuries.

"Haven," she heard Iain call, a trace of alarm in his voice. "What did you find in there?"

Haven crammed the painting back into the closet. "I'll be ready to go in ten minutes," she answered, ignoring the question. "Ask the driver to get here as soon as he can."

CHAPTER TWO

Haven had seen it all before. Strolling along the banks of the Arno River, she was overwhelmed by the sensation that she had walked the same path countless times in the past. Most people would have glibly dismissed it as déjà vu. But Haven knew better. If she had the feeling she'd seen Florence before, then it was fairly certain she had. Just not in *this* lifetime.

Haven's gloved hand squeezed Iain's arm. "I know this place." Ahead of them, a bridge spanned the narrowest part of the river. It was flanked on both sides by rickety buildings—orange houses and saffron-colored dwellings that jutted out over the Arno. In the icy gray waters below, two fat muskrats paddled around a pier. "I saw that bridge get swept away by the river. I must have been very young when it happened, but I remember it clearly. And then I watched them build it all over again."

Iain's frozen breath hung in the air when he laughed. "I was wondering when you might say something." His memories of the past

9

were much better than Haven's—his memories were better than *everyone's*. "It's called the Ponte Vecchio. It was destroyed by a flood in 1333. They rebuilt it in 1345."

"Were we here then?" Haven asked. "In 1345?"

"*You* were here in 1345," Iain replied. "I died the year before, when I was sixteen years old."

Haven still winced whenever Iain mentioned one of his deaths, even if it had occurred hundreds of years in the past. It didn't matter how many previous existences they'd shared. Every life that had been cut short reminded her how fragile their current lives could be. "You died at sixteen?"

"I fell off my horse on the road to Rome. Broke my neck. But a lot of people would say I was lucky. Half of Florence died three years later—of something much worse than a broken neck."

"What's worse than a broken neck?"

"The black death." Iain took Haven's hand in his and pulled her away from the river and between the tall gray columns of the Uffizi Gallery. The winter sun was losing its strength, and the courtyard of the museum felt frigid. Patches of black ice expanded and multiplied in the shadows. A group of Spanish tourists shivered inside their goose-down parkas. The women among them gaped at Iain as if one of the museum's statues had suddenly sprung to life. A few pointed and whispered. Iain didn't notice—he rarely did—but Haven smiled and pulled the handsome boy even closer.

When the couple emerged in the Piazza della Signoria, Haven's feet froze. The square was empty but for a man dressed in a black robe so long that it swept the street behind him. Beneath a wide-brimmed leather hat, he wore a hideous mask with a long white beak. Spectacles with red-tinted lenses shielded his eyes. He might have been a monster from the depths of hell. But Haven recognized his costume as the protective suit of a medieval plague doctor. She watched as the man stood over a motionless body that lay on the paving stones and poked at it with his cane. Then the doctor glanced up at Haven. His face was hidden, but she could sense his disapproval. She, of all people, didn't belong in the plaza. Haven blinked and the whole scene disappeared.

"Come on. I have something to show you before it gets dark," Iain urged, and Haven realized he'd seen nothing unusual.

EIGHTEEN MONTHS HAD passed since Haven had learned the truth about the strange visions that came to her. They weren't hallucinations or fantasies. She now knew they were memories—scenes she'd witnessed in previous lives. The doctor in the terrible mask didn't belong in the twenty-first century, but he had once been as real as the boy who was holding her hand.

The visions had started when she was just a small child. For years, Haven would faint and find herself inside another life—that of a beautiful young woman named Constance who had perished in a fire. Haven's uncontrollable "fits" frightened most people who witnessed them. They insisted the girl must have been sick or disturbed. Only Haven's father suspected that his daughter was visiting the past each time she fainted. When he died unexpectedly, he took that secret to his grave, where it had remained for almost a decade.

Shortly after Haven turned seventeen, the visions returned, and it was then that their true meaning was finally revealed to her. The glimpses of the beautiful young woman were memories of one of the many lives that Haven had led. Driven by the need to know more about Constance's untimely death, Haven had fled her hometown in Tennessee and made her way to New York. There she discovered her murderer, her soul mate, and the dark figure who'd been chasing her across oceans and continents for more than two thousand years.

Still, the visions hadn't stopped once the mystery of Constance's death had been solved. Haven seldom fainted now, but at night she journeyed to distant times and exotic lands. In the darkness, her dreams were vivid, but they always faded at dawn. Most days, while the sun was shining, Haven remained free from her visions of previous lives. But the whiff of a familiar fragrance, the sound of a long-forgotten name, the sensation of Iain's breath on her skin could blend Haven's pasts and her present together. She would find herself giddy with love for a boy who had shared Iain's lopsided grin. Or overwhelmed by a potent mixture of old fears and desires that she still couldn't comprehend.

"DOES THAT PALAZZO REMIND you of anything?" Iain released Haven's hand and pointed at a mansion at the end of a cramped little square. Haven looked up at his face before she followed his finger. She still felt a rush of excitement whenever she locked eyes with him. Even with his wavy brown hair tucked under a knit cap—and his nose red from the bitter cold—he barely passed for a mortal. For a moment she couldn't have cared less about her former life in Florence. If she hadn't been able to share it with Iain, it must not have been worth living.

Haven reluctantly turned toward the building in question. It looked more like a fortress than a palace. The bottom floor had been constructed with huge square blocks, and enormous metal doors were set in three separate arches. Each door was high enough for a giant to enter, and all three were tightly sealed. But Haven knew that beyond them lay a courtyard. And she knew the stairs that led to the living quarters on the second and third floors could be withdrawn if the house were ever attacked. The world had been a dangerous place when the building was erected, and the wealthy had been determined to defend their fortunes.

Haven's eyes fluttered. She felt her legs pumping, fighting against heavy skirts that encased them. All around her, the walls were painted in dazzling colors, reds and golds. The wooden floorboards protested as she ran to the open window. She wasn't quite tall enough to see out of it, so she hoisted herself up on the sill and surveyed the square below, her little body dangling dangerously over the edge.

A teenage boy was sprinting away from the palazzo. His blue tunic and red stockings looked two sizes too large for him. "Run! Run!" she shouted at the kid, laughing so hard there were tears in her eyes. "Don't let them catch you!" The words sounded foreign to Haven's ears, though she had no trouble understanding their meaning.

"Beatrice!" A woman's sharp voice came from behind her. "Get down from that window. What has your brother done now?"

"I LIVED HERE," Haven mumbled as the twenty-first century took shape once again. "My name was Beatrice, and I had a brother."

"So you saw him?" Iain asked with his crooked grin. "Was it anyone you recognized?"

"Recognized? I didn't really get a good look at the kid. I only saw him running away." Haven stopped. "Wait, are you saying . . ."

Iain crossed his arms like a pompous professor and began to deliver a lecture fit for a history class. "The palazzo before you was purchased in 1329 by Gherardo Vettori, a wealthy wine merchant. Observe the Vettori family coat of arms above the door. It features three rather sinister dolphins carrying bunches of grapes in their mouths. . . ."

"Drop the act, and stop teasing me!" Haven demanded, knowing that if she let herself laugh, it would only encourage him. "Are you telling me that my brother in that lifetime was . . ." She couldn't quite say it.

"Despite a raging libido and a roving eye, Gherardo Vettori only managed to sire two children. You were one of them. Your friend Beau was the other. His name back then was Piero Vettori, and he was a world-class delinquent."

For a moment Haven found herself at a loss for words. She'd known for some time that Beau Decker, her best friend from Tennessee, had been her brother in a previous existence. But she had never expected to find herself gazing up at the house where they had fought and played and consoled one another seven hundred years earlier.

"I've been meaning to bring you here since we came to Italy," Iain explained. "I've been saving it as a surprise."

"You knew Beatrice's brother too?!"

"I was friends with Piero before I died. And I was madly in love with his little sister. He wasn't terribly happy about that."

Haven recalled the boy in the oversize tunic and the love his young sister had felt for him. Beatrice Vettori had worshipped Piero. He couldn't have been more than thirteen at the time of Haven's vision, but his sister would have told anyone who would listen that he was fearless and brilliant. She knew other things about her brother as well, secrets only the two of them shared.

"I wish I had seen more," Haven said sadly. "I wish I had seen you, too. I hate that my visions are always so random."

"Maybe someday you'll see everything," Iain consoled her. "And then you'll be the one telling *me* stories."

"Maybe," Haven said, though she held no hope of that ever happening. She had managed to recall a few fragments of the many lives she'd led, but most of her memories were still lost in time. She might have tried harder to conjure them, but she suspected there were things she wouldn't want to remember. Iain's memories, on the other hand, were perfectly preserved. Of all the people who had returned to earth time and time again, Iain was the only one who could recall each of his incarnations. It was a skill that made him dangerous to all the wrong people—most notably the man in black.

"I should take a picture of the palazzo for Beau," Haven said.

"In a minute. There's something I need to get out of the way first. When you told me you wanted to take a trip, this is why I suggested Florence. Now I can do what I didn't have the chance to do before I fell off that damn horse."

"What?" Haven asked.

Iain removed his gloves and stuffed them in the pocket of his coat. Then he gently took Haven's face in his hands. Her eyes closed, and she could feel his warm breath on her skin. With his lips on hers, time came to a halt. She let her hand slip between the buttons of his coat until her fingers rested against his chest. It was something she did from time to time—just to prove to herself that he was real.

She had no idea how long they stood there, locked in an embrace that had waited seven hundred years to happen. But when Haven opened her eyes again, Florence was already dark.

CHAPTER THREE

Haven and Iain were greeted at the door of the restaurant by a pretty young hostess in a dress that must have inspired more drooling than the food being served. Haven took note of the woman's surgically sculpted chest and leonine hair extensions and grinned. She knew exactly what was about to transpire. Just as she'd anticipated, the hostess ignored Haven and beamed at her handsome companion instead. Haven had watched countless females offer Iain the same smile, and it almost never meant "hello."

"Good evening, *signore*," the hostess flirted in beautifully accented English. "Do you have a reservation?"

Iain shot a quick wink at Haven before he flashed the hostess a rakish grin. "*Buona sera, signorina.* Do I need one?"

The young woman's seductive smile turned scandalous. "Not tonight," she whispered, as if they were sharing a secret.

The exchange was deliciously corny. Haven gritted her teeth and tried not to giggle. The Colosseum itself couldn't have held all the bodies that were thrown at Iain every week. Whenever Haven left him alone in a store, she'd return to find him surrounded by salesgirls, all as hot and bothered as goats in a pepper patch. A policewoman had once slipped Iain her phone number while she wrote Haven a parking ticket. Waitresses plied him with free drinks and desserts. Haven teased Iain about his "fans," and a year earlier she might have bristled at the hostess's boldness. But now that she knew what Iain had gone through to find her, jealousy seemed completely absurd. There was no harm in letting silly girls flirt with someone whose heart belonged only to her.

"May I take your coats?" the hostess asked, her eyes practically fondling Iain.

"Yes, you may," Haven replied with a smile, stepping between the two and finally drawing some attention of her own.

As she peeled off her gloves and removed her hat, Haven sensed she was being appraised like a sculpture at an auction house. Fortunately, the dress she wore underneath her coat was one of her own designs. Made of red silk and lacking all frills, it was cut so perfectly that Haven's every flaw was hidden and every asset enhanced. Two men near the entrance turned to gawk when she and Iain were escorted to their seats. The restaurant's tables were crowded together, and as Haven squeezed by, a hundred eyes traveled from her dress to her face to her wild black hair before returning to the plates on the tables in front of them. One man's gaze remained locked on Haven's chest until he received a subtle but unpleasant jab from Iain's elbow as the couple passed by him.

It was hardly the first time that all eyes had been on Haven. Growing up in tiny Snope City, Tennessee, she'd always been keenly aware that the whole town was watching. But people had been scared of her then. A little girl with mysterious visions of other places simply couldn't be trusted—particularly when the girl's own grandmother claimed the visions had been sent by the devil himself. Now Snope City was five thousand miles and a whole year behind her. Haven was a different person, and for the first time in her life she was starting to enjoy attention whenever she received it. She liked the way people looked at her, with a mixture of admiration and envy. She welcomed their gazes and enjoyed dressing to draw them. Even though she and Iain were supposed to be hiding.

"Sorry the restaurant is so packed," Iain whispered once they were seated. "My mother always said that the food here is much better than the atmosphere."

"Aside from all your fans, the atmosphere isn't that bad," Haven said, breaking away from a staring contest with a love-struck girl on the other side of the room. "But I doubt there's a chef in Italy who can cook anything as good as one of your omelets. Now, Mr. Morrow, no more small talk. It's time to get down to business. You've made me suffer for three whole hours. Tell me more about Piero and Beatrice. How did you meet them? What were they like?"

"Wild. I met Piero on my fifteenth birthday. He tried to bash my brains in with a rock."

"Charming," Haven laughed. She loved Beau, but everyone knew he wasn't exactly a pacifist.

"Yeah. Piero was a good guy, but he had the world's worst temper. He accused me of stealing his horse. He'd left it untethered, and I happened to walk by just after it wandered off after a vegetable cart. We were pounding the pulp out of each other when the horse came back to search for its owner. Piero apologized, so we called a truce and decided to join forces. A few days later he invited me to his house, where I happened to spot his little sister slaving away on a gown for their mother. If I recall correctly, she was being punished for sneaking out of the house the previous night. Beatrice was always in trouble, just like Piero. They egged each other on. And, as you know by now, some things never change."

"So when you found Beatrice, was it love at first sight?"

Haven had been trying to tease him, but Iain's answer was serious.

"It always is. I didn't even have to speak to her. I knew it was you the second I saw Beatrice with a needle in her hand. I spent the next few weeks loitering outside the Vettori house, trying to catch glimpses of her. It nearly drove Piero insane. He was always annoyingly overprotective."

"What was your name in those days?" Haven asked.

"Ettore," Iain said.

"Ettore," Haven repeated, enjoying the way the name made her heart skip a beat. Haven loved nothing better than to listen to tales of her own romances. Every story was different and every setting unique. Just when she thought she'd heard them all, Iain would lead her into another existence in some faraway land. But exploring their pasts was not without peril. As many times as they'd found happiness together, there were just as many lives that had ended too quickly or were spent searching for each other in vain. Haven couldn't remember those dark days, and Iain rarely spoke of them, but she knew the memories remained fresh in his mind.

"Did you ever have a chance to talk to Beatrice?" Haven asked more cautiously. "Did you tell her how you felt?"

"Yes, but it wasn't easy. Beatrice's parents were not pleasant people. They made her life miserable—and they were incredibly cruel to Piero. You would have been beaten if they'd seen us together, so we used to whisper though the hedges in the courtyard. Beatrice was terrified that her father would force her to marry one of his business associates. I promised her I'd never let that happen. But as you know, I didn't live long enough to keep my promise."

"So what *did* happen to Beatrice?"

"I'm not sure," Iain admitted.

Haven leaned back in her chair as the waiter approached. Iain examined the menu and ordered for the two of them in fluent Italian. A question waited, poised on the tip of Haven's tongue.

"You're not sure?" she asked as soon as the waiter was gone. It wasn't the first time Haven had wondered if Iain might be protecting her from an unpleasant truth.

"I guess Beatrice must have died of the plague," Iain replied. "Most people in Florence did. All I know is that the Vettori family abandoned the house we saw today. From what I've read it was taken over by a bunch of rogue doctors who gave up trying to heal everyone and decided to save themselves. They hid out in the palazzo and drank all the Vettoris' wine and ate all their food and then proceeded to drop dead of the plague. One of the doctors kept a journal until the day he died, but even he didn't seem to know what happened to the Vettoris after they fled Florence. Chances are, the whole family's in one of the mass graves outside of the city."

"That's a terrible story," Haven said, suddenly sorry she'd asked.

"True," Iain acknowledged. "But don't dwell on it. We've had our share of happy endings as well. In our next lives we were peasants in Kathmandu. We got married when we were seventeen, and we lived together for more than forty years."

"Did we have any kids?" Haven asked a little too loudly, and a man at the next table shot her a puzzled look. "Did we?" she repeated in a whisper.

"No, but we had three lovely yaks," Iain said, as two glasses of water were set in front of them. "And thirty-six nieces and nephews."

"Thirty-six?" Haven's head ached just thinking of it. "Was it just our families or did everyone hump like bunnies back then?"

Iain choked on his water, barely avoiding a spit take. "Such a *sweet* little Southern belle," he laughed from behind his napkin. "There wasn't much else to do in fourteenth-century Nepal. It could get a little dull at times, but I've always considered it one of our best lives together. I still wake up some mornings craving yak-butter tea." He seemed to savor the grimace on Haven's face. "You used to love it too," he insisted. "I'll take you back to Nepal someday so you can acquire the taste again."

"As long as I don't have to milk any yaks," Haven quipped. "I wouldn't say I'm a princess, but I can't see myself getting too friendly with livestock."

"Is that right?" Iain teased. "I think you might be surprised to find out what you're capable of doing."

"Okay then, surprise me," Haven challenged.

"Let me think for a second. . . ." Iain tapped his temple and arched an eyebrow. "I'll come up with something suitably shocking."

As she waited, Haven's attention was drawn to a woman who had risen from her seat at the back of the restaurant. She was making her way toward the exit, draped in a fur that she hadn't deigned to leave at the coat check. Haven couldn't figure out which unfortunate animal had given its life for the sake of fashion. The pelt was as exotic as the woman herself, who didn't appear to be entirely human. As the lady passed by, the empty sleeve of her fur brushed against their table, and Haven grabbed her glass to keep it from toppling. Startled by Haven's sudden movement, the woman clutched her fur to her chest before it could be sullied by a stranger's touch. A single platinum ring adorned one of her hand's elegant fingers. It was in the shape of a serpent swallowing its own tail. An ouroboros.

"Haven, are you all right?" She barely heard Iain's voice over the pounding of her heart. She scanned the crowd, checking every face in view. Seated at a table against the far wall, beneath a painting of a Renaissance nobleman with a shifty smile, were two men in suits. They were too plainly dressed to be Italian. They could have been traveling businessmen. Or vacationing undertakers. Or men sent to find her.

Haven flagged down a waiter and requested the check, just as their first course arrived.

"Is something wrong?" the waiter inquired.

"Haven?" Iain joined in.

"I'm not feeling well," Haven managed to explain as she dug

through her purse and fished out a credit card. Once the waiter had disappeared, she leaned across the table toward Iain. Protecting him was the only thing that mattered now. "You have to get out of here," she whispered. "There's a chance they haven't figured out who you are."

"Who?" Iain asked. Haven nodded toward the two men in suits.

Iain stole a quick look and laughed with relief. "Those guys? They're not from the Ouroboros Society, Haven. They're copy machine salesmen. From Cleveland. I could hear them talking when we walked by."

"You're sure?" Haven asked. "There was someone from the Society here tonight. The woman in the fur—she had a ring. An ouroboros ring. I saw it."

"Haven, it's okay. It was just a coincidence. Why don't we stay and have our dinner? There's something—" Iain started to say.

"No, we're not safe here!" Haven insisted. "I felt it in Rome, and now I feel it here. He's looking for me, Iain."

"*Signora*, I'm terribly sorry." The waiter was hovering over them. "I'm afraid your credit card has been declined."

"That's impossible," Haven snipped.

"No, *signora*," the waiter said, growing snootier by the second. "It is not. Perhaps the *gentleman* has a card?"

Of course he doesn't, Haven wanted to say. *The gentleman is supposed to be dead.*

"I'll be happy to pay with cash," Iain told him.

CHAPTER FOUR

There was no one on the streets of Florence. Snowflakes swirled in the air, never seeming to land, as though repelled by the ground's icy touch. The night was silent, and the lights from the restaurant didn't stretch far into the darkness. Haven surveyed her surroundings and recognized nothing. She couldn't even recall which route they'd taken from the hotel.

"I gave that waiter all of my cash," Iain told her. "I don't have enough money left for a taxi." Haven was surprised to see that he didn't appear worried. He even grinned as he tightened the scarf around her neck and tucked it into the collar of her coat. "Are you going to be okay if we walk?"

"Am I going to be *okay*? Iain, listen to me," Haven pleaded, her teeth already chattering. "He's got to be here somewhere." She half expected to see the figure in black emerge from around a corner or behind a car. There was no dark crevice that couldn't have held him. "He's followed us from Rome. We can't stay here anymore."

"Haven, I *promise* you. He's not in Florence. I would know if he was. And in any case, my question was rhetorical. Unless you'd like to hitchhike, walking is our only option."

"Then let's hurry." Haven led the charge in her three-inch heels.

"Haven!" Iain called out to her. She turned to see him pointing in the opposite direction. "Our hotel is *that* way."

Behind her cashmere scarf, Haven bit down on her lip until she could taste her own blood. She wasn't insane. She knew what she'd seen. The woman's ring—the platinum snake swallowing its own tail—marked her as a member of the Ouroboros Society. The secret organization run by the man in black. Adam Rosier. And when Adam was involved, there were no such things as coincidences. Haven had been a fool to imagine she could ever deceive him.

MANY MONTHS HAD passed since Haven had last set foot in the Ouroboros Society headquarters. But while the organization lay on the other side of the Atlantic, it was never very far from her mind. Housed in a stately, ivy-covered mansion on the edge of Gramercy Park in Manhattan, the Society had once been devoted to the scientific study of reincarnation. Its benevolent founder had always maintained that people born with knowledge of previous lives—people like Iain Morrow and Haven Moore—should devote themselves to improving the world. Adam Rosier had changed all that. Since he had taken over the OS, he had turned the organization into his own sinister social club. Individuals with unusual memories still flocked to Gramercy Park from all over the world, hoping to learn more about the lives they'd once led. Many of them arrived with remarkable skills they had built over multiple lifetimes. There were medical savants and mathematical geniuses. Artists and actors. Politicians whose words could fire up crowds or leave them in tears. Pianists who could conjure heaven with their fingertips.

It didn't matter who they were or what their abilities might have been. Once they became members, they found themselves slaves to the OS's system. The Eternal Ones (as they called themselves) were all given accounts and instructed to earn valuable "points" by helping one another. The system seemed perfectly harmless until members discovered that OS points could buy anything the heart secretly desired—fame, fortune, drugs, or sex. Eventually, power and points became every member's obsessions. Those who refused to play the game were visited by Adam's obedient army of "gray men"—and some were never seen again. But few refused, and each time the Society recruited a new member, the world grew just a little bit darker.

That was Adam Rosier's plan, after all. He was the subject of Marta Vega's eerie paintings—the dark figure who set tragedies in motion. *What* he was could only be answered by scholars, shamans, or priests. For thousands of years he had wandered the globe, wreaking havoc, spreading lies, and feeding chaos wherever he found it. But in 1925, he had made Manhattan his home. The Ouroboros Society allowed him to continue his dark work while he waited for the only girl he had ever loved to arrive in New York and fulfill the destiny he had designed for her.

Adam may have preyed on people's darkest desires, but he had a weakness of his own. Haven Moore. They had been married once in a life two thousand years in the past, but Adam's fear of losing her had led him to lock Haven away. She escaped from confinement with the help of a servant she'd come to see as her soul mate, but Adam was unwilling to let her go. Instead, he had followed Haven across countless lifetimes, and there were few crimes he hadn't committed in his pursuit of her.

In this lifetime, Adam had located Haven when she was too young to run from him. He had been watching her since she was nine years old—keeping her safe and waiting for her to come of age. But despite Adam's best efforts, Haven and Iain were drawn together once more. In order to live out their days in peace, they'd had to trick the man in black. Haven had convinced Adam that she'd fallen out of love with her soul mate, and Iain had faked his own death. Believing he'd defeated his adversary, Adam promised Haven one life of freedom. He would patiently wait until she was reborn to make her his wife once again.

It was a promise Adam made because he believed that his rival was dead—and that the love that brought Haven and Iain together again and again had finally been destroyed. If Adam discovered that Iain was alive—if he knew they were still madly in love and living in Italy—there was no telling what the consequences might be. Before Iain "died," Adam had framed him for the murder of a musician named Jeremy Johns. One call to the police, and Iain could be locked away. But prison might be the least of their worries if Adam Rosier was in Florence. If Iain were to lose his life, there was no telling how long it might take before he and Haven could be reunited. A year without him would be terrible. A century would be torture.

Which is why it surprised Haven to hear Iain speak as though Adam were no longer a threat. As if an ocean could keep him at a distance. Haven knew they hadn't escaped him. Adam might have stayed behind in New York, but a part of him still followed Haven wherever she went. He frequently appeared in her dreams of the past. And while she rarely recalled many details, there was one terrible fact Haven couldn't forget. Not all of those dreams were nightmares.

FEAR HAD SHARPENED her senses, and Haven heard the Vespa's motor long before its headlight came into view. It appeared at the intersection ahead of them and sat idling at the stop sign a little too long before it turned toward them. Blinking in the harsh light, Haven and Iain paused to let the scooter pass. As it rumbled by, Haven fought the urge to flee. The last time she and Iain had faced death, it had come in the guise of two OS members on a motorbike. But the person riding the Vespa wasn't one of Adam's gray men—it was a teenage girl in a long brown coat and motorcycle boots. She wore neither helmet nor hat, and the snowflakes in her blonde hair sparkled like glitter. The Vespa slowed, and the girl stole a long look at Haven. She showed no interest in Iain. Even in the darkness, there was something about the rider that struck Haven as familiar. She knew they'd met at some point in the past, and the smirk on the girl's lips seemed to suggest that she knew it too.

Several blocks later the Vespa's motor could still be heard in the distance. The rattle kept Haven marching on, though her feet had lost all feeling. She imagined the girl on the scooter circling near-by blocks, like a predator waiting for the right moment to make its kill. Even when the lights of their hotel appeared through the swirl-ing snow, Haven wouldn't allow herself to feel any relief. She knew there was still a chance she'd never make it to safety—that she'd be snatched up like a rabbit at the edge of its burrow. The girl was follow-ing them. Haven was sure of it.

Once they were inside the doors of the hotel lobby, Haven spun around and peered outside with her nose almost pressed to the glass.

"Do you see something out there?" Worried at last, Iain put a hand on her shoulder and looked out into the night.

"Shhh," Haven told him. The streets were empty, and the shadows didn't move. Several blocks away, a tiny light flickered. She thought at first that it might be the Vespa, still circling, until the light stayed in place for more than a minute. Then Haven's anxiety began to fade into the desire for a long, hot shower. She let Iain take her by the hand, and together they forged their way through the lobby.

"Excuse me, Miss Moore." A prissy woman from hotel reception was blocking their path to the elevators. Despite her small stature, she made an effective obstacle. "May I have a word?"

"We're in a bit of a hurry," Haven said wearily, attempting to step around the woman, only to find the way blocked once more.

"It will just take a moment." The woman pointed toward the open door of an office. Haven and Iain reluctantly followed her inside.

"Yes?" Haven asked, feeling like a naughty child who'd been sum-moned to the principal's office.

"There's been a problem with your credit card. The hotel has been instructed to decline any additional charges."

"Instructed by whom?" Haven demanded. She could feel the crimson blotches growing on her face and chest.

"The issuing company. Now, would you like to settle your bill in cash, or would you prefer to check out early?" It was no secret which option the woman would have chosen for them.

"We'll pay in cash," Iain stated for the second time that evening. "I had an envelope placed in the hotel safe. Would you mind retrieving it for me?"

"Not at all," the woman responded curtly.

"*Now* do you believe me?" Haven asked as soon as she and Iain were alone in the office. "Someone's shut down my accounts. It has to be Adam. Who else would be able to do this to us?"

"Let's not jump to any conclusions," Iain said, still determined to comfort her. "It's only four thirty in New York. We should have time to deal with the problem. Check your e-mail first, and see if there's anything new. Maybe the credit card company sent you an alert. It's probably a misunderstanding."

"A misunderstanding? Then how do you explain the girl on the Vespa? She was watching us."

"This is Italy, Haven," Iain said. "Do you know how many girls here ride Vespas?"

"In snowstorms?" Haven countered.

"Please, Haven. Check your e-mail."

Haven rifled through her handbag for her phone. Sure enough, a message had arrived two hours earlier from Haven's lawyer in New York. She scanned the note.

"Well, *that* explains it," Haven announced. "Your mother is suing me."

"She's *what*?" Iain's calm façade finally cracked.

"She says I forged your will."

"Read me the note."

"'Dear Miss Moore, I regret to inform you that your accounts have been temporarily frozen. Your late boyfriend's mother, Mrs. Virginia Morrow, has filed a lawsuit accusing you of inheritance fraud. She believes the signature on Iain's will may not be authentic. A Manhattan judge has ordered that the Morrow family fortune be placed in escrow until the issue is resolved. He has also requested that the original document signed by Iain Morrow be forwarded to Mr. Harold Tuckerman, a noted expert on the subject of forgery. Please telephone me at your earliest convenience. We need to discuss this matter at once.'"

"I can't believe it," Iain muttered. "I left that woman five million dollars in my will. I thought it would take her a decade to drink her way through it."

"Well, let's look on the bright side," Haven said, though she could barely see one herself. "At least Adam isn't behind it."

"Don't underestimate my mother," Iain replied. "When it comes to pure evil, she makes Adam Rosier look like the Easter bunny."

In the past year, Haven had heard dozens of stories about Iain's father, who'd passed away shortly before she and Iain had reunited. A difficult man, Jerome Morrow had made Iain's childhood far more complicated than it had to be, escorting his son to countless psychiatrists, each with a different flavor of pill to prescribe. Yet it was clear that Jerome Morrow had loved his son, even if that love had been poorly expressed. However, Iain rarely spoke of his mother. Whenever the subject came up, he would always do his best to change it.

"You're exaggerating," Haven said softly.

"No." Iain was adamant. "I'm not. She once held me hostage at her villa until my father agreed to increase her alimony payments. I missed an entire month of sixth grade. Believe me, she'd let us both starve if she thought there was the slightest chance of getting her hands on the Morrow fortune."

"We're not going to starve, are we?" Haven laughed nervously. "We must have *some* money set aside for emergencies."

"Some," Iain admitted. "But it won't last forever."

"Well, there's always my boutique. We should be able to live off the shop's profits for a while."

Iain shook his head. "They'll shut it down. The building and the supplies were all purchased with Morrow money. You're worried," he added when he saw the horror on Haven's face. "Don't be worried. I can always hop on a flight to New York. I still have a few contacts there. I can try to get my hands on some cash while we fight the suit."

"Contacts? Since when do dead guys have *contacts*?" Haven sighed and rested her cheek against Iain's chest. His heartbeat was still slow and steady. She wondered what it would take to make it race as fast as hers. "It doesn't matter anyway. I want you here with me. Virginia Morrow can take our money, but I'm not going to let her separate us."

She felt Iain plant a kiss on her neck. "My mother isn't going to get her hands on our money, Haven. She'll just make our lives unpleasant for a while. We've been poor before. We'll survive."

"I know," Haven said, though the thought of scrimping and saving held little appeal. She was already wondering how she might plead for a loan from her loathsome grandmother back in Snope City.

"We'll just have to be careful for a while. We won't write any big checks."

The last two words hit Haven hard. She broke out of Iain's embrace and stumbled backward. "Oh my God!" she gasped. "I sent out a check right before we left Rome. It probably hasn't even gotten there yet."

"A check for what?" Iain asked.

"Beau's college tuition. The payment is due next week."

CHAPTER FIVE

"Well, if it isn't Haven Jane Moore, formerly of Snope City, Tennessee. To what do I owe this rare pleasure?"

Haven's heart surged at the sound of Beau's deep drawl. They communicated mostly by e-mail these days, and she hadn't seen him face-to-face in six months—since his visit to Rome the previous July. She had never expected to miss him so terribly. Being away from Beau was one of the few disadvantages of living in Italy. Having seen him every day for almost a decade, Haven still found it hard to believe that she couldn't just jump in her mother's car and drive up to the old Decker farmhouse whenever she needed to talk.

Beau had been like family since the day they'd first found each other, and when Haven had learned that Beau had once been her brother, she hadn't felt a single twinge of surprise. Beau knew all about Haven's many faults, and, like a brother, he loved her anyway. So when she'd inherited the Morrow family fortune after Iain faked his own death, Haven's first act as an heiress had been to foot the bill for Beau's college tuition. It was the least she could do to repay him. Telling him that the Morrow money was gone was one of the most painful tasks she'd ever had to take on.

"I wish this was going to be a pleasure, but I've got some bad news." Haven heard her own Tennessee drawl return in full force, as it did every time she spoke to Beau. "You better get ready for it."

"Uh-oh," Beau responded. His moods—good or bad—were often hard to break, and he still sounded relentlessly cheerful. Haven could hear him moving about his bedroom. Wire hangers jangled in the background. He was already packing to go home, she thought miserably. "Well, I've got *good* news," he said, "so maybe they'll balance each other out. But you called me, so go ahead and get yours out of the way."

"It's about your tuition." Haven paused, trying to summon a second part to her sentence.

"Oh, *that*," Beau jumped in. "Yeah, the Vanderbilt registrar called this morning. They said your check for the spring semester didn't clear. I already told them it had to be a mistake. . . ."

"It's not."

The incessant activity on the other end of the line came to a sudden halt. "Well, how's that possible? I've never seen you buy anything but sewing supplies, cappuccinos, or hair relaxer. Did you blow your whole fortune on sequins?" He still didn't sound terribly upset.

"My accounts have been frozen," Haven tried to explain. "Iain's mother has accused me of fraud."

"*Fraud?*" Beau choked on the word. "*You?*"

"She claims I had someone forge Iain's will."

"What! Who does she think you are, some sort of criminal mastermind?"

"I know, I know. It's totally insane, but she seems to have found a judge in New York who's willing to believe her. I just got off the phone with my lawyer. It looks like I might have to fight Virginia Morrow in court."

"This sounds like the sort of thing that ought to be discussed woman-to-woman."

"Are you *kidding*?" The notion hadn't even occurred to Haven. "She'd hang up if I tried to call her."

"I'm not saying you should *call* her. Iain's mom lives in Italy, right? Why don't you go see if you can talk some sense into her? And if you can't, you can just give her a good punch in the gut. Or hand her a big wad of cash. That's probably what she's after anyway."

"You know, that might not be such a bad idea," Haven mused. Virginia Morrow lived in the Tuscan countryside, not far from Florence. Haven had come across the address on the papers she'd signed after Iain's staged death.

"And did you ever consider telling Ms. Morrow that her son isn't really dead? That would probably put a serious crimp in her plans."

It had been the first thing Haven had suggested, and Iain had instantly vetoed the option. His mother was the last person he wanted to know that he was still among the living.

"Iain doesn't think that's the answer," Haven offered diplomatically as she glanced over at the young man sitting in front of a computer on the other side of the hotel room. Still dressed in the sleek navy suit he'd worn to dinner, he was scanning the documents their lawyer had e-mailed, searching for a solution. Iain's confidence was usually contagious, but this time Haven had a hunch that there weren't any easy answers to be found. "But look, Beau, we'll figure this out and get your tuition paid. It just might take a while. There's not a whole hell of a lot I can do right now."

"Don't worry about it. It's all good," Beau assured her. "I was planning to take a little time off anyway."

"Time off?" Haven repeated. "To do what?"

"Well, that's *my* news," Beau said. "I've met someone."

"Fabulous," Haven said with as much enthusiasm as she could muster. As the only openly gay kid in Snope City, Beau had endured four years of high school without so much as one date. His dry spell had ended the day he arrived at college, where there were plenty of people who could appreciate someone with the charm of a Southern gentleman and the looks of a Norse god. But Beau quickly discovered that he wasn't equipped for the blood sport of dating. He'd had his heart badly broken in his second semester, and Haven had hoped the experience would make him a little more wary.

"It's not like that," Beau countered. "This guy is the real deal."

"That's what you said about Stephen," Haven pointed out.

"Yeah, but this guy is different. He says he used to know us."

Haven snorted. "He's been to Snope City? Not much of a recommendation, if you ask me."

"No. It's so much better than that." Haven could hear Beau's excitement bubbling up. "He says he knew us before Snope City. *Way* before Snope City. In a previous life. When you and I were brother and sister."

Feeling light-headed, Haven lowered herself down on the side of the bed. "What exactly did he tell you?" she asked.

"This is going to knock your socks off. He said my name was Piero. His was Naddo. Yours was Beatrice. We all lived in Florence in the middle of the fourteenth century. Beatrice and Piero were rich. Our house was a palace with three large doors. Piero and Naddo met when they were sixteen years old and started a secret affair. He makes it all sound so romantic. Tights and tunics and palaces. Rendezvous by candlelight . . . "

"Hold on just a second, Romeo," Haven butted in. "How does this guy know *I* was Beatrice? How does he know me at all?" Across the room, Iain set aside his work and started to listen.

"He *doesn't* know you," Beau snipped. "I was the one who made the connection. He said that Piero had a sister he adored, despite the fact that everyone else thought she was a massive pain in the ass. Who else could it have been?!"

Beau kept talking while Haven pressed the phone's mouthpiece to her chest. Iain was watching her. "Does the name *Naddo* ring any bells?" she asked him.

A wide grin spread across Iain's face. "I didn't meet the guy," he said. "But Piero never shut up about him."

"Hey, I just heard you talking to Iain," Beau said when Haven lifted the phone back to her ear. "What did he say? Was he in *that* life too? Don't I ever get you to myself?"

"Guess where I am right now," Haven said.

"What?"

"Guess where I am right now," she repeated.

"How am I supposed to know?" Beau barked. "Can I *please* get back to my story?"

"I'm in Florence."

"You're in *Florence*?"

"I'm in Florence. And guess where Iain took me today?"

She could hear Beau breathing heavily on the other end of the line. "No!" he managed to whisper.

"*Yes.* A palazzo with three enormous doors. The same place we used to live when we were brother and sister."

"It's still there?"

"It is. And I just asked Iain if he knew the name Naddo."

"And?!"

"Going by his grin, I'm guessing there's a chance that this Naddo character might be someone you're supposed to find," Haven announced.

"Oh my God," Beau said. They both sat in silence for a moment, allowing the information to sink in. "Is it really supposed to be this easy?"

"I don't know," Haven said. "How'd you come across this guy, anyway? Does he go to Vanderbilt too?"

"No, he lives in New York. And he found *me*. He saw my picture on Facebook, and he says he just knew that I was the one he'd been searching for."

"And you? Did you feel anything when you saw his picture?"

"No. Not really," Beau admitted. "Though believe me, the boy ain't hard to look at. But you didn't know Iain was 'the one' until you met him in person, so I'm flying up to New York tomorrow to see the guy face-to-face."

"When were you planning to tell me all of this?" Haven demanded, feeling a little hurt. She rarely made a move without e-mailing her best friend first.

"I was going to tell you if it turned out to be the right guy," Beau said. "I didn't want you to get all excited for nothing."

"Are you *sure* you have to meet him in New York?" Haven asked. Maybe she was being paranoid, but something didn't seem right. "You know it's not safe for you there. If Adam sees you . . ."

"Adam? I thought El Diablo was supposed to leave us alone for the next six or seven decades."

"He's supposed to leave *me* alone. He didn't make any promises when it came to you. And after you threatened to send the Ouroboros Society's membership list to the *New York Times* . . ."

"Okay, okay, Haven. I get it. But New York's a city with eight million people. And Roy goes to Columbia. He lives up in Morningside Heights, for God's sake," Beau said. "I'm not going anywhere near Gramercy Park or the Ouroboros Society."

"So his name is Roy now?" Haven finally cracked a smile.

"Roy Bradford," Beau confirmed. "He sounds like a movie star, don't you think?"

"He does." Haven's smile faded fast. "You will be careful, won't you? I don't want you to get your feelings hurt if he ends up being a psycho." Most people might not have felt the need to protect a six-foot-four football player with a terrible temper, but Haven knew that

Beau's Achilles' heel was his heart. After he'd watched Haven find the person she was meant to be with, Beau's own search for a soul mate had begun in earnest. The only problem was that he had mistaken him for half of the men he'd met. As hard as she tried, Haven couldn't shake the feeling that Roy Bradford might be another wrong number.

"I'm not going to let my imagination run away with me this time," Beau vowed, as though he'd been reading her thoughts. "And you watch yourself too. Don't let some old lady rob you blind. Go see Virginia Morrow and let her know who she's dealing with."

"I'll think about it," Haven said, though she'd already made up her mind.

CHAPTER SIX

The villa perched on a small, overgrown hill that rose above the emerald green Tuscan fields surrounding it. From the road, all Haven could see of the building was the clay tiles of its roof, which looked badly in need of repair. As she turned into the driveway, she noticed that a cypress tree had grown to engulf one corner of the house while grape vines scaled the walls, pinning the last chunks of the villa's crumbling plaster to the bricks beneath.

Haven pulled her car as close to the house as she could. She'd hoped to complete her errand quickly and return to Florence before sunset. Iain thought she'd gone window-shopping, and if the trip took less than three hours, his suspicions might not be aroused. Now there didn't seem to be any reason to rush. The villa looked deserted, and Haven wondered how long Virginia Morrow had been gone. Still, she decided to fight her way through the vines to the front door. A cold wind rustled the vegetation, and Haven was assailed by the faint smell of rotting flesh. She looked down to find herself standing at the edge of a swimming pool. The corpse of a bird floated in the icy, algae-filled rainwater that had collected inside. Startled, Haven almost turned back toward the car, but she stopped herself. It would be ridiculous to drive so far only to leave without knocking.

As she stood outside the villa's front door, a cat emerged from under a bush and brushed against Haven's ankles. She reached down to scratch behind its ears. Abandoned on a desolate hill in the middle of Tuscany, the creature had the protruding ribs of a castaway. Haven wondered if she should take it back to the city, where it might stand a chance of survival.

"Who's there?!" a voice inside demanded.

Haven jumped, and the cat slunk silently back into the bushes. "Mrs. Morrow?" Haven replied.

"I don't talk to reporters."

"I'm not a reporter, but I would like to speak with you if you have a moment. My name is Haven Moore."

Haven thought she heard a throaty chuckle. "I'm busy. If you have something to say, you can say it to my lawyer."

"I was hoping that wouldn't be necessary. I'd like to settle this issue out of court, if possible. I'm prepared to make you a deal."

The woman laughed louder. "What kind of *deal*?"

"I could tell you if you let me in," Haven said.

"Fine." The door opened. "*This* should be entertaining." It was half past two, but the woman standing in front of Haven was still wearing her nightgown. Her right hand clutched a crystal glass half filled with an amber liquid. Scotch, Haven surmised, judging by the aroma that wafted by on the breeze.

One night back in Rome, while teetering on the edge of sleep, Haven had been quietly flipping through television channels when she'd come across an episode of Virginia Morrow's old cooking show, *The Sophisticated Chef*. Wary of waking Iain, Haven had kept the volume low as she watched his mother sleepwalk around a set that was designed to resemble a humble Tuscan kitchen. The style of the host's attire told Haven that the show had been taped in the late nineties, shortly before Virginia's spectacular self-destruction. There were already signs of the trouble to come. Her eyes were hollow and her rouge a bit too bright. She resembled a painted corpse—one that had risen from the dead to take its revenge on the living.

Curled up beside Virginia Morrow's slumbering son, Haven had watched the woman on TV and wondered how long it would be until she taped the show that was destined to become a YouTube classic. Leaked to the press by a cameraman who'd finally tired of his boss's abuse, the footage captured the sophisticated chef hurling eggs, pork products, and curses at her studio audience. A Parma ham had briefly knocked a woman unconscious. Virginia Morrow fled the U.S. shortly after the video made the evening news. People still speculated about the cause of her public meltdown, and from time to time an enterprising journalist would attempt to put the big question to her. But in the end, it remained one of the few mysteries of the gossip age. Only Haven and Iain knew the unsavory truth. Virginia had been destroyed by the love of her life—a love she'd discovered at the bottom of a bottle.

Now, here she was in the flesh. She looked older, of course, but age seemed to suit her. The woman's razor-sharp features had softened, and a little extra weight had filled out her figure. There was no doubt that she was the parent responsible for her son's good looks. Though her hair had turned prematurely white, it still fell in elegant waves over her shoulders. With her white gown and unnatural pallor, she looked like a glamorous ghost. But not a particularly friendly one.

"You look younger than I expected," Virginia observed before promptly turning her back on her guest and disappearing down a hallway. "Follow me." Haven heard the command but remained frozen in the doorway. Without Virginia there to block the view, she saw that the house was little more than a ruin—as dilapidated on the inside as it was on the outside. And the air felt even colder. The villa was at least two hundred years old, Haven thought. Two decades of neglect couldn't be responsible for all the damage it had suffered. She spied a meat cleaver embedded in the foyer's wall and knew that some of the destruction had been wrought by human hands.

"Do you see how I am forced to live?" Virginia Morrow inquired without looking back at her guest. "This is what I get for wasting my youth on Jerome Morrow. Are you coming or not?"

"Sure, yes," Haven said, scrambling to catch up.

They reached a room filled with dusty antiques—the first furniture Haven had noticed anywhere in the house. The chambers they'd passed on the way had all been empty. Here, rotten floorboards were covered by threadbare rugs, and a few meager flames danced around a broken chair leg that had been tossed into the fireplace. Haven waited for Virginia Morrow to offer her a seat, but the woman ignored her. Instead she refilled her own glass with liquor from a cheap-looking bottle and propped up one arm on the fireplace mantel.

"So, what kind of deal are you offering me?" Virginia asked, playing innocent. "Enough to fix this place up, I hope?"

"I was told you'd been left five million dollars in Iain's will," said Haven, hesitant to probe much farther.

"And I suppose you're wondering what happened to it?" Virginia said, finishing Haven's thought. "Taxes and debts, my dear. Twenty years of debts. When Iain died, the IRS and every credit card company on earth came calling. They took it all."

"Well, I'm sure I could give you enough money to—" Haven stopped. The woman was slowly shaking her head, warning her guest that the effort was pointless. Haven realized then that Virginia wouldn't settle for less than every last cent of the Morrow family fortune.

"How long were you and Iain together before he died?" the woman asked. "In *this* life, I mean."

"You know?" Haven was caught off guard.

"How long?" Virginia repeated with a satisfied smirk.

"Long enough." Haven dug her hands deep into her pockets for warmth. Even with the little fire, the house was freezing. How could Virginia Morrow bear to wander its shabby rooms in nothing but a tattered silk gown?

"I was twenty-five when I met Iain's father and thirty-seven when we divorced. By the time he was done with me, there wasn't much left. So that's what? Twelve years? I think I deserve more than what I've been given. Don't you?"

"It's not for me to say," Haven replied. "It was your son's decision to make me his primary heir. I would think you'd want to respect his wishes. Still . . ."

"*My son?*" The phrase struck Virginia Morrow as amusing. "Iain Morrow was never *my* son. I still don't know what he was. Can you *imagine?* You sacrifice your body and your freedom to have a child, and as soon as he's able to talk, you discover that he doesn't really belong to you. He says he's had other mothers—dozens of them. Then when he's older, he tells you that you're the worst of the lot. You called him my son? The boy was a changeling. Someone stole my baby and left that creature in his place." By the end of her tirade, Virginia's mouth had puckered with bitterness.

"I can't believe you would say such things. Iain must have loved you. You were his mother."

"You're confusing love and need. They are two very different things, Haven. And as I just said, he was never my son."

"Of course he's your son! If nothing else, he looks just like you." Haven knew she'd made a mistake the instant the words were out of her mouth.

"Looks?" Virginia took a gulp from her glass, and her face returned to its previously placid state. Haven wondered how much scotch it took to control the demons inside her. "An interesting choice of verb tenses. Anyway, don't look so appalled, Miss Moore. You may think I'm a monster, but you're really no better than I am. You'll hurt Iain more than I ever did."

"You don't know the first thing about me." The woman finally had Haven seething.

"Oh, yes, I do. I know you far better than you could ever imagine. You've had quite a few names. Constance. Cecile. Bao. Beatrice. But you're always the same."

"How—"

"You think I neglected my little changeling? You think I wasn't listening when he started telling his stories? Even when he was three years old, Iain was already a strange boy. Everywhere we took him, he always tried to break free. Finally, we found out why. He told my husband that he was looking for someone he'd known in other lives. As you might imagine, Jerome dragged him to see a psychiatrist the very next day. It took a few sessions, but Iain finally confided in the doctor. There was a girl he was desperate to find. He claimed that someone else was searching for her as well. He needed to reach the girl before his rival had a chance to win her."

"*Win* me?" Haven hoped her laughter could hide her shock. Did Iain really see Adam Rosier as a rival? "I'm not a carnival prize."

Virginia seemed to know that she'd found Haven's weak spot. "Those might not have been Iain's exact words. But he seemed convinced there was someone else. Someone you might choose instead. He was terrified that you'd break his heart one day."

"That's the most ridiculous thing I've ever heard," Haven scoffed, though the suggestion was worming its way into her brain. "I could never break Iain's heart."

"*Is* it ridiculous?" Virginia asked. "Most people know their mailmen better than they know themselves. They'd never guess what they're capable of doing. Do you think most people would ever believe they're capable of murder? Or breaking their spouses' hearts? Or destroying their careers with a carton of eggs and a ham? Of *course* not. We all like to think that we're models of integrity. We have no idea what we might do if the gods decided to turn against us. But those of us who've seen the worst in ourselves—let's just say that we can spot potential in others. And you, my dear, are simply bursting with potential."

Virginia downed the last of her drink and deposited the glass on the mantel with a loud bang and a mean grin. A gust of wind swept down the chimney, making the fire surge and surrounding the house's mistress with smoke. The woman was poisonous, Haven thought.

"I will never be like you."

"Well, here's your opportunity to prove me wrong." Virginia Morrow was starting to slur her words. "I'll guess you've gotten quite comfortable spending all of my money. That dress alone must have cost a small fortune."

"I *made* this dress," Haven snarled.

Virginia pinched Haven's sleeve and rubbed it between her fingertips. "And I don't imagine this fabric was free. You appear to have exceptional taste. So let's see what happens when all the money is taken away. Do you think you can go back to being the middle-class hick you once were? What do you think you'll do to prevent that from happening? Who will you turn to when Iain can't afford you anymore?"

"He put you up to this, didn't he?"

"He?" Virginia Morrow asked. "Who's *he*?"

"*Adam*. Adam Rosier."

"I have no idea who that is," the woman sneered. "Why would you assume that there's a *man* pulling my strings? I think my motives are completely transparent. I want my life back. I want to live in a house without mice. I want to dress in beautiful clothing. I want people to be nice to me whether they like it or not. I want what I lost, and soon

44

I'll be able to buy it back. My attorney is convinced we can win, and he stands to get a nice, big check if we do."

"Don't think I won't fight you every step of the way," Haven said.

"I wish you the very best of luck," said Virginia. "Which of us do you suppose has the most to lose?"

CHAPTER SEVEN

Back inside the hotel room in Florence, everything was still. Outside, the world was growing dark. The last light of the afternoon filtered through the sheer curtains and tinted the room's walls a pale silver. Haven thought of the little house in New York where she had shared her very first night with Iain. The light had been the same in the bedroom upstairs, beneath the skylight, with the clouds overhead. Sometimes it was hard to believe that their house was gone, destroyed in a fire that had almost killed them both. Haven paused to take in her surroundings and commit them to memory. She knew there was no guarantee that this world could last. It was already starting to fall apart.

Iain lay on the bed fully clothed, his finger tucked inside a book. He'd fallen asleep waiting for her to come home. She stood over him, her eyes tracing the faint scar on his forehead. He hadn't escaped from the fire unscathed. Haven often found herself longing to let her fingers brush over it. She knew the scar was there to serve as a warning.

It was meant to remind her that Iain was human. No matter how brave or powerful he seemed, he wasn't completely invincible.

An image passed through her mind—Iain's beautiful mother standing among the ruins of the life she'd let her drinking destroy. The rage that followed in the wake of the memory made Haven's body stiffen and her teeth clench. On the drive back to Florence, she had cried so hard at the thought of Iain being raised by that monster that she'd had to pull to the side of the road. She understood better than anyone could how lonely he must have been as a boy. From the age of eight, Haven had been an orphan of sorts—her father was dead and her mother's mind unsound. Raised by her grandmother, she knew what it was like to suffer at the hands of someone consumed by bitterness. But Haven had always had Beau. She still imagined the two of them as fairy-tale siblings, forging their way through a dark, dismal forest with little more than a basket of bread crumbs to mark their trail. Together, they had been able to make it to safety. Alone, there was little doubt they'd have perished.

Haven kicked off her shoes and crawled onto the bed. She slid one arm around Iain's waist and pressed her body against his warm back. Tucking her face into the nape of his neck, she inhaled deeply. He smelled just like home. Whenever she felt anxious or unhappy, the scent that rose from his skin could flood her mind with a thousand beautiful memories. Sometimes she'd sort through them and choose a clear one to savor. But more often, Haven would simply bask in the sensation of reunions, first kisses, and long-awaited caresses. It was as close to heaven as the living could come. That was why Virginia Morrow's words had to be meaningless. Haven could never love anyone but Iain. She wouldn't risk her paradise for anything.

Or would she?

Haven's eyes popped open again. She hadn't told Iain about her visit to his mother. Instead she had lied to him, broken his trust. And for what? A fortune that was never hers to begin with? Haven felt fear grab her by the throat. For a moment she could scarcely breathe. Had Virginia Morrow been right? Was this the first sign of the terrible things that she had predicted Haven would do?

IAIN ROLLED OVER to face Haven. "You're back," he said. "I was starting to worry." He drew her closer and kissed her. The world could have ended, and Haven wouldn't have noticed. Then, at last, she pulled away.

"I went to see your mother," Haven confessed. "I rented a car and drove out there this morning."

"I know," Iain said. "The car company called to confirm the reservation."

"You knew? And you didn't try to stop me?"

Iain grinned at the thought. "Haven, I've loved you for two thousand years. I figured out a long time ago that once you get an idea in your head, no one can stop you from seeing it through. Anyway, I thought it might be good to let you meet Mommy Dearest. Now you know what kind of a fight we're in for."

The fact that he'd known about the trip just made Haven feel worse. "You were right all along, Iain. The woman's a monster. I don't know how you managed to survive with a mother like that."

Iain propped himself up on one elbow and looked down at Haven lying beside him on the bed. "You don't know? I do," he said as if it should have been obvious. "I knew you were out there, and I had a feeling that this time I'd find you. That's how I got through the first nineteen years of my life. It's as simple as that."

"Still," Haven said. "She didn't have to make it so hard for you. A mother should love her child no matter how many lives he's led."

"That's over now. You're all the family I've ever needed. Which reminds me," he said, suddenly jumping up from the bed. "There was something I meant to give you before you hauled me out of that restaurant last night."

He went to the closet and searched through the pockets of the jacket he'd worn the previous evening. When he returned, he held a small wooden box in his hand.

"I did manage to make one final purchase before we lost the farm."

Haven opened the box without a word. Inside was a simple ring with a wide gold band and a cabochon in the center.

"It's glass," Iain remarked nervously as Haven watched the golden flecks inside the pale blue gem glitter in the light of the bedside lamp. "Just like the last one. I mean the first one. The first ring I ever gave you."

"When we ran away to Rome together two thousand years ago?" Haven asked.

"Yes. And I spent our last penny on that ring too, and I didn't have many pennies to spend back then. That's why the jewel was glass, not something fancier. But now it's an antique and . . ."

"It's perfect," Haven announced.

"Good." Iain exhaled with relief. "I saw it in a shop right before we left Rome and I—"

"What does it mean?" Haven asked.

Iain sat down beside her and swept away a curl that had fallen across Haven's cheek. "It means that we belong to each other and always will. It means that whenever you're ready, we can get some government's stamp of approval. Or we can continue to wallow in heavenly sin for the next sixty years. It means whatever you want it to mean, Haven."

"Thank you." The lump in Haven's throat kept her from saying any more. She had never thought of herself as the kind of girl who could get weepy over a piece of jewelry. And Iain's feelings came as no surprise to her. But somehow Haven felt different with the lovely Roman ring on her finger. It had a power she'd never anticipated. She knew her mother would have argued that Haven was too young for such things. Mae Moore still prayed that her nineteen-year-old daughter would one day return to east Tennessee. She didn't seem to understand that Haven was already home.

"You're very welcome," Iain said, ending the conversation with a kiss.

LATER, AS SHE lay beside Iain, with little more than a sheet twisted around them, Haven dreamed of the Florentine girl she'd been seven hundred years before. Beatrice was standing in an empty room, examining a fresco. The house's furniture was gone, strapped to wagons that had fled the city the day before. Looters were bound to follow, stealing whatever was left and leaving only the brightly colored paintings that decorated the walls. The one Beatrice was studying showed the massacre of the innocents—the execution of all the male infants in the village of Bethlehem as ordered by King Herod. Frantic women ran through the streets of town, trying to save their babies from the swords of Roman troops. In the top left corner of the fresco, a motionless figure watched the slaughter from a window.

The girl in Haven's dream had just stepped toward the painting for a better look when she heard the sound of footsteps behind her. She turned to see a group of women enter the room, some young and some old. Some were peasants and others the daughters or wives of rich men. There was even one woman disguised as a soldier. At the head of the group stood a young girl who couldn't have been more than eleven years old. Her face was dirty and her clothing torn, yet she spoke with an unexpected authority.

"You've changed your mind?" she demanded to know.

"I have," Haven heard herself say.

She woke suddenly to the ringing of the phone.

CHAPTER EIGHT

"Mom?" Haven groaned into the receiver. The room was perfectly dark, and all Haven could see was a faint glow from her phone's screen. "You do remember we're six hours ahead of you, right? It's three o'clock in the morning here."

"I'm sorry for waking you, honey," said Mae Moore. "But Ben Decker just asked me to call. It's a little bit urgent."

Haven sat up. "Is something wrong with Beau?" she asked, a thousand horrific scenarios bombarding her mind at once.

"Well, see, that's the problem. We don't know. We were hoping you might."

"Might *what*, Mama?" For most of Haven's life, her mother had done her best to avoid the real world. Devastated by cruel rumors surrounding her husband's death, Mae Moore had turned inward. She rarely spoke above a whisper, and she couldn't look anyone in the eye. In the year since the truth had finally come out, and her husband's name had been cleared, Mae Moore had made remarkable progress.

She was almost the sunny, charming woman she'd once been. But she still had a hard time getting straight to the point.

"We were hoping you might know where Beau is."

Haven fell back on her pillows. It was typical Beau—leaving town without letting anyone know where he was going. "He went to New York," Haven said. "I'll tell you everything in the morning once I've had some sleep."

"Ben knows about the trip," Mae said before Haven could hang up. "Beau was supposed to call when he got there last night. The plane landed at ten, but he never phoned. You haven't heard from him, have you?"

"No." Haven felt suddenly cold.

"Oh." Mae's voice was small.

"Is Mr. Decker really worried?" Beau's father had spent twenty years in the Army. He wasn't the sort who fretted for no reason.

"He's getting there," Mae said. "I guess he wasn't too happy about Beau going up to New York in the first place, but there wasn't much he could do. Now that he hasn't been able to reach him, he's feeling pretty nervous. Ben said Beau's usually real good about checking in. Unlike some people I know."

Haven let the jibe pass without comment. "I'm sure he's fine," she said, more to convince herself than her mother.

"So you know this person he went to see?"

"I haven't met him, but I know his name. Roy Bradford."

"That's what Beau told his father. He said he met this Roy character on some website. But Ben visited the site this evening, and he couldn't find anyone who goes by that name."

"Tell Mr. Decker he should call Columbia University," Haven said. "Beau said the guy goes to school there."

"Ben tried that too. They don't have any students named Roy Bradford."

"Did he check the telephone listings?" Haven asked.

"There were three people with that name in Manhattan. None of them had ever heard of Beau."

Haven searched her brain for another clue, but there wasn't one to be found.

"Haven?" Her mother interrupted her thoughts. "I know you're officially an adult and all. And I know you have your own money, but don't you think it might be time to come home? It would sure help Ben if you were here."

"Beau's fine," Haven repeated. This time she didn't believe it. "He'll call one of us soon."

Mae sighed. "If he calls you, would you tell him to phone his father?"

"Of course," Haven promised.

"Well then, you go back to sleep, honey," Mae said. "I'm sorry I had to wake you."

There was no way Haven was going back to sleep. After the call, she sat with the phone still gripped in her hand.

"What is it?" Iain asked. "What's wrong? Was that your mom?"

"Beau's missing." The light radiating from the phone's display switched off, and Haven stared into the darkness. She had tried to sound upbeat on the call, but now her fears were threatening to swallow her. "He left for New York last night, and no one's heard from him since. Beau's dad has been trying to find Roy Bradford, but the guy doesn't seem to exist."

Iain's warm hand gripped her shoulder. "Is there a chance Beau might have sent you a note?"

Haven felt a rush of hope. She'd been traveling all day, and she hadn't had a chance to check her messages. "Maybe," she said, typing in the password to her e-mail account. "Yes!" she shouted at the sight of an unopened envelope next to Beau's name. She clicked the icon and the note opened.

PAN-PAN, PAN-PAN, was the only thing he'd written. The phone slipped out of Haven's fingers as soon as she saw the words. Seized by terror, her mind was no longer in control of her body.

"Haven, are you okay?" Iain picked up the device and read the note for himself. "What's 'pan-pan'?"

"It's something Beau and I used to say when we were kids," Haven said as soon as she was able to speak. "It means he's in trouble. Beau sent that note a few hours after his plane landed. Something must have happened when he got to New York, but he hasn't called anyone for help. Which probably means he *can't*. Either he's hurt or being held against his will. *Dammit!* I should have known Roy Bradford was too good to be true! Just because he knew Beau in another life doesn't mean they were meant to be together. What if Naddo was some kind of psychopath? What if Piero broke his heart, and Naddo's been waiting seven hundred years to get his revenge? What if . . ."

There were too many terrible possibilities to contemplate. When Beau had told her about his trip, Haven had hoped for the best. But she should have prepared for the worst. She knew better than anyone that reincarnation was responsible for creating as many vendettas as soul mates.

"Well, that settles it," Iain announced. Haven felt him climbing out of bed.

"What?" Her sight blurred by tears, she followed the sound of Iain's voice across the room. "Settles what?"

"I'm going to book a flight to New York right now. I'll scrape together enough money when I get there to hire a detective to hunt down Roy Bradford. There's someone I used to know. . . ."

"We don't need a detective, Iain. We need the *police*. I've got to call Beau's dad and have him contact the NYPD."

She heard the flip of a switch, and a lamp lit up the room. When Haven wiped her tears, she could see the worry on Iain's face. "They might not start looking right away, Haven. Beau's an adult, and he's been missing for less than a day."

"But they can't wait! What if Beau's already been hurt?!" Her fists clenched at the thought. If only she could travel back in time, she'd kill Naddo with her own hands before he had a chance to harm Beau. She could feel her fingers around a throat, but she still couldn't visualize a face. "Hold on! What do you remember about Naddo? Was there anything unusual about him back then? Was he like us—did he have a talent that set him apart? Don't most people who've been reincarnated have a special gift of some sort?"

"Let me think for a second." Iain closed his eyes. "I remember Piero telling me that Naddo was well-spoken. He worked for one of the men who ran Florence. But that's not going to help us identify Naddo in this life. I wish I'd had a chance to meet the guy before I died."

An idea was starting to form in Haven's mind. "Do you think I might have known Naddo back then?"

"It's possible, I guess. Piero and Beatrice were really close. He would have wanted his sister to meet his boyfriend."

"Then maybe I know something." Haven peered up at Iain. "Do you think I might know something about Naddo that could help us find him?"

Iain sat down on a chair by the window and ran a hand through his hair. "It's a long shot, Haven."

"Are you sure?" It was Haven's best hope and she clung to it. "I already had one vision of that life today. Maybe if I go back to that palazzo we saw I can summon another one!"

"Hold on, Haven. Let's think this through for a second. Suppose you find out that Naddo *did* have an unusual talent. Maybe he was the greatest lute player in Italy. Or a gifted equestrian. What would you tell the police? If you start talking about reincarnation, they'll think you're nuts. We need to find someone who would take us seriously. That's why—"

"Iain, I've got it!" Haven cried, unable to contain the bombshell that had just gone off in her brain. "If Naddo lives in New York now, and he knows he's been reincarnated, I bet he's been in touch with the Ouroboros Society. Even if he's not an actual member, they'll probably have a file on him—and I bet they'd know how to reach him too!"

She had expected Iain to applaud her discovery. Instead he was staring at her in disbelief.

"Do you realize what you just said?" he asked. "We can't contact the Ouroboros Society, Haven."

"There's got to be a way," Haven insisted. "It's *Beau*, Iain. I *owe* him."

CHAPTER NINE

One Friday morning in the seventh grade, Haven had found a frilly pink card tucked inside her homeroom desk. It was an invitation to a Saturday slumber party, and the party's hostess was Morgan Murphy, the most popular girl in school. She and Haven had been best friends until Haven's visions had frightened away everyone but Beau. Now Haven saw her chance to reclaim her rightful place at Morgan's side.

She ate next to Morgan in the school cafeteria that day, gossiping with girls who hadn't spoken to her in three years, while Beau had his lunch alone outside. After school, Haven had run home to brag to her grandmother, who saw the invitation as a sign that the family's troubles were finally coming to an end.

The next evening, Mae Moore dropped Haven off at the Murphy house. The girl lugged her sleeping bag to the front door and rang the bell. It took several minutes for Haven to realize that there was nobody home. The Murphys were gone. There wouldn't be any party.

Haven should have called her mother to come pick her up, but she didn't. The light was fading, and she started looking for a place to roll out her sleeping bag. The thought of spending the night alone in the Murphys' yard terrified her. But she couldn't face owning up to the shame. The last thing she wanted to do was tell her grandmother she'd been the butt of a horrible joke.

That's when Beau showed up. He didn't say much; he just took Haven's sleeping bag in one hand and threw his other arm around her.

"Next time you need me, just text *pan-pan*," he told her. "P-A-N P-A-N. You don't need to say anything more than that."

"Pan-pan?" Haven had asked. "What's *that* mean?"

"My dad told me it's what they say in the Army. I think it's French or something. It means you need help."

"Why don't they just say 'help'? Why do they have to get all fancy and speak French?"

"How would I know? Stop asking so many questions and let's get a move on. I'm hungry as a horse. You wanna eat hot dogs?"

"Yeah," Haven said. She hadn't eaten in hours, and her mouth was already watering.

Together, they walked the mile back to the Decker house. That night, they camped out in the yard. Beau's father built a fire for them, and they stayed up late roasting marshmallows. No one mentioned the party. It was one of the best nights of Haven's life.

Haven had sifted through her childhood memories and found dozens of similar scenes. Beau had always been there for her—even when Haven hadn't deserved his friendship. Now she had a chance to repay him properly. Whatever it took, she wouldn't let him down. Wherever he was, she would find him and take him home.

TWO DAYS HAD passed since Beau's disappearance—long enough for the police to officially declare him a missing person. Ben Decker now had the NYPD searching for his son, but no one was satisfied with the progress they'd made. There were no leads. No clues. Beau seemed to have stepped off a plane at LaGuardia Airport and vanished without a trace. The cops had warned Beau's father to brace himself for bad news. But Haven was certain that there was still time to save her best friend. It was this one little hunch, with no proof to support it, that managed to keep her sane.

Two mornings in a row, she dragged herself out of bed before dawn and returned alone to the palazzo Iain had shown her. Haven stood in the square from sunup to sundown, letting her body freeze in place as she tried to invite more visions from the past. She didn't notice all the tourists who snapped photos of her—or the locals who whispered and laughed. Iain offered to keep her company, but Haven couldn't allow anything to distract her. She needed to see more of the life Beatrice and her brother had shared in the mansion at the end of the square. More importantly, she needed to see *Naddo*.

But the vision Haven craved never revealed itself. There were a few tantalizing glimpses of medieval Florence—a rope being tossed out of a third-story window. Piero shimmying down the side of the building and Beatrice pulling up the rope once he'd landed. Or Beatrice hiding in a cabinet while her furious mother searched the house for her. But Haven saw nothing that could help her find Beau. Still she waited. The longer she stood in front of the palazzo, the darker the visions became. She watched the Vettori family's belongings be loaded into carts and hauled away in a hurry, the carts' drivers steering around bodies that lay in the street. Later she saw the plague doctors descending on the house like a flock of vultures, each dressed in a dark overcoat and a terrible, birdlike mask. Their parties lasted late into the night. Until they stopped altogether.

On the third day of Haven's vigils, Iain took a train back to Rome to pick up some much-needed cash and a few changes of clothes. The night before, they had lugged their suitcases from their luxury lodgings to a run-down youth hostel at the edge of town. Their new room reeked of pot smoke and bug spray. Next door, four British college girls partied with a local soccer team while Haven and Iain huddled together on the lumpy mattress, their arms locked tightly around each other. Unable to sleep, Haven gazed at the golden ring on her finger and wished it had the power to transport them back to their apartment in Rome. At dawn, she and Iain rose and began the long trek to the center of Florence When they reached the palazzo, Iain tucked Haven's scarf into her collar and filled her coat pockets with snacks he'd purchased along the way. Haven didn't tell him they'd never be eaten. There was too much on her mind to worry about food.

Hours later, Haven's stomach remained empty, but her head had filled with terrible thoughts. Church bells were tolling two o'clock when her phone began to ring. Thinking it must be Iain calling from the train, she answered without bothering to check the number.

"Haven Moore? That you?" Haven recognized Leah Frizzell's nasal mountain drawl in an instant. She and Leah had grown up together in east Tennessee. Both had been outcasts in tiny Snope City, but Leah would have stood out in any town. Raised in a family of snake handlers, the girl had been granted the gift of prophecy. Like Haven, she knew how it felt to possess abilities that frightened lesser folk. They could have been—should have been—friends from the start. But when Haven had looked at the scrawny redhead who paired old-fashioned dresses with combat boots, she'd seen the same freak everyone else saw. For years, Haven hadn't bothered to find out what lay beneath Leah's eccentric exterior. It was a mistake she had come to regret.

During Haven's encounter with Adam Rosier and the Ouroboros Society, Snope City's town freak had proven to be a critical ally. Now she and Haven were full-fledged friends. Leah was one of the three people Haven trusted with her secrets—and one of the six people on earth who knew Iain Morrow was alive. Leah was special—even more special than Haven had realized at first. Over the months, Haven had discovered that there were others who shared her own ability to peer into the past. But Leah was still the only person she'd ever met who was able to see the future.

"Leah, thank God you called! Beau's missing!" Haven blurted out.

"I heard." Haven had never known Leah to mince words or indulge in small talk. She got right to the point and said what she thought— no more, and no less. It was a trait that took some getting used to.

"Have you seen something? What was I thinking?! I should have phoned you at Duke days ago!" Haven said, scrambling for any scrap of hope. Her desperation was so obvious that two passersby cast pitying looks in her direction. "Do you know where Beau is? Can you tell me how to find him?"

"Slow down, Haven," Leah urged. "Mama just called to tell me Beau's vanished. Too bad she doesn't get into town very often—the news has been all over Snope City for days. But nobody seems to know much else. I thought you might be able to fill in a few blanks for me."

Haven opened her mouth, but all that emerged was a sob.

"Haven? You okay?"

"He met someone online," Haven explained through her tears. "A guy who claimed his name was Roy Bradford. He said he'd known Beau in another life, and he invited him up to New York. I should have stopped Beau from going, but I didn't even try."

"Beau went to visit some man he met on the *Internet*? And you didn't try to talk him out of it?" Leah asked.

"You're right, it was stupid! But he knew Beau in fourteenth-century Florence. I was Beau's sister when they first met. I've seen bits and pieces of that life myself, so I know he was telling the truth about some of the stuff he said. Beau thought Roy Bradford might be his soul mate. I should have realized that the guy might be dangerous."

"So you think you met Roy Bradford in person in one of your previous lives?" Leah asked.

"His name then was Naddo. I may have met him, but I can't remember!"

"Okay, Haven. Don't go getting all hysterical," Leah said. "We're starting to make a bit of progress here. I had a vision of you last night, and I think I just figured out what it means. I'm pretty sure you need to see more of the life that you and Beau shared. I think there could be some sort of clue hidden deep in your memories."

"I *know*. That's why I'm still in Florence."

"You're in *Florence*?" Leah repeated as if it made no sense at all. "*Italy*?"

"I've been standing in front of the place where Beau and I used to live, trying to summon a vision of Naddo. There might have been something unusual about him back then—a skill or talent—something that could help me find him today. But I haven't seen a single useful thing!"

"I don't think you're supposed to be in Italy," Leah said. "You need to get back to New York. There's someone there who can help."

"What do you mean?" Haven sniffled.

"In my vision, I saw you talking to an old woman. It's gonna sound crazy, but she had a towel on her head. And she was surrounded by smoke."

"Smoke?"

"Yeah, I don't get it either. But this woman is important. I think she helps people see into their past lives."

"Is that possible?" Haven asked. "I've never heard of anyone who can do stuff like that."

"Anything's *possible*," Leah said. "But you should ask Iain. He knows the old lady. I'm surprised he hasn't mentioned her yet."

"Iain knows the woman surrounded by smoke?"

"I can't say for sure, but I heard her mention him in my vision. She called him Mr. Morrow."

"And you say this woman lives in New York?"

"Yep. Do you think you can make it there?"

"I'll be on the first flight I can get," Haven said. Even if it took her very last cent, she'd be in Manhattan by morning.

"Good. Maybe I'll see you there soon," Leah said. "I'm planning a little trip for spring break."

"You're going to New York?" Leah Frizzell and New York didn't belong in the same sentence.

"I've been meaning to call you for the past few days. I keep having visions that seem to take place in New York. In most of them, I see a thin man with a stick walking through a garden. There are flowers and trees all around him. At first I figured he was in the woods. But then I spotted a round subway entrance in the distance. It's shaped like a little temple. Anyways, I'm pretty sure the man's somewhere in Manhattan, and I'm supposed to go find him. Any idea where I should start looking?"

"For a man with a stick . . ." Haven gasped. "Wait a second. What does he look like?"

"Don't worry, it's not him," Leah assured her. "It's not Adam Rosier."

"You're positive?" Haven asked.

"You told me that Adam's always the same age, right? That he doesn't get any older? Well, this man I'm looking for is probably sixty or so. And bald. But does the rest of it ring any bells? The flowers and trees and the round subway entrance shaped like a temple?"

"There are an awful lot of parks and subway entrances in New York," Haven said. "You remember anything else?"

"There was a bird. Looked like some kind of hawk."

"Well, that doesn't help much," Haven said. It was the sort of weird detail that only Leah would recall. "But I'll keep an eye out for subway entrances when I get to the city. I'll ask Iain too. Maybe he'll know where your man is."

"No, don't go talking to Iain about this," Leah insisted. "Let's keep it between us for now, okay?"

"Why?"

"'Cause the future has a way of shifting. I'm only telling *you* because I have a feeling the man with the stick and the woman sur-rounded by smoke are connected somehow, which makes me wonder if you might be mixed up in this too. But the more people who know about my prophecy, the more chance there is that something will change and the man won't be there when I finally figure out where to find him."

"What do you think he's going to tell you?" Haven asked.

Leah snorted. "If I knew that, I wouldn't bother paying for a plane ticket, now would I? But my guess is that he wants to warn me. I have a feeling something bad is going to happen."

"How bad?" Haven wasn't sure she wanted to know.

"*Real* bad."

"And I'm mixed up in it?"

"Dunno," Leah said. "Maybe."

Just give me a chance to save Beau first, Haven silently prayed. *Before Leah Frizzell tries to save the world.*

BY THE TIME Iain arrived back at the hostel, Haven was sitting on the bed waiting for him. She was wearing her coat, and their suitcases were packed.

"What's going on?" he asked, bending down to kiss her cheek.

"I have to leave tonight," Haven told him.

"So I see," Iain said with a nod at her luggage. "Where are you going?"

"Why didn't you tell me you know someone back in New York who might be able to help me find Beau?"

"I do?"

"I spoke to Leah Frizzell. She had a vision of an old woman who can see other people's past lives. She says the lady was surrounded by smoke. And Leah thinks you know her."

Iain remained silent. Haven wished she could pry open his skull and see what was going through his head.

"It's not smoke," he said at last. "It's steam."

"So it's true?" Haven asked. "You know her?"

"The woman's name is Phoebe," Iain said. "It never even occurred to me that you might want to meet her. She works for the Ouroboros Society. They call her the Pythia."

"But she could help me see the life I had in Florence?"

"She might be able to," Iain admitted reluctantly.

Haven stood up and grabbed the handle of her largest suitcase. "Let's get to the airport. We can't waste any more time in Italy if the woman I need to see is in New York."

Iain took the suitcase from her and set it back on the floor. "Hold on, Haven. This isn't as simple as you think."

"Really? It seems pretty simple to me," Haven said.

"It's not. No one knows how much of what the Pythia says is true. She only works with the high-ranking members of the OS. She claims she helps them remember more of their previous lives. But there are a lot of people in the Society who recall being famous or royal—and not that many who remember being peasants or chambermaids. It's just not realistic. We've *all* been peasants. The Pythia has to be making a lot of stuff up."

"But if we told her it was a matter of life and death, she wouldn't lie, would she?"

"There's no way to be sure," Iain said. "And there's something else you should know."

"What?"

"The Pythia is one of the people who know about Adam. She speaks to him on a regular basis."

He waited for Haven to respond, but for once she kept her lips sealed. When her mother had called to say that Beau was missing, Haven had made a secret deal with the gods. She'd promised them any sacrifice if Beau Decker's life were spared. But now Haven's resolve was being put to the test. How far was she really prepared to go?

"If you visit the Pythia, you'll be putting yourself in danger. We both know we'll have to deal with Adam and the OS someday. But we came to Italy to get away from him for a few years. Then we left Rome because you thought he had followed us there. Now you want to go to New York and run right back into his arms?"

"His *arms*?" After Haven's conversation with his mother, Iain's words felt like a slap in the face. "When was I ever in Adam Rosier's arms? Is there something you want to tell me?"

"He's obsessed, Haven. . . ."

"What does that have to do with *me*? Women throw themselves at you every day, Iain. I trust *you*."

"I trust you, Haven. It's just—"

"I have to go, Iain. It's *Beau*. Do you know how many times I've let him down?" The panic surged, and her voice squeaked. "I won't do it again."

"You don't need Phoebe's help. We'll find another way to rescue Beau. I can't let you take this kind of risk, Haven. It's not what Beau would have wanted. We managed to fool Adam once, but I doubt we'll be able to fool him again. And this time I may not be able to rescue you."

"Rescue *me*?" Haven's temper flared. "As I recall, the last time we were in trouble, I rescued *you*. I'm not some damned damsel in distress. You can come with me or stay here. I'm leaving for New York tonight."

At last Iain seemed to realize that Haven's mind was made up. "Fine," he announced. "We'll go back together. On one condition."

"What is it?"

"I'll tell you where to find the Pythia. You'll gather whatever clues she can offer you and take them straight to the police. And then we leave New York. *Immediately*. Do we have a deal?"

"Deal," Haven agreed. Her anger was fading, and the need to embrace him was growing in its place. She knew just how much she was asking. But Iain had barely put up a fight. In return, Haven took a second silent oath. She would sacrifice anything for Beau. But she wouldn't let the quest to save her friend lead her away from the person she loved.

"I'm sorry, Haven," Iain said. "I should have remembered the Pythia. I want to do everything possible to find Beau. I'll fly halfway around the world to look for him. I'll spend every dime we have left. I'll search New York City by foot if I have to. But I won't risk losing you. I'm sorry if that sounds selfish."

Haven couldn't hold herself back any longer.

CHAPTER TEN

Haven opened her eyes when she felt the plane being pulled back to earth. The cabin lights were out, and most of her fellow passengers were dozing in their seats. Over the hum of the engines, she could hear machine-gun fire and angry voices. The little boy to her left had been playing the same war game since they took off from Florence. She wondered how many enemy soldiers he'd managed to dispatch during their eight-hour flight.

Iain didn't wake when she tucked a blanket around him, but he grumbled in his sleep as she reached over to slide open the window shade. As she got closer, Haven couldn't resist the urge to kiss him. Her lips lingered on Iain's cheek, and she prayed he wasn't worrying about all the wrong things. Adam Rosier was dangerous. They were putting their lives in jeopardy, no doubt. But Haven wondered if that was what bothered Iain most. In the heat of the moment, he'd accused Haven of running back into Adam's arms. What exactly had he meant? Had his mother been telling the truth after all? Did he really see

Adam Rosier as a rival? Didn't Iain know that there was nothing on earth that could ever tempt Haven to stray?

As usual, Beau Decker took any opportunity to make a cameo appearance inside Haven's head. "I suppose all that jealousy was just his conscience talking. Like my grandpa used to say, a guilty dog always barks the loudest."

It was a snippet of a conversation now months in the past, and Beau hadn't been referring to Iain. He'd been talking about Stephen, the boy who'd broken his heart. He'd been flattered when Stephen hadn't wanted to share him with anyone else. Amused when the boy imagined every male on campus was a rival for Beau's affections. And horrified to discover that the first person to whom he'd given his heart had been sharing his body with half of Nashville.

The plane sank again, dipping low over Manhattan as it prepared to land on the other side of the river in Queens. Haven looked up from Iain and out the window. Not far below, the roofs of the sky-scrapers that rose out of midtown seemed so close that Haven briefly wondered if the pilot planned to fly through the streets. An entire avenue turned a bright, blaring red as drivers hit their brakes for a traffic light.

Her best friend in the world was down there somewhere. Haven could feel it. But the city was vast—even from the air it didn't seem to end. *Poor Beau,* Haven thought. *He came all this way to find his Iain.*

"Can I see?" asked a voice. The ten-year-old boy seated on the aisle had dropped his video game and was kneeling on his seat cushion for a better look.

"Sure." Haven sat back in her chair and let him lean over her.

"Just like I remembered," the boy said solemnly.

"Have you been to New York before?" Haven asked.

"Mmm-hmm. A long time ago."

"He has *not,*" the boy's mother chimed in from across the aisle.

Haven hadn't realized she was awake. "He just has an overactive imagination. How many times have I told you not to lie, Jordan?"

"I'm not lying," the boy insisted. "I flew here in a giant balloon."

"See what I mean?" the woman told Haven, her eyes searching for sympathy. "I don't know where he gets it."

"What kind of giant balloon?" Haven asked the boy quietly once his mother was no longer listening. "Do you mean a blimp? Did you fly here in a blimp?"

"Forget it," Jordan said, sulking.

The boy was still out of sorts thirty minutes later when she and Iain found themselves trapped behind his family in the taxi line at the airport. The icy wind rushed around them all, sneaking up Haven's sleeves and worming its way through the buttonholes in her coat.

"Have you ever been this cold?" she asked, trying to make small talk with the miserable little kid. He snorted once with contempt before pulling out his video game and ignoring her all together.

"Jordan!" his mother admonished him. "Don't be rude!"

"Leave me alone," he demanded.

"It's okay," Iain assured the boy's mother. "It's late and we're all exhausted."

Once they'd been ushered into a cab, Haven huddled next to Iain and tried to fight the dread that was gnawing away at her. As their taxi raced toward Manhattan, she watched the buildings across the East River grow until they loomed over the car, each a monstrous shadow bedecked in glittering lights. The city was beautiful, but it wasn't safe. Haven felt as if eyes were following them as they cut across town. Riding through wild, wintry Central Park, she began to imagine an ambush. An obstacle would appear in the road. The cab-driver would hit the brakes, and dark figures would emerge from behind the snow-covered trees. She gripped Iain's hand and pressed her face into his cashmere-clad shoulder. But the ambush never came to pass. They arrived safely at their destination on the west side of Central Park—an enormous building with towers that resembled a pair of horns. She and Iain hurried into the lobby of the Andorra apartments, Haven with the collar of her coat turned up, and Iain with a baseball cap pulled down to hide his face. On the seventeenth floor, they knocked at a door.

"Come in, come in!" Frances Whitman beamed at the pair of them. The chipper, thirty-something blonde had answered the door of her opulent apartment in tattered flannel pajamas. She looked like a peasant who'd inherited a palace. "I'm so thrilled you're here! It gets lonely in this big old place with no one around."

"Iain, I'd like you to meet Frances, my . . ." Haven paused. "What would you say we are, Frances?"

"Third cousins, one lifetime removed." Frances winked at Iain. She and Haven had met for the first time eighteen months earlier, when Haven had been researching her previous existence as Constance Whitman. Haven was surprised to learn that Constance had one distant relation left in Manhattan—and shocked to discover that Frances had inherited the apartment where Constance's parents had once lived. The last time Haven had spoken to Frances was outside Iain's Manhattan funeral, but when Haven had phoned her out of the blue, Frances treated Haven like nothing less than a long-lost relative.

"It's a pleasure to meet you," Iain said as he took off his hat.

"Oooh, he's *so* handsome!" Frances informed Haven in a stage whisper. "No wonder you keep searching for him in every life. I wouldn't let that get away either." She turned back to Iain and offered him her hand. "I can't tell you how happy I was to find out that you didn't die in the fire. It would be a shame if the rest of us couldn't enjoy that face while you have it."

"Why thank you, Ms. Whitman," Iain said, planting a kiss on her knuckles. The woman's eyes widened with surprise. She hadn't expected him to play along.

"So charming!" she mouthed at Haven. "But please, Iain, call me *Frances*. Haven told me what happened. It's like something out of some tawdry romance novel. And I mean that in the very best way, of course. I hope you guys won't mind if I live vicariously for a little while."

Iain laughed. "Not at all," he said.

"Thanks so much for giving us a place to stay," Haven added. "You're the only person in New York that I know we can trust."

"And I imagine it's hard to rent a hotel room in a city where one of you is supposed to have died," Frances observed.

"It's even harder when you're both broke," Haven added.

"Pssh," Frances dismissed all talk of money with a wave of her hand. "You have no idea what I'd give to be young and poor and in love. The only things my money seems to buy are lawyers and gold diggers. You should enjoy your poverty while you can."

"That's what I've been trying to tell Haven all along," Iain said.

"Then I guess you've learned a thing or three over your past hundred lives," Frances fired back flirtatiously.

Iain peered down at Haven. *What exactly have you told her?* his eyes seemed to ask.

The message in Haven's smile was clear. *Not everything*, it said. Haven had given Frances all the romance she'd been craving—nothing more.

A clock chimed and Frances jumped. "What am I thinking?!" she exclaimed. "It must be two o'clock in the morning your time. Come on. I'll show you to your room. We can catch up over breakfast."

Haven and Iain followed Frances as she shuffled down the hall in her slippers. The corridor's walls were lined with art purchased by generations of Whitman family collectors, and Haven recognized most of the works. Her eyes had just passed over a small watercolor that Constance Whitman's mother had bought on their trip to Rome in 1924 when Haven suddenly heard shouting in a nearby room. At first she wondered if a television had switched on. But the three voices were familiar. Constance and her parents were at war once more, and the subject of their argument appeared to be a young man named Ethan. Haven gripped Iain's hand, and the noises began to fade away. The past and the present were not mixing well.

"Here we go. This is where you'll both be staying." Frances opened a door and stepped to the side, thrilled to prove her coolness by allowing two young people to share the same bed. "I just had it completely redone."

"This is Constance's room," Haven gasped. Though the furnishings were different, she recognized the view. She remembered standing in front of that very same window, wishing she were somewhere—anywhere—else.

"Oh dear. I thought you'd be pleased. Is it going to be a problem?" Frances said, clearly horrified that she'd committed such a terrible faux pas. "Do you want me to put you up somewhere else? It won't take a minute to get another room ready."

"No, no, this is fine," Haven insisted, feeling a little bit queasy.

BUT IT WASN'T fine. Even with Iain's warm body beside her, she tossed and turned all night until she was trapped somewhere between exhaustion and delirium. Her eyes opened, and she found herself in a restaurant, wearing an uncomfortable white dress composed of layers and layers of ruffles. She was Constance again, and it was her sixteenth birthday. It would be years before she would meet the love of her life. She was having lunch with her mother, who had temporarily abandoned Constance to go gossip with a friend on the other side of the room. Constance waited, idly plucking petals off the roses in the middle of the table. A waitress arrived and placed an enormous sundae in front of her. It wasn't the same woman who had taken their order.

"I didn't ask for this," Constance said. She might have accepted it, but she could see her mother watching from across the restaurant. Having been plump as a girl, Elizabeth Whitman kept a close eye on her daughter's figure.

"No?" said the waitress with a smile that was a little too familiar. She was not much older than Constance—perhaps eighteen or nineteen. "I'll take it away then."

The waitress picked up the sundae and placed it back on her tray. Left behind on the table was an envelope with *Constance Whitman* inscribed on the front. Constance looked up, but the waitress had disappeared through the door to the kitchen. She slid the envelope down into her lap and opened it as stealthily as she could.

SHE WOKE DISORIENTED. When she finally remembered who and where she was, Haven snuck out of bed and left Iain sleeping. She found Frances sitting on the sofa in the living room. Behind her, a large window framed the sky. Haven felt like she was floating.

"Sit, sit," Frances said, her eyes lingering on the morning headlines for a moment. Then she folded the newspaper and made room for Haven on the couch. "Do you want coffee and toast?"

"I'd love some," Haven said, her voice still raspy.

"Is Iain asleep?" Frances asked. She clearly had something on her mind.

"He is," Haven confirmed.

"In that case, do you want to tell me what you're doing back in New York?" Frances asked as she poured Haven a cup of coffee. "You were rather enigmatic when you phoned."

"My friend Beau has disappeared."

"The big, handsome kid you were with at Iain's funeral?"

"That's him. He came to New York a few days ago to meet a guy who claimed to be his soul mate. No one has heard from him since."

"I'm so sorry," Frances said.

"No need to be sorry." Haven took a bite of toast and washed it down with black coffee. She felt more confident now that she was finally in the same city as Beau. "He's alive, and I'm going to find him."

Frances watched Haven. She seemed to sense that there was more to the story.

"*You're* going to find him?"

"I have to."

"And not the police?"

"They're looking too. But they won't be looking as hard as I will."

"And I suppose I shouldn't remind you that you're still just a kid?"

Haven almost laughed. She'd never been just a kid. "Go right ahead. It won't do any good."

Frances crossed her arms, and for the first time since Haven had met her, the petite blonde could have passed for a real adult. "Well, you're certainly risking a lot coming back to New York. If anyone here catches sight of your boyfriend, the whole jig will be up. Is he ready to explain to the world why he's been playing dead for over a year?"

"We're hoping no one will find out he's alive," Haven said.

"I hope so too. Weren't the police looking for Iain before he supposedly died in the fire? Wasn't he the main suspect in the death of that musician? What was the guy's name? Jeremy . . ."

"Johns. Iain had nothing to do with it."

"I believe you. But the police might not."

Haven wished Frances would find another dead horse to beat. She was well aware of the risks she and Iain were taking. Now that they were in New York, there wasn't much point in rehashing the list. "You're right, Frances. I should have come back by myself, but Iain never would have let me. Still, I don't know what he expects to do while he's in New York. He'll probably end up spending most of his time with you. It's too dangerous for him to tag along with me."

Frances took a sip of coffee. As she lowered the cup, there was a hint of a smirk on her lips. "This may be my first time on this planet, but I still know a thing or two about men. You really think that gorgeous boy is planning to hang out on the Upper West Side with a lady who's old enough to be his aunt?"

"What else is he going to do?" Haven asked.

"Oh, I'm sure he has a few ideas." Frances paused for another taste of coffee. "But right now I'm more interested in *your* plans. What exactly do you have in mind? Do you have any idea where your friend might be?"

"No, but I know where to start looking," Haven said. "The guy Beau came here to meet seemed to know details about a life we all shared in fourteenth-century Florence. I figure I might stand a chance of identifying the person who took Beau if I can find out more about our life back in Italy."

"How are you going to do *that*?"

Haven hesitated. If she told Frances what she knew about the Ouroboros Society, she'd be putting her in terrible danger. "There's a woman here who claims to see into other people's past lives. I'm going to pay her a visit today."

"That sounds like it ought to be interesting," Frances said.

"Yeah, and I haven't even told you the best part yet," Haven said. "Apparently the woman works out of a spa."

"A spa?"

"That's what Iain says. She does a lot of her consultations at some fancy ladies' spa that only the super wealthy can afford."

"You don't mean the one down on Morton Street, do you?"

"That's it!" Haven exclaimed. "How do you know about it?"

"Well, I'm hardly strapped for cash," Frances said with a modest chuckle. "I went there a few times when I was in college. I haven't been back lately. The crowd there is rather cliquish. But I'm happy to go with you today if you feel like some company."

"Thanks," Haven demurred. "But that won't be necessary."

"You may want me there," Frances insisted. "There's something odd about the place. You'll see what I mean. It's . . . *unusual*."

"Why should that bother me? My whole life is unusual," Haven said.

Frances laughed. "It is, isn't it, you lucky girl. Oh, that reminds me! I have something for you." She jumped up from the couch. "I'd have given it to you last night, but Iain was there, and I thought you might want to take a look at it alone first." Haven watched Frances digging through a drawer of the desk that sat in one corner of the room. Finally, the woman held up a scrap of paper triumphantly. "A workman found this when they were renovating Constance's room. It was hidden under a floorboard. . . ."

Haven recognized the note, though its heavy white paper had long since turned yellow.

Keep this to remind you. You're not who you think you are. When he comes to you, you must find us. Don't dare trust yourself. Telephone LE4-8987.

"Weird, right?" Frances said. "Do you know anything about it?"

"I had a dream about this note last night. I saw a girl give it to Constance."

"Do you think she was being warned about Ethan?" Frances had a nose for gossip.

"I have no idea," Haven said, grabbing a clean cup off the table. "I'll take Iain some coffee and see what he knows. Maybe Constance told him about it."

"MORNING, GORGEOUS," Iain said when Haven threw open the door to their room. She'd hoped to find him in bed, with his hair rumpled and his pajama top half buttoned. Instead he was already dressed and scrolling through messages on his phone.

"I brought you breakfast in bed," Haven said, setting down the tray she'd filled with toast, bagels, coffee, and jams. "You're going out?"

"Yes." Iain grabbed a sesame bagel and ripped it apart. "Thanks, Haven. You wouldn't believe how much I've missed these things."

"Where are you going?" She had to wait until he'd swallowed a mouthful of bread.

"To see what I can do to find Beau."

"But . . ." She wanted to argue that it wasn't what they had agreed. But the look in Iain's eyes said he wasn't about to listen to reason.

"You can't expect me to come to New York and do nothing, Haven. I know I can't talk you out of visiting the Pythia, so please don't talk me out of trying to help."

"But—"

"No more *buts*. Come here."

Once she was close enough, he grabbed her arm and pulled her down on his lap. "We'll *both* be careful," he said, just before his lips met hers. By the time they parted, Haven had forgotten both her worries and her mission.

"So what else did you bring me?" Iain asked, plucking the yellowing note from Haven's hand.

"Oh! Right! God, I almost forgot. Frances found it. I'm pretty sure it belonged to Constance. Did she ever mention it to Ethan?"

Iain seemed to read the note three or four times before looking back up at her. "No, I don't remember her saying anything. Do you know who sent this to Constance?"

"A waitress in a restaurant delivered it to her. I think I saw the incident last night in a dream. What do you think it means, 'You're not who you think you are'?"

Iain shook his head. "I have no idea."

"Iain, is there something you're not telling me?"

"Like what?" he responded cryptically.

"If I knew, I wouldn't have asked!"

"Okay, don't go all Southern spitfire on me. I think the note means that you need to be very, very cautious while we're here."

"I still don't understand. Why would these people want me to call them when I met you?"

Iain frowned as he returned the piece of paper to Haven. "You think it's *me* they were talking about?"

"Who else would it be?"

"Can't you see, Haven? The note must be referring to *Adam*."

CHAPTER ELEVEN

The street entrance to the baths was unmarked. All Frances and Haven found was a faded blue door with a hand-painted address. Beyond it lay a set of stairs that led downward. The air grew hotter and more humid with each step they took. At the bottom, deep below the New York streets, they entered a tiny white room where a receptionist was stationed behind a desk. She was extremely attractive, though she'd done her best to disguise the fact. Her hair was pulled back from her face in a tight ponytail, and the lab coat she wore was large enough to make her look lumpy.

A sign on the wall politely refused all visitors under the age of eighteen. Once Haven had shown her ID, Frances handed the secretary her credit card without waiting to be presented with a bill. Anyone who knew how to find the baths didn't care what they cost, she'd explained to Haven in the cab downtown. Once the transaction was complete, the woman stood up and led the way to the dressing room.

Haven had expected to find a sumptuous setting with pristine white tiles and gilded fixtures. Instead, she entered a cavernous room that looked as though it had been carved out of Manhattan's bedrock. Benches that were little more than slabs of granite were the chamber's only furniture. The woman in the lab coat placed two wire baskets on one of the benches. Inside the baskets were simple white cotton robes.

"Please leave all of your personal belongings in the baskets," she instructed. "I will take them when you're finished. You'll find the baths through the door on your right." After that one brief announcement, the receptionist left Haven and Frances alone to change.

With her skimpy robe covering far less than she'd anticipated, Haven opened the door to the baths and was enveloped by a cloud of hot air. She and Frances followed a long corridor until they arrived at a pool surrounded by tall marble columns and wooden lounge chairs. Steam issued from the pool's murky green waters, and the air stank of something like sulfur. The light was weak. There was barely enough of it to make sense of the scene. Ghostly figures floated through the mist. A glistening naked body rose from the pool and lay facedown on a nearby lounge chair.

"They say the water comes from an underground river," Frances whispered.

"That must be one nasty river," Haven remarked. "It looks more like runoff from a sewer to me."

"The green stuff in the water is supposed to be good for you. But it's whatever they put in the *air* down here that makes you feel nice and relaxed."

"There's something in the air?" Haven asked.

"Take a good whiff," Frances said. "That's not steam you smell. I have no idea what it is, but I've heard that people have hallucinations sometimes. A girl I knew in high school had a ten-minute conversation with a wall sconce. She thought it was God."

"How long have these baths been here?" Haven wondered. They looked old enough to have been built by the Romans.

"I don't know," Frances admitted. "But my grandmother used to talk about them. She claimed they were the only thing that helped her rheumatism. She also told me that back in the old days rich New York girls would be given the address of this place for their eighteenth birthdays. Do you think Constance ever dropped in for a *shvitz*?"

"What's a *shvitz*?" Haven asked.

Frances shook her head sadly. "You need to spend more time in New York. You're not getting enough culture in Italy. Now where's this woman you're looking for?"

Haven began to circle the perimeter of the pool. There were clusters of white-robed women wherever she looked. "Her name is Phoebe. She's old. I'm not sure what she looks like, but I doubt she's alone."

"Is that the lady?" Frances asked. In a dark corner of the room, a tall, thin figure sat upright on one of the chairs, a towel draped over her head. All Haven could see of the woman was her moving lips. Two other women leaned toward her, trying to catch every word that was uttered.

"Could be," Haven said. "I'll check it out. You go relax. Have a swim or something. I'll find you when I'm done."

"I don't know." Frances hesitated. "I promised Iain I wouldn't let you go off by yourself."

"She's just an old woman," Haven said with a huff. "What could possibly happen?"

She didn't wait for an answer and left Frances standing alone by the pool. She chose a lounge chair not far from the Pythia and lay down with her eyes closed and her ears open.

"You were a queen, and you were murdered by your very own husband," Haven heard the old woman say. Her voice was deep and mellifluous and somehow familiar. "He had changed the world to be by your side, but when you gave him a daughter instead of a son, he turned against you. He may not have killed you with his own two hands, but he might as well have. He accused you of witchcraft, infidelity, and incest, and he had your head removed for the crimes he concocted."

"This doesn't sound like a very nice life," the woman whined.

"Not all of our lives are *nice*," the Pythia responded wearily. "But your life changed the course of history. And your daughter was one of the most powerful women the world has ever known."

"My *daughter*?" the woman whined again. "Not me?"

"I've got it!" The woman's friend gasped. "Oh Joan, you must have been Anne Boleyn!"

"Who's *that*?" the first woman asked.

"You know, that wife of Henry VIII. He chopped off her head so he could marry someone else. Have you ever had any headaches or neck pains that you couldn't explain?"

"Now that you mention it, yes!" The first woman could barely contain herself. "I do have migraines sometimes! And I've always been terrified of axes!"

"Well, there you go!" her friend exclaimed. "Now you know why! And don't forget your terrible taste in men. That last husband of yours would have murdered you too, if he'd had the chance."

The first woman turned back to the Pythia, her enthusiasm renewed. "Can you please tell me more?" she pleaded. "What else do you see? Did I really have affairs? Were they as exciting as they sound?"

"I see nothing now," the Pythia said. "My energy is spent. You must go."

"Oh no! Please! You see I'm having a little get-together this weekend, and I was hoping to invite Miranda Bennett, and she won't even *talk* to people who don't have the right pedigree. . . ."

Phoebe held up her hand. "Stop. Come again in two days, and I will attempt to see more."

"Oh, thank you!" the first woman gushed. "This has been *so* fascinating."

"Go," Phoebe urged them once more.

The two women wandered off arm in arm, whispering in each other's ears. Once they had disappeared in the mist, Haven rose and approached the Pythia.

"How much of what you told them was true?" Haven asked.

The woman glanced up at Haven. Half hidden beneath the towel, her face appeared old and frail, but her hazel eyes were dancing. "You're very bold," she noted without seeming offended. "Didn't one of your mothers teach you that it's not polite to eavesdrop?"

"I'm sorry," Haven said. "I just got the sense that you were telling them what they wanted to hear so they'd go away."

"Yes, I doubt Ms. Mortimer would be interested to know that she's been ignorant and useless in every life she's led. I imagine the only notable thing she's done is perfect the art of divorcing rich men. But these people all want to hear that they changed the course of history. If I told them the truth, they would just keep pestering me until I gave them the lies they were looking for."

"So she wasn't Anne Boleyn."

"Goodness no!" the Pythia exclaimed. "I *knew* Anne Boleyn. She would have *my* head if she knew what I've done. Fortunately for both of us, Anne never came back to earth. She had enough of this planet the first time around. Now. What can I do for *you*?"

"You can tell *me* the truth," Haven said. "I need to know more about one of my previous lives, and I was hoping you might be able to help me."

"No." The Pythia shook her head. "I can't help you. I am expecting another client in just a few moments."

"If you can't help me now, maybe I could make an appointment with you? The sooner the better, if possible. A friend of mine is missing. He came to New York to meet someone we both knew in another existence. I have to find a way to travel back to the fourteenth century. It's a matter of life and death. . . ."

"It is always a matter of life and death, Miss Moore," the old woman told her.

Haven froze. "You know me?"

"Yes. And Mr. Morrow as well. You were reckless to come here. Do you know where you are? Do you know who these people are?"

Haven glanced back at the pool and felt eyes regarding her through the steam. How long had they been watching her? What did they want? Haven's fear only grew when she realized she didn't know what was scaring her. It was the blind terror of a trapped animal. The panic of a beast that's been dragged out of hiding. Haven frantically searched for Frances, who was nowhere to be found.

"Relax, my dear. They aren't going to hurt you," the Pythia told Haven. "Some of them have even been waiting for you to return. But I'm afraid I can't help you. It has been expressly forbidden, and the walls here have ears."

"Forbidden by whom?" Haven demanded.

"I know that I don't need to tell you that," the Pythia said.

Haven turned and bolted for the dressing room.

CHAPTER TWELVE

The dressing room was deserted. There was no attendant. No Frances. No wire basket with Haven's belongings. She stood there in the cavernous space, considering her options. She couldn't leave the spa in her cotton robe. She'd freeze to death before she had a chance to catch a cab, and she couldn't pay the fare if she caught one. Haven was stuck.

She poked her head into the lobby and saw no one at all. Tiptoeing out, Haven picked up the receiver on the phone that sat on the receptionist's desk. There was no dial tone, just the soft whistle of wind. Returning to the dressing room, she checked under the stall doors in the bathroom, desperate to find Frances—or anyone else who might help her collect her things and escape. Finally, she took a seat on a bench in the far corner of the room, hoping to stay out of sight until she could decide what her next step should be.

The women inside the spa—were they all members of the Ouroboros Society? How did they know who she was? Which of them had been waiting for her? Iain had been right to worry, she now realized. They should never have come back to New York. The Morrow money, Beau's disappearance—they both must have been part of a plot to lure her here. How long would it be before Adam came to claim her? She caught sight of her own reflection in a mirror across the room and immediately looked away. Huddled on the bench, pale and practically naked, her black curls shooting in every direction, Haven barely recognized herself—the mirror showed a girl she'd never wanted to be.

The door to the lobby swung open, and a great gust of steam was sucked out the exit. A tall figure in a dark, knee-length overcoat appeared at the opposite end of the dressing room. Haven didn't wait to see his face. She silently rose from her bench and crept into one of the bathroom stalls, where she perched on top of the toilet, praying under her breath.

She heard the sound of footsteps on the granite floor. They came to a halt in the middle of the room.

"Haven." The name echoed. "I'm afraid I saw you just now. Would you mind coming out?"

It could have been mistaken for a polite request, but Haven knew she had no choice but to obey. She stood up and adjusted her robe, wishing it covered more than the bare minimum. Then she opened the door and marched out into the dressing room like a condemned woman greeting her fate.

Haven hadn't forgotten how handsome he was—how dark and debonair. He still had the same aura of power about him, as though he could snap his fingers and turn the world off. But he looked younger than Haven remembered, no more than twenty. He was dressed for the winter weather in a perfectly cut cashmere coat. His hands were clad in black leather gloves and a charcoal scarf was tied around his neck. It was nothing more than a costume, she realized. He needed no protection from the cold.

"Hello, Adam." Haven felt light-headed, short of breath. But much to her surprise, she no longer felt any fear. Maybe it was because Haven was older now. Or maybe Adam had improved his human disguise. But something had changed since they'd last been together.

At first Adam said nothing in response. His jaw was set, and his cheekbones sharp. He stared at her as if he couldn't quite believe his good luck. He took off his gloves and ran his fingers through his lustrous black hair. Once he'd finished, he shoved his long white hands in his pockets, and Haven wondered if he was trying to restrain them. She knew those same hands had been allowed to caress her skin in the past. Adam knew it too.

"I was told you were here," he said. "I was certain it was a mistake. But here you are, indeed. And you're more beautiful than ever."

There was something about the way Adam looked at her—as if nothing could draw his attention away. Haven had never been the type to take compliments to heart, but when Adam said she was beautiful, she had to believe him.

"A mistake?" The words fell just short of mocking. Haven couldn't muster the indignation she needed. "Do you really expect me to believe that you didn't plan this whole thing?"

"What *thing*?" Adam looked confused. It wasn't an expression that came naturally to him. "Perhaps you can tell me what I've done? I refuse to take credit if I don't deserve it."

"My friend Beau disappeared three days ago. He came here to meet someone, and he vanished without a trace. Where do you have him? I won't leave with you unless you let him go. I need to know he'll be safe."

"I'm sorry." Adam shook his head. "You've been misinformed. I didn't have anything to do with Beau's disappearance. You must be terribly worried. Is there anything I can do to help?"

Haven studied Adam, trying to figure out what his angle might be. "You can let me speak to the Pythia. I was told she's forbidden to help me."

"Yes," Adam said. "She is. Now and in the future."

"Why?"

"Because she's a fraud. Nothing she says is true. Her name is Phoebe, and she is an employee of the Ouroboros Society. I pay her to keep our senior members happy. They enjoy hearing tales of illustrious lives they never lived. But Phoebe is just a storyteller. She doesn't *see* anything. No one is able to peer into the past lives of others. It's simply not possible."

"Oh," Haven said. Her best hope of finding Beau had evaporated, and the disappointment hit her hard.

"I didn't intend to upset you." Adam took one step forward and reached out to touch her before he thought better of it and let his arm drop to his side. "Why did you think the Pythia could help you find your friend?"

The question had a simple answer, Haven realized at once. Leah Frizzell had instructed her to find the woman surrounded by smoke. It was Leah's vision of the future that had led Haven to the spa. Which meant there might be a reason Haven needed to come face-to-face with Adam. She just had to figure out what it was.

"I was told I'd have to see into one of my past lives if I want to find Beau. So I came here to speak to the Pythia. Are you sure you didn't know I was back in New York?"

"You still believe I arranged this encounter?" Adam asked. He almost seemed wounded by the suggestion. "Do you really imagine that I couldn't have found you before this if I'd wanted to? I promised you this lifetime. To be honest, it's a promise I often regret. But it's not one I intend to break. The reason I'm here now is because you came to *me*. The Ouroboros Society has owned this spa for decades. I thought you knew that. Apparently you did not. So you're free to go whenever you like. I only wanted to say hello." He started for the door.

"Wait," Haven called. "That's it? But the Pythia said there are people here who've been waiting for me."

"I don't know what she's talking about," Adam said. "I suspect Phoebe may spend too much time inhaling the fumes down here. I didn't expect to see you again until your next lifetime. This has been a very pleasant surprise, nothing more. However . . ."

"Yes?" The word slipped out and the conversation continued. Somewhere inside, Haven wasn't quite ready to see Adam leave.

"If you do want my help, the Society has a number of contacts in the law enforcement community. I would be happy to call in a few favors. I could have head of the NYPD searching for your friend in the next fifteen minutes."

"Why would you do that?" Haven asked warily. Nothing was making sense to her. "You hate Beau. A year and a half ago you wanted him dead. Why would you help me find him? What's in it for you?"

"The chance to spend a little more time in your company, of course," Adam said with a spark of hope in his eyes. "That's worth more to me than anything. But beyond that, the only thing I'd get is the opportunity to prove that I'm not what you think I am."

"Not what I think?" Haven laughed bitterly. "Adam, you burned down two of my houses. You murdered my father!"

"I did *not* kill your father," Adam insisted. "I thought you understood. Tidmore was working alone. As for the houses—no one was meant to be harmed in those fires."

"Dr. Tidmore . . ." The name still left a terrible taste in her mouth. He was the man Adam had sent to Tennessee to watch over Haven until she came of age. "How is he, anyway? Enjoying his reward for ruining my childhood?"

"I can't say. He left the Society months ago. I haven't seen him since."

"Really?" Haven laughed bitterly. "After all of his hard work, I would have thought you'd keep Tidmore on as your right-hand man."

"Things have changed. I no longer have need of his brand of services," Adam said.

"What—so you're claiming you've been rehabilitated? Does that mean you won't be ordering any more fires or executions?" The idea was too ludicrous to consider.

Adam seemed to absorb the affront. "I'm merely saying that I've come to *understand* a few things. If there's a chance you'll be mine in your next life, I want to be worthy of you. That's why I've offered to help you. It's the only reason."

"You'll never be worthy, and I don't want your help," Haven said. "I'd like you to leave."

Adam didn't move. He stood with his hands still deep in his pockets while his dark eyes swept across every inch of her skin.

"Now."

"Very well. If that's what you would like," he agreed at last. "It's been a pleasure to see you again, Haven. I'm sorry you don't feel the same way."

He disappeared through the door to the lobby, and Haven quickly checked behind her, half hoping someone had been there to witness the exchange. She had asked Adam Rosier to leave, and he had obeyed. Haven felt like she'd lifted an eighteen-wheeler with her bare hands or ripped a door off its hinges. Somehow she had summoned a power she'd never known she possessed. There was no other way to explain her escape.

The door from the baths flew open with a bang, and Frances rushed in.

"Haven! Where the hell did you go?" she screeched as if Haven were a toddler who'd wandered off in a shopping mall. "I've been looking all over the spa for you!"

CHAPTER THIRTEEN

Haven and Frances parted ways outside the entrance to the baths. Haven no longer had any need for an escort. Adam didn't seem to be a threat to her, and Haven wanted some time alone. It had been a strange experience, having all her darkest fears realized, only to see them fizzle away in the daylight. Was it possible that Adam had somehow been reformed?

Haven wandered north, through Washington Square Park, and stopped outside the Washington Mews. Once, in the middle of that narrow cobblestone lane, there had been a white cottage with a red door and green velvet curtains. Haven couldn't count the times she had stood by its windows, waiting breathlessly for the sound of a key in the lock. She and Iain had called the cottage home in two different lifetimes, and when she closed her eyes, Haven could hear Iain charging up the stairs to the bedroom. She could feel him wrapping her up in his arms. The site had been as sacred to Haven as the memories themselves. She had lived, loved, and died there.

But the cottage was gone now, burned to the ground. Haven's heart broke to see the modern eyesore that had been built in its place. It was all Adam's work—he'd wanted to erase all traces of the lives she and Iain had shared. Haven's anger and fear returned in a rush. The same being who'd destroyed her home could never be anything more than a monster.

SHE HOPPED ON the subway at Union Square. A woman dressed like a backup dancer in an old-school rap video boarded behind her. She wedged her spandex-covered butt into the seat beside Haven and proceeded to further invade Haven's space by unfolding a copy of the *New York Daily News*. As the train left the station, the woman spoke.

"You've let down your guard," she said, keeping her face buried in the newspaper.

"Pardon me?" Haven demanded, her senses instantly on full alert.

"Don't look at me," the woman ordered. "There's a gray man seated on the other side, half a car down on the right."

Flustered and frightened, but trying her best to look casual, Haven turned and spotted a man dressed in jeans, sneakers, and a baseball cap with no logo on it. She caught the motion of his head swiveling back in the opposite direction. He'd been watching her. A brief glint of metal told her he was wearing an earpiece. Adam had ordered one of his men to follow her. Haven could feel her veins throbbing and her palms sweating inside of her gloves.

The woman spoke again. "At the next stop, I want you to get off the train. Walk two cars down and get back on. I'll do the rest."

"Why should I trust you?" Haven tried to speak without moving her lips.

"Because we've helped you many times in the past," the woman told her.

"We?" Haven asked.

"Shhh," the woman commanded.

THE TRAIN RUMBLED into the Twenty-third Street station. As soon as the subway doors opened, Haven leaped up and joined the crowd shoving each other out onto the platform. Then, exactly as instructed, she hurried toward the back of the train and reentered it two cars down. Gripping a pole, she heard a commotion outside in the station.

"Pervert!" the woman in the spandex pants was screaming at the gray man who'd been tailing Haven. "How dare you grope me! I'll teach you to touch a lady's ass!"

The crowd was cheering her on as she pummeled the man with her oversize handbag.

"Dirty, dirty, dirty bastard!" she shouted, punctuating each word with a whack of her purse.

"Ladies and gentlemen." It was the voice of the subway conductor. "I'd like to stay here and watch justice be served as much as the rest of you, but I have a schedule to keep. So if you're coming with me, please step back inside the train and stand clear of the closing doors."

With that, the doors slid shut, and the train lurched forward. Haven scanned the rows of passengers packed onto the plastic benches that lined both sides of the car. Most were reading, some stared into space, and a couple were either napping or recently deceased. One, a pretty Indian girl with long black hair and ruby bindi, was smiling straight at her. To Haven's relief, none of the passengers could have passed for a gray man. She closed her eyes and took a deep breath of stale subway air.

"Hello."

Haven jumped. The Indian girl had risen from her seat and come over to share Haven's pole. "Remember me?" she asked.

"What?" Haven's dread had returned in full force.

"Do you remember me?" The girl enunciated each word.

94

"Ummm." Haven bit her lip and tried to concentrate. The girl's face *was* familiar, but she couldn't quite place her.

"We met at an Indian grocery on Lexington Avenue. You and your brother stopped by one night over a year ago, when there were some men chasing after you."

A memory flashed through Haven's mind. She was huddled with Beau in a hidden storage space while Adam's men searched the girl's shop. Beau held Haven pressed to his side, and she knew that if the men ever managed to find them, Beau would fight to the death to protect her.

"Of course!" Haven exhaled with relief. "You hid us until they were gone. I always meant to come back and thank you."

"But you didn't," the girl noted.

"No," Haven admitted, taken aback. "I didn't. I'm sorry."

The girl reached out a dainty hand. "My name is Chandra," she said.

"Haven Moore."

The girl nodded as though she already knew Haven's name, and her smug smile suggested she knew much more than that. Chandra was toying with her, though it was hard to tell what her motive might be. Now that Haven was no longer frightened, the games were beginning to piss her off.

"Look, Chandra." Haven took a step toward the girl, but Chandra held her ground. "This is all just a little *unusual*. What exactly is going on here? Were you with the woman who just helped me?"

"Her name is Cleo. And yes. We belong to the same organization. I've been asked to speak with you on behalf of Phoebe."

"*Phoebe?*" Haven sputtered. There had been too many surprises in too short a space.

"Some people call her the Pythia. You met her earlier today."

Haven had just opened her mouth to respond when the train screeched into another station.

"Wait," Chandra ordered as a small group of European tourists crammed into the car. Haven watched Chandra examine each individual face. A businessman with his eyes glued to a BlackBerry was the last person to board. When he blindly grabbed hold of their pole, Chandra tapped his shoulder. "Don't stop here, big shot. Move it along," she barked. The man peered down at the pretty girl and shook his head in disbelief. One look at her face, though, and he chose not to argue.

"I know who Phoebe is," Haven continued once the man had edged further down the car. "What does she want?"

"She wants to help you," Chandra said. "We all do. We want to help you see the life you need to see."

"How is *Phoebe* supposed to help me?" Haven asked. "I know she's a fraud. She invents stories to make rich people happy."

Chandra giggled girlishly. "And who told you that?"

Haven chose not to reply.

"Exactly," Chandra told her. "Your sources have not been reliable. Phoebe is undercover at the Ouroboros Society. She pretends to be a charlatan, but her gifts are very real."

"And who are *you*?" Haven demanded. There was something slippery about the girl, and Haven was impatient for her to get to the point.

"I am one of a group of sisters. We call ourselves the Horae. Like you, we have all lived many lives. Unlike you, our lives have been devoted to saving mankind from his influence."

"His?"

"You call him Adam, but that's not his real name. He has no real name."

"And how exactly do you save mankind from his influence?"

"Why don't I let Phoebe explain? She has a proposition for you. One that may benefit us all."

"That sounds great," said Haven dismissively. "But I'll have to think about it. I didn't come to New York to make new friends. I have things to do while I'm here."

"We know, and that's part of our plan," Chandra replied. "You told Phoebe that a friend of yours has vanished. You help us with the one you call Adam, and we promise to help you locate your friend."

"I don't know. Like I said, I'll have to think about it."

"You mean you need to discuss the idea with Iain Morrow."

Spoken at full volume on a crowded subway car, the name was clearly meant to provoke. "Excuse me?" Haven asked, glancing around to make sure no one else had heard.

"Yes, we know about Mr. Morrow. We know he's still alive. And we can help him stay that way. We can even ensure that the two of you never need to hide again. You'll be able to live wherever you like without having to watch over your shoulders for gray men."

"And how are you going to make that happen?"

"Meet us at 623 Lenox Avenue." Chandra handed Haven a business card. "This evening at six. Be sure to bring Mr. Morrow. Phoebe will explain everything to you both."

Haven looked at the card. It was dirty and crumpled, as if it had been picked up off the street. Stamped on the card was the address and a phone number: 534-8987.

The train pulled into Grand Central Station, and the mob inside the car traded places with the one waiting on the platform. Haven stepped aside to make way for a woman pushing a baby carriage filled with old, dirty dolls. When she returned to her original spot, Chandra was gone.

CHAPTER FOURTEEN

"You saw him! And you *talked* to him?" They were outside on Frances Whitman's terrace, and Iain was pacing back and forth. Haven watched his feet, worried that he might slip on a patch of ice and plummet down to the park below.

"I didn't have much of a choice. Someone at the spa must have told him I was there." Haven could see Frances peeking out at them through a crack in the living room drapes.

"You had a choice not to speak to him, didn't you?"

Haven wrapped her arms around herself. Seventeen floors above the streets, the wind was wild. "What was I supposed to do, just stand there and say nothing?"

"You should have run," Iain said.

"I was wearing a tiny little spa robe with nothing on underneath! Where was I supposed to go?"

"You were wearing *what*?" Iain exclaimed a little too loudly. A light flipped on in an apartment one floor above them, and Haven saw a figure peering out into the twilight. "Never mind. You can spare me the details. I don't need that image seared into my brain for the rest of eternity. So what did Adam say to you?"

"He promised again that he'd leave me alone. He said he had nothing to do with Beau's disappearance."

"Now that he knows you're back, do you really expect him to keep any promises? I *knew* we shouldn't have come here! You realize what this means? He probably had you tailed. There could be gray men waiting outside the building right now."

"No, there aren't," Haven insisted. "I lost the one guy who was following me."

Iain stopped pacing, but his eyes were everywhere at once, as if he were surrounded by unseen assailants. "So there *was* someone following you."

"I think so, but—"

"We've got to get you out of town. You saw Phoebe. It didn't work out. So it's time to go. That was the deal." Iain took her wrist and headed for the terrace door.

"Hey!" Haven twisted her arm free. "Let me finish. There may be another way to find Beau."

Iain froze. His chest heaved as he inhaled the night.

"There was a woman on the train uptown. She spotted a gray man following me and helped me lose him."

"Some ordinary woman on the train spotted a gray man?" Iain repeated in disbelief.

"I didn't say she was ordinary. She's a member of a group that's been looking for me. They're called the Horae. They must be the same people I've been dreaming about. The ones who sent the message to Constance."

Iain looked stunned. "The woman in the subway told you that she was one of the Horae?"

"Well, a girl named Chandra did. You'll meet her tonight." Haven pulled the card out of her coat pocket. "The Horae want to see us. So you've heard of them?"

"Yes." Iain examined the card. His confusion seemed to have calmed him. "But I thought they were just a legend. I had no idea they were real. Are you sure the woman you spoke with is dependable?"

"She saved me and Beau the last time we were in New York. She hid us when we were being chased by gray men. I suppose that makes her dependable, right? Why? What do you know about the Horae?"

Iain passed the card back to Haven. "Not much. They say there are twelve of them. They follow Adam wherever he goes. They were sisters once. Adam did something terrible to them, and now they spend each lifetime trying to punish him."

"What did Adam do?" Haven asked.

"I have no clue," Iain said. "But I have a hunch it was pretty awful."

"So will you come with me to meet them?" Haven asked, recalling the promise she'd made to herself. Wherever her quest took her, she'd make sure Iain came with her. She just hoped she wasn't pushing him too far too fast. "I need you there, and they want me to bring you."

"They know I'm alive?"

Haven nodded and Iain sighed.

"Then I guess we have to go. Do you have any idea *why* they want to meet with us?"

"The Pythia is one of them," Haven said. "She pretends to be a fraud, but her powers are real. Chandra said she can help me see the life that I shared with Beau."

"And what are they expecting in return?"

It was the same question that had been nagging at Haven. "I don't know. But if the Horae want to stop Adam, they can't be all bad."

"You're being naive, Haven. Do you want to get caught up in a feud that's lasted for millennia? Do you know what can happen to people who hate for that long?"

"Whatever the Horae want from me, they can have it," Haven stated bluntly. "If they can help me save Beau, I'll give them anything they need."

Those words seemed to shock Iain more than any others she had uttered.

"Don't make any promises until you hear their demands," he warned. "Just because they're Adam's enemies doesn't mean they're our friends."

CHAPTER FIFTEEN

Across the dark street sat an empty storefront. The space had once been home to a church. A faded purple awning read TEMPLE OF POWER, and the location was still marked by a flashing neon sign that read SIN WILL in blazing red, followed by FIND YOU OUT in brilliant white. Plastered in the plateglass windows were yellowing newspapers. It had been quite some time since the Temple of Power had heard anyone's prayers.

"That's the place," Haven said before she could read the numbers on the door. "I'd bet you anything."

"You really want to do this?" Iain asked, making it perfectly clear that he didn't.

"Absolutely." Haven said. Determined to answer his uncertainty with confidence, she hopped off the curb and into the street.

The door wasn't locked, and chimes rang when Iain stepped forward to open it. Inside, it took Haven's eyes a few moments to adjust to the darkness, but she felt the bounce of plywood flooring under her shoes and knew at once that the building had been gutted. Soon she could see electrical cables snaking down from the ceiling. Multicolored wires poked out of the walls. The storefront had been stripped of anything of value. Everything left behind was coated with layers of spray paint and decorated with the tags of New York's most prolific vandals.

"Lock the door behind you and come with me," said a voice. "Quickly. You should never be late for a meeting with Phoebe." Chandra appeared, wearing a blue denim jumpsuit and a baseball hat.

"Where are you taking us?" Iain asked.

"You'll see."

"Phoebe isn't here?" Haven had risked enough already. She couldn't ask Iain to take another leap into the unknown. "This was the address you gave me."

"Do you really think we'd write our real address down for you?" Chandra's girlie laugh sounded slightly brittle. "Or let you lead a team of gray men to see us?"

"No one followed us," Iain snapped. He seemed to have taken an instant dislike to Chandra.

"We were very careful," Haven added, trying to smooth things over.

"You're sure about that?" Chandra inquired. Haven couldn't help but look over her shoulder at the street outside the glass windows. She didn't see anyone, but that was no guarantee that there wasn't anyone out there.

"Yes," Iain said. "Because if Adam's men had followed us, I'd be dead by now."

"Maybe," Chandra replied. "Or maybe they'd wait to see where you led them first."

The girl had a point, though Haven didn't dare agree out loud. Iain's mood was growing darker by the moment and getting him as far as they'd come had been quite a challenge. She almost had to push him when Chandra headed for the back door of the store. Outside in the alley, an electrician's van sat idling. Emblazoned on its side was a cartoon god with a lightning bolt in one hand. Below the image was a company name: TITAN ELECTRIC.

"Get in the back," Chandra ordered.

Haven and Iain settled in among a jumble of extension ladders and other equipment. Chandra drove for ten minutes before she pulled the van over. "Hop out," she called to her passengers. "It's the first house on your left. Go through the door on the ground floor. There will be someone inside to greet you."

"Where the hell are we?" Iain asked as the van sped off. "Is this New York?" They were standing at the end of two rows of wooden houses that faced each other across a narrow lane. The buildings dated from the nineteenth century, and they were all painted a sunny yellow, with green shutters and brown trim. Light pooled around the gas lamps that lined the street. Haven spun around. Behind them, an old white mansion sat perched on a hill. It was so quiet outside, they could hear the streetlights humming.

"We didn't go very far," Haven noted. "We've got to be somewhere near Harlem."

The door that led to the ground floor of one of the nearby buildings opened a crack. A strip of bright light cut across the road.

Haven took Iain's hand, but he hesitated. "Let's go," she insisted, almost dragging him behind her.

A woman in her twenties met them at the door. She wore a chocolate-colored sheath dress, and her electric-blue hair was swept into a chic chignon.

"Welcome to Sylvan Terrace. My name is Vera. Please, come inside. You must be freezing."

"Do I know you?" It was hard for Haven to place Vera's face when she couldn't stop staring at her hair.

"This is the second time we've met in this lifetime." The woman had the friendly, patient smile of a kindergarten teacher. "The first was at a café in Greenwich Village. But I feel as if I've known you forever. May I take your coats?"

"That's right! I remember now," Haven said as she loosened her scarf. "A gray man followed me to a café. You were my waitress. You told me to slip out the bathroom window. How did you . . ."

The thought was shoved to one side as a million new questions jostled their way to the front of the line. With her coat half off and still dangling from one shoulder, Haven stopped to take in her surroundings. She and Iain had entered a large round chamber. Four closed doors were set in the parchment-colored walls that encircled them. On one side of the room, an elliptical staircase rose like a twisting ribbon of sandstone. With no banister and no obvious means of support, it seemed to have been carved from a single piece of rock. Beyond the stairs was a sitting area. Chairs and sofas covered in honey-colored velvets were turned toward a blaze in a marble fireplace. A large clock on the mantel kept the time. Haven glanced up at the ceiling. The room was lit by two chandeliers that gave off a pale, golden light. High above, where the staircase reached its apex, an enormous skylight framed the moon. The whole house may have looked modern and empty, yet somehow it felt warm and alive.

"This can't be the same building we saw from outside," Haven said. "It's much too large."

"Oh, but it is the same," Vera assured her. "My sisters learned long ago how to make the most of a space. Many homes are filled with useless nooks and crannies. We allow nothing to go to waste. I would love to give you a tour, but it wouldn't be wise to keep Phoebe waiting. We prize punctuality here. Asteria!" she called, and a young girl appeared. "Would you mind taking our guests' coats while I escort them to the fourth floor?"

"I'd be delighted." The girl's face was childlike, but her expression said she knew things no child could know. "It's a pleasure to see you again," she told Haven. "And you as well, Mr. Morrow," she added with a grin.

"*Thank you,* Asteria. You may see to your chores now," Vera dismissed the girl. "Haven? Iain? Will you follow me, please?"

She led them up the magnificent staircase that rose in an ever-tightening spiral. Women buzzed by them along the way. Each nodded politely, but none stopped. They appeared to be following a strict schedule. A willowy girl with the regal bearing of the Masai glided down the stairs with a stack of leather-bound books under one arm. Haven spun around for a second look, certain she'd seen the lovely young woman somewhere before. A prim lady hurried past with a basket filled with plant trimmings. She shared the face of a Japanese tourist who had once purchased four dresses from Haven's boutique in Rome. Behind her, a tiny child who couldn't have been more than six groomed a wig as she walked. Even she was familiar. They all were. Haven stopped on the stairs when she spotted a young woman who had sold her a pair of shoes on her first trip to New York. Iain paused as well, and Vera looked concerned by the unexpected delay.

"You've all been watching me," Haven said, feeling suddenly trapped—like a wild creature that's woken to find itself on display at a zoo.

"Yes. Phoebe will explain." Vera pointed to one of the tall clocks that stood on each landing. The minute hand had almost reached the top of the hour. "We must hurry."

Bells began to toll just as they arrived at the fourth floor. There, a girl with blonde hair was unlocking a room to their left. She wore a long brown coat and motorcycle boots. The same outfit she'd worn in Florence. Haven had just reached out to tug at Iain's arm when the clocks stopped striking. In the house below, a dozen doors shut at once. Another opened in front of them.

"We're here," Vera called out.

In a brightly lit sunroom, the little group discovered the Pythia watering tidy rows of plants. At the spa she'd seemed ancient, but now Haven saw that Phoebe couldn't be much more than sixty. All of her mystical trappings were gone, and her hair was styled in a sleek silver bob. To the average eye, her simple beige dress might have appeared unremarkable. Haven recognized the work of a master tailor. And Phoebe wore it exceptionally well. Even in New York, few women could manage such effortless elegance.

"Please, take a seat," Vera told Haven and Iain. Three wicker chairs waited for them in one corner of the sunroom.

"Hello." Phoebe greeted the couple warmly. When she saw Haven's alarmed expression, she smiled. "You must be shocked to find me looking so normal."

"A little," Haven admitted, relaxing a bit.

Phoebe chuckled. "I have to put on a good show at the spa. My clients would be terribly disappointed if I arrived at work dressed in my usual garb. And this must be Mr. Morrow." She didn't just look at Iain—she examined him. Haven was amused but hardly surprised. Even older ladies couldn't resist Iain's charms.

"We've met," Iain replied flatly. "At the Ouroboros Society."

"Yes, of course. How could I forget?" Phoebe glanced at the blue-haired girl who still stood by the door. "Vera, dear, would you mind if I chatted with our guests in private?"

"Not at all," Vera said, though Haven suspected she'd wanted to stay.

Once Vera had closed the door behind her, Phoebe finished watering the plants that lined the sunroom's windowsills. They weren't typical houseplants, Haven noticed. The tall, leafless stalks resembled the sort of reeds that might grow on the banks of faraway rivers. They exuded a faint fragrance that reminded Haven of something, though she couldn't quite figure out what it was.

"What is that you're growing?" Haven asked. "The plants' scent—it's familiar."

"No living language possesses a name for this species. It's been virtually extinct for centuries." Phoebe closed her eyes and inhaled deeply. "To me, it smells of cypress groves and olive blossoms. I would imagine that's not the scent you're experiencing. The fragrance is different for everyone. That's one of the reasons these plants are so essential to my work. But I'll explain more later. You must have many other questions to ask me. Shall we attempt to get a few of them out of the way?"

"Sure," Haven agreed, searching for a good place to start. "I recognized half the women in this building. How long have you all been following me? Who are you? What do you want?"

Phoebe chuckled again. "I'll answer one question at a time, if you don't mind. We have been following you since your first trip to New York eighteen months ago. I knew you would find your way to the Ouroboros Society, and my sisters and I were waiting for you to arrive. We lost track of you for a year after you moved to Italy. Then we found you in Rome and followed you to Florence. We would have made contact there, but you disappeared once again. I must admit— you caught me by surprise when you arrived at the spa."

"That's just *this* lifetime," Haven said. "I know you've been following me much longer than that. In the nineteen twenties my name was Constance Whitman. I have a note someone once wrote her—a note that instructed Constance to call a certain telephone number if *he* ever found her."

"Yes, I wrote that note myself. Constance never called. I assume you know what happened to her? She might have lived longer if she had taken my advice."

"The *he* was Adam Rosier, wasn't it?" Iain asked curtly.

Phoebe turned to Iain. "Yes, but we don't call him that. We call him the magos. He's the reason I asked you both here this evening." She took a key from her pocket and unlocked an old ebony cabinet on the far side of the room. A work of art built by craftspeople using skills that no longer existed, it had always been meant to hold precious things. Reaching inside, Phoebe withdrew a large hand-bound book, which she passed to Haven with great care. "This is our story. We keep it with us at all times to remind us of the importance of our mission. It contains every scrap of information we have collected on our adversary."

Haven gingerly flipped though the book. Only the last few pages were typed in a language she could understand. Other sections were handwritten in everything from hieroglyphics to Old English. Tucked into the book's spine, however, were dozens of photographs. The first showed Adam strolling through a cemetery. The style of his suit dated the photo to the late nineteenth century. He wore a beard that ended in a neat little point at the tip of his chin. Otherwise he hadn't changed at all. On the back of the photo, someone had written *Cimetière du Pè re Lachaise, 29 Mai 1871.*

The next photograph Haven found had been taken in New York. In the background she spotted the stock exchange building on Wall Street. Thousands of men in hats and 1920s-style suits jammed the area, blocking traffic. A gentleman peered out a window of one of the cars stalled in the street. Haven felt her pulse quicken. She knew the handsome face well.

"I recognize Adam, but I can't read most of this," Haven said, her hands shaking too badly to turn another page. "Can you tell me what it says?"

Phoebe settled into a seat, and Haven felt as if the old woman were bestowing an honor upon her, like a queen taking time to have tea with a subject.

"Perhaps I should start our story at the beginning. There are twelve of us," Phoebe said. "Today we look nothing alike, but once we were all sisters. We lived in a small town on the eastern coast of Greece. Our father died, and because there were so many of us, we were forced to take in washing to make ends meet. It was a hard living but an honest one. Then a rumor started. A man passing through town had seen the twelve of us. He told the townspeople that we had offered him more than our laundry services. He claimed we were running a brothel. They stoned us to death in the streets. I was the oldest. I was twenty. The youngest of us was eleven. She was only a baby."

"I'm so sorry," Haven said. "And the man who started the rumor—it was Adam?"

"There's no doubt that it was. In fact, he looks exactly the same today as he did thousands of years ago."

"Do you know what he is?" Iain asked.

Phoebe took the leather volume out of Haven's hands and closed it. "That's the one answer you won't find in this book. The truth is, even we don't know. He may not be truly eternal, but he's as old as mankind. All cultures have had a name for him. In Greece, he was Chaos. In Egypt they called him Seth. In India some still call him Ravana. I've heard people here refer to him as the devil, but that's not quite right. The Christian devil has a reason for doing the things he does. The magos does not."

"Chandra told me that the Horae spend each lifetime fighting him," Haven said.

"My sisters and I are drawn back to earth for one reason: to find the magos and exact our revenge. We are born into families scattered all over the globe. But we each hear the call the moment we draw our first breaths. Just as honeybees always find their way back to the right hive, we always return to each other. It often means traveling thousands of miles, but we reunite with our sisters as soon as we can. Even as children we devote our lives to the cause."

"So you're the leader?" Haven asked.

"I am the oldest. When I am able, I take care of my sisters as I always have."

"And you've been returning to earth for two thousand years?"

"Much longer than that," Phoebe said. "The Horae have been fighting the magos for so many centuries that we've become part of a system of checks and balances. Without us, the world could plunge into darkness."

"How do the Horae keep the world from 'plunging into darkness'?" Iain didn't bother to conceal his skepticism. Haven cringed, but Phoebe appeared unperturbed.

"That is an excellent question, Mr. Morrow. We cannot kill the magos, so we lock him away whenever possible. It's not easy to do. He is usually difficult to locate. And quite slippery when we do find him. But during the decades he's imprisoned, the human race thrives. The Renaissance, for instance—it wouldn't have been possible without us."

"And Haven's role in all of this would be?" Iain asked.

"She can help us put him where he can do no harm for a while. You see, none of the Horae can get close enough to the magos to imprison him. We've tried, and we invariably fail. But Haven is his weakness. He can never resist her. In fact, she's the reason we've been able to keep track of him. He's never remained in one place for so long. He's been in New York for almost ninety years, waiting for Haven to return to him. Now that she's here, we finally have what we need to lure him into our trap."

"Forget it," Iain said. "You're not going to use Haven as bait."

"Iain!" Haven protested. "Don't you think we should hear the rest?"

"She's not going to tell you the whole story, Haven." Iain glared at Phoebe. "You say you've locked Adam away before. That means he must have escaped. Am I right?"

"Yes," Phoebe said.

"So what's going to happen to Haven when he gets out again?"

Phoebe nodded. "I can't predict the future, Mr. Morrow. I don't know what will happen should the magos escape. But you must understand—if Haven doesn't agree to assist us now, she'll have no hope of finding her friend. I am the only one who can help her see the life she needs to see." She turned her attention to Haven. "This friend of yours who's missing. Is he the one Chandra met when you were running from the gray men?"

"Yes. His name is Beau," Haven said.

"Chandra sensed a special connection between you. He's more than just your friend, isn't he?"

It felt like the old woman had reached into Haven's chest and seized her heart. "He was my brother."

"Chandra suspected as much. When we met at the spa, you told me your friend came to New York to meet someone from his past."

"That's right," Haven confirmed.

Phoebe's face was grim. "I don't want to frighten you, Haven, but Beau may be in grave danger. There have been similar incidents in the past. Not long ago, a Society member disappeared shortly after she was reunited with a lover from one of her previous lives. I tried to warn her that the man wasn't who he claimed to be. The woman's corpse—what little was left of it—was discovered months later. They say she'd been tortured for weeks."

No. Haven shook her head at the thought. Things like that never happened to people like Beau. *They might,* a voice whispered, but Haven refused to listen. She knew that if she indulged her worst fears, her hopes wouldn't stand a chance.

"Who was the woman who died?" Iain demanded. "Why didn't I read about her murder in the papers?"

"Ouroboros Society scandals rarely make the papers," Phoebe noted.

"I'll do it, Phoebe," Haven interjected. "Whatever you want, I'll do it if you promise to help me find Beau."

"Hold on—both of you. I agree that we've got to act fast to save Beau," Iain said. "But why do we have to deal with Adam *now*? He isn't going to leave New York anytime soon. Why can't we work together and come up with a plan that won't put Haven in danger?"

"You have a habit of letting emotions cloud your thinking, Mr. Morrow," Phoebe told him. "I assure you there's very good reason for our haste. As I mentioned, the magos has been in Manhattan since the 1920s. He still travels the world, of course, spreading chaos and discord. But at this point, we could have read the newspapers and known which city he calls home. All the stock market crashes and financial bubbles—he's even started to repeat himself. And it's made him very conspicuous. But the fact that he's been here for almost a century isn't a good thing for anyone. When the magos isn't on the move, chaos becomes concentrated in one spot, and the world becomes unbalanced. It could cause irreparable harm to this city— to the entire country. We can't afford to wait. We must take action immediately."

"What do you think is going to happen?" Haven asked.

"We don't know," Phoebe said. "But we do know that the magos has been working on a new scheme—one that has the potential to be extremely dangerous. You've been to the Ouroboros Society head-quarters, have you not?" she asked Haven.

"I have," Haven confirmed.

"And who did you see while you were there?"

Haven thought back, trying not to forget anyone. "I saw a few low-level OS employees. And a bunch of kids who'd come for past-life analysis."

"That's right," said Phoebe.

"I don't get it," Haven said. "Did I miss something?"

"Did you happen to notice that the children in the waiting room were all the same age?"

"They were?" Haven remembered a little blonde girl she'd spoken to in the lobby of the OS, Flora, who claimed she'd once been a renowned epidemiologist named Josephine. Flora had been small, perhaps only eight or nine. Haven felt a pang of panic and hoped no harm had come to the little girl.

"Until ten years ago, children were not welcome in the Ouroboros Society," Phoebe said. "With one or two exceptions, they were rarely allowed inside the building. Then suddenly, one day, it was announced that the OS would begin recruiting children who were nine years of age."

"Is this true?" Haven asked Iain. "You must have met some of the kids while you were a member of the Society."

"Sure," Iain said. "But they were just little kids. I was more interested in what the adults were up to. I didn't think a bunch of nine-year-olds could do the world much harm."

"At the moment, we are more worried about what's being done *to* them, Mr. Morrow," Phoebe explained. "In that first year alone, the Ouroboros Society recruited twenty children. We've tried to contact some of the young members. They're alive—we know that for certain—but it's impossible to speak to them. All of the OS children are sent to a boarding school north of the city. It's called Halcyon Hall. The security around it is impossible to breach, and as far as I can tell, the children only return to New York once a year, on their birthdays. Even the parents refuse to speak about the OS. They've been bribed, I believe."

"What do you think Adam has planned?" Haven asked.

"We suspect he's building an army of sorts. Children's minds are easily warped, and the ones the magos has recruited are no ordinary souls. They all possess astounding abilities. We don't know how he plans to use the children—or how much damage they're capable of inflicting. But we do know that Adam's first recruits are starting to come of age now. And that's what frightens us." She fixed her cool stare on Iain. "Now do you understand why we can't wait any longer to deal with the magos? Whatever he's doing at Halcyon Hall must be stopped."

"I understand," Iain said. "But I still don't know why you need to put Haven in danger. There must be another way to destroy the Ouroboros Society. I'll help you. I'll do whatever it takes."

A flicker of annoyance lit the old woman's eyes. "Please forgive my candor, Mr. Morrow, but you've had your chance. We've been watching you too. We know you failed to destroy the Society when you were last in New York. What makes you think you might succeed this time?" she asked. "If I thought we could proceed without Haven, we would surely try. But I've watched one of my very own sisters be ruined by the magos. You, too, have seen firsthand what can happen to people who spend time in his presence. No one else can help us but Haven."

Iain said nothing, but Haven could see he was far from convinced.

"And so," Phoebe continued, "that is the deal I'm offering, Haven. You help us capture the magos, and I will help you locate your friend. Do you agree?"

"Yes," Haven said. "I'll help you."

Phoebe rose from her chair. "Then please follow me," she said.

CHAPTER SIXTEEN

They found themselves outside underneath the stars. The skylight in the roof glowed like amber. Phoebe led them around the glass, toward a water tower set on steel stilts in a dark corner of the building. She scaled a short ladder and opened a door cut into the side of the round wooden structure.

"This is where you give past-life readings?" Haven asked, her teeth chattering. If she'd known they'd be making a trip outdoors, she would have asked for her coat. When she reached the top of the ladder, she could see the vast city beneath her. Hundreds of water towers stood watch on the rooftops. How many were still filled with water, she wondered. And how many were used to store secrets?

"The closer we are to the heavens, the easier it is for the soul to travel," Phoebe replied. She pointed up at the sky, where the stars gathered in predictable patterns.

The empty space inside the tower was twelve feet in diameter and carpeted with a mat made of woven straw. Burning embers in a stone hearth set into the floor lit the room. A wicker basket waited beside the fire. The heat in the small chamber wrapped around Haven and squeezed. Struggling to breathe, she hurried to peel off her heavy winter sweater.

Phoebe removed her shoes and floated down to the floor, where she perched on her heels like a seasoned geisha. The heat didn't appear to bother her any more than the cold had.

"Please, join me by the fire," she said.

Haven and Iain sat cross-legged on the floor. Phoebe pulled a few twigs out of the wicker basket and tossed them onto the hearth. A wave of heat washed over Haven's face. Her eyes dried out, and she blinked furiously as a strong fragrance filled the room. It was a mixture of honeysuckle, Play-Doh, fresh-cut grass, sawdust, and the other scents of Haven's youth. Milky white smoke curled upward and disappeared through a hole in the domed ceiling above.

"Would you mind wearing one of these, Mr. Morrow?" Phoebe handed Iain a white surgical mask.

"You're burning the plants from your sunroom, aren't you?" Iain asked. "Isn't the smoke safe to breathe?"

"The mask is meant to block the fragrance. Scent and memory go hand in hand. The aromas released by the plants can summon memories buried deep in the past. You and I must remain here in the present while Haven travels back in time. But I assure you, there's no need to worry. I've been performing this ritual since the ancient Greeks perfected it." Phoebe fitted an identical mask over her own nose and mouth. "Now," Phoebe said, her voice muffled, "which life-time will you be visiting today, Haven?"

"I would like to visit the life of Beatrice Vettori," Haven said. "Her brother's name was Piero. They lived in Florence, Italy, in the middle of the fourteenth century. I need to go back to 1347 and see a friend of Piero's. His name was Naddo."

"Did you know this Naddo well?"

"I don't think so," Haven admitted. "I'm hoping I met him at least once."

Phoebe's brow furrowed. "I'm afraid my gift has its limits. I can guide you to the right year and place. But I cannot show you a specific scene unless I witnessed it as well. It is difficult to locate a precise moment in time. It may take you several attempts before you find the young man you need to locate. And I can only allow you to visit the past for a few minutes each session. If you do not see what you want to see this evening, you will have to return to us in a couple of days."

"Why can't I just stay in the fourteenth century until I get what I'm after?" Haven asked.

"Past-life regression strains the body and brain. If you stay too long, your mind could end up mired in the past. And your body in this life would die."

"I had no idea this would be so risky," Iain whispered to Haven. "Are you sure you're up for it?"

"I'm sure," Haven said. "And I'm ready to start."

"Then close your eyes," Phoebe said.

Haven complied.

"Inhale deeply and concentrate on my voice. You are in the darkness, but your soul is traveling across time and space. You're searching for your brother. Let the fragrance carry you. Keep traveling backward, two hundred, three hundred, four hundred years. Every era has its own aromas. Every person has his own signature scent. Now you're approaching the fourteenth century. You can smell the air of Florence. . . ."

There's no way this is going to work, Haven thought. All she could smell was something like dirt. Then she opened her eyes.

SHE WAS LYING *facedown. Her tears watered the soil as the cold crept through her velvet dress and seeped into her skin. He was resting deep beneath her, encased in the frozen ground. Beatrice lifted her head. It had only been a few months since she had buried his body here beneath the oak tree. The land around it had once been a beautiful field. Now it was a patchwork of freshly dug graves that extended as far as the eye could see. Half of Florence had come to keep Piero company.*

Beatrice prayed to be among them soon. She deserved to suffer for the things she had done. But the pestilence had passed her by. She stayed with the sisters from the convent, watching from her window as Florence died all around her and trying not to think of the man she'd trapped deep underground. She left her room only twice a week, when she went to sit with her dead brother and beg for forgiveness.

WHEN HAVEN WOKE, the sadness stayed with her. The Beatrice she'd seen had been barely alive. She had no faith left in anyone, not even herself. Everything she believed in had been destroyed, and everyone she loved had been taken away. Haven knew the vision should serve as a warning. She would share Beatrice's fate if anything were to happen to Beau.

"Well?" asked Phoebe.

"It was horrible." Even in the heat of the room, Haven was shivering. "Piero was dead. My family was dead. Everyone was dead. I was scared and alone."

"Did you see Naddo?" Iain asked eagerly. "Do you know anything that might help the police identify him in this life?"

"I didn't see anyone," Haven said. "Beatrice was in a field that had been turned into a cemetery. I was lying on Piero's grave, begging him for forgiveness. For some reason, I felt responsible for his death."

"Do you know why?" Phoebe probed.

"No," Haven told her. "I didn't see how he died."

"Then we will need to meet again," the old woman stated. "In two days."

"Two days!" Iain exclaimed. "How much longer is this going to take?"

"As long as it needs to take," Phoebe said calmly. "Now let's discuss Haven's responsibilities."

"But—" Haven started.

"I believe I've made it perfectly clear why we can't delay our plans," Phoebe said. "I thought you would be anxious to get started as well. Every minute could mean the difference between life and death for your friend. And I'm certain you wouldn't want to feel responsible for what might happen to the children at the Ouroboros Society."

"No! but . . ." Haven struggled to free herself from the quicksand of Phoebe's logic, but she was already in too deep.

"Well then, let's not waste any more time. First I must insist that you never return to this house on your own. We'll collect you every couple of days for a session. In time, you'll have the vision you need." Phoebe paused for emphasis. "As long as you continue to do what you're told. Now are you ready to hear the plan?"

Haven sighed. "I'm listening."

"Tomorrow morning, you will visit the Ouroboros Society and request to see Adam Rosier."

"What?!" Iain rose to his knees and yanked off his mask. "You never said she had to *see* him!"

Phoebe calmly removed her own mask. "Allow me to finish, Mr. Morrow. Tomorrow Haven will visit the magos. She will ask for his help finding her friend. She will also allow him to provide her with lodging."

"Why?" Haven asked as Iain seethed.

"Because you will need to stay very close to him in order to accomplish the second phase of your task. You must lower his defenses enough for us to strike."

"How am I supposed to do *that*?" Haven asked.

"By pretending to fall in love with him." Phoebe held up a bony finger, silencing any objections. "I'm aware that it may take some time to convince him. The magos is naturally very suspicious, and he knows he has enemies. But he also has great faith in his own powers of persuasion. Let him think that he's winning you over little by little. Then, when the moment is right, you will find an excuse to bring him to the first address you visited tonight—the storefront on Lenox Avenue. There was a bank next door for many years. Its vault is still in the basement of the building, and we have prepared a cell for him there. "

"No." Iain wouldn't hear any more. "Absolutely not. There's *no* way I'm going to let this happen. Maybe you'll trap him for a few decades, but he'll know Haven was the one who betrayed him. What do you think Adam will do to her when he finally breaks free?"

Phoebe didn't demur. Like a diligent lawyer, she had come prepared with answers to every question. "If Haven does her part, there's no reason to believe that the magos will break free this time. My sisters and I own the buildings on Lenox Avenue. As soon as we give the word, they will both be torn down. The vault will be buried, and a modern apartment building will be erected on the site. There will be no way to get into—or out of—the prison that will hold the magos."

"We're talking about Adam," Iain reminded her. "He'll find a way."

"I knew you might object to my plan, Mr. Morrow. That's why I insisted you accompany Haven tonight. I want you to hear her make her choice. And may I remind you—it is *her* choice to make."

"What if he locks you away again?" Iain asked Haven before setting his frustration and anger loose on Phoebe once more. "You have no idea what he's done to her in the past. He's imprisoned her for entire lifetimes! He has a cabinet filled with her bodies!"

"That may well be the case. But why would the magos harm Haven if he believes she's falling in love with him?" Phoebe countered, her voice still cool and rational. "And remember, all twelve Horae will be watching out for her. We managed to keep Haven safe the last time she was in New York, did we not?"

Iain fumed. "No," he said. "Just no."

"If Haven's safety is no longer in question, what is the source of your anxiety, Mr. Morrow?" Phoebe's question had an edge to it. "Surely you aren't worried that Haven might actually fall in love with the magos? I suppose he *does* have his charms."

"That's ridiculous!" Haven blurted out. "Iain and I are meant to be together. I couldn't love anyone else if I tried!"

"Would you agree, Mr. Morrow?" Phoebe asked.

"My feelings are none of your business." Iain glowered.

"Well, if what Haven says is true, then no one—not even the magos—will be able to come between you two. There should be no cause for concern . . . unless you have reason to question the strength of your bond. Is that the problem? I don't mean to be rude, Mr. Morrow. I'm merely trying to understand."

"I've already made myself clear," Iain said. "I don't have to explain anything to you."

"That is true," Phoebe acknowledged. "But I imagine you'll need to explain your objections to Haven."

"Okay!" Haven broke in. "I know you're trying to be helpful, Phoebe, but you'll have to excuse us. Iain, may I speak to you alone?"

THEY SAT ON the ledge that circled the roof. On the street below, a battered minivan sped through a traffic light, and three police cars gave chase while a helicopter kept watch from above. Its blue searchlight passed over the roofs of nearby buildings, catching lovers, delinquents, and drug dealers in action.

"We made a big mistake coming here," Iain said once the cold air had tempered his rage. "The Horae don't have your best interests at heart. You're just a pawn. Phoebe will do whatever it takes to win her war against Adam. She won't hesitate to sacrifice you if she thinks it's necessary."

"I don't like any of this, either." Haven kept her voice low. "But unless we can get our hands on some of those weird herbs, I'm going to need Phoebe's help if I want to see Naddo. And if I do find a clue that could identify him in this life, I might have to contact the Ouroboros Society anyway."

"We'll find another way. Phoebe wants too much. No one should be asked to take such a risk."

"I'm willing to risk my life if it means saving Beau."

"I know that, Haven. But I'm not sure if I can take the risk that the Horae have asked *me* to make."

"You?" Haven asked.

"Don't you see? They've asked me to risk losing you. If something happened, I could end up searching for centuries to find you again. You know, Haven, sometimes I think you're the lucky one. You forget everything each time you're reborn. But I always remember. Do you have any idea what that's like? Knowing the person you need is out there—and not being able to find her? It's torture. I wouldn't wish it on anyone."

Haven kicked the brick ledge with the toe of her shoe and wished there were a simple solution.

"So what do you think I should do?" she asked Iain. "I can't sit back and let something terrible happen to Beau. If I didn't do everything in my power to save him, I wouldn't be able to live with myself. And I don't think *you* could live with me, either."

"Beau wouldn't want you to do this for his sake." Iain was right and Haven knew it.

"We both know it's not just about Beau anymore. Whatever Adam has planned for those kids at the Ouroboros Society, it can't be good. I don't want them on my conscience, Iain. But if we're going to save them, you're going to have to let me deal with Adam. Unless . . ."

"Unless what?"

"Unless Phoebe was right," Haven whispered, worried she wouldn't find the courage to complete the thought. "Are you really worried that I might fall in love with Adam?"

Iain sighed. "Phoebe's trying to stir up trouble, Haven. I can't tell you *why*, but she is. I'm not worried that you'll fall in love with Adam. But I don't think you realize just how dangerous he is. Have you ever wondered why the Ouroboros Society is so successful? Why do you suppose so many people get sucked in?"

"Most people are greedy and weak."

Iain shook his head. "I spent years at the Society. I know more than a few of the members. They're not all bad. Some of them are actually pretty decent. But they've all gotten in over their heads. They've found themselves doing things they'd never have believed themselves capable of doing. It starts with one little lie. Or a single bad habit. I knew a nice girl there who was really insecure. She spent all of her points on plastic surgery and ended up delivering drugs to pay off her debts."

"But Adam never managed to corrupt *you* while you were at the OS. What if I'm incorruptible too?"

"You give me far more credit than I deserve." Iain leaned over the ledge and examined the drop, as if he were measuring the exact distance to the ground. "I'm far from incorruptible. I've done things in the past I'm not proud of. And I've been around long enough to know that everyone has their price, even me. But Adam can't give me what I want. Because all I've ever wanted is *you*."

The confession kindled a dozen questions, but Haven knew it was not the time to ask them. Instead, she took Iain by the elbow and turned him to face her. "And all I want is you, and Adam can't give me that, either. Besides, I know who I'll be dealing with. I know not to do anything I shouldn't."

"And you think it's always so easy to tell?" he asked.

"Yes, I do."

"You're wrong. That's why Phoebe's plan is too risky. Especially when we have other options."

"*What* other options?"

"I met with someone this afternoon while you and Frances were at the spa," Iain said. "Remember that detective I told you about? Her name is Mia Michalski. I still want to hire her to search for Beau."

Haven dropped Iain's hands. "You met with a detective? How do you know her? Are you sure she's any good?"

Is she cute? Is she another member of the Iain Morrow fan club? The questions seemed to come out of nowhere. Haven hadn't felt any jealousy in over a year. She forced the thoughts out of her mind. She wasn't going to let any useless emotions get in the way of finding Beau.

"Mia's our age, but she's the best detective around. We met a couple of years ago at the Ouroboros Society. She's not an active member anymore, but she won't laugh if the subject of reincarnation comes up."

"Then great." Haven tried to sound pleased. "I officially welcome Mia Michalski to the team. When does she want to meet with me?"

"She doesn't need to meet you," Iain replied.

"What? But I'm the one who knows everything about Beau!"

"Mia's too young for a private investigator's license, so she does almost all of her work online. She told me she has enough information about Beau to get started. I'll call her tonight and let her know that we're moving forward full steam. So does this mean you'll tell Phoebe no?"

He sounded so optimistic, and Haven hated to dash his hopes. "I'm sorry, Iain. I have to say yes. Just think about the students at Halcyon Hall! Can you imagine what's being done to them? And even if your detective friend finds Beau, there's nothing she can do to shut the school down. It's up to me to find some way to save all those kids!"

"But why do you have to do it all on your own? Why won't you let me help you?"

"You will help me! You'll come to every meeting I have with the Horae. You'll hire your detective to look for Beau. You'll give me advice.

The only thing I have to do on my own is see Adam!"

Iain studied Haven's face. "You're not frightened of him, are you?"

"I'm scared. But I'm not scared of Adam anymore."

"Why not? You should be."

"Because I don't think Adam will hurt me. And because I know that nothing's ever going to take me away from you."

"Do you swear?" Iain was serious, but Haven wanted to laugh. It was the most ridiculous question she'd ever heard.

"I swear." She lifted herself up on her toes and kissed him.

CHAPTER SEVENTEEN

A dozen little heads were bobbing around the bland waiting room of the Ouroboros Society. Haven stood for a moment and watched the children busy themselves while they waited to be called in for their interviews. There were a few rowdy types, a couple of studious kids, and a handful who merely looked bored out of their minds. But none seemed particularly noteworthy. Haven wondered which, if any, would be invited to join the Society. And what might happen to those who accepted the invitation.

"Excuse me? Excuse me, miss?" The receptionist's voice was grating, borderline rude.

"*What?*" Haven spun around to face the weasel-like man who was waiting behind her with a clipboard pressed to his chest. "Yes?" she tried again with a softer voice and a smile. She'd felt jittery all morning. An attack of nerves during the drive downtown had almost made Haven lose her breakfast in the back of the cab.

"Do you have an . . ." The receptionist's words trailed off as Haven removed her hat. She put her hand to her hair. It must look awful, she thought, if it had the power to render someone speechless. "Oh. It's *you*," the man added in a reverent tone. Haven peered over her shoulder, certain he was addressing someone else. But the only person behind her was a nine-year-old boy who'd escaped from his keepers and was making a run for the door.

"Jeremiah!" A woman sprinted after the kid and caught him before he could flee the building.

"Do you know me?" Haven asked the receptionist.

The man grimaced nervously and fumbled with his clipboard. "Please wait here, Miss Moore," he almost begged. "I'll only be a moment."

Haven watched as the receptionist hurried back to his desk to use the phone. She couldn't make out his words, but their effect was immediate. Haven heard a door open on the second floor and the sound of footsteps on the stairs. In less than a minute, Adam Rosier was standing in front of her. He was wearing the chunky black glasses he favored, along with slim black pants and a sweater. The outfit looked casual, cool, and astronomically expensive.

"Haven, you're back!" Adam exclaimed with a smile that was a little too broad. Otherwise there was nothing about his handsome face that suggested he might be anything other than human. It was hard to believe that this could be the monster Phoebe called the magos—the one responsible for countless deaths, disasters, and random acts of cruelty.

"I am." Haven's mind was already feeling a bit hazy in his presence. She struggled to remember the script she'd practiced. "I need to talk to you. I need your help."

"Certainly," Adam replied. "Shall we take a walk? I could use some fresh air."

"Yes," Haven agreed, hoping the cold could keep her alert. "Let's do that."

As they made their way toward the door, the little boy who'd tried to escape broke loose again from his mother's grip. With a lightning-fast movement of his arm, Adam snatched the back of the boy's sweater as he passed, bringing the child to a sudden halt.

"Hello." Adam kneeled down to face the stunned little boy. "Where are you off to?" Coming from most adults, the question would have sounded patronizing. Adam, however, seemed genuinely interested.

"Outside." The mesmerized child breathed in great gulps of oxygen, but his eyes never left Adam's face.

"Thank you so much for catching my son!" The boy's embarrassed mother had arrived on the scene. She was older than most of the other parents, with the air and the outfit of a woman who'd once been accustomed to success. It had taken a child to finally humble her. "Jeremiah has gotten to be such a terror these days!"

"No trouble at all." Adam didn't look up at the woman. He only had time for the boy. "And what's outside that you want to see?" he asked the child.

"Birds," said the little boy. His breathing had slowed and he even smiled, grateful to finally find someone who was willing to take him seriously. "I think I spotted a black-legged kittiwake in the park. They're really rare, you know."

"I see. Have you always been interested in watching birds, Jeremiah?"

The boy's mother opened her mouth to speak, but Adam raised a single finger to his lips.

"Jeremiah?" Adam probed.

"Watching birds helps me relax."

"Your life must be very stressful, then?"

Haven almost laughed until she realized it wasn't a joke.

A dark cloud passed over the boy's face. "I used to work as a biological engineer at . . ." He stopped briefly and his brow furrowed as if he were straining to remember. "At some school in Boston."

"You didn't care for your job?"

"I wanted to do something good. But they used everything I invented to hurt people or to make billionaires even richer."

"Ah. I understand. That would be stressful, wouldn't it? Then what do you say we get your interview over with quickly so you can go outside and see your rara avis?" Adam stood up and signaled to the receptionist. "Let's move Jeremiah up to the top of the waiting list," he said to the officious man who'd rushed over.

"Really? Oh, thank you! Thank you!" Anyone watching Jeremiah's mother gush would have thought her son had just won the lottery.

"No, thank *you*, madame," Adam said, grabbing his coat from a hook near the door. "I have a feeling we'll be seeing a lot more of your son here. Now, if you'll excuse us." He opened the front door of the Society and stepped aside to let Haven pass. "What do you say you and I go sneak a peek at that black-legged kittiwake?"

Outside on the stoop of the Ouroboros Society, Haven paused to survey Gramercy Park. As usual, its paths were empty and its benches deserted. The private garden was surrounded by a wrought-iron fence that had protected it from New York's rabble for more than 150 years. At the center of the enclosure stood a statue of Edwin Booth, an actor whose brother had murdered Abraham Lincoln. He looked cold and lonely, trapped for eternity in his landscaped cage. Haven had visited the statue in two separate lives, and she had hoped to never see him again.

When Adam reached the bottom of the stairs, he stopped to wait for his guest. "We don't have to visit the park. Would you prefer to go elsewhere?"

Haven hesitated. The last time she'd set foot in Gramercy Park, it had been summer in New York. The flowers had been blooming and the trees still leafy and green. She'd watched passersby stop outside the park's gates and gaze through the bars at the beauty they were only allowed to admire from a distance. Now no one seemed eager to enter the icy, desolate space.

"No," Haven said, forcing herself down the stairs. "The park will be fine."

Across the street, Adam opened the gate with a key that he took from his pocket. Inside, they walked in silence, the gravel crunching under their feet.

"That ring you're wearing—it's lovely," Adam remarked. "I haven't seen one like it in many years. It must be an antique. Am I right?"

There couldn't have been a worse way to start. She should have removed the ring Iain had given her. Haven commanded her lungs to keep breathing.

"That's what they told me in the shop," she said. She found her gloves in her coat pocket and pulled them on. "I probably paid way too much for it, though."

"It was worth any price," Adam said. "The stone is the same color as your eyes."

"Thank you . . ." Haven searched for another topic of conversation. "So when did the Society start recruiting children?" She winced. The question felt forced and awkward.

"About ten years ago," Adam told her. "It makes perfect sense, wouldn't you say? I'm surprised I didn't think of it earlier. Childhood is when most people are able to recall their previous lives. They often lose those memories as they grow older. It's best to record their stories before they forget."

"How old are the kids you recruit?" Haven asked. "The ones in the waiting room looked about the same age to me."

"They're all nine years old," Adam said.

"Why nine?"

Adam smiled as if he were embarrassed. "I suppose the number has a sentimental significance. You were nine years old when I found you in this lifetime. In fact, you were the inspiration for the initiative."

"How flattering," Haven said flatly. "I heard you opened some sort of academy for your little recruits?"

"Certainly. They have unique educational needs," Adam said. "Most would only be bored in an average school. You can't ask a child who once designed space shuttles to listen to teachers drone on about long division or spelling rules. It would be almost cruel. But why do you ask? I never knew you were terribly interested in children—or school for that matter."

"I'm not," Haven said. "I'm just trying to make small talk."

"Ah. I see."

The conversation stalled, and Haven pretended to admire the lifeless park all around her as she searched for something to say. The trees' branches were bare and the grass brown. Patches of snow still lingered beneath the trees. The space felt smaller, more confined. A peculiar aroma seemed to rise from the ground—the scent of things hidden away from the sun, like the gills of toadstools or the soil dug up to make room for a grave.

As they passed a redbrick mansion a few doors down from the Ouroboros Society, Haven felt a sudden rush of panic. It was so easy to forget that the charming, handsome young man at her side was responsible for the most horrific crimes she could ever imagine. Yet the redbrick mansion was undeniable proof. The things she'd seen in that building still kept her awake some nights. The top floor of the mansion, she'd once discovered, was devoted to a museum of sorts, filled with artifacts from Haven's many lives. Adam had collected them over the centuries. There were dresses and jewels and photographs brittle with age. And tucked away in a large wooden cabinet were six desiccated bodies. They all belonged to women Haven had once been—women who had fallen into Adam's trap. If she wasn't careful, Haven knew there was a good chance she might join them.

"Haven? Are you there?"

She jumped at the sound of Adam's voice. Had he somehow managed to read her thoughts?

"Sorry," she said, surprised at how easily she was able to

manufacture a smile. "I was searching for the little boy's bird. Did you say something?"

"Nothing important," Adam replied. He stopped on the path without warning, and Haven took several steps past him before she caught on. When she faced Adam, she found his arms were crossed and his expression businesslike. In the afternoon light, his pale skin had a bluish tinge, and his lips were a crimson red. It was a striking combination, one that reminded Haven of black-and-white photographs colored by an artist's hand.

"I wish you were here for the pleasure of my company, Haven. However, I know that can't be the case. Why do you want to talk to me today?"

Reminded of her mission, Haven felt her fears begin to fade once more. "Beau is still missing. The police are looking for him, but they haven't made any progress. I've thought about the offer you made me. If you're still open to it, I really could use your help."

"You must be terribly worried," Adam noted, "if you're willing to turn to me for assistance. I will make a few calls as soon as I'm back inside. "

"I appreciate it. But there's one more thing. I hate to ask."

"Anything. Just tell me what it is and it's yours." He made the promise without a pause, and Haven knew that whatever she asked for, Adam would deliver it. She seemed to have a power over him— one that surprised even her.

"I'm having a few financial problems. You probably heard that I inherited Iain Morrow's fortune."

Adam blinked at the mention of Iain's name. "I did," he said.

"Well, I've lost it. His mother claims that I forged his will. All of my accounts have been frozen."

"I can fix that too," Adam said. "I knew Virginia Morrow. She won't pose a problem at all."

"How do you know Virginia Morrow?" Haven asked, trying not to make the question sound like an accusation. Still, the true meaning of the words wasn't lost on Adam.

"I *knew* Virginia," he corrected Haven. "She spent some time at the Society in the early nineties. I haven't seen or spoken to her in years. But I suspect she hasn't changed. If she's harassing you, I can put an end to it."

His offer was tantalizing. Virginia Morrow deserved whatever punishment Adam could deliver. "Thank you," Haven forced herself to say. "But that's not what I'm after. What I really need is a place to stay while I'm searching for Beau."

"You want *me* to find you a place to stay?" Adam seemed certain he'd misheard. When Haven nodded, his face remained somber, but his dark eyes flashed. "This is quite unusual. I never expected you to return to me—to New York—like this."

Haven's heart was racing again, but she played her part to perfection. She could even feel tears welling in her eyes. "I'm alone and broke and my best friend is missing. I don't have anyone else to turn to."

"So you're using me," Adam said.

"No! It's not like that. . . ."

"It is—but I don't mind. We all have to start somewhere, don't we? I want to take care of you, Haven. That's all I've ever wanted. I've made a mess of things in the past, but I'll help you in any way that I can."

Haven's sense of relief was so strong that the smile she presented to Adam was almost entirely genuine.

"I will have a suite reserved for you at the Gramercy Gardens Hotel," he continued, once again leading the way along the park's gravel path. He seemed more relaxed, less suspicious. "You can check in as soon as you like. And I'll have a bank account opened in your name."

"That's okay. I don't need money," Haven insisted. "Or a fancy suite. I just need someplace to sleep. I can live without everything but a bed."

"It seems your one necessity is my ultimate luxury," Adam mused. "Sleep is the only thing I can't afford."

Haven thought of her last visit to Adam's house, an ancient building on Water Street. Most of the rooms had been empty. She remembered finding a wall covered with Marta Vega's disaster paintings. And Haven would never forget the pit she'd discovered in the basement. But she didn't recall having seen a bed.

"You don't sleep?" she asked.

"I never have time," Adam said. "There's too much to be done."

"Do you eat?"

Adam glanced at Haven out of the corner of his eye. At first she worried she'd gone too far, but he only appeared amused. "I could eat, but I'm rarely hungry. This is an odd line of questioning, Haven. Are you trying to determine whether I'm human?"

"I'm just curious. I hope you don't mind."

"The truth is, I don't know what I am. I never have. Most of the time, I feel very little. I don't experience hunger or fatigue. I usually have no urges or desires. That all changes when I'm with you. I come alive in your presence. I feel things. It doesn't matter that it's mostly pain. At least for now it's something."

"I cause you pain?" Haven slowed her stride. She could see it when he turned to her—the grimace that he forced into another toothy smile.

"I once spent a long winter traveling across Russia with Napoleon's army. The French soldiers told me that it doesn't hurt to freeze. The pain comes only when you begin to thaw." Adam pointed to the space between them. "Keeping this distance prolongs the agony. I want nothing more than to absorb as much of your warmth as I can. I could end my torture by touching you. But I can't do that—I won't do that." His attention turned to the sidewalk beyond the park's fence. A homeless woman was staring back at him. "Pardon me for a moment."

Adam stepped off the gravel path and charged across beds of dead flowers toward the woman standing outside the park. Haven could hear his voice rise in anger as he spoke with her. Finally, a car pulled over, and two men in suits picked up the woman and deposited her in the car's backseat. Adam's face was dark as he trudged back toward his guest.

"Who was that?" Haven demanded. She had almost let down her guard again. She'd almost forgotten who Adam was. "What did you do to that poor woman?"

"Poor woman?" Adam's laugh sounded sharp and bitter. "That 'poor woman' is the former president of the Ouroboros Society. The same woman who tried to murder you twice and succeeded once."

"Padma Singh?" Haven gasped. "I thought—"

"You thought I'd had her executed."

"I read in the papers that she disappeared. And you *did* tell me you'd make her pay for the things she'd done."

"Believe me—Padma is suffering for her sins," Adam assured her. "But I did nothing to harm her physically. I banished her from the Society instead. Every few days, she comes to beg my forgiveness. Tonight she claimed to have information I'd be willing to buy. The woman is a nuisance I would rather not endure, and I could strangle her with my own hands for what she's done to you. But I know you would not want anyone executed in your name. Or was I mistaken? Would you rather I have her killed?"

"No! Of course not!" Haven exclaimed.

"That's what I thought. So I won't," Adam said. He seemed almost proud of himself. "I am a very old creature, and I'm set in my ways. I learn slowly. But I learn." He was suddenly pointing toward the sky. "Look! There he is!"

"Who?" Haven asked.

"Jeremiah's black-legged kittiwake."

A small gull sat perched on a tree branch, shivering as it tried to blend in with the overcast skies. It must have been blown off course, Haven thought. Just like her, it belonged somewhere warm and green. Not in this cold winter wasteland. She wondered if either of them had any hope of finding their way home.

CHAPTER EIGHTEEN

Haven's hotel room was set in a corner, and from the tall windows she could see the frozen rivers on either side of Manhattan. Flat slabs of ice floated on the surface of the East River, and the Hudson was almost a solid, snow-dusted sheet. Down in the dark trenches that passed for city streets, it was easy to forget the rivers were there, encircling the island like a moat designed to keep residents in—and the rest of the world out. At the far end of Manhattan, where the waters merged, a clump of skyscrapers stood like steel sentries, towering over the boats that sailed into the harbor. Haven felt like a spy inside an enemy fortress—a saboteur sent to destroy the opposition on his own home ground. There would be nowhere to flee if she didn't succeed.

Twenty-four hours had passed since she and Iain had last been together. It had been more than a year since they'd been apart for so long. Haven felt empty and numb, as if she'd spent the night on an operating table. Something inside her had been removed, and the anesthesia wouldn't wear off. She couldn't recall falling asleep—just staring into the darkness for hours on end and praying she could find Beau quickly and satisfy the Horae.

Haven's stomach grumbled, and she unwrapped an energy bar. There was a small pile of them on the bedside table. They tasted no better than sugared dirt, but they were all Haven could afford. And each bite helped remind her why she was standing in room 2024 of the Gramercy Gardens Hotel. Eighteen months earlier, after the fire that had "killed" Iain Morrow, Beau had refused to leave Haven's side. She hadn't asked him to stay in New York—he just had. With little money between them, they ate energy bars three meals a day. Beau must have been starving, Haven realized. But he had waited patiently until Haven was ready to say goodbye to the city, and only then did he toss her bags into the bed of his truck and drive her back down to east Tennessee.

Now, room service carts laden with delicacies arrived at Haven's hotel room door every three or four hours. She let the carts sit untouched until the food grew cold, then wheeled them out into the hall to be collected. She didn't dare sample a thing on the trays. There had been other deliveries too. A bank card presented by a dapper man who might well have been the bank's president. Flowers of every imaginable hue and variety. Haven refused all of Adam's gifts. But it was impossible not to appreciate the aura of decadence that surrounded her at the hotel. The staff bowed and scraped before her as though she were vacationing royalty. Everyone knew her name, and her every desire was anticipated.

Haven swallowed the last chunk of the energy bar and checked her reflection in the mirror. She'd chosen a simple gray dress from her own collection for the meeting Adam had arranged with the police. But even with its high neckline and knee-length hem, the outfit seemed a little too sexy for an afternoon appointment. Haven knew the Horae would approve.

She frowned and tried to shove the twelve sisters out of her head.

She didn't relish being their bait. Adam Rosier had to be locked away. But Haven hated that she had been recruited to do Phoebe's dirty work. If there was a chance Adam's feelings for her were real, it would be cruel to use his love to destroy him. But Haven had no choice in the matter. Whatever it took, she'd do it for Beau.

As the elevator slid down its shaft toward the lobby, Haven removed the ring Iain had given her and dropped it into her handbag. She rubbed at the impression on her skin until there was no evidence that the golden band had ever graced her finger. As much as it hurt her, there was no other way. She couldn't afford to make any more mistakes. She couldn't leave behind any more clues that Iain Morrow was still alive. Maybe Adam did love her, but Haven had no intention of testing his powers of forgiveness.

ADAM WAS WAITING for her in the reception area of the Ouroboros Society. Haven arrived to find him lounging in one of the beige leather chairs, his long, pale fingers laced together with his chin resting on top. Two boys chased each other around the room. A little girl was wailing. The child who had apparently walloped her with a textbook was being lectured by her father. The bedlam hadn't disturbed Adam's calm. Before he saw her, his expression was serene, even vaguely amused. Yet Haven thought she noticed him twitch when he spotted her coming toward him across the room, as if her presence had briefly knocked him off balance.

"You look stunning." Adam stood to greet her.

"Thank you." Haven wished Adam would look at something other than her dress. His gaze seemed almost obscene, and she could feel herself beginning to blush. He wanted her badly, and he could have taken her whenever he liked. Why was he so willing to wait?

At last Adam's eyes rose to meet Haven's, and she wondered if he had read her mind. "Follow me," he said with a hint of a smile on his lips. When he put his hand on her back to guide her, Haven could feel his icy touch through the wool of her dress, and a pleasant chill tickled her spine. "They're waiting for us in the conference room."

At the end of the hall, Adam opened a door to reveal four men and one woman sitting around a long glass table, their hands in their laps. They were in their forties or fifties, hardened professionals whose faces bore wrinkles and grooves etched by decades of stress. Yet they all regarded the youthful-looking man in black with a mixture of respect, curiosity, and fear.

"Ladies and gentlemen," Adam announced, "this is my friend Haven Moore. Haven, I'd like to introduce you to Gordon Williams, New York's police commissioner." A burly man in double-breasted suit rose to shake Haven's hand. "Commissioner Williams has brought two of his finest colleagues, Detectives Harvey and Hayes. We also have two representatives from the Federal Bureau of Investigation, Agents Jackson and Agnelli." Adam pulled out a chair for Haven and she sat. "So, shall we begin?" he asked the group.

"May I say a few words first?" the police commissioner inquired.

"Certainly," Adam said.

"Thank you." The commissioner spoke in a thick Brooklyn accent that sounded quaint to Haven's ears. "I would just like to remind the law enforcement professionals gathered here that you were chosen for your discretion. Nothing you hear today will ever leave this room. If there are any leaks, I will personally punish the person responsible. Do I make myself clear?"

The other guests exchanged anxious glances, none of them sure what to say.

"Do I make myself clear?" Gordon Williams repeated.

"Yes," someone offered.

"Good. So, Miss Moore—what seems to be the problem?"

Haven glanced over at Adam, and he gave her a nod of encouragement. She suddenly realized that he hadn't told his guests anything. They had gathered at the Ouroboros Society without knowing whether they'd be tasked with rescuing a kitten from a sewer drain or saving the city from terrorists.

Haven cleared her throat. "A friend of mine has disappeared. The police have been looking for him for almost a week, but they haven't found him yet. He flew here from Nashville, Tennessee—"

"Wait one second," interrupted Gordon Williams. Haven braced for a lecture. She expected him to say that an ordinary missing-person case wasn't worth the police commissioner's valuable time. Instead, he pulled a pencil and small notebook out of his jacket's inside pocket. "Sorry about the interruption, Miss Moore. I just want to make sure that I get all of this down."

THE BRIEFING LASTED for more than two hours. The lawmen wanted to know everything about Beau—from the color of his hair to his father's war record. Haven supplied all the details she could while Commissioner Williams and his colleagues nodded solemnly and took copious notes. When she touched on the subject of Beau's trip to New York, she could see one of the FBI agents growing increasingly agitated.

"Is there something wrong, Agent Jackson?" Adam asked at last. He, too, had noticed the man fidgeting.

"Look, I don't want to sound disrespectful, Miss Moore," the man told Haven. "I know you and Beau Decker are from a very small town and you've probably led sheltered lives. But how could you let your friend visit a stranger he met online? Don't you read the news? That's just asking for trouble."

Haven had tried her best to steer clear of reincarnation. Now she saw that the topic was unavoidable.

"Beau believed he knew the man who called himself Roy Bradford in a previous life. He said I knew him too. But you're right. I should never have let Beau go."

"Wait a second. A previous life? You really believe—" the man began.

"This is the Ouroboros Society, Agent Jackson," Adam cut him off. "We *all* believe."

"And please remember that this information is privileged, Agent Jackson," Commissioner Williams barked. "You say you may have known this man in another existence, Miss Moore? Do you have any information that might help us identify him?"

"No," Haven admitted. "Not yet."

"Yet?" Agent Jackson asked.

"I'm trying to remember more of the life Beau and I shared," Haven explained.

"And you think—"

"Agent Jackson," Adam said firmly, "you came highly recommended, and your superiors assured me that you were a man with an open mind. But if your skepticism is going to interfere with your job, I suggest you find another case to pursue. Or perhaps a new line of work altogether."

Even the briefest glimpse of Adam's power was enough to silence the room.

"Thank you, Miss Moore," Commissioner Williams finally said. "I think this has been a very productive meeting. Do you have anything else you'd like to add at this time?"

"No," Haven said, glad the experience was almost over.

"In that case," the man said, rising from his seat, "we will speak to Mr. Decker's father and the NYPD officers who've been working on the case. We'll find your friend, Miss Moore," he assured her. "You can be sure of it."

"Thank you, Gordon. I have every confidence in you," Adam told the man. Haven detected an ultimatum in his tone. "Thank you all. You're free to leave. I'd like to chat privately with Miss Moore."

After the NYPD and the FBI obediently filed out of the room, Haven turned to Adam. Having seen his power put to work, it was impossible not to feel a little awestruck.

"I'm sorry about Agent Jackson," Adam said. "He's not one of us, and it may take him a little while to get used to the way things work around here. I hope you didn't find his outburst discouraging."

"Forget Agent Jackson. I'm totally thrilled. I can't believe I just had the New York City police commissioner writing down every word I said."

"You're surprised?" Adam asked.

"He's the *police commissioner*," Haven replied. "I doubt he spends much time searching for nineteen-year-old boys who go missing. How did you manage to convince him to come?"

"I didn't need to convince him. He's a member. He volunteered."

"To please you?"

"To earn points," Adam corrected her. "He doesn't know that he needs to please me. He doesn't know who I am at all, aside from a fellow member with a bottomless account."

"So the police commissioner is a member of the Ouroboros Society?" Haven asked, wondering how Commissioner Williams planned to spend the points he would earn. What was his secret weakness? Whatever it was, Adam must have already found it.

"Yes, he's a member, but not a very important one. Only those in the upper ranks are aware of my role here at the Society. I'm afraid Gordon Williams will never reach such heights."

"If the police commissioner isn't high-ranking, who is?" Haven asked, hoping for a rare glimpse of the Society's inner workings.

"Would you really like to know?" His smile had turned sly again.

"Absolutely!" Haven replied.

"Then come with me."

Adam led her out of the conference room. The clock in the reception area said 6:12. Ouroboros Society business hours were over, and the children had all disappeared. In their place were three elegant young women. A curvy redheaded creature in enormous sunglasses jumped up when she saw Adam and rushed over to greet him.

"Hello!" The girl almost came close enough to peck Adam's cheek before she caught herself and lurched backward like she'd bounced off an invisible force field.

"Good evening, Alex," Adam said. "I apologize for making you wait. Allow me to introduce my friend Haven Moore."

Alex removed her sunglasses, revealing a face that appeared clean-scrubbed and unremarkable. Yet Haven felt a jolt of recognition. She knew the face well. Almost everyone did. Without makeup, it could have been that of a Midwestern cheerleader. But it belonged to Alexandra Harbridge, one of the most famous young actresses in the world. Haven felt as if she'd just been introduced to someone she'd been spying on her entire life. Beau had avidly followed Alex's career since the girl had made her acclaimed film debut at the age of thirteen. Alex had never lived up to most critics' expectations, but at age nineteen, she was a worldwide star nonetheless. Half the romantic comedies churned out by Hollywood now featured Alex in a leading role. Most were so saccharine that they left Haven feeling physically ill, but Beau gobbled them up like bonbons. And for six years, he'd regaled Haven with tales of Alex's disastrous relationships, emergency appendectomies, weight fluctuations, and fashion blunders.

"Haven, this is Alex Harbridge," Adam said. "She has been kind enough to offer her help with our Society recruitment efforts this year."

"Hi," Haven croaked.

"Hello to you too! So sorry for butting in like this! I never pass up an opportunity to meet Adam's friends. He knows the most *fascinating* assortment of people." Alex paused, bit her lip, and grinned as if she were contemplating something naughty. "May I ask you something personal? Where *did* you get that dress? I noticed it the second you stepped into the lobby. Would you mind?" Alex twirled one finger, and it took Haven a moment to realize she was being asked to spin around. The gesture might have seemed obnoxious if anyone else had made it, but somehow Alex made it feel friendly and familiar.

"I designed it," Haven said, modeling her own dress.

"You *designed* that?" the girl gasped. "Do you have your own fashion label? Where is your store? Can I stop by tonight?"

"I don't have a store in New York," Haven informed her. "I just design for myself these days."

"How can you deprive the rest of us like that? It's just *cruel!*" Few people could make such a pronouncement sound natural. For the first time, Haven knew what Beau saw in Alex. "Do you think I might be able to persuade you to sew up a little something for me?"

"I'd love to, but I'm living out of a suitcase right now," Haven said. "I'm afraid I didn't pack any of the supplies I'd need."

"And you don't think I can get my hands on a little fabric and thread? Just say yes and I'll have everything delivered to you! And I'll pay you whatever you want."

Haven could see that Alex wasn't inclined to take no for an answer, and Haven did need the money. "What would you want me to make for you?" she asked. "*If* I decided to do this."

"First, I want a dress exactly like *that*," Alex announced, right before inspiration seemed to strike. "*Actually* . . . how about a gown? Do you make gowns?"

"That depends. What kind of gown?"

"Something I can wear to the Oscars. The date is just around the corner, and I still haven't found a single thing I like. My stylist is hopeless. I'm starting to suspect that she's secretly employed by one of my rivals."

"The Oscars?" Haven grimaced. Designers' careers were made— or destroyed—on the Oscars' red carpet. "I'm not sure I'm ready for—"

The girl clutched Haven's arm. "Oh, please don't say no! Please!" she pleaded. "Did you see what I wore when I won my Oscar for *Promises, Promises*? The dress with the purple ruffles? *Star* magazine said I looked like a teenage mutant sea slug. If I don't come up with something good this year, I'll never be able to show my face on a red carpet again."

It *had* been a hideous gown, Haven recalled. Beau had bitched about it for weeks. He'd even unearthed one of Haven's old Barbies, renamed her Alex, and sewn the doll a more suitable dress.

"Okay," Haven reluctantly agreed. "I'm at the Gramercy Gardens Hotel. Room 2024. Would you have time to stop by tomorrow morning? I could take your measurements and possibly show you some sketches."

"Perfect! Let's say nine o'clock," Alex announced, plugging the appointment into her phone.

"Come along, Haven," Adam said. "I'll walk you to the door. Alex, will you excuse us?"

"Did you do that?" Haven asked once they were out of Alex's earshot.

"Pardon me?" Adam said. He retrieved Haven's coat and helped her into it.

"Did you just arrange for me to meet Alex Harbridge?"

"Is that what you think?" Adam opened the mansion's front door for her. It had started to snow, and the scene outside was a blur. Frosted with snow, the trees of Gramercy Park formed a dense white net of branches and limbs. "Did you happen to look in the mirror before you left? That dress you're wearing is a masterpiece. You're very talented, Haven. Why would you need any help from me?"

"Thank you for saying so, Adam. But I want you to know—I'm only taking the job so I can afford to stay in New York while I search for Beau."

"I understand," Adam assured her. "This is a difficult time for you. But let something good come out of a horrible experience. Your friend wouldn't want you to throw away a diamond just because you found it in the mud. Would he?"

He wouldn't, Haven thought as she hurried down the steps of the Ouroboros Society. In fact, she knew *exactly* how Beau would react if he ever got wind of Alex Harbridge's offer. She still remembered the morning she'd shown him her acceptance letter from the Fashion

Institute of Technology in New York. Beau hadn't even paused to consider what it might mean for him—that his one and only friend would be moving a thousand miles away. Instead, he'd let out an ear-shattering victory whoop and carried Haven through their high school's halls on his shoulders, shouting out the good news to hundreds of kids who couldn't have cared any less.

But Beau's approval wasn't what mattered. His safety was Haven's only concern now. Still, she needed money to search for him—and a movie star's cash was as green as the next person's. It would be fine, Haven told herself. As long as the Oscars dress remained nothing more than a job.

EAGER TO GET to work, Haven took a detour on her way back to the hotel. At a drug store on Third Avenue she bought a drawing pad. It was the price of a day's worth of energy bars, but Haven decided to call it an investment. Outside, she stopped on the corner to sketch out some ideas. They were arriving too fast to get them all onto paper, and the snowflakes were causing the pages to warp. A rowdy group of teenagers ran past, shouting colorful insults at one another as they slid down the snow-dusted sidewalks. It looked like fun, Haven thought. She watched as a boy and a girl hung back from the rest and kissed in a shadow between the streetlights. Her inspiration deserted her, and Haven closed the drawing pad. As she made her way back to the hotel, she couldn't help feeling a bit sorry for herself.

When she reached the door of her room, Haven tucked the pad into her coat pocket while she fiddled with the lock. She took one step inside the room and froze. She was certain she'd left all the lights on, yet the room was dark. She checked the outside door handle and found the DO NOT DISTURB sign still dangling there. When she looked up, she spotted a figure sitting in the armchair by the window. The light from the hallway fell across a pair of men's shoes. Haven's hand shot toward the switch on the wall. It wasn't where she remembered it. As she groped in the darkness, the figure rose and made its way toward her. The man was only a few feet away when Haven's fingers made contact with the switch.

"Keep the lights off. The curtains are open, and someone might see us."

"Iain!" Haven gasped.

"Shhh." Iain pushed the door closed and pulled Haven into the room. When his lips found hers, the numbness Haven had felt melted in an instant, and her body began to burn. In Iain's arms, with the smell of his skin all around her, she was perfectly content. Nothing else mattered. She wouldn't risk losing the feeling for anything . . . except. A quick stab of panic made her shove him back.

"What are you doing here?" she asked Iain. "How did you get into the hotel?"

"I snuck in through the delivery entrance. I had to see you."

"I *know*. I miss you too, Iain, but do you realize how dangerous this is? We can spend every minute together as soon as we find Beau. Besides, we both have another meeting with the Horae tomorrow. We could have seen each other then."

"You're right. I promise I won't do it again. But I needed to let you know that I've come up with a plan. Mia told me Padma Singh is still alive, and I think I know where to find her."

Haven briefly wondered if all the stress had sent Iain over the edge. "Why would you want to do *that*?" she asked.

"Because Padma is Adam's first huge mistake, that's why!" It had been a while since Haven had seen him so energized. Even when he was still, he seemed to be moving. "I have no idea why he let her live. Padma kept secret files on OS members back when she was president. She knows every terrible thing they've ever done. If Padma still has access to the files, she has enough evidence to send half the members to prison. It would destroy the OS!"

"But Padma doesn't want to destroy the OS," Haven argued. "I saw her yesterday begging Adam to take her back."

"Even better!" Iain exclaimed, clearly thrilled by the news. "If Padma saw you and Adam together, she probably lost all hope of ever being allowed back in the OS. She'll be even *more* likely to help me now!"

It made sense, Haven thought as she turned to face the windows. Outside, fat flakes of snow fell down from the heavens. Far below lay a white void where Gramercy Park had been just a few hours earlier. Still, one lonely soul was out for a walk.

"Just give me one week," Iain said. "That's all I'm asking. Keep your distance from Adam for seven days while I try to find Padma. And if I fail, you can always go ahead with the Horae's original plan."

"But what about Beau?" Haven asked.

"Mia's looking for him. The police are looking for him. And you can inhale as much of Phoebe's smoke as you want. No one's going to put Beau on hold. I'm only asking that you stay away from Adam."

"I don't have any problem with *that*," Haven assured him. "But I don't know how you're going to convince Phoebe to go along with all of this."

"I'll talk to her at our meeting tomorrow, but why would she argue? If the Ouroboros Society is shut down, then that boarding school upstate will have to close. The kids Adam's recruited will be sent home to their parents, and we'll have enough time to come up with a better plan to get Adam into that vault."

"I guess you've got everything figured out," Haven said, trying to identify all the feelings that were clouding her thoughts. At least one of them was relief.

"Well, there is one little hitch," Iain said.

"Oh no," Haven sighed.

"It's nothing major. I'll just have to be out of touch for a while. Adam probably has people watching Padma. I'll be careful, but if

I'm spotted, I don't want them finding a phone with your number on it."

"You mean I'm not going to be able to talk to you for a whole week?" Haven moaned.

"Don't worry," Iain said. "I'll try to find other ways to stay in touch."

Haven felt her coat being unbuttoned and removed. The sketch pad in the pocket landed with a thump when Iain let the coat drop to the floor.

CHAPTER NINETEEN

Alex Harbridge arrived at nine on the dot with two coffees and a bag filled with croissants. Dressed in jeans and a black turtleneck, her signature copper-colored hair pinned back with a simple barrette, she seemed like any other New York girl. But Haven knew most designers would have strangled their mothers for a meeting with the actress, and she'd gone to great lengths to make sure she was ready. After Iain had departed in the wee hours of the morning, Haven stayed up sketching dresses until her new book was completely full. Then, at seven, she had found herself pleading with a tailor at a nearby dry cleaner. At seven fifteen, he finally agreed to lend Haven his measuring tape in exchange for her very last twenty-dollar bill.

"They're all so gorgeous." Alex sighed, paging through Haven's illustrations. "I don't know how you do it. I'll never be able to choose. I'm good at a lot of things, but dressing myself has never been one of them."

"Would you like me to make a recommendation?" Haven asked nervously.

"I'd *love* it." Alex sounded relieved.

"How about something like this?" Haven flipped to a page toward the back of the sketchbook. There she'd drawn a sophisticated ankle-length dress with a jeweled neckline. "I didn't have my colored pencils with me, so you'll just have to imagine that the fabric's a shimmering green."

"Am I going to look like a giant beetle?"

Haven laughed. "I'm shooting for butterfly."

"Do you really think I could pull off a color like that?"

"With your hair? I think you'd look stunning," Haven assured her.

"And what about my giant ass? Is there anything you can do to make it look smaller?"

Haven was beginning to like the girl. "You know, there's nothing wrong with the size of your butt. In the right dress it could be your biggest asset."

"Oh, it'll be my biggest asset all right, if I don't stop eating these things." Alex threw herself back on the couch and bit into her second croissant. Haven wondered how much Beau would have given to see Alex Harbridge with pastry crumbs all over her sweater. "If you knew how many hours I spend in the gym every day trying to work off the crap I stuff down my throat."

"Why don't you stop working out for a while?" Haven asked. "You've been rich and famous since you were thirteen years old. Maybe you should take some time off to live a little."

"That's what my mom always says. But I'll have plenty of time soon enough," Alex said. "I don't plan on working this hard forever. But right now I make the front cover of half the magazines in the country every time I gain five pounds. I've been called everything from Princess Porky to America's Fattest Sweetheart. Not that I give a damn. I've been through all of this before. I know what it's like. But the problem is that no one will hire me if I'm too tubby. So until it's time to retire, I'll just have to keep dragging myself to the gym so I can keep doing what I love."

"You've really done all this before?" Alex was such amusing company that Haven had almost forgotten she was a member of the Ouroboros Society—and she was far too important to be innocent.

"Oh yeah. I've been acting for seven lives now. This is my second time in Hollywood. A lot of people at the Society think I've come back for the fame, but they couldn't be more wrong. Fame sucks. You think I like having gross men with cameras follow me around all the time? I only put up with it all because I'm finally getting to be a good actress!"

"Were you someone famous your first time in Hollywood?"

Alex grinned sheepishly. "You could say that."

"Who were you?"

"Maybe later. It freaks people out. Everyone used to laugh when I told them. No one ever believed me before I met Adam. Wait, that reminds me. I've been meaning to ask. How do *you* know Adam, anyway? I haven't seen you around the club before."

"Oh, we've known each other forever," Haven said, sticking uncomfortably close to the truth. "I can barely remember how we met. Do you know him well?"

"As well as anyone, I guess. You know how mysterious he is. I used to . . ." Alex bit her lip and blushed.

"What?" Haven prodded.

"I used to have a terrible crush on him. He's so good-looking, and he was so sweet to me when I was a kid. My parents thought I was totally nuts, but Adam took me in and made me feel special. He arranged for tutors and coaches. He even helped me get a nose job."

"A nose job!"

"Believe me, I needed it. I would have been playing the homely sister or bitter best friend for the rest of my life without it. Anyway, that was years ago. I got over my little crush. I've heard he's got a girl-friend now, anyway. By the way, have you ever noticed . . ."

Haven raised an eyebrow, and Alex leaned in.

"Adam doesn't seem to age. I'm nineteen, and I look older than he does!"

A sudden chill made Haven shiver. "I have noticed."

"So do you know?"

"Know what?"

"They say when you reach the highest level of the Society, you're told the big secret. I think the secret's about Adam."

"You're not in the top level of the Society?" Haven asked. "You must be pretty high up there if you know Adam at all."

"Yeah, but I still have one level to go. So do you know what the secret is?"

Haven laughed nervously. "I'm not even a member of the OS. But if I find out, you'll be the first person I tell. Why don't we go ahead and take your measurements?"

She pulled out her measuring tape and had Alex stand in front of the full-length mirror on the bathroom door.

"You're not a member of the Society, but you *are* one of us, aren't you?" Alex asked, staring at Haven's reflection in the mirror.

"One of us?" Haven measured the movie star's waist.

"An Eternal One. Someone who keeps coming back. How else could a person our age have a talent like yours?"

"Yes, I guess I am."

"Are what?"

"An Eternal One."

"Well, if you're ever interested in joining the club, I'd be happy to introduce you to a few people. Is there anyone at the OS you've been dying to meet?"

Haven couldn't resist. "Do you know someone named Mia Michalski? I think she's some kind of detective."

"I could introduce you to movie stars, Nobel Prize winners, and the editors of every fashion magazine in town, and you want to meet *Mia Michalski*?"

"She's a friend of a friend. So you do know her?"

"Not well," Alex said. "Mia doesn't spend that much time at the OS anymore. I have a feeling she's avoiding Adam."

"Why?"

"Have you ever seen Mia?"

"No," Haven admitted.

"She's gorgeous," Alex said, and the measuring tape almost slipped from Haven's fingers. "When she first joined, half the guys at the OS would have traded every point in their accounts for a night with her. She set her sights on Adam, of course. But I don't think he knew she existed until she started throwing herself at him every chance that she got. I have it on good authority that he ended up telling her to back the hell off. I gotta say, the whole episode was rather hilarious."

"Sounds like it," Haven said mirthlessly. She should never have asked.

"But why are we talking about boring old Mia Michalski, anyway? So you say you're one of us? Does that mean you know who you were in your previous lives?" Alex asked.

"I've had a few visions here and there, but my memories aren't very good. Do you mind if I move your hair? I need to measure your neck."

"Not at all." Alex pulled her hair up and held it in a pile on the top of her head. At the base of her hairline was a tattoo of a serpent swallowing its own tail. "A lot of my lifetimes weren't that clear, either," Alex continued. "But then I heard about this woman who can see into other people's past lives, and she told me some amazing stories. You should go see her."

"Oh crap! Phoebe!" Haven dropped the measuring tape, and it rolled across the floor.

"Is that her real name? I've only heard people call her the Pythia."

"Sorry, Alex. Listen, I just remembered I have another appointment. I think I have all the measurements I need. Can I call you when I have some fabric samples to show you?"

"Sure," Alex said, gathering her things. "But I wouldn't make any more appointments if I were you."

"Why?" Haven asked.

Alex's grin was mischievous. "Because I gave your number to a friend of mine who needs a gown too. You're gonna be pretty busy for the next few days."

THE STORM THE night before had deposited more than a foot of snow on the city, and icy white corridors branched in all directions from the Gramercy Gardens Hotel. The doorman guided Haven through the passage that led to the curb and opened the door of an idling taxi. She climbed inside and discovered Chandra sitting in the driver's seat, wearing a military-style coat over a sparkling sari.

"It's twenty past ten." Chandra's gold bangles tinkled when she pointed at the clock on the dashboard. "You're going to be an hour late, and Phoebe's *not* going to be happy."

"Sorry. Where's Iain?" Haven asked. "Are we picking him up on the way?"

"That's Vera's job," Chandra said. "My job is losing the two gray men who are following you. Look out the back window. They're getting into a car parked down the block."

Haven watched two men with no distinguishing features duck into a beige sedan. The sight left her trembling. "Does this mean Adam's having me followed? Do you think he suspects something? Am I in trouble?"

"I doubt it. We've been careful. He probably just wants to protect his favorite girl. Now pay attention, princess. At the first stop light we come to on Park Avenue, I want you to get out of the cab. There will be a blue minivan stopped on the corner facing the other direction. Walk across the street. A bus will drive by. Wait until you're hidden from view and get into the minivan. Don't hesitate or the timing will be off. You'll recognize Cleo. She's the other woman you met in the subway. She'll take you straight to Phoebe."

"Wow," Haven said. "That's some pretty impressive planning."

"We never forget who we're dealing with," Chandra noted humorlessly as she started the engine. "You shouldn't either."

The switch went off without a problem. In the thirty minutes they spent driving along the East River, Cleo said nothing to Haven. Her eyes, hidden behind black Gucci sunglasses, seemed to be checking the rearview mirror as often as they watched the road. When they reached Sylvan Terrace, they found Phoebe peering down at them from the house's stoop. With her silver hair, pale skin, and sleeveless ecru shift, she could have been mistaken for an ice sculpture.

"You're *very* late." Phoebe's voice had taken on an imperious tone. Haven felt like a chambermaid being scolded by her mistress.

"I apologize," Haven said. "I was working, and I lost track of time."

"Working?" Phoebe scoffed. "At what? Don't you have all the work you need for now?"

"Yes, but I'm totally broke," Haven tried to explain. "I need to work if I want to eat, so I'm making a dress for a friend. I promise—I won't let it interfere with our plans again."

"Is this 'friend' someone you met through Adam?" Phoebe inquired.

"Yes," Haven admitted.

"Excellent," Phoebe said, friendly once more. "Take some of what he gives you. It's the first step toward convincing him that he's won you over. But don't be too obvious. No money, no jewels—just little favors. Otherwise he'll suspect you're up to something."

"I don't think you understand," Haven couldn't help but bristle. "This job wasn't a *favor*. I'm a good designer. I don't need Adam Rosier to sell my dresses."

"Of course you don't," Phoebe said. "But please. Don't be late again. Even a talented designer should take the time to save her best friend. It would be a shame if something happened to him while you were sewing pretty dresses."

Haven opened her mouth to argue, but there was no argument to be made. Phoebe was right.

"We should get started." The old woman ushered Haven inside and directed her toward the stairs. "I must return to the spa soon. I have an appointment with a woman who's certain she was Joan of Arc." She sighed dramatically. "They *all* think they were Joan of Arc."

"Wait a second. Where's Iain? Vera was supposed to pick him up."

"And so she did," Phoebe said. "He came, we talked, and then he said he had to leave. It's too bad you missed him; I hear he'll be out of contact for a while."

"You spoke to him? Did Iain tell you about his plan?"

Phoebe stopped on the stairs. "Yes, and I gave him my blessing. But I also explained why the Horae can't afford to put our own efforts on hold. You and I will continue just as we discussed."

"But—"

"If Iain succeeds, I promise to reevaluate the agreement I made with you. Until then, our deal stands. Your friend may be in the hands of a psychopath, Haven, and I know you want to do everything you can to help him. Surely you see that two plans might be better than one?"

THE SNOW ON the rooftop had melted in a perfect circle around the water tower. Haven stripped off her outerwear as soon as they entered the hot, dry room inside. The air already bore the familiar fragrance of Phoebe's strange herbs. Haven dropped down to the floor by the hearth, and Phoebe took her place at Haven's side. It was all a waste of time, Haven decided. There was no way a vision would come when she was feeling so agitated. Why had she let herself be late for the meeting? How could she have missed her last chance to see Iain? And why was Phoebe being so stubborn?

"Close your eyes," Phoebe said as she threw more twigs on the coals. "Try to remember the odors you encountered on your last voyage through time."

Haven recalled the scent of the dirt on Piero's grave, the mustiness of the robes she'd worn. Then another fragrance came to her. It was delicate and floral, a perfume Beatrice had loved. It was still there, beneath the stenches of the fourteenth century.

"Let the smells pull you back. . . ."

TWO SERVANTS ARRIVED *in the room, each bearing a large trunk. Several of the girls gasped. Beatrice enjoyed watching the rest of her friends struggle to hide their envy.*

"They're from Adam. Open them," she ordered the servants. She had trained her voice to sound both bored and haughty, but she was excited. Gifts were the only thing that could drag her out of the land of the dead and make her feel truly alive. But the satisfaction never lasted very long.

The trunks' locks were opened and the lids flipped back. The first was filled with silks too beautiful to imagine. The second contained linens, laces, and furs. A bejeweled box rested on top. Six young women gathered around the treasure. One reached out for the small box, but Beatrice was too fast for her. She slapped the girl's hand and snatched the box away. Inside were three golden necklaces.

"Put this one on me," she ordered a friend, whisking her long blonde hair away from her neck. The other girls wore their hair up, twisted and coiled like rope. But Beatrice refused to follow the fashion. Hair like hers was meant to be admired, and she could do as she liked now. Beatrice stood in front of the glass. Even in her simple gown she was radiant. Somehow her sorrow had made her more beautiful.

"You dare wear such things?" a friend whispered. "You're only a merchant's daughter. The nobles won't be happy."

"And soon I'll be the wife of the man who loans them all money. I can do as I please."

"Do you know when you'll be married?" a girl asked.

"When it's time," Beatrice said. The wedding was the price she would pay for the presents, but she could settle that debt whenever she chose. Her mother and father wanted the marriage to take place as quickly as possible, but they no longer held any sway over her. Her fiancé had set her free to do as she liked. Only her brother, Piero, was unafraid to speak his mind. He said she was reckless, that nothing good could come of the union.

"Fortune has smiled on you," a friend told her.

"At last," Beatrice added.

HAVEN WOKE ON the floor. She could feel the woven mat etching a pattern onto her cheekbone.

"Tell me what happened," Phoebe said.

"This is getting ridiculous!" Haven struggled to rise. She was still in shock—the horrible vision had taken a toll on her. The scent of Beatrice's perfume lingered, making Haven feel nauseous. "You're supposed to show me Naddo!"

"Tell me," Phoebe repeated.

"No. What I saw was too personal." Haven didn't want to admit that she'd once been the vain, greedy creature with the lovely face and the stunning blonde hair. And she didn't dare mention the girl's fiancé. There was no doubt about it. Beatrice Vettori had been on the verge of marrying Adam Rosier. But Haven wasn't about to let Phoebe know that.

"Nothing I saw today is going to help me find Beau."

"How can you be so certain?" Phoebe asked.

"I just am," Haven announced.

"You're pale. You must have seen something that disturbed you," Phoebe probed. "There's no need to keep any secrets from me."

"Please," Haven begged. She couldn't bear any more probing. "I'm not feeling well. I need to go home."

Phoebe's mouth curled up at its corners. If she hadn't known better, Haven would have guessed the older woman was delighted. "Very well," Phoebe said. "Go back to your hotel. We will come for you again in a couple of days."

Outside, Haven searched for a cab, but the slush-covered streets were deserted. Eager to escape from the Horae, she set off into the grounds of the rickety white mansion across the street. Perched on a hill in the middle of a neighborhood just north of Harlem, it had once been a stately country home, surrounded by an ancient forest. The man who had built it in the eighteenth century could never have imagined it would one day be enveloped by a bustling city filled with people from every known land.

Trudging through snow, Haven circled around to the back of the building where the Horae would neither see nor hear her. There, a porch offered welcome shelter from the bitter wind that blew west off the Harlem River. A strip of yellow police tape stretched across the stairs, but Haven ducked beneath it and shook the snow from her shoes. With Sylvan Terrace out of sight, she pulled out her phone and tried to call Iain. There wasn't an answer—not even a voice mail greeting. Frustrated, she sat down with her back against the wall of the house. She needed to talk to someone she could trust, so she scrolled through her phone's list of received calls. When she found the number with a North Carolina area code, she pressed dial.

"Hello?" The person on the other end of the phone had a mouth full of something crunchy. When they were kids, Leah Frizzell had always carried a bag of chips in her hand or a candy bar in her pocket. Yet she never managed to gain an ounce. There seemed to be a beast inside of the girl, demanding to be fed. It might have had something to do with the rumors she'd heard about Leah's family, but Haven had imagined a giant snake coiled inside the girl's belly, gorging on a never-ending supply of junk food.

"Leah, it's Haven. Do you have a minute?" Haven's mouth was watering. She had no idea what Leah was chewing on the other end of the line, but she'd have given almost anything for a bite.

Leah swallowed. "D'you find Beau?" she asked, as if Haven had been given the simplest task in the world.

"No, not yet. But I'm in New York now."

"Have you been to see the woman surrounded by smoke?"

"Her name is Phoebe. I've talked to her. Three times, as a matter of fact."

"And?" More crunching.

"It's not been very helpful. She takes me back to the life I need to see, but never the right parts. I wish there was some other way."

"I'm sorry to hear that. If I knew of another way, I'd tell you. I suppose you'll just have to keep trying for now."

"Yeah. It's just . . ." Haven sighed. "It's just that my visions haven't been all that pleasant. Turns out I wasn't a very good person back then. Actually, I was pretty damn horrible. I was mean and vain and greedy. And I have a sick feeling I was engaged to Adam Rosier—and that I might have had something to do with my brother's death. I don't want to see any more, Leah. If I hurt Piero, I don't know how I'll live with myself."

"I'd be real surprised if you hurt anyone. But even if you did, it was a long time ago. Have you ever considered that you might have learned a thing or two since the fourteenth century?"

"Sure, but—"

"I mean, isn't that the whole point of this reincarnation stuff?" Leah continued. "To learn from the mistakes you've made?"

"To be honest, I don't know what the point is," Haven said. "But if we really learn from our mistakes, wouldn't we all be much better people by now?"

"Maybe you *are* better," Leah said. "Or maybe there's something out there that holds people back. You know, like they say in physics, for every action, there's an equal and opposite reaction."

"Never had much time for physics," Haven said.

"That's a shame. It explains an awful lot, you know. But I'm afraid I don't have much time for it either right now."

"No? Why not?"

It was Leah's turn to sigh. "These visions I'm having—they're getting so bad that I can't hardly think straight."

"Are you still seeing the man in the garden?" Haven looked out from the porch at the grounds of the mansion and tried to imagine how lovely they would be in the spring when the snow finally melted away. There were hundreds of gardens hidden all over Manhattan. Any of them could be the one Leah needed to find.

"Yeah," Leah said. "It's like he doesn't want me to wait anymore. He wants me to come now. I've never felt this sort of pressure before. Something big is going to happen. I'd be in New York today if I knew where to look for the guy. You haven't had any ideas, have you?"

"No," Haven admitted. In the distance, a fire engine wailed. "Can you give me any more clues? Do you hear anything in your visions? Smell anything?"

"Now that you mention it, there's something that smells nasty. Rotten—like the time a possum crawled up into my uncle Earl's carburetor and died."

"That's what New York smells like all summer," Haven said. "What about noises. Do you hear anything in the visions? A church bell, maybe, or an ice cream truck?"

"No," Leah said after a long pause. "I don't hear anything."

"Are you sure? Not even sirens or horns or traffic?"

"Nope," Leah said. "Nothing. It's totally silent." Haven heard

Leah's hand rustling around in a bag, then the crunching commenced once more.

"Well, I don't know what to tell you, then," Haven said as her stomach began to growl. "I'm having a hard time thinking straight myself. I've hardly eaten all day."

"Why not?"

"It's a long story," Haven said. "Let's just say I'm trying to avoid temptation."

"By starving yourself?" Leah scoffed. "A hamburger's not going to get you in trouble, Haven. Go find some food. You ain't gonna save anyone if you let yourself die of hunger."

"Good point," said Haven.

"My points always are. And Haven?"

"Yeah."

"Don't worry so much about temptation. Just trust yourself, and you'll do the right thing. Whatever that turns out to be."

CHAPTER TWENTY

Haven raced to board the last car on the train. The seats were packed with weary passengers on their way home from work. She leaned her back against the door of a conductor's booth and watched the subway tunnel recede in the distance. Even in the most desolate stretches, she could see signs that the tunnels weren't entirely vacant. A mangy couch. A stuffed suitcase. A baby stroller. There were people living beside the tracks, fumbling their way through the darkness.

Haven felt just as blind. Her vision had illuminated a single scene in the past. Beatrice hadn't been Adam's prisoner. She'd been his fiancée. But the revelation was like striking a match on a moonless night. How many times had Haven chosen Adam of her own free will? Had Iain known all along? As much as she dreaded the answers, she knew she needed to ask.

When the subway stopped at Seventy-second Street and Central Park West, Haven got out. As express trains swept through the station, she sat on a bench and waited for the platform to empty. Chandra might have lost the gray men who'd been following Haven earlier in the day, but there was always a chance that they'd picked up her scent once more. When no one else stayed behind, Haven charged up the steps. Ducking between cars stopped at the traffic light on the avenue, she made her way to the wall that circled Central Park. There, across from Frances Whitman's apartment building, she lingered once more to make sure no one was watching. She shouldn't have risked guiding gray men to Iain. But she'd tried calling a dozen times with no success, and her desire to hear his voice had grown too strong to resist.

She was scanning the street for suspicious sedans when she saw the young man emerge from the Andorra apartments and begin walking uptown. Iain's face was hidden under a Yankees hat, but Haven recognized his gait in an instant. The traffic was heavy, and she couldn't cross the avenue. Shouting would draw unwanted attention. So she trailed Iain from the opposite side of the road until he disappeared down a side street. When the streetlights finally turned red, she hurried to catch him. But the trail had gone cold by the time she reached the sidewalk. Jogging west, she searched for Iain's black coat and cap. Finally she spotted him on a corner of Amsterdam Avenue slipping inside a dingy bar with a neon sign.

She had plenty of time to call out to him, but she didn't. Instead, Haven crept down the sidewalk and hid behind a tree outside the bar. Why was Iain out drinking while she was busting her butt to save Beau? And who in the hell was he meeting? Peeking though the soot-smeared windows, Haven could see a small, shabby room with a pool table at one end. Three booths lined the right-hand wall. A long oak bar ran opposite. There, Iain was greeting a girl who must have been waiting for him to arrive. Mia Michalski. Haven's stomach turned when she saw Iain kiss the girl's cheek.

She didn't look for long, but she saw enough of Mia to see the detective was too young for barhopping—and every bit as beautiful as Alex Harbridge had described. Haven wondered why someone so attractive would choose to do most of her business over the Internet. One flutter of Mia's eyelashes or flip of that long blonde mane could draw secrets out of almost any man alive.

Haven slid back behind the tree and thumped her head against the bark. She'd lost another opportunity to speak to Iain. If she stepped into the bar, he would realize she'd followed him. How would she explain her actions if she couldn't understand them herself? What was wrong with her? Why hadn't she called out to Iain when she'd had the chance?

You're not who you think you are, the Horae once warned her. Virginia Morrow had said the same thing. Haven thought of selfish, spoiled Beatrice. The girl who lived only for gifts and had agreed to marry Adam Rosier. Was that horrible girl still somewhere inside of her? Was *she* the reason Haven had been too dazzled by Alex Harbridge to remember her meeting with the Horae? Was *she* the reason Haven had gone behind Iain's back to save a fortune that wasn't really hers? Was *she* the reason Haven was spying on the person she loved most— the person who was risking everything to help her?

Trust yourself, and you'll do the right thing. This time it was Leah's words that Haven heard in her head. And Leah Frizzell never lied. She never tidied up the truth or softened her words just to save some-one's feelings. If Leah trusted her to do the right thing, then Haven knew she was capable of figuring out what it was. So without a single glance at the bar behind her, Haven stepped out of her hiding place and followed her heart down Amsterdam Avenue.

She bought a small spiral notebook at a deli, intending to write Iain a note—an apology, a thank-you, and a love letter all wrapped into one. But words couldn't capture everything she needed to say. So for the next two hours, Haven sat at a café and sketched scenes of their happiest memories. The little white cottage in the Washing-ton Mews. Eden Falls. The basement of the Apollo Theater. The bal-cony of their apartment on the Piazza Navona. The winding streets of Rome. On the very last page of the notebook, Haven wrote, *I keep missing you.*

The doorman at the Andorra apartments took the notebook and placed it in an envelope that he labeled *guest of Frances Whitman.* Her errand finished, Haven stepped to the curb, hailed a cab, and gave the driver the address of the Gramercy Gardens Hotel. When she arrived, she rushed straight for her room. The right thing to do going forward, she'd decided, was keep herself out of trouble. But Haven was only halfway across the lobby when she heard her own name.

"Excuse me! Miss Moore!" A woman dressed in a chic black suit was chasing her.

Not again, Haven thought as she reluctantly came to a halt. She recognized the woman as the manager who had greeted her at check-in, and Haven hoped she wasn't about to be sent packing from another hotel. Then she remembered: The Ouroboros Society was footing the bill. She could probably demand that the manager strip to her underwear while belting out "The Star-Spangled Banner," and the woman would happily obey.

"I'm so glad I caught you!" The manager was out of breath but still struggling to keep a broad smile on her face.

"Is there a problem?" Haven asked.

"Oh no, no problem at all, Miss Moore! I just wanted to let you know that you received a delivery earlier this afternoon. I hope you don't mind, but I instructed my staff to take it up to your room."

"That's fine," Haven said. Whatever Adam had sent could go right in the trash.

"It was a rather unusual delivery," the manager said.

"I'm sure it's fine," Haven assured her.

Upstairs, she opened the door to her hotel room and stopped in her tracks. There was a figure standing by the windows.

"Iain?" Her head told her it couldn't be possible, but her heart kept dancing. When the lights came on, she gasped. The figure was a dressmaker's dummy. Bolts of fabric in every shade of green were leaning against the walls. The desk held a state-of-the-art sewing machine. On the table by the window was a gift basket the size of a garbage can overflowing with pink frosted cupcakes and champagne. An envelope lay beside the basket.

I had them bring every green in the store.
Call me as soon as you're ready. No pressure!

xx Alex

CHAPTER TWENTY-ONE

Haven sat at the sewing machine, letting the fabric flow through her fingers as it passed under the needle. She hadn't bothered to cut a pattern for the dress she was making. It wasn't the dress she'd agreed to make, but she knew it was the gown Alex needed to wear. She was creating it from memory, and for the first time since she'd returned from spying on Iain, her mind was unclouded. She kept the phone nearby in case he called, but she knew Iain had gone ahead with his plan. A whole week might pass before she'd have word from him. All Haven could do now was wait—wait for the right vision to come. Wait for someone to save Beau. Wait for Iain to find Padma Singh. While Haven waited, she'd work. The more time she spent alone in her room, the less likely she was to screw everything up.

She cut and pinned and sewed through the night, stopping briefly around three in the morning to attack a cupcake from Alex's basket and wash it down with a glass of champagne. She dropped the cupcake wrapper onto the floor alongside scraps of fabric and rejected zippers.

Four hours later, she collapsed on top of the trash and fell fast asleep. The room was a disaster, but in the center stood the dressmaker's dummy, wearing one of the most beautiful gowns Haven had ever created. She would have been the first to admit that it wasn't her own design.

Beau visited Haven in her dreams. She was sitting at the table in his father's kitchen, eating a bowl of Froot Loops. Beau came in and plunked down a doll in a slinky green dress.

"Who is that, Hooker Barbie?" Haven had asked, dribbling a little milk down the front of her shirt.

"Do you have to be so crude? That's Alex Harbridge," Beau said. "I've freed her from the tyranny of bad fashion."

"Alex Harbridge would never wear that."

"She would if *I* made it for her," Beau argued. "It's designed for a girl with a little flesh on her bones. Barbie doesn't quite cut it, but she's all I had to work with."

"I'm not saying it wouldn't look good. I'm saying Alex Harbridge would never wear it. She's obviously neurotic about her weight. You may think she's hot, but most girls have no idea what they really look like. We see something totally different when we look in the mirror."

"And that's why every lady needs a gay best friend to set her straight."

HAVEN WOKE WITH a start when someone screamed. Daylight streamed through the windows, and a woman with a vacuum cleaner was standing in the door. At first Haven imagined that the maid was horrified by the mess she'd left. Then she realized she was lying on the floor of a room that looked like the scene of a violent crime.

"It's okay! I'm not dead!" Haven said, just as the woman fainted in the hallway.

*   *   *

ALEX HARBRIDGE TOOK off her sunglasses and began chewing on one of the tips. "I wasn't expecting to hear from you for a few days. You made *that* in one night?" she asked skeptically. "The whole thing?"

"I have the calluses to prove it," Haven said.

"It isn't the dress we discussed." Alex stepped forward and spun the dummy around slowly. The disappointment on her face was clear. "A little skimpy, isn't it?"

"You're nineteen years old. You don't have anything that you need to keep hidden. I know the dress doesn't look like much on a manne- quin, but it was designed by someone who's been dying to dress you for the last six years."

"You've been dying to dress me since we were in the eighth grade?"

"No, not me," Haven admitted as she carefully removed the dress from the dummy. "I borrowed a friend's design. He always thought you should flaunt your curves—not hide them. Do you think you could give it a shot?"

"I suppose," Alex said with a forced smile. Then she took a deep breath. "Oh, why the hell not?"

Haven handed her the dress, and Alex carried it into the bathroom and locked herself inside. The door remained closed for ten full min- utes before Haven worked up the courage to knock.

One of Alex's eyes appeared in the crack. "How did you do this?"

"Do what?"

Alex opened the door. The gown hid nothing, and it couldn't have been more flattering. Without her flesh zipped, crammed, and tucked into a prison of fabric, Alex appeared larger than life, like a goddess or a mythical being. "How did you make me look like this? I've spent hundreds of thousands of dollars on doctors and trainers, and all it took was a dress."

"It's you," Haven said. "Not the dress."

"No, it's not. I've worn a million gowns, and none of them made me look this good."

"Well, I'm glad you like it," Haven said, her spirits higher than they'd been in days.

"Like it? After I take this off, we're going to celebrate the fact that I'm no longer on a diet. I'm meeting a friend downtown for lunch at Amrita. Why don't you come with? You'll love him—he's amazing."

"I should probably take a nap. I didn't get much sleep last night."

"Are you kidding? Have some coffee if you're tired! You're going to need to get out of the house as much as you can before Oscars night. After that, you're going to be very busy—and very famous."

EVEN A GIRL from Snope City, Tennessee, knew that you didn't just stroll into a place like Amrita and expect to be fed. At brunch time on a Saturday, the bar of the restaurant was already crammed with people who'd been waiting for more than an hour to be seated. And it wasn't the food that had drawn them to Amrita. It was the chance to be seated near the rich, famous, and beautiful and pretend for a while they were one of them. The crowd parted with an excited murmur as Alex sashayed up to the maître d's stand. Haven trailed behind in her wake, wishing Beau were there to enjoy the spectacle.

"Miss Harbridge," the man gushed. "Such a pleasure to see you. Right this way, please. Your party has already arrived."

Past the bar were two dozen tables covered in modest white table-cloths. The white walls bore black-and-white photos of ancient ruins. The restaurant itself could have passed for almost any other if not for its patrons. Every single guest was familiar, even if Haven couldn't quite remember their names. But she could see in an instant that they were different from the crowd waiting by the bar. No one looked up as Alex Harbridge passed, and they didn't need to pretend that they belonged. It was as if Haven had stumbled across the hidden nest of the *hoi oligoi*.

Haven spotted a sandy-haired young man waving furiously to Alex from the best table in the house. Slim and impeccably groomed, he wore a shirt tailored to display his sculpted chest. She recognized Calum Daniel's face from a top-rated teen drama that she'd never bothered to watch more than once or twice. He played the billionaire bad boy who'd seduced every character on the show. Rumor had it that the role didn't require Calum to do much acting.

Calum's companion smiled but didn't wave. He was darker, burlier, and even better looking than his friend. He couldn't have been more than eighteen or nineteen, but Haven sensed a serious soul hidden behind the boy's youthful features.

"Calum!" Alex exclaimed. "I didn't know you were coming. Did you invite yourself as usual?"

"Hello to you too, sweetie!" the first boy greeted the actress. As they hugged, he shot Haven a wink over Alex's shoulder. "Who *is* this remarkable creature you have with you today?"

"Haven Moore, this is Calum Daniels. And the strong silent type is Owen Bell."

"Hello," Haven said.

"My God! Look at this hair! I've never seen anything like it," Calum raved. Haven had assumed Calum Daniels was gay, but now, with his fingers in her hair and his eyes roaming all over her body, she figured omnisexual was much closer to the mark. "Where did you find this little goddess, Alex?"

"Let Haven sit down," Owen said. "You're embarrassing her."

"'You're embarrassing her.'" Calum's impersonation of Owen's baritone was pitch-perfect.

"Come on, Calum," Alex agreed. "She hasn't had a chance to build up immunity to your bullshit yet."

"Oh, please. With hair like that she must be accustomed to having people ogle her," Calum argued, but he still pulled out a chair for Haven and allowed her to sit unmolested. "So, how *do* you two know each other?"

"Haven just designed an Oscars dress for me. It's so amazing I can't even begin to describe it."

"An Oscars dress?" Calum asked. "I thought you'd decided to go with Chanel this year. I wasted three hours of this life watching you try on dresses the other day!"

"I changed my mind. You'd know why if you saw Haven's gown."

"Well, I hope you charge a truckload of points, Haven," Calum said. "Don't let Alex cheap out on you just because you're a newbie."

"Actually, I'll be paying in cash," Alex said. "Not that it's any of your business."

"Cash?" Calum looked confused. "But *why*?" It was as if Haven had asked to be paid in manure.

"Apparently Haven's not a member of the Society," Owen explained.

"Oh *really*?" Calum's nose wrinkled as he prissily refolded the napkin on his lap. "That's too bad."

"She's not in the OS, but she *is* one of us," Alex hurried to add. "How else could a girl our age do the things she does?"

Calum shrugged. "Stranger things have happened."

"And she's friends with Adam too."

"*Good* friends?" Calum asked, his interest piqued once more. "You're not the new lady in his life, are you? Where does a girl go to meet someone like Adam, anyway?"

"It's a long story," Haven said.

"Perfect. I've got plenty of time," Calum said.

"Leave her alone," Owen insisted.

"Fine. But if you're one of us and you're friends with Adam, why aren't you a member of our club?"

"I couldn't say." Haven hoped Calum would move on to another subject, yet it was still flattering to have someone famous making a fuss over her. She could tell he wasn't the sort to waste his time on just anyone.

"Don't bother," Alex told Calum. "I've already tried to tempt her. I said I'd be happy to introduce her to some of our esteemed colleagues. But the only person she wanted to meet was Mia Michalski."

Haven grimaced with embarrassment.

"*Who*?" Calum asked.

"*Exactly*," Alex said.

"Oh, come *on*, Haven," Calum groaned. "You *have* to join! All the cool kids are members. And I can prove it too." He appealed to his companions. "How about a game of 'Spot the Snake'?"

"I'm hungry," Alex moaned. "Can't we just order some food?"

"I'm trying to make an important point, darling! Okay, I see one. Haven, in a moment I want you to turn around and take a good look at the very serious gentleman sitting two tables behind you. And I want you to pay close attention to his cuff links."

Haven slowly turned and peeked over her shoulder. A distinguished-looking man was signing his bill. She caught a quick look at one of his cuff links before it vanished beneath his suit sleeve. It was a platinum snake swallowing its own tail.

"Did you see it?" Calum asked, and Haven nodded mutely. "That man runs the biggest bank in New York. And you know what's funny? They say he hasn't touched cash in forty years. He only deals in Society points. The woman with him is a member too. She's responsible for all those hideous celebrity portraits you see in the magazines. I have it on good authority that she hides her snake tattoo somewhere the sun should refuse to shine. Ooh," he interrupted himself. "There's another. To your right, against the wall. Take a look at his tie clip."

Haven snuck a peek at the patron in question and swiveled back around in an instant. "That's the *mayor*," she whispered.

"It is indeed," said Calum, acknowledging the man with a nod.

"Why does everyone have a snake somewhere? I thought Society membership was supposed to be secret?"

"It *is* secret. Nobody knows to look for the snakes but us. And you. Besides, the mayor needs to advertise a little right now. Word has it that he used up most of his points during the last election. Anyone here need a favor? There's a bar two doors down from my apartment. The customers have been getting rowdy while I'm trying to get my beauty sleep. And all their nasty cigarette smoke must be terrible for my skin. Maybe I'll have him shut it down for me."

"You're just upset because their bouncer carded you last week," Owen said. "Let the other young people have their fun. You'll be twenty-one soon enough."

"Are you kidding? I can't wait two whole years. I depend on that bar for all my fresh meat. I'll just have that bouncer fired. The owner needs me to keep the place classy. But do you see my point, Haven? Haven?"

"Sorry. Hold on a sec," Haven said. Her phone was ringing. She'd just fished it out of her bag when Calum snatched it out of her hands.

"No, no, no," he admonished her, switching the phone off and dropping it back into her bag. "Not at the dinner table, darling. *Anyway*, as I was saying, the members in this room alone could make sure you have everything your little heart desires. And for a pretty girl like you? Who knows? You might even get a few freebies."

"I don't need their help," Haven sniffed, annoyed by Calum's etiquette lesson. She hadn't recognized the number on the caller ID. But it must have been Iain, and she was dying to speak to him. "I prefer to get by on my own hard work and talent."

"That's sweet," said Calum. "But you're awfully naive for an Eternal One. *Nobody* gets by in New York without a little help. It doesn't matter if you sew the most beautiful dresses the world has ever seen if there's no one to spread the word about you. Or give you a loan to open your first shop. Or convince the department stores to carry your line. Or get you in the pages of *Vogue*. You can't do it alone, my dear. Either you accept your friends' help or you get used to obscurity. It's really as simple as that."

"Calum." Owen tried to stop him. "That's enough. We both know there are plenty of people who've managed to succeed without the Society's help."

"Maybe," Calum said. "But if they're lucky enough to come back, they'll certainly join us the next time around. Who would be stupid enough to turn down an invitation?"

"I might," Haven ventured. "I've heard some things about the OS that aren't very flattering."

"Like what?" It was Owen this time. He seemed so genuinely concerned that Haven half expected him to whip out a pen and start taking notes.

"I've heard about what some of the less fortunate members are forced to do to keep their accounts in good standing."

"Oh God. You heard about all that nasty stuff? That was back when Padma Singh ran the show," Alex said. "She was a *terrible* president."

"Such a troll," Calum agreed. "But you gotta admit—"

"Admit what?" Alex asked.

"That it was a lot more interesting back then. It was like the Roaring Twenties or the Weimar Republic. You knew something terrible was going to happen, but it was a whole lotta fun waiting for the ship to go down."

"Your memory is crap," Alex said. "You're just pining for the days when you were Adam's number-one boy." For once, Calum didn't have a quip ready. But only Haven seemed to notice the stunned look on his face. How had he fallen from Adam's good graces?

"Did you know Padma too?" Haven asked Owen, hoping to shift the conversation.

"No, I never had the pleasure. I just joined last year," Owen said.

"*Owen's* part of the new regime," Calum explained. He'd recovered quickly. "He's one of the people who are cleaning our little dump up."

"I do what I can," Owen said, embarrassed by the sudden attention.

"Yes, and you do it so *well*," Calum said, licking his lips.

"Okay, Calum," Alex said with a roll of her eyes. "Owen may let you kiss his ass, but that's the most you can hope for. Let's talk about something else. I haven't seen you for ages. I assume there's a young stud somewhere who's a little worse for wear?"

"You're an evil little strumpet with a diseased mind," Calum said. "For your information, I've been honing my *art*. There's a juicy role I'm hoping to land any day now."

"And you haven't told your very best friend?" Alex asked, batting her eyelashes.

"Why? So you can leak it to *Us* magazine? No thank you, Miss Harbridge. You can find out along with the rest of the world. Now." He grabbed Haven's hand and leaned in close. "Tell me every single thing there is to know about the fabulous Haven Moore."

IT WAS THREE o'clock by the time all the dishes were cleared away, the bill paid, and the handsome waiter generously tipped. Haven could barely believe she'd stayed for so long. And though she didn't want to admit it, she'd almost enjoyed herself. Listening to Alex and Calum bicker like foul-mouthed siblings had taken her mind off her troubles. But it was Owen Bell who'd impressed her most. He hadn't uttered more than two dozen sentences, but his each and every word had left a mark. She knew now that Iain had been right. Not everyone in the Society had started life as a terrible person. She didn't hold out much hope for Alex—and none for Calum—but Haven prayed there was still a way to save Owen's soul.

"There she is!" a man shouted as the group left the restaurant. Haven blinked, blinded by the flash of cameras.

"Alex!" yelled a man with a five o'clock shadow and a beer belly. "Give me a smile, beautiful!"

"You're looking good, Alex," another man shouted. "D'you lose a couple of pounds or sumthin'?"

"Someone tipped off the paparazzi," Alex muttered, managing to sound annoyed even as she blew a kiss at the camera. "It wasn't you again, was it?" she asked Calum.

"Oh, please," he responded. "It's been ages since I had to resort to such tactics."

Together the foursome pushed their way toward the street. As Calum hailed a cab, one of the men grabbed Haven's arm.

"Hey! Who are you?" he demanded. "She look familiar?" he asked the colleague standing beside him.

"Yeah, now that you mention it, she does a bit," the other man concurred.

"What's your name, sweetheart? You famous?"

"Let her go," someone growled. Haven saw Owen barreling toward the paparazzo. He was half a head taller and twenty years younger than the out-of-shape man with the camera.

"Okay, buddy!" Haven's arm was released, and the paparazzo backed up with his hands held in the air. "No harm done, right?"

"You get a picture of that girl?" Haven heard as she ducked into the taxi.

"Yep. I know I've seen that hair somewhere before."

CHAPTER TWENTY-TWO

The walls, carpet, and ceiling of the corridor that led to Haven's room at the Gramercy Gardens Hotel were all the same shade of burgundy. There was never any noise and barely any light. Traveling the fifty-five paces to her door was like coursing through the veins of an enormous beast. Whenever Haven had passed other guests in the hall, they always seemed to be moving as quickly as she. It wasn't a place one wanted to linger. Yet Haven stopped halfway to her room the moment she remembered the call. Cursing her absentmindedness, she dug through her handbag. Her fingers brushed against a ring at the bottom before they located the phone. She switched on the device, and a message light began to blink.

"Haven. It's me." Beau. Haven couldn't breathe. She dropped to her knees as the walls seemed to pulsate. "I hope that text didn't scare you too bad. Listen, I know I'm not supposed to call, but I just wanted you to know I'm here. Be brave and I'll see you real soon. Okay? Love ya."

She instantly dialed the number from which the call had come. She lost count of the number of rings.

"Yeah?" The voice was gruff.

She cleared her throat. "I'm trying to reach Beau Decker."

"Don't know him. You got the right station?"

"Station? I don't understand. Where am I calling?"

"It's a gas station. This is a pay phone."

"A gas station? Where?"

"Eighth Avenue and Central Park North," the man huffed. "Look, lady, I gotta get back to work. I only answered 'cause the ringing was driving me nuts. There's nobody named Beau here. Don't call back."

He hung up.

"Shit!" Haven shrieked, staring down at the phone. Her hands were shaking, but she managed to call Iain. No answer, no voice mail. Why had he insisted on pursuing his own plan? Why wasn't he there when she needed him most? "Shit." This time a whimper. She dialed a third number. There was only one person left to call.

"Ouroboros Society."

"I need to speak with Adam Rosier."

"Certainly, Miss Moore. One moment, please."

"Haven?"

The sound of his calm, concerned voice brought tears to her eyes. "Adam. Something's happened. He called! Beau called! And I missed him!"

Five minutes later, Haven was still slumped in a stupor on the hallway floor when Adam rushed to her rescue. She had been trawling her memories again, trying to recall a single time that Beau Decker had ever let her down. But he'd always seemed to know if Haven needed help. When two freshmen had tried to curry favor with Haven's high school enemies by running off with her clothes as she showered after gym, Beau had appeared in the locker room with a lab coat he'd pilfered from their chemistry class. He had cinched the smock's waist with his very own belt, creating a little white dress that almost looked chic. Then there was the day Bradley Sutton had cornered Haven in an empty classroom and attempted to kiss her. Beau had blackened both of the boy's eyes and promised much worse if the offense were ever repeated. Those and the other scenes Haven remembered could have filled a dozen films. And yet when Beau had reached out to *her* for help, Haven had missed the call. She'd been out hobnobbing with silly celebrities when she should have been searching for her best friend.

Gordon Williams and his men arrived at the hotel just moments after Adam. Haven was still too frazzled to speak. Thankfully, Adam did most of the talking while Haven sat in a corner of her room and replayed Beau's message fifty times, trying to decipher its meaning. When her head started pounding, Haven closed her eyes and felt the fatigue wash over her. Shortly after eight o'clock, the cops finally left. Haven was already dozing on the couch when Adam bid her good night. The last thing she remembered was his promise to phone the second he heard any news. In her drowsy state, Haven had almost asked him to stay.

IN HER DREAM, Haven was back in Snope City. She knew the day. She recognized the clothes she was wearing, the lunch on the cafeteria tray in front of her. It was a day that could still send a shiver of shame though Haven's soul.

She was alone. Beau had been out of school for two weeks, and for seven hours each day, Haven was silent. No one spoke to her, and she spoke to no one. If Beau didn't come back soon, she worried she might lose her voice all together. But she couldn't complain. She had to wait. Beau couldn't be rushed. Haven knew what it felt like to lose a parent, but her father had died suddenly. He hadn't suffered the way Beau's mother had.

She heard the trays slam down on the table behind her. She

listened to three boys gossip the way she'd imagined only girls could. It was like she wasn't even there. *Maybe,* she thought, *I'm not.*

"I didn't see Decker this morning. I guess he's gonna miss another practice," Dewey Jones noted.

"A couple more and Coach'll have to name a new quarterback," said Justin Snead.

"Goddamm. That'd just about kill Decker's daddy."

"Yeah, well, he already killed his mamma," Bradley Sutton said. "She got sick right after she found out he was a faggot. My uncle says she must've died of a broken heart."

The rage was unlike any Haven had ever experienced. She wanted to turn around and hurl their table against a wall. Rip out Bradley's throat with her own teeth. Kick Dewey Jones until he was just a lifeless mound of flesh. She should have defended Beau, whatever the cost. But she didn't. She picked up her tray and walked away, angry tears blurring her vision. It was a decision she'd regret for the rest of her life.

CHAPTER TWENTY-THREE

"Oh my God, is this *you*?" squealed the young woman being mea-sured for a gown. She was an up-and-coming starlet whose face was plastered on movie posters all over town, but Haven couldn't recall her name. She'd shown up at Haven's hotel room door at the crack of dawn with a text message from Alex Harbridge on her phone and a checkbook in her hand. Haven had dragged herself out of bed, thrown on a bathrobe, and grabbed her measuring tape. The events of the previous day still cluttered her head. Beau's bizarre call, Ad-am's kindness. Haven couldn't stop digging through details in search of some truth. A single fact she could rely on. But nothing made sense anymore.

As a kid, she'd discovered that her mind was clearest whenever she held a needle between her fingers. Haven had welcomed her new client, hoping that a little hard work might help her put her thoughts back in order. But the girl refused to stop babbling. In the time it took to take her measurements, Haven had heard about the starlet's hair extensions, workout routine, and all the famous actors she was dying to bed.

"Is what me?"

The girl bent down and shoved her phone under Haven's nose. "*This!*"

On the screen were two pictures that had been posted on a gossip site. The first showed Haven, Alex, and Calum exiting the restaurant the day before. The second photo was almost two years old, and it was the only picture ever taken of Haven and Iain together in Rome. She remembered the moment well. They had been standing on the Ponte Sant'Angelo. Iain was begging her to stay in Italy with him. If only she had given him what he'd wanted back then. Haven let the thought go before it could break her heart.

MORROW HEIR SPOTTED IN NEW YORK, read the post's headline.

"Yeah, that's me," Haven said, returning to her work. There was no point in denying it.

"*You're* the girl who inherited all of Iain Morrow's money?" the starlet asked, nearly swooning at the thought. "You must be rolling in cash! Why do you still bother making dresses?"

"I actually like doing this," Haven snipped. "I'm an artist, not a seamstress."

"Yeah, but you could just come up with the ideas and pay someone else—"

"Wait!" Haven said, holding a finger up to her lips.

Once the girl stopped yapping, Haven could hear someone knocking on the door of her room. She tiptoed across the carpet and pressed her eye to the peephole. A young man in a crisp white shirt and unfashionable glasses was staring straight at her, as if he had x-ray vision.

"Yes?" she inquired through the door.

"Hello, Miss Moore. I'm from the Ouroboros Society. Adam was wondering if you might have a moment. He said to tell you there's been some news."

Haven shoved on her sneakers. Any news had to be about Beau.

"Wait—you're leaving?" the starlet whined. "What about my dress?"

"I have all your measurements," Haven told her. "Come back tomorrow."

"Tomorrow?" the girl repeated in astonishment. "So soon?"

"Yep."

"Wait!" The girl shouted as Haven sprinted out the door and down the hall. "Aren't you going to put some clothes on?"

PEDESTRIANS BUNDLED UP in their warm winter coats turned to stare as Haven ran around the park in a terry-cloth robe emblazoned with the logo of the Gramercy Gardens Hotel. She paid no more attention to the people on the sidewalks than she did to the wind that was doing its best to shove her all the way back to the hotel.

It was a quarter to nine. The Ouroboros Society wasn't open for business. Two fathers waited across the street, impatiently checking their watches while their nine-year-old children tried to shimmy over the gate that surrounded Gramercy Park. Haven bounded up the mansion's stairs, and the door opened to admit her.

"Right this way, Miss Moore," said a woman wearing the standard OS uniform. She guided Haven up the stairs and delivered her to an office the size of a closet. Its only furnishings were two black chairs, a wooden desk, and a rotary phone. Adam was sitting with his feet propped up on his desk.

For a moment, Haven almost forgot the purpose of her visit. "*This* is where you work?" she asked. A cardboard box would have had more character.

"I have more than one office," Adam said with a smile. His eyes traveled from her head to her feet. "For a person who designs such beautiful clothing, you spend a surprising amount of time wandering around town in robes. I think I prefer the one you were wearing last week at the spa."

"What have you heard about Beau?" Haven asked, uninterested in wasting time on flirting or small talk.

"Right." Adam slid his feet off the desk and got down to business. "I received a call from Commissioner Williams this morning. He told me there's been a break in the case. They've been showing Beau Decker's photo to people who work in the vicinity of the gas station where your friend placed his call. Last night they came across a vendor selling umbrellas on the corner of Frederick Douglass Boulevard and 112th Street. Several days ago, he saw a young man matching Beau's description hop out of a cab with a suitcase. He thought Beau might have gone into one of the buildings on 112th."

"Did the police find him?" Haven asked breathlessly.

Adam held up a hand to prevent her from jumping to any more conclusions. "No, not yet. The umbrella man didn't see which building Beau entered. They're searching the entire block as we speak. I'll phone you the moment I hear any more. But there's something else you should know."

"What?"

Adam frowned. The news wasn't all good. "Another pair of officers happened to speak with a deli owner in the area. She claims she saw Beau too. Apparently he passed by her store yesterday afternoon. There were two people with him—a man and a woman—but she didn't get a good look at either of them."

"Was he okay?" Haven held her breath while she waited for the answer.

"Yes, but there was a reason she remembered seeing him," Adam said. "The deli owner said he looked as if he'd been in a fight."

"A fight?" Haven gasped.

"Beau's face was bruised, and he was walking with a limp."

"Oh my God! What have they done to him?!" She couldn't help but recall the terrible story Phoebe had offered up as a warning. Until then,

Haven had avoided thinking about the Society member who'd been tortured and murdered by a lover from another life. If Haven stepped into that darkness, she knew she might never find her way out. But now she had to consider the possibility that Beau's tale would also have a tragic ending.

"Haven." Adam's voice pierced her frenzied thoughts. "Don't let your imagination go wild. Try to focus on the facts right now. Beau is alive. He's not critically injured. And now that the police have zeroed in on a block, it shouldn't be long before he's back at home."

"Are you sure?" Haven asked through her tears.

"Gordon Williams gave me his promise."

The relief was so powerful that Haven nearly dropped to her knees. She could hardly believe that the ordeal might soon be over. Once Beau was home, there would be no more horrible visions to endure. No more sleepless nights spent worrying about the two people in the world she loved most.

"I really hope Commissioner Williams is right," she said, wiping the tears from her eyes. "Thank you, Adam. I can't tell you how grateful I'll be. I promise I'll never forget it."

She wanted to leave, but she could see that Adam hadn't quite finished with her.

"It has been my pleasure, Haven," he said. "I suppose you'll be leaving New York as soon as Beau has been rescued. I know the timing isn't ideal, but I may not have a chance to see you again for quite some time. May I ask for one simple favor before you go?"

"Of course!" Haven blurted before she had a chance to stop herself.

"Will you have dinner with me?"

Haven struggled not to grimace. She should have realized there would be a catch. That was why Adam had summoned her to the OS instead of calling the hotel. Now that he had helped her, he expected to be repaid. "I wish I could, but I'm going to be busy." The excuse sounded rushed and insincere. "Alex Harbridge gave my name to one of her famous friends. The girl needs a gown as soon as possible, and I'm already behind schedule."

"I understand," Adam said.

Haven waited for him to insist, but he didn't. "I'm really sorry," Haven told him, and this time she meant it. He had gone out of his way to assist her, and he hadn't really asked for that much in return. "I guess I should go."

"Stop," Adam commanded. Haven's heart began to pound.

"Yes?"

"I can't let you go outside in a bathrobe. It's the middle of winter. At least allow me to find a proper coat for you to wear." He stepped out of his office and called down the stairs. "Madison, will you please bring a coat for Haven?"

In less than a minute, a stunning young woman was hurrying up the stairs with a lustrous fur cradled in her arms.

"Haven doesn't wear fur," Adam informed the girl. He didn't even look at her. "Go find something else."

"I believe it's faux, sir," Madison replied.

"It doesn't matter if it's real or not. I can't accept it," Haven told Adam.

"Accept it? Who said I was *giving* it to you, Haven? It belongs to one of my people—I'm merely *loaning* it to you." Adam helped Haven slip into the coat. With her arms inside, she felt instantly warm. "I'll have a hotel employee bring it back."

Once she was bundled up, Adam put his hands on her shoulders and held Haven in place while his eyes took her in.

"Will you come and say goodbye before you leave?"

"I will," Haven said, making a promise she wasn't sure she'd be able to keep.

OUTSIDE, THE SUN felt a little brighter, and the wind had calmed. Gordon Williams had promised Beau would be home soon, a bit battered perhaps, but alive. For the first time in days, Haven didn't feel panic pushing at her back. She'd been trapped in a dark and confusing maze—rushing down the wrong passages, reaching dead ends, and confronting monsters at every turn. At last she might have found the right path. Beau was waiting at the center of the maze, and Haven was almost there. She imagined throwing her arms around him, feeling her feet leave the ground as he spun her around. She would guide her best friend back to safety. Make him swear he'd never return to New York. Then they could both finally go home.

Home. The thought of Rome almost stole the spring from Haven's step. She had been so focused on freedom that she hadn't considered what she might find when she reached it. Thanks to Virginia Morrow's lawsuit, the apartment on the Piazza Navona would be off-limits. Haven's boutique on the Via dei Condotti would be shuttered. Haven knew that her golden city was now little more than a memory. She and Iain would need to find a new place to live.

But that was a dilemma for another day. As Haven rounded the park, she spotted a familiar taxi idling across the street from the Gramercy Gardens Hotel. Chandra sat behind the wheel, waiting to ferry Haven to her next appointment with the Horae—an appointment Haven was now able to cancel. She didn't need Phoebe's help to find Beau. The Horae could lock "the magos" away on their own. Adam was the one who had come to Beau's rescue. Haven wouldn't need to repay his kindness with treachery.

When she reached the taxi, Haven motioned for Chandra to roll down the window.

"What'd you have to do to get that coat?" the girl asked. "Looks pretty fancy."

"It's just a loaner," Haven informed her.

"Are you ready to go?" Chandra asked. "You don't want to be late again."

"Please thank Phoebe for all of her help, but I won't be visiting the Horae anymore," Haven said. "I'm on the verge of finding my friend."

Chandra laughed. "You're joking."

"Not at all. I wish I could thank Phoebe in person, but I should stay here and get more work done. I need to make some money before I go home."

"Have you lost your mind?" Chandra demanded as if the exchange didn't make sense to her.

"I don't think so," Haven replied.

"But what if you're wrong? What if you don't find your friend and he ends up getting hurt? What if he winds up *dead*?" Chandra spat the last word at Haven, as though the thought were one that she savored.

"I'm not wrong," Haven insisted, taken aback by the girl's tone. She had known the Horae wouldn't be happy, but she hadn't expected such fury.

"You made a deal with us, Haven!"

"I'm sorry. The deal's off," Haven told her. She backed away from the car and marched toward the hotel entrance. Behind her, Chandra's cab screeched into the street.

ONCE HAVEN WAS in her room, she resisted the urge to make any calls until she had real news to share. Instead, she started work on the starlet's dress, using one of the bolts of fabric leaning against the walls of her room. She worked with an eye on the phone. But as the minutes ticked by, Haven began to suspect that she should have kept her hopes in check. Something was wrong—she could feel it. If the police knew where to find Beau, what could possibly be taking so long?

Three hours later, Haven finished the last stitch on a stunning green version of a pale blue gown that had been a top seller in her boutique in Rome. Just as she was carefully draping it on a hanger, a flashing light on her phone told her an e-mail had arrived. She dropped the dress to the floor and opened the message.

"Welcome to the Ouroboros Society, Haven Moore," read the note. "An account has been opened in your name, and a deposit has been received from Lucy Fredericks."

"What the hell?" Haven muttered, finally recalling the young actress's name. She had told the girl to pay her in cash. Now Haven had an OS account she'd never wanted. She needed to close it as quickly as possible, but there was only one person she dared ask for instructions.

Haven dialed Frances Whitman's number. If she couldn't reach Iain by phone, she'd have Frances deliver the message the next time she saw him.

"Haven? How are things going?" Frances asked.

"Great. We may be close to finding Beau." She wished she sounded more certain.

"That's wonderful news!" Frances exclaimed. "Where has he been?"

"I'll tell you all about it later, but I was hoping I could speak with Iain for a moment."

"Iain? I haven't seen him in days," Frances said. "I thought he was keeping you company."

"You haven't seen him in days?" Haven asked, warning herself to stay calm. "Hasn't he been sleeping at your house?"

"Not for the past few nights. Where do you think he's been staying?" Haven could hear Frances's anxiety mounting at the same pace as her own. "Isn't he worried someone will see him? For God's sake, Haven. Do either of you have *any* sense? Iain's supposed to be dead!"

There was a beep on the line. "Hold on, Frances," Haven said. "I've got another call. Maybe it's Iain." She switched over. "Hello?"

"Haven Moore?" The man spoke with a familiar Brooklyn accent.

"Yes?"

"This is Gordon Williams of the NYPD. I was asked to call you directly. I know you were informed that we would be spending the day following up a promising lead. However, I'm afraid we have been unable to locate your friend, Beau Decker."

"What? But you promised!" Haven almost shrieked.

"I apologize, Miss Moore. I should have been more cautious."

"So what—are you just giving up? You can't stop! You've got to find him! That deli woman said he'd been hurt!"

"Let me assure you that we're going to keep looking. I've been in-structed to extend the search to neighboring blocks." Commissioner Williams sounded resigned, like a man sent out on a snipe hunt. "But if you happen to remember anything else, please contact me immedi-ately. Any new clues would be welcome right about now."

"I will," Haven muttered.

"Don't lose hope," Commissioner Williams said.

"I'll try," Haven said. She hung up, forgetting Frances on the other line. The panic was back. She'd reached another dead end. The maze was closing in all around her. She needed to act, but there was noth-ing she could do.

The hotel phone rang. Haven grabbed for it like a rescue rope.

It was someone from the front desk. "You have a delivery, Miss Moore. May I send it up?"

"Yes." Haven felt herself slipping back into despair.

The deliveryman who knocked at the door was completely engulfed by flowers. The huge bouquet of snow-white peonies in his arms was perfect. There wasn't a petal out of place.

"Where would you like me to put this?" he asked.

"The dresser, I guess," Haven said, too distracted to send them away. She pulled a card out of the bouquet as the man passed by.

I heard the news. It's just a setback. We won't give up. Love, Adam

Terrible thoughts began to take root in Haven's mind. Could

Adam have sabotaged the investigation just to keep her in town? Had the search been a sham from the very beginning? What if she'd made a terrible mistake? What if she'd trusted the wrong person? But the fear came with a pale glimmer of hope. If she'd made the right choice, Beau still had a chance. If anyone could find Beau, it was the head of the Ouroboros Society.

The deliveryman left without closing the door, and Haven heard someone humming the theme song from a Disney movie outside her room. A little girl no more than seven or eight was skipping down the dark hall. She wore a wide smile on her pretty face and held a cluster of daffodils in one hand. She stopped in front of Haven and thrust the tiny bouquet at her.

"Are you Haven?"

"That's me."

"Then these are for you," the child said.

"For me?" Haven asked. "Did you pick them?"

"No, they're from a *boy*. He said to tell you . . ." The little girl closed her eyes and tried to remember her lines. "He said they remind him of Rome. He said he misses you. But he's almost got everything fixed, and he will come see you soon."

Iain.

"Where did you talk to him?" she asked the little girl.

"In the park," the child said, skipping down the hall.

"Georgia!" A woman's voice called from a room around the corner. The little girl offered Haven a wave, and then she was gone.

HAVEN FOUND A glass in the bathroom and placed the daffodils inside. The flowers' heavy heads hung over the side of the cup. During the single spring she and Iain had spent in Rome, Haven's apartment had been filled with yellow blooms. Every time Iain ran an errand, he'd come back clutching a fistful of daffodils. By April, all the apartment's vases were in use, and flowers spilled out of tumblers, pencil holders, and empty cans, brightening every room like patches of sunlight.

Haven placed the daffodils beside her bed and prayed that Iain really had everything fixed. She was more desperate now than she'd ever been. She wanted Iain to be the hero, but if he couldn't come through, Haven would no longer hesitate to turn to Adam.

CHAPTER TWENTY-FOUR

"We brought him to Florence! You swore you would help!" the little girl snarled. She had come to Beatrice as she had in the past, disguised as a daughter of one of the servants. At first Beatrice had been shocked to hear a child speak as she did. But Beatrice had seen things since that very first meeting that made the girl seem quite ordinary now.

"I had nothing to live for when I agreed to assist you," Beatrice told her. "This house was a cage. I've been set free."

"And you don't care what will happen to the people here?"

"Why should I sacrifice my freedom for them when they've never lifted a finger to help me? I've seen no proof of the claims that you make. My fiancé does whatever I ask. Even if he is everything that you say, I can ensure that your prophecy never comes to pass."

The girl regarded her with sheer disgust. "You have sold your soul, Beatrice Vettori. Whatever happens now will be on your head."

*   *   *

"HELLO?" HAVEN MUMBLED into the telephone.

"I'm here with Calum." It was Alex Harbridge. "We're in the lobby. You have exactly ten minutes to brush your hair and get your ass down here."

"Don't tell her to brush her hair," Haven heard Calum moan in the background. "That could take *hours*."

"I can't hang out right now," Haven said. "I just got up from a nap, and I have a million things to do."

"What 'things'?" Alex asked. "I know for a fact that you don't have any more dress orders to fill at the moment. I got a call from Lucy Fredericks this morning saying how thrilled she was with your work. I just hope her dress isn't nicer than mine. So you're done. Enjoy it. Now let's spend some of the points you've made."

Haven frowned. She had twenty points sitting in the Ouroboros Society account that Lucy Fredericks had opened without her permission.

"I told you I'm not a member, Alex," Haven said. "And I never will be."

"Fine with me," Alex said. "But that doesn't mean the points you have should go to waste. Come on. You can find some way to thank me for turning you into a rock-star fashion designer."

"I really can't."

"Yes, you *can*, Haven," Alex chided her. "Lucy told me that when she picked up her dress this morning, you were wearing the exact same thing you had on yesterday. She said you looked like you were starting to go all bag lady on us. I had to assure her that you bathe regularly."

Haven glanced around at the room she had barely left in two days. Lucy was right. She hadn't bathed in a while. She hadn't wanted to risk missing a call. But the phone hadn't rung. Beau was still missing. Neither Adam nor Iain had made good on their promises, and Haven was starting to wonder if she'd made a terrible mistake by breaking off contact with the Horae.

"You're down to eight minutes," Alex informed her. "You don't want to see what kind of scene I'm capable of making."

"All right," Haven said with a huff. "But give me twenty. I need to take a shower."

SHE FOUND ALEX and Calum huddled together on one of the love seats in the hotel lobby. They made such a beautiful pair that it was hard to imagine they were real. Perfect, porcelain features, and hair that gleamed like copper and gold. Alex wore a coat in a deep shade of purple that perfectly complemented the lavender scarf tucked into the collar of Calum's jacket. They looked like they'd stepped out of a Fitzgerald book or off the cover of some vintage fashion magazine. Haven wondered if their matching ensembles could have been a coincidence.

"Oh baby, you *are* looking a little rough," Calum announced as soon as he saw Haven. "Maybe you should have brushed your hair after all."

"I gotta go with Calum on this one," Alex agreed. "What do you say we dump our male escort and pamper ourselves a little? I know this spa on Morton Street—"

"No!" Haven blurted out with a little too much force.

"See? She can't bear to be away from me." Calum stood and flung an arm around Haven's shoulders. He gave Alex a smug little grin. "It's not just the gentlemen. All the ladies love me too."

"If not the spa, then how about a little culture?" Alex asked.

"That sounds splendid," Calum replied in a perfectly posh English accent. "I believe some culture may be just what this young lady needs." It was clear they had a plan. They both linked arms with Haven and virtually dragged her through the lobby to the sidewalk. A black SUV was waiting for the trio.

"The Metropolitan Museum of Art," Alex told the driver.

"It's Monday," Haven said. "Aren't most museums in New York closed on Mondays?"

Calum and Alex both laughed. "Not for *us* they're not," Calum said.

A WOMAN MET them inside the front doors of the museum. Dressed in a white shirt and a shapeless gray suit, she was clearly a Society drone. They had even infiltrated the venerable Met.

"Everything has been arranged as usual, Miss Harbridge," the woman informed them. "Do you remember how to get to the gallery?"

"Of course!" Alex swept past the woman with barely a second glance. Calum and Haven trailed behind her as she made her way through the vacant maze of the museum's first floor and down a set of stairs. At last Alex arrived at her destination. Outside a gallery stood a small table. On top of the table sat three crystal glasses and a bottle of champagne. Alex popped the cork and poured.

"Thank you," Haven said, accepting a glass, though it was barely noon and a little too early for underage drinking.

"Here's to Haven." Alex lifted her champagne flute. "May her designs be displayed in this museum one day." She drained her wine and poured herself another glass. "Let's go explore."

Haven stepped into the gallery and found herself surrounded by pale, thin mannequins whose soulless eyes peered out from glass cages. Each wore the costume of a distant era. There were Spanish court dresses embroidered with gold looted from Aztec temples, and nineteenth-century gowns with bustles that would have rendered a lady unable to sit. A few of the mannequins posed for invisible cameras while others hid their faces behind hand-painted fans. Haven found the effect unnerving. The museum's perfect white wraiths had no business impersonating the flesh-and-blood women who'd died and left their belongings behind.

"What is this place?" Haven asked.

"It's the Costume Institute," Alex explained. "I come here all the time. I try to imagine myself in other lives, wearing something like that." She stopped in front of a scarlet dress adorned with pearls and garnets. "I wonder what it was like," she said wistfully before moving on.

"Alex doesn't remember much about her past lives," Calum confided in a whisper. "Her parents never kept track of the things she said when she was little. They thought she was bonkers, and I have a hunch they still do. I met Ma and Pa Harbridge over Christmas. Don't tell Alex I said so, but they're the dullest people on earth. They get fidgety if you talk about anything other than football or the weather. But sweet little Alex thinks they're *fabulous*."

"Alex *must* remember a few things," Haven said. "She told me she's been an actress for her last seven lives."

"All she knows is what the Pythia has told her. By the way, did Alex happen to mention she was Marilyn Monroe?"

"You really believe that?" It had to be one of Phoebe's lies. "Alex seems smart. Wasn't Marilyn Monroe a bit dim?"

"Not in the slightest. She had a wicked sense of humor. The critics might have noticed she was a pretty good actress too, if they hadn't been so focused on her ta-tas."

"And you?" Haven asked. "How much do you remember?"

"Me? Not much anymore. I'm lucky my mother brought me to the OS when I was still very young. Back then, I used to talk about three different lives. I claimed I was a famous thespian in the seventeenth century. In fact, Shakespeare may have written the role of Hamlet for me. A century or two later I was a well-known child actor, but I died of some horrible wasting disease. And in my last life I was Wallace Reid."

"Who?" Haven asked.

Calum frowned. "Wallace Reid was a silent film star. 'The screen's most perfect lover.' Anyway, it all goes to show that my mother was convinced I was bound for great things."

"She must be very proud," Haven said. "You've done so well for yourself."

"Everything's relative," Calum replied with none of his usual snarkiness. "We don't talk much anymore."

"Hey, you two. Want to see something amazing?" Alex called back to them. "Let me show you what I spotted a couple of weeks ago. It must be new, 'cause I'm sure I'd have noticed it before." She was standing in front of a shimmering flapper dress covered in thousands and thousands of golden beads. There were 10,725 beads to be exact, and each was pure twenty-four-carat gold. Haven knew this for a fact because the dress had been hers when her name was Constance Whitman. Feeling light-headed, she used the plaque placed near the mannequin's toe as an excuse to crouch down for a moment and catch her breath.

EVENING DRESS, SILK WITH GOLD BEADING, CA. 1924.

GIFT OF A WHITMAN FAMILY FRIEND.

"What are you doing down there?" Alex asked.

"Reading the description," Haven answered.

"Well, stand up and take a look at the mannequin's arm."

Haven still felt a little dizzy when she pulled herself up, and her knees nearly gave when she spied the golden band on the ghost-white arm. It was a snake with two ruby eyes, its tail clamped inside its jaws. An ouroboros.

"Do you think it belonged to one of us?" Alex asked.

"I don't know," Calum said. "When was the Society founded?"

"Nineteen twenty-three," Haven answered, and they both swiveled to stare at her.

"How do *you* know?" Calum inquired. "You're not even a member."

"I was back then," Haven said. "I made this dress, and that was my jewelry."

"No shit!" Alex exclaimed. "I *knew* there was a reason I was supposed to bring you here. Do you think I might be psychic or something?"

"Stop congratulating yourself and let the girl talk!" Calum demanded. "I'm *dying* here."

"No, no, wait!" Alex insisted. "This is too good to discuss standing up. Let's go have lunch and Haven can tell us all about it."

"Excellent suggestion," Calum trilled as they both set off up the stairs to the first floor.

"Hey," Haven called when they headed into the Egyptian art gallery. "I don't think the exit's that way."

"Of course it isn't," Alex said. "We just got here. Why would we want to leave?"

Together they drifted by the ancient stone Temple of Dendur, past gleaming suits of medieval armor, and around a statue of Andromeda chained to a seaside cliff. Inside one of the French period rooms, Alex and Calum hopped over a velvet rope and made themselves at home on a pair of plush chairs with gilded legs. The three walls of the room featured white paneling trimmed in gold. The atmosphere was refined and opulent, despite the unmistakable smell of sausage in the air.

"Help yourself," Alex said. An eighteenth-century French console held several covered silver platters. Calum jumped up and lifted one of the lids.

"Hot dogs?" he groaned. "We're sitting in a room taken from the home of the Marquis de Cabris, and we're going to eat *hot dogs*?"

"I *like* hot dogs," Alex said. "And so do French people. Don't be such a snoot, Calum. It's not very attractive. Besides, the people who built this room weren't as fancy as you'd think. They used to pee in the corners."

"You remember that?" Calum squealed with laughter.

"No, I read it in a book," Alex said.

Haven passed on the hot dogs, but she did pour herself a cup of coffee from a silver pot that looked as if it had been snatched from another part of the museum.

"Crap!" Calum yelped. He'd accidentally smeared some carnival mustard on the three-hundred-year-old upholstery and was dabbing at it with a white cotton napkin.

"All right," Alex said, ignoring Calum's cursing. "Spill it, Haven. Who was the girl with the golden dress?"

"What do you know about the history of the OS?" Haven asked.

"Not much," Calum said, looking up from his chore. "The only history that fascinates me is my own."

"You're stalling." Alex huffed comically.

Haven hesitated, but she couldn't think of a reason not to tell them. "In the 1920s, I was a girl named Constance. She was one of the original members of the Ouroboros Society. I started having visions of her life when I was just a little kid. She and her boyfriend died in a fire in 1925. I knew the fire hadn't been an accident, so I came to New York about a year and a half ago to find out what had really happened."

"What *had* happened?" Alex moved to the edge of her seat.

"They were both murdered by a girl who was in love with Constance's boyfriend." Haven neglected to add that the murderess had since been reborn as Padma Singh.

"Oh my God!" Alex said. "That's horrible! So did Constance really love this guy—the one she died with?"

"Yes."

"So maybe you'll find each other again. You know that sort of thing happens all the time. There are lots of people at the OS who think they've discovered 'the one.'"

Haven resisted the urge to share too much. She still didn't know Alex and Calum that well, but she knew better than to trust them with secrets.

"We did find each other."

"And?!" Calum prodded.

"What happened?" Alex asked.

"First he disappointed me. Then he died. In another fire."

"You're talking about Iain Morrow, aren't you?" Alex asked.

"How do you know?"

"Oh, come on, Haven, you think we don't read the gossip pages? You're the heir to the Morrow fortune. To be honest, we're a little hurt that you didn't tell us yourself. I thought maybe Iain had said terrible things about us or something."

"You knew Iain?" Now Haven was surprised.

"Sure," Alex said. "We met at the Society. We were friends for a while. I even went out with him a few times. It was only for show, of course. We both needed the publicity."

"Iain's a jerk," Calum blurted out. "Hot as hell, but still a jerk."

"Yeah," Alex agreed sadly.

"Why do you say that?" Haven asked. "What did he do?"

"We used to be close," Alex said, "and then one day he just decided that he didn't want to be my friend anymore."

"For no reason?"

"Well . . ." Alex looked to Calum.

"Go ahead and tell her," he urged.

"So a couple of years ago, I let my OS account get low. I'd just used a bunch of points for a little nip and tuck here and there. And I was busy with my Oscars campaign. You have no idea how expensive those things can get. I felt like I was transferring points to every person I met. Anyway, the old president of the Society—that bitch Padma Singh—was really tough about making people keep points in their accounts. I dropped under the fifteen-point minimum, and I was informed that I'd have to earn more immediately if I wanted to stay in the club.

"Iain promised to loan me the points, but then Padma called

and offered me a job. She needed someone young and innocent looking to deliver some drugs to a Society bigwig on vacation in Paris. It would take less than a day, I'd get a free trip to France, and I'd make enough points to drag myself out of debt. The offer was too good to refuse, and I was pretty naive back then. I told her I'd take the job."

"You delivered drugs?" Haven asked.

"No. I decided against it in the end. I found another way to refill my account."

"Alex won't even tell *me* what she had to do," Calum said, and the girl glared at him.

"I tried to talk to Iain, but he was so pissed that I'd even considered helping one of the drug dealers that he refused to speak to me."

"He always looked down on us," Calum sniffed. "Like we were tainted."

"Yeah," Alex agreed, "and I never understood why. He wasn't exactly a model citizen himself. He'd gone through every pretty girl at the OS by the time he turned eighteen."

"So I've heard," Haven said. A few years earlier, Iain had infiltrated the Society disguised as a womanizing playboy to hide his true identity from Adam. Apparently, his disguise had fooled Alex and Calum as well.

"Is that why you were curious about Mia Michalski?" Alex asked.

"Iain and Mia?" Haven remembered the kiss Iain had planted on Mia's cheek. She'd convinced herself it was innocent. It probably had been. But why hadn't Iain mentioned that Mia was one of the girls he'd "dated"?

"Yeah, they tried to keep it hush-hush, but everyone knew they were together. And then Mia disappeared, and Iain decided he preferred old ladies and started sniffing around Padma Singh's wrinkled old carcass. But"—Alex bit into a hot dog—"that was back in the dark days of the Society. It isn't one big orgy anymore."

"No, everyone's a model citizen now," Calum complained. "If you ask me, Iain was always more like one of the creepy robot kids than one of us."

"Robot kids?" Haven mumbled, finding it hard to keep up her side of the conversation. If Iain's womanizing had really been nothing but a disguise, why had he kept his relationship with Mia hush-hush? It didn't make any sense.

Calum rolled his eyes as if the mere mention of the subject annoyed him. "Have you met many young people at the OS?"

"No," Haven said.

"I call them the robots. Most of them take the Eternal Ones thing *way* too seriously. All they think about is their glorious future."

"Yeah, it's amazing how much the OS is changing," Alex said.

"For the *worse*," Calum groaned. "Can you imagine what it's going to be like now that the little robots at Halcyon Hall are starting to graduate?"

"You mean the kids at the school Adam started? What are they like?" A wave of guilt washed over Haven. She had almost forgotten about Adam's young recruits.

"They're not allowed to talk to the likes of me," Calum said. "But their leader is this guy named Milo Elliot. He's a total tool. I bet he was shopping at Brooks Brothers when he was in the third grade."

"Adam *loves* Milo," Alex said.

"Yeah," Calum agreed. "I suppose the rest of us should just face it. Adam has big things planned for his robot army. My guess is it starts with world domination."

"World domination? What in the *hell* are you talking about?" Alex rolled her eyes. "The Halcyon Hall kids are just goody-goodies. They're not *evil*."

"That's what *you* think," Calum said solemnly. "My sources tell me otherwise."

"You and your 'sources' have always been full of it," Alex replied.

"I'm not going to sit here and let you fill Haven's head with this crap. Let's take her to the fund-raiser and let her decide for herself."

"Forget it!" Calum squawked. "I'm not going to be responsible for Haven dying of boredom."

"Fund-raiser?" Haven repeated.

"What are you doing tonight?" Alex asked innocently.

CHAPTER TWENTY-FIVE

When Haven saw all the studious Society members filing up the steps of City Hall, she was glad she'd worn her most conservative dress. Alex's plaid skirt and pearls made her look more like a kindergarten teacher than a movie star. Even Calum had buttoned his shirt and topped it with a crimson and navy striped cravat.

"You forgot to mention that the party was going to be *here*," Haven whispered. Bathed in spotlights, the two-hundred-year-old landmark was breathtaking.

"Don't be so dazzled, darling." Calum was out of sorts. He didn't want to waste an evening at a fund-raiser, and he'd complained non-stop until Alex had threatened to kick him out of the car on the way downtown. "This is just the mayor's way of earning a few precious points."

"You're saying the mayor rents out City Hall?"

"If you know the right people, everything in New York is for rent," Alex explained. "You could have a cocktail party inside the Statue of

Liberty for fifteen points. If you ever decide to join the OS, I'll throw you a midnight bash on the top of the Empire State Building."

Inside, the trio flitted past the security guards in the building's magnificent white rotunda, where the coffin of Abraham Lincoln had once been on view. Following the other guests, they then scaled the grand stairway and entered a bright green room, its walls decorated with priceless paintings framed in gold.

Despite the grandeur of the Governor's Room, the atmosphere was somber. Unlike the other OS parties Haven had witnessed, this one seemed to be short on booze and scantily covered skin. The snippets of conversation Haven picked up as she and her companions traipsed through the crowd were too dull to lodge in her memory.

"Look. There's the man of the hour," Calum said, grabbing Haven's hand and whispering in her ear. "That's Milo. What'd I tell you? Is that kid a robot or what?" He pointed to a clean-cut young man in his late teens. Milo was blond and fair and unremarkable in almost every way. Even his off-the-rack suit was just a notch above the uniform favored by the Society's drones. And yet Milo was clearly important. Haven recognized the bald man with whom he was chatting as the tycoon who ran the biggest bank in New York. Milo said something that made the man chuckle.

"I thought you guys didn't give a damn about changing the world." Haven spun around to find Owen Bell looking dashing in a conservative suit. He smiled at Haven. "It's nice to see *you* again, though. I'm glad they finally dragged you out of that fancy hotel."

"Thanks," Haven said. "What are you doing here?"

"Yeah, what *are* you doing here, Owen?" Calum demanded, as if Owen had crashed the party.

"As you may recall, Calum, I'm employed by the Ouroboros Society. I get paid to be here."

"That's right. How could I forget? Owen has dedicated his talents to helping the robots seize control," Calum explained. His tone was flippant, but his eyes were serious. "He's a traitor to the human cause."

"Who knows? Maybe I'm a double agent," Owen quipped. "Maybe I'm protecting the human race from Milo."

"Joke all you want, but I still don't know why Adam wastes his time on that kid," Alex said. "You're the one with all the big ideas, Owen. You're the one Adam really listens to."

"Adam listens to you?" Haven asked Owen, trying not to show the disappointment she felt. Maybe she had been wrong about Owen. Maybe his soul was already too polluted to save.

"He humors me," Owen corrected her.

"Owen's just being modest," Alex jumped in. "He has all of these great ideas for improving the OS. He told Adam about them, and Adam's been making the changes."

"You're exaggerating, Alex," Owen said, embarrassed.

"Am I? You convinced Adam to forgive debts for members under twenty-one, and you helped kick out the serious drug dealers."

"Adam really agreed to do all that?" Haven asked in astonishment. If it were true, it was the first real proof she'd found that the OS was evolving.

"Yes, soon everything at the Society will appear completely dull and legitimate," Calum jumped in. "We wouldn't want rumors of criminal activity to jeopardize Milo's career, would we?"

"My suggestions were never meant to help Milo," Owen said. "I don't like him any more than you do. But if Adam's convinced that Milo's the future, I'm going to do what I can to make sure that future is one I can live in. So if you'll excuse me for a moment, it's time for me to get the Society's great hope to take the stage."

"How long have you guys known him?" Haven asked as Owen disappeared into the crowd.

"Just a year or so," Alex said. "Calum took one look at Owen after he joined the OS and decided to make himself Owen's own personal welcoming party."

"Didn't work out," Calum explained. "Apparently I'm not Owen's type. Which is totally crazy—I'm *everyone's* type."

"Owen's been a member for a single year, and he already has Adam's ear?" Haven asked.

"He's a talented boy, that Owen Bell," Calum snipped. "I wish I could come off so sincere."

"Excuse me, ladies and gentlemen!" An older gentleman in a tweed suit had stepped up to the podium at the front of the room. "May I have your attention, please?"

"Who's that?" Haven whispered to Calum.

"Jeffrey Lemke. The new president of the OS. He replaced Padma. Lemke's about as interesting as a ball of lint compared to the diabolical Ms. Singh."

"Maybe that's not such a bad thing," Haven remarked just as Lemke started to speak.

"I'd like to introduce the young man you've all come to hear. At age nine, Milo Elliot was the first student accepted at Halcyon Hall. In May, he will graduate with top honors, and come September he'll be joining the freshman class at Yale. Milo's not only one of the Ouroboros Society's brightest lights, he's the future of our organization. Tonight, he's going to give us a peek at what that future may hold."

The crowd clapped politely.

"Thank you, Jeffrey," Milo said. He looked down at his notes and then up at the portrait of George Washington on the wall above his podium. When he faced the audience once more, Milo had been transformed. Gone was the bland blond boy. In his place was a confident leader with a warm, winning smile. "When I look around the room at the faces gathered here tonight, I see this country's best and brightest. Artists, businesspeople, philanthropists, inventors, scientists—there's enough money, talent, and brainpower in this one room to change the course of history.

"That was, after all, what the Ouroboros Society was *meant* to achieve. Lasting change. When August Strickland started this organization in 1923, he brought the first Eternal Ones together with a purpose in mind. He had a vision of a world in which our unique skills and knowledge would make a difference. Unfortunately, over the last ninety years, that vision has remained unfulfilled. Ironically, as the Ouroboros Society has grown more powerful, our impact on the world has diminished. We've come to focus on our own petty needs and desires. We've forgotten that we were sent back to earth not to line our own pockets, but to shape the future and to lead those less fortunate than ourselves."

Haven shivered. A figure in black had materialized only inches away from where she stood. Adam smiled down at her before returning his attention to the speaker. Haven sensed an invisible shield surrounding them both—a bubble that couldn't be burst. It felt like nothing could ever threaten her while Adam was at her side.

"Ladies and gentlemen," Milo continued. "I believe that the time has come to devote our talents to a higher cause. The day I graduate from Yale, I intend to pledge my life to serving others. By seeking public office, I can do my small part to influence the future of our city, our state, and our country. And I'm not the only student at Halcyon Hall with such goals. The next generation of Society members knows it's our *destiny* to lead the world. In a decade, we will be America's politicians, its scientists, and its businesspeople. With your support, in the next twenty-five years, we will be its presidents, Nobel Prize winners, and CEOs.

"So I've come here tonight to ask for your help. This is your chance to use your wealth and power to begin shaping the future. Simply transfer as many points as you can spare to the Halcyon Hall Endowment Fund. We'll be keeping records of contributions, and all donations will be much appreciated. Thank you, and enjoy the party."

The applause this time was louder and more heartfelt.

"Good evening, Haven," Adam said once the room had quieted down. "I didn't expect to see you here tonight."

"Alex and Calum brought me." Haven gestured toward the spot where the two had been standing, but the couple had vanished.

"And what did you think?"

Haven glanced over at Milo, who was shaking hands with members of his awestruck audience. Calum and Alex were now standing to the side of the crowd, snickering at the scene.

"He's a powerful speaker. I didn't expect someone that young to be so charismatic," Haven said. "But I'm a little confused by his speech. Milo just said he wants the Society's members to start changing the world around them. Doesn't that go against everything you stand for? I thought you wanted members so focused on the points in their accounts that they *couldn't* change the world for the better."

"I suppose you could say that my strategy has shifted," Adam replied. "I've decided to take a different tack. The Society of the future will look quite different from the one you've come to know."

"Alex says you've been working with Owen Bell. She told me that he's dedicated to cleaning up the OS—and that you've been making all the improvements that Owen's recommended. Is it true?" Haven still found it hard to believe.

"Yes. Owen is very talented," Adam confirmed. "It's always easier to have someone so gifted working *for* you than fighting against you. In fact, I've come to rely on Mr. Bell. Milo is only the *face* of the future. Owen will be its heart and its voice. He wrote the speech you just heard."

"He did?" Haven searched for Owen and found him glaring at Milo from the far corner of the room. His arms were crossed, and he looked livid.

"I wish Mr. Bell could give the speeches as well as write them, but there are reasons he prefers to work behind the scenes." Adam's eyes landed on the young man in question. His gaze was that of a zoologist observing a rare and remarkable creature. "I've encountered Owen in several of his lives, and his way with words has always impressed me. But until recently, I considered him a waste of my time."

"Why?" Haven asked.

"As far as I can tell, Owen Bell is incorruptible," Adam said, almost sounding surprised to hear himself utter the words. "I can't say I've ever met anyone like him. Owen has more than three thousand points sitting in his OS account. He's never spent a single one, and I doubt he ever will. I'm pleased that you two had a chance to meet. Owen could use a good friend. It's a shame you'll be going away." The final sentence seemed to trigger a thought, and Adam's voice shifted from friendly to formal. "I shouldn't take any more of your time, Haven. I only came over to offer my apologies. I'm sorry that we haven't found Beau yet. Commissioner Williams has assured me it's only a matter of days—if not hours—before we do. In the meantime, will you let my people at the Society know if there's anything we can do to make your stay in New York more pleasant?"

"Sure," Haven said, feeling more than a little confused. Had he given up trying to win her?

"Then please excuse me. As much as I would love to spend my evening with you, I must attend to my guests."

"You're leaving me all alone?" Haven heard herself flirting.

Adam nodded solemnly. He was even paler than usual, Haven noticed, and his eyes had lost their luster. He looked like someone in terrible pain. Was it possible to fake such suffering, she wondered. "I *must* leave. For your sake," Adam said. "Yesterday, I had to face a terrible truth. For the past week, I've tried to ignore the fact that you're not in New York to stay. I gave into temptation, Haven. I allowed myself to feel things that I promised myself I wouldn't feel. But soon, Beau will be located, and I'll lose you once more. If I don't put some distance between us, the pain will be too much to bear. I'm afraid I may not be able to let you leave when the time comes. I know how that must sound, but I have to be honest with you. I hope you forgive me."

"But . . ." Haven started to argue before she truly understood what he'd said. The Adam Rosier she'd once known would never have warned her. He wouldn't have denied himself pleasure, even if it came at another's expense. Until that moment, Haven hadn't considered taking Adam at his word. She had allowed him to help her, of course. And she was grateful for his assistance. But it had never occurred to her that the love Adam felt might be completely sincere—or that her happiness could be more important to him than his own. Maybe it was all just a ruse—a new trick he'd dreamed up to lure Haven back into his arms. Or maybe—just maybe—the man standing beside her was a different Adam Rosier.

"Goodnight, Haven," he said.

Haven watched Adam cut through the crowd, leaving her behind.

"What did you say to the boss, Haven?" It was Calum, with Alex in tow. "I've never seen him like that. And look at you blushing like a virgin in a sex shop! Are you still going to tell me you two are just *friends*?"

"What do you care?" Haven asked, suddenly annoyed. "Why were you watching me, anyway?"

"Oh, don't mind Calum," Alex advised with a roll of her eyes. "He may be nosy, but he rarely means any harm."

CHAPTER TWENTY-SIX

Haven thought of the days when her world had been simple. Iain was her soul mate. Beau was her best friend. The Ouroboros Society was hopelessly corrupt. Adam was evil. Just a few weeks earlier, she'd been blissfully unaware that the Horae were watching her every move. And Mia Michalski had been nothing more than a name. In two short weeks, that world had been blown apart. Haven would have to piece the fragments together again. She'd start with one of the few things she still knew for certain. Beau was her best friend, and until she found him, nothing else mattered.

She fled City Hall Cinderella style, dashing down the stairs and heading toward the traffic circling the grounds. She never noticed the van parked on Broadway, and it wasn't until she felt arms grab her from behind that Haven realized Chandra and Cleo had been waiting to ambush her. Cold and miserable, Haven was bounced around in the back of the Horae's van long enough to build up a powerful rage. Finally the vehicle stopped, the doors opened, and Chandra hopped inside.

"Put this on," she ordered, handing Haven a blindfold.

"Kiss my ass," Haven snarled.

"Put it on," Chandra repeated.

Haven complied, and her captors dragged her out of the van like a sack of groceries. Each woman grabbed an arm and guided her forward. Snow filled Haven's shoes and brush slapped at her ankles. They were in the woods. Finally, her arms were released.

"Count to sixty before you take off the blindfold," Chandra commanded.

Haven could hear them returning the way they'd come. When she removed her blindfold, she found herself in a dense forest. Between the trees, she could see a flickering blaze. She trudged through the woods and into a snowy opening in the middle of the wilderness. A campfire lit the center of the clearing. Seated on a log, a few feet from the flames, was Phoebe. She seemed perfectly at home, though her beige suit and overcoat were better suited for a boardroom than the boondocks.

"I can't believe you just had me kidnapped! Where am I?" Haven demanded. All around her, a thick web of pine branches formed an impenetrable barrier.

"Try to remain calm, Haven," Phoebe cooed as if pacifying an overwrought child. "You haven't been abducted. This is merely a place where we can speak without interruption."

"Speak about *what*? There's no way I'm going to help you after what you've just done. We've got nothing to discuss."

"I can't force you to talk, but I wouldn't recommend leaving here on your own." Phoebe gestured to the forest that surrounded them. "I know for a fact that there are monsters in these woods."

"Stop trying to scare me!" Haven snarled as she took a step toward the fire. She didn't like feeling the darkness at her back.

"Chandra delivered your message. You've decided not to honor your deal with the Horae. Is that correct?"

"That's right. I don't want your help anymore. I can find Beau on my own." Haven began to doubt her words the second they left her mouth. But she'd learned something important in the back of the Horae's van. Haven had discovered the lengths to which the sisters would go to make her cooperate. Something told Haven that she and Beau might be better off without them. But she couldn't be sure.

Phoebe laughed. "On your *own?* Do you really believe that the magos has the police searching New York for your friend? How do you know that he wasn't the one responsible for Beau's kidnapping? How do you know that he doesn't have his gray men torturing the boy as we speak?"

"He doesn't," Haven insisted. She could still see Adam walking away from her, leaving her all alone at the party. If he had used Beau to lure her back to New York, he wouldn't have let her go. Somehow that one simple gesture had led Haven's heart to a startling conclusion that her mind was still trying to explain. "He's different now."

"Is he? And how many people's lives would you be willing to bet on that?" Phoebe stirred the fire with a stick, and its embers crackled and sparked. "I was hoping you'd be more intelligent this time around. But you're as foolish now as you've ever been."

"I'd go easy on the insults if I were you," Haven warned the woman. "Do you have any idea what Adam would do if he knew you kidnapped me tonight?"

"Yes, your knight in shining armor would arrive on his noble steed to rescue his princess and punish her enemies," Phoebe sneered. "He won you over quite quickly this time, didn't he? He tells you he's seen the light, and you fall at his feet. Have you forgotten that there are lives on the line? What about the children—the little ones the magos has been recruiting for the past ten years? Don't you care what will happen to them?"

"Of course I *care.* But I haven't seen any proof that the Society kids are in any danger. I was just at a fund-raiser for Halcyon Hall. . . ."

"Yes, the magos has been holding quite a few fund-raisers lately. Whatever he has planned must be very expensive."

"Well, I thought the party couldn't have been more respectable," Haven countered stubbornly. "I've watched Adam interact with some of the younger kids too. He's very sweet to them."

"Sweet to them?" Phoebe said. "Oh, you poor, silly creature."

"I don't care what you think of me." Haven glowered. Having been the butt of countless jokes as a child, she didn't enjoy being laughed at. "Call Cleo and Chandra and tell them to take me back to my hotel. I'm finished with the Horae."

"Don't be ridiculous. The magos has found your weakness, and he's exploiting it. It's all an *act*, Haven. He wants you to believe you've inspired him to become something different—someone better. But don't forget—the magos has spent thousands of years spreading misery and pestilence. He's murdered and maimed. I've seen things so terrible that you couldn't possibly comprehend them. If you give me a chance, I'll let you see for yourself."

Haven didn't need to witness any of Adam's crimes. She thought of her own father, who'd been killed by one of Adam's men. Adam could inspire his minions to do horrible things. But there was no way to rid the world of him forever. Phoebe had admitted as much herself. Locking him away was nothing more than a temporary solution. Changing him could be permanent. Was it foolish to think she might be the one who could do it?

"I don't think Adam is still the same person," Haven argued. "He's cleaning up the Ouroboros Society. He's encouraging the young members to devote their lives to improving the world. Maybe he's just trying to win me over, but what does that matter? Think of all the good Adam could do."

"Your argument has two serious flaws, Haven. *People* can change—but the magos isn't a person. And *you* don't have the power to change him."

"I guess we'll just have to wait and see," Haven replied with a sarcastic shrug.

Phoebe shook her head. "I'm afraid that isn't going to be an option. I asked Chandra and Cleo to bring you here because you have a decision you must make. *Tonight*. You can agree to help the Horae bring our plan to fruition. Or you can take a chance and pray that the magos is the saint he's pretending to be."

Haven opened her mouth to make her choice, but Phoebe stopped her.

"Before you decide, perhaps it's best to examine the dangers involved. We'll start with the children at Halcyon Hall. You've made it clear that you don't mind risking their lives. Fine. What about your friend Beau? Are you willing to gamble his life as well? And Iain's life? You do remember Mr. Morrow, don't you? You must realize that if you're wrong about Adam, Iain could pay the price. Is that a chance you want to take?"

Phoebe was right. Haven couldn't deny it. Even if her heart told her that Adam was different, there was still no way to be certain. It was one thing to make that leap of faith on her own. She couldn't demand that Iain and Beau make it too.

"There's only one sure way to protect your friends," Phoebe said. "Honor the deal that you made with me and my sisters. I know you don't want to betray Adam. I know that you'd rather not lock him away. But is his freedom worth the lives of the people you love? It's time to remember what matters most to you, Haven."

Haven couldn't speak, and Phoebe's satisfied smile was that of an archer whose arrow had found the right mark.

"As I said, this is your last chance." The old woman gestured to the log in front of the fire. "I won't extend this offer again. Do you accept it?"

"Do I have any choice?" Haven mumbled. She took a seat and felt the warmth of the fire spread over her.

"In time, you will see what a wise decision you've made." Phoebe threw a handful of twigs on the flames, and the sweet, cloying scent of perfume filled the clearing.

BEATRICE WAS LYING on her bed, staring up at the ceiling, tracing the flower garlands painted on the exposed beams. Her new gold necklaces were hanging heavily across her throat, and she fought the urge to gag. Only when she heard the door of her chamber open did she lift one hand to adjust her jewelry.

"It's not true, is it?" said a voice. "Tell me you haven't agreed to a date."

"I have. The wedding will be on the third of next month."

"It's not possible. He can't have bought you so cheaply. Is this the price you put on your soul?" She felt a fur land on her chest. "You let him buy you for a few measly trinkets?"

The rage inside her boiled over, and she sat up to confront her brother. Piero was tall, well built, and nearly as beautiful as Beatrice. "I don't care about any of this, you idiot." She flung the fur across the room, and it landed in a pile in the corner. "The only thing I want is something you take for granted. Haven't you noticed? Since my engagement, no one has been able to tell me where I can go or what I can do. Father, Mother—they're all too afraid of him. Adam gave me my freedom, Piero. And the price won't be my soul—it will be my body. My soul left me when Ettore died. I couldn't give it to anyone else if I wanted to."

Piero sat on the side of the bed. "I'm sorry," he said, staring down at the floor. "I'm sorry I couldn't save Ettore. But you can't throw yourself away just because he's gone."

"What does it matter?" Beatrice asked. "I'll have to marry someone anyway. Why shouldn't it be Adam? There's no doubt he adores me."

"Anyone else would be better," Piero said. He thought for a moment before he spoke once more. "Have you heard of the sickness making its way through the city?"

"I've seen the doctors in the streets wearing those hideous masks."

"The pestilence arrived in Genoa on Adam's ships, and now it has come to Florence. They say his crews were already dying when the boats docked. Even the rats didn't survive in the end. He brought this plague to our city. Dozens have died, and he is responsible."

"This is insane!" Beatrice snarled. *"How dare you come to me with such outrageous lies? You say my husband-to-be managed to summon a pestilence? Only the devil could do such a thing!"*

"I'm not the only one who believes Adam brought the disease. Naddo told me that the city leaders all think he's responsible. They say he's trying to rid Florence of rivals. Once everyone is gone, he can seize control."

"Ridiculous. Adam's right about you, you know. You're jealous, Piero. You and Naddo have to sneak and hide. If anyone found out about your love, you would both be dead within a week. You can't stand that the rest of us are able to live openly. You want to rob me of my freedom—of the one scrap of happiness I've had in years." It was the first time she had ever spoken of such things at full volume. She knew anyone could be listening, but she was too angry to care.

"Is that what you really believe?" Piero asked.

"It is."

"Then I'm sorry I disturbed you. I shouldn't have wasted my time appealing to your sense of reason. I'll have to take this matter into my own hands."

"Don't you dare," Beatrice spat.

"DID YOU SEE HIM this time?" Phoebe wanted to know.

Haven rubbed her eyes, which were still stinging from the smoke. She had a hunch that Phoebe was talking about Adam. But Haven refused to give the woman any satisfaction.

"I saw Piero. He was with Beatrice. He mentioned Naddo as well. But I still don't know enough to find him. I knew this would be pointless."

"You're wrong," Phoebe insisted. "The visions are building to a revelation. The very next one may hold the memory you need."

"Then take me back now," Haven said.

"No, it's too dangerous," Phoebe said with a shake of her head. "I refuse to endanger your life while you still have work to do. You must return to the magos and convince him of your love. Soon we shall put our plan into action."

"Not until I see Naddo!" Haven insisted. "Not until I can find the man who took Beau! If I'm going to honor my end of the deal, you have to honor yours too!"

"You can't afford to wait, Haven. Your boyfriend—the human one—is getting quite reckless. One of my sisters spotted him talking to a little girl in Gramercy Park. It was the middle of the day, and he was in full view of the Ouroboros Society. If you don't put an end to all of this soon, Iain Morrow may find himself face-to-face with the magos. And who, do you imagine, would win such a contest?"

Haven didn't need to respond. The answer was obvious.

"You should be very concerned about Iain," Phoebe continued, determined to press her point. Haven could tell there was a surprise on the way—one the old woman had been saving for just such a moment. "This isn't the first time his foolishness has put lives at risk. The boy has always acted without thinking, and he's never listened to reason. On at least one occasion, he managed to get you both killed."

"How would *you* know?" Haven scoffed.

"I know because I personally witnessed the tragedy. Twelve hundred years ago, you were the daughter of the Emir of Cordoba, and your father had arranged your marriage to an important ally. You had lived in the emir's harem your entire life. You had never spoken to a man outside your family—neither your future husband nor the young tutor your father had brought to Spain to instruct his sons. Three of the Horae were palace slaves, and we recognized both men immediately. I spoke to Iain. I couldn't reveal my true identity, but I pleaded with him not to interfere with your marriage to the magos. I swore he would disappear shortly after the wedding, and Iain could have you for the rest of your days. But Iain refused to compromise. One night he broke into the women's quarters and carried you away. Your father sent men after him. They slaughtered Iain for his crime. And they executed *you* for bringing shame upon your family. Your deaths weren't necessary. Iain's impulsiveness condemned you both. I suggest you act quickly before it happens again."

"Great story, Phoebe. Are you sure I wasn't Anne Boleyn? Or Joan of Arc? How do I know that wasn't just one of your lies?" Haven said, though the tale had the ring of truth. She knew Iain sometimes trusted his instincts too much. And his convictions were never easily challenged. Even Haven could find it difficult to make Iain listen to her side of an issue. A stranger would barely stand a chance.

"I believe there's another person who can confirm my account," Phoebe said. "And now that I've said my piece, you're free to go ask him." She dismissed Haven with a wave of her hand.

"Go? We're in the middle of a forest. Where the hell am I supposed to go?"

"Follow the path behind you," Phoebe told her.

Haven turned around. Somehow she had overlooked a gravel trail that cut through the trees. It was several feet wide and perfectly maintained. When she glanced back at the fire, Phoebe was gone, and the light was growing fainter. Haven hurried along the path, wondering where it might lead and why the sky above seemed to glow. There was a sound in the distance. The blare of a car horn. She began to sprint. The forest thinned until there were hardly any trees at all. Haven found herself in a meadow. And that's when she saw them—the massive structures circling the wilderness. She was standing in the middle of Central Park.

CHAPTER TWENTY-SEVEN

THE CITY HAD frozen again overnight. Icicles dangled from doorways, a fire hydrant spewed a river of solid ice, and the mounds of snow that lined the streets were hard to the touch. The sidewalk seemed to crackle with each step Haven took. The cars on Lexington Avenue plowed through the slush.

As Haven approached the Ouroboros Society, she spotted a group of people clustered on the building's salt-sprinkled stairs. Parents and their progeny waiting for the doors to open, she assumed at first—until she saw there was only one adult among them. As she drew closer, she realized it was Adam, surrounded by half a dozen children. None of them noticed her. They were all silent and perfectly motionless as they stared straight ahead at the park. Haven had never seen six children sitting so still or concentrating so intently.

Haven was almost upon them when she heard one of the little boys whisper, "There it is." She wheeled around to see what he'd spotted. A majestic brown bird landed on the statue at the center of

227

Gramercy Park. It perched there for a moment, observing them all. Then it stretched out its massive wings and took one turn around the garden before it flew off toward the East River. As soon as it was out of sight, the group of children seemed to exhale in unison.

"In the ancient world," she heard Adam say, "people believed that the will of the gods could be determined by studying the flight of birds. The priests who read the signs were called augurs. A hawk landing on the head of the statue would have been seen as a powerful omen."

"What does it mean?" inquired one of the children.

"We'll have to find an augur to know," Adam said. "Very few of us are allowed to see the future. In fact, there's only one . . ." He looked up. "Haven." A smile spread across his face.

"You're bird-watching?" she asked.

Adam slid an arm around the kid sitting next to him, and the little boy beamed. "Jeremiah saw a red-tailed hawk and thought we should all take a look."

"And who are the rest of your crew?"

"James, Hunter, Olivia, Avery, Jeremiah," Adam pointed to each of the kids. "And Flora. Everyone but Jeremiah is in town to celebrate a birthday."

"Then happy birthday to you all!" Haven smiled down at the cherubic little girl sitting to Adam's right. She was taller than Haven remembered. Even with her hair still in pigtails, she seemed much more mature. "Hi, Flora," she said. "We met once a long time ago in the waiting room here. Do you remember me?"

"I'd never forget you," Flora said affably. "We met the same day I met Adam."

"That's right," Adam said, patting Flora on the knee. "Such an excellent memory. No wonder you're at the very top of your class." He rose from the stoop. "Will you ladies and gentlemen excuse me for a moment?" he asked. "Why don't you go inside and ask Madison to make you some hot chocolate? I'll join you in a minute."

Squealing with delight, the kids jumped up and scrambled into the building. The children might have been prodigies, but their hearts still raced at the mention of cocoa.

"IS THERE SOMETHING you need?" Adam asked Haven once the children were gone. He sounded guarded; his politeness was a shield.

"No. I . . . I was wondering if you might like to have dinner with me," Haven said, staring at her cuticles. She'd never hated herself more. If Adam really loved her, what she was doing was almost indefensibly cruel. *Do it for Beau,* she reminded herself. *Do it for Iain.*

"Would it be a date?" Adam asked warily. "Does this mean you're considering staying in New York?"

"Maybe. I think so. I mean yes. I'm thinking of staying. Look, if you're busy tonight that's okay."

"No, no. Not at all," Adam assured Haven, unable to disguise his pleasure. "I have an important meeting at seven, but it shouldn't last very long. How does eight o'clock sound?"

"Perfect." Haven took a step backward. With her mission accomplished, she was eager to leave. "I'll pick you up here."

"I'm afraid I'll be working at our other offices this evening."

"Oh," Haven said, casting her eyes at the redbrick mansion that lay east of the Ouroboros Society on Gramercy Park South. The first time she had visited, there had been a small bronze sign identifying the building as the Gramercy Park Historical Society. The sign was gone now, replaced by an even smaller plaque engraved with a silver ouroboros. Long an annex of the Ouroboros Society, the mansion hosted Adam's secret meetings with the organization's most esteemed members.

Haven couldn't stop her eyes from scaling the brick walls to the fourth floor of the building, where Adam kept his macabre museum. The sight that had once inspired terror now brought her relief. Maybe she was doing the right thing after all.

"You needn't worry. There's nothing there anymore," Adam said.

"What?" Haven pretended she hadn't understood.

"The room at the top. It's empty."

Haven could hardly believe that he'd broached the subject. She thought of all the things she'd seen in that horrible room—her possessions from previous lives and the corpses of six women she'd once been.

"It's not in my interest to remind you, but I thought you should know," Adam said. "A moment of discomfort is better than a lifetime of uncertainty. I had all of your belongings removed. Some were donated to museums. Others were packed away in a storage facility. The key is yours if you'd like it."

"And the bodies?" Haven asked.

"They've been laid to rest. I had a mausoleum built for them in Brooklyn. Have you ever visited Green-Wood Cemetery?"

"No," Haven said.

"It's lovely," Adam told her. "There are tall trees, and hills that look out over the city. The mausoleum itself is quite simple. A man-made structure couldn't have added to the beauty of the surroundings. So I had the tomb constructed beneath one of the hills. Only the entrance is visible. There's a lake a few yards away, and in the summer you can watch the swans gliding by. Even I find it peaceful. Though I must admit, I haven't visited since the mausoleum was finished. After all these years, I thought you deserved your privacy."

"You really have changed." The words almost caught in Haven's throat. She didn't want them to be true. But now that she was finally looking, she could see that he had.

"I'm merely a work in progress," Adam corrected her. "The truth is, I didn't expect you to return in this life. I thought I'd have more time to get things in order. I want to build a Society you'll be proud of. One you may even choose to lead by my side."

"Will I really have a choice?"

"Yes," Adam promised. "You will."

*   *   *

AT EIGHT O'CLOCK, Haven stopped half a block from the redbrick mansion, unable to convince her feet to move any farther. She simply couldn't go through with the Horae's scheme. Haven's heart ached for Iain and Beau, but she couldn't bear the thought of betraying Adam. He adored her, and she pitied him. It seemed a cruel twist of fate that she might have to trade Adam's freedom for the lives of the two people she loved most. If only there were another way. She'd spent hours trying to reach Iain, hoping to learn what progress he'd made—and to warn him to be more careful. But her calls never went through, and Frances Whitman hadn't seen Iain in days.

Haven felt her heart slow and her body begin to freeze. Still, she couldn't turn back or propel herself forward. Then she saw the door of the redbrick mansion open. Commissioner Williams charged down the stairs and turned toward Third Avenue. *Remember what matters to you most,* she heard Phoebe say. Haven set off in a sprint.

Adam caught her as she flew into the mansion's foyer.

"Did you run all the way from the hotel?" he quipped. "Who would have guessed that my company could be so alluring?"

"I saw Commissioner Williams outside," Haven said, struggling to catch her breath. "Was he your seven o'clock appointment? Was he here to talk about Beau?"

Adam let her go. "I didn't mention anything earlier because I didn't want to worry you without cause. There has been some news. Would you care to have a seat?"

Haven looked around. Her former bodies might have been moved to Brooklyn, but the mansion still made her skin crawl.

Adam seemed to sense her discomfort. "I have a better idea. Why don't we walk toward the restaurant? I made reservations at Amrita." He held the door open for Haven. It wasn't until they were a block away that she realized Adam hadn't bothered to wear his coat. It couldn't have been more than twenty degrees outside. Seeing Adam outside in his thin cashmere sweater was a bit like glimpsing Clark Kent without his glasses.

"Tell me," she said.

"Haven, do you think there's a chance that Beau may have vanished on purpose?"

"No!" Haven insisted. "Why would you even say such a thing?"

"Gordon Williams thinks it's odd that Beau left school right before his midterm exams."

"He was excited," Haven argued. "He thought he was flying to New York to see a man he was meant to meet. I doubt he even *remembered* the exams."

"Gordon also found it a bit strange that Beau was seen on the street uptown. It doesn't sound like someone being held against his will, does it?"

"What are you talking about? He had bruises all over his face! Where is all of this going, Adam?" Haven demanded.

"You've been paying for Beau's tuition, is that right?"

The reminder of her poverty made Haven's frown deepen. "I was until Virginia Morrow accused me of fraud. But what does that have to do with anything?"

"Gordon told me that Beau hadn't been striving for academic excellence this semester. He was skipping classes, and his grades were atrocious."

"He wasn't even halfway through the semester!" Haven countered. "Beau had plenty of time to turn his grades around."

Adam softened his tone. "But perhaps he didn't expect to. Perhaps he was embarrassed that your money wasn't being put to good use."

"Right. I see what's happening," Haven glowered. "Instead of looking for Beau, Commissioner Williams has been busy finding excuses for his own incompetence. Is that why he came here tonight? To convince you that Beau disappeared, so I wouldn't know he was flunking out of Vanderbilt?"

"It's just a possibility Gordon felt he had to put forward." Adam stopped. "Haven, I'm able to see the sides of people that they would prefer to hide. Do you think there's a chance that Beau doesn't want to be found?"

"No!" Haven insisted once more. "I can't believe this! Does Commissioner Williams really think Beau beat himself up?"'

"There could be another explanation for the bruises."

"No! Just no, Adam! Beau would never scare everyone he loves just to save face. Besides, if Beau had been failing all of his classes, he'd have told me!"

"And risk ruining the perfect image you have of him?"

"He'd have told me!" Haven cried, refusing to question one of the last things she still knew for certain. She'd felt it too. There *was* something odd about Beau's disappearance. Maybe he *had* been in trouble at school. But he wouldn't have willingly put Haven through hell. It didn't matter what evidence there might be to the contrary. Beau Decker couldn't hurt her. And *that*, Haven knew, was an indisputable fact.

"I'm sorry," Adam said, backing down. "It was merely a suggestion. Gordon was surprised that his men haven't solved the case yet. He wondered if Beau might have gotten word we were looking for him and moved on."

Haven chewed on her lip, trying to hold back her rage.

"I'm sorry," Adam told her. "We'll keep searching for Beau. And I'll put more pressure on Gordon. Don't worry about that. Can we try to forget this conversation and enjoy a pleasant dinner together?"

"I'M AFRAID I'M not very hungry anymore," Haven grumbled.

They were already on the far side of Madison Square Park, with the Flatiron Building in front of them when Haven stopped. The triangular tower had been constructed a few short years before Constance Whitman was born. As a little girl, Constance had marveled at the skyscraper, which even then was one of the most famous buildings in the world. Haven had a vision of wild winds stirring women's skirts as crowds of men dressed in old-fashioned three-piece suits held on to their hats and waited for a glimpse of a lady's ankle.

"May I ask what you're thinking about?" Adam asked, and the vision ended. "You had the funniest look on your face just now."

"Sometimes the past and the present mix together," Haven explained. "It makes me feel like I'm losing my mind."

"It happens to all of us," Adam assured her. "Time isn't the straight arrow that most people imagine."

On another day, in another mood, she might have asked for an explanation. "You're making my head hurt," Haven told him instead.

"I apologize. What do you say we skip the restaurant? Are you feeling up for a stroll?"

She wasn't. She hadn't worn the right shoes for a walk, and her thin dress and wool coat weren't enough protection from the cold. But Haven knew she shouldn't say no. A romantic stroll was the perfect opportunity to finish the terrible task that Phoebe had set her.

"Where do you want to go?" Haven asked, trying to forget that the previous conversation had taken place.

"This way. There's something I'd like to show you."

They ambled west toward the Hudson River. Twenty-fifth Street was lined with antique stores and mannequin makers. Behind the metal mesh that shielded one of the shop fronts, the bald plastic heads of a hundred beautiful women had been mounted on a wall. Each wore a different expression—some laughing, others somber and composed, like an audience unable to interpret the show. Haven and Adam were almost to Tenth Avenue when Adam came to a stop in front of a rusting gate beside an old brownstone. He bent and removed a brick from the building's wall. Behind the brick lay a key.

"We're here," Adam said as he unlocked the gate. "Don't worry, I'm allowed to visit whenever I like. Come, take a look."

"Whose house is this?" Haven asked. A tight alley led to a garden. She stepped into the passage and let the gate close behind her.

"A very old man named Matteo Salvadore. He's a friend of mine. Follow me."

The garden behind the brownstone was barren. There were no plants or trees, just marble statues lit by the moonlight. They were all so lifelike that they might have been real women frozen in place by a spell. Adam approached one of them. It was the figure of a girl dancing alone. Her dress, which she wore draped around her body in the style of the ancients, clung to her skin, revealing every curve. Her long, curly hair floated freely, and her crown of flowers had come loose and threatened to slip to the ground. Adam reached out and caressed the statue's cold, dead arm. It was the first time Haven had seen his eyes come alive in another woman's presence.

"Do you recognize this girl?" he asked.

"No," Haven said, jealous to think that the lovely creature might once have been real. "Should I? Is she someone I've known?"

"It's you."

"Me?"

"This is what you looked like when we first met. I saw you dancing in the gardens behind your father's house in Crete." He smiled at the memory. "Do you know what I did when I saw you there, spinning around to the music inside your head? I laughed. You might not believe it, but I'd never laughed before. But you were so young and beautiful, so full of life and passion. You were everything that I wasn't. Matteo must have seen you too. The resemblance is uncanny. I often wonder how many lifetimes it took him to acquire the skills needed to craft such a masterpiece."

"Is Matteo Salvadore a member of the Society?"

"No," Adam said firmly. "He visited the OS back in the 1940s. He was only eighteen when I first met him, but he said he'd been sculpting for well over a decade. He remembered little snippets of previous lives. Nothing remarkable, just the sort of meaningless memories that stick around for no reason. I asked for a chance to inspect his work, and he brought me here. He'd just completed this statue. He said it was a girl he was sure he'd once seen, but he couldn't remember where or when. Of course I recognized you in an instant. It was so soon after losing Constance, and the pain was still fresh. I asked him if I could sit with you for a while. I stayed here in this garden for three days. Matteo never asked a single question.

"He wanted to join the Society, but I refused. I couldn't bear to see his talents be misused or destroyed. So I became his patron instead. I gave him the money he needed to pursue his art, with no strings attached. In the past seventy years, I've asked only three things of him. I asked him never to sell your statue. I asked that I be allowed to visit this garden whenever I like. And a year ago I asked Matteo to create two statues for the mausoleum I had constructed in Green-Wood Cemetery."

"He's known you for seventy years? Has he ever wondered why you still look the same as the day you first met?" Haven asked.

"Matteo knows I'm not like everyone else."

"Is he frightened of you?"

"Why would he be?" Adam asked. "I've never been anything but kind to him. May I ask you a question?"

"Yes."

"Are *you* still frightened of me?"

"A little," Haven admitted. "When I was last in New York—when we were upstairs in that room together. You were going to . . ." She couldn't say it. "What would have happened if Beau hadn't shown up?"

"I don't know," Adam confessed as his eyes swept the ground. "I look back at that moment, and I don't recognize myself anymore. I'm ashamed to remember the events of that day."

Shame. He had put a name on the emotion still building inside of her. She was ashamed that she'd bartered Adam's heart for Beau's safety. Ashamed to let Adam hope that his love might be returned. And ashamed to realize that a bit of it already was.

"Haven? Is something wrong? Have I made you unhappy?"

"No. It's not you," Haven told him, trying to keep the tears from her eyes. "You've been so kind to me. Helping me find Beau, getting me a room at the hotel, convincing Alex Harbridge to let me design a dress for her . . ."

"I told you I had nothing to do with Alex's dress," Adam said. "As for the rest, it has been my pleasure. I only wish I could do more for you. But I'm willing to wait." He turned his gaze to the statue of the first girl he'd loved. The first of many who had fled from his embrace. "Haven, when you asked me to dinner, it was more than I could ever have hoped for. The idea that you might come to me of your own volition. Quite frankly, it's astounding."

"I guess I'm just grateful," Haven said. "And I can see that there is something different about you now."

"For the first time, I'm looking forward to the future," Adam responded, the life returning to his dark eyes. "Before, all I had was the past. That's why I hoarded everything that you'd touched. Now I don't need those things. I'm sorry," he added when he caught sight of the flush creeping up Haven's neck. "I didn't want to embarrass you."

"You didn't," Haven lied. "I was just wondering why you weren't like this before. If you had been, I might not have kept running away from you."

"It's not always easy to know what someone wants most," Adam said. "At first I imagined that your affection could be purchased with gold and jewels. Those efforts to win your heart were spectacular failures. Then I tried solving the problems you encountered in each lifetime. That worked for a while. There were a few years in Constantinople when we both were happy. Then you discovered the truth about me and threw yourself into the Bosphorus. Later, in Florence,

I lost my chance again. But now I know what it is that you desire. I know the one thing I can give you that you can't ever refuse."

"What?" Haven asked.

"Someone good. Someone you can trust. I saw how distressed you were when Iain disappointed you, and I realized that if I wanted to be with you, I would need to be the man that he wasn't. So I began making the necessary changes. I'm trying to reform the Society. I want to give our members a new mission. One day you may choose to rule by my side, and I want you to be proud of what we have. Think of what we might be able to accomplish with the OS behind us. It can be a force for good, just as August Strickland intended it to be."

"But I still don't understand, Adam. You once told me that chaos is necessary. You said that without you, the world would grow stagnant. What's going to happen if you become someone different?"

"The universe has ways of keeping its balance," Adam replied. "I have a plan, but I won't lie to you, Haven. What I'm attempting might be dangerous. I don't know what the results may be."

"But you're still willing to change?" Haven asked. "Just for me?"

Adam gazed down at her. "I love you," he said simply. "I have from the moment I first laid eyes on you. I don't think you realize how important you are to me, Haven. You're my only imperfection."

"Your *imperfection*?" It wasn't quite the compliment Haven had anticipated.

"Nothing in creation was made without flaws. For thousands of years, I thought I was the exception to that rule. I believed I was a superior being sent to lead a race of weaker creatures. I despised humans, who could be manipulated by desires they couldn't control. Then I discovered you, and I realized that *I'm* the one to be pitied. Only when I'm near you do I feel fully alive. I suffer the lust and the longing that mortal men must endure. I've become addicted to the sensation, and I'm jealous of the creatures I scorned. You were sent to humble me, Haven. I'm human whenever you're by my side."

Haven knew Phoebe would be pleased by Adam's admission. But she felt no relief or delight. She wished there was a way to give him the one thing he wanted. All Haven could offer Adam now was a brief glimpse of the way things might have been if her heart had never belonged to someone else. She reached out and took one of Adam's hands. His fingers felt as smooth and cold as those of the statues in the garden. Adam gazed at her until his wonderment turned to joy.

"Come," he said. "I'll walk you home."

They strolled hand in hand to the Gramercy Gardens Hotel. By the time the pair reached the lobby, Adam's fingers had absorbed her warmth. They could have passed for human, Haven thought.

"Would it be all right if I—"

"Yes," Haven said. She had known the moment was coming, and she closed her eyes and waited for Adam's kiss. It finally arrived, and the chill of his lips spread through her body. Her fingers tingled as they touched his back, and a wonderful numbness washed over the rest of her. Soon she realized Adam's arms were all that was keeping her from collapsing to the floor. She'd let him kiss her because she pitied him. But Haven suddenly felt herself kissing Adam back.

And that was when she knew she could love him. She had always imagined that there weren't any forks on destiny's path—no hard choices that would need to be made. She was meant to be with Iain. That was it, end of story. But now she saw another life she could easily have chosen. One with a man who adored her enough to do whatever she asked of him. A man with the power to alter the course of history. A beautiful being whose kiss, when it ended, left her stupefied.

"Good night," Adam whispered softly in Haven's ear. "Will I see you soon?"

"Yes," Haven promised, staggering a little as the feeling returned to her legs and toes. "You will."

She stood in the lobby and watched Adam leave. She remained frozen in the same spot after he was gone, wondering what it was she'd just done—and what exactly it meant. Part of Haven wanted to slink upstairs in shame. Another part would have rushed after Adam.

"Phoebe will be pleased," said a young female voice with a faint accent. A girl with blonde hair passed within whispering range. Haven recognized her motorcycle boots before she managed to place the girl's face. "That kiss almost looked a little *too* real."

When the girl pushed through the hotel's glass doors, Haven's ears caught the sound of someone whistling in the darkness outside. Just a few notes of the ancient tune were all she needed to identify the song she'd waited to hear every night back in Rome. Iain was letting her know he was on his way. Haven turned toward her room. Her choice had been made.

CHAPTER TWENTY-EIGHT

There was no way to tell if it had been a dream or a memory. She could feel a man's hands unfastening her clothing, exposing the flesh beneath it. She could hear him breathing, but she didn't see his face. Whoever it was, she helped him with the last few buttons. At last she was fully exposed. She waited for him to touch her. When his fingers brushed against her skin, they were as cold as a corpse.

Haven woke with a gasp. Someone was sitting on the end of her bed.

"Iain?" Haven's voice was thick with sleep.

"Yes."

She dove across the bed and threw her arms around him. She hadn't realized how much worry had been weighing her down. Now that she knew for a fact that Iain was safe, Haven felt lighter than she had in days. "Oh my God, Iain! I'm so glad you're here! I'm so glad you're okay!"

But something was wrong. He wasn't responding to her kisses.

"I saw you, Haven."

Haven lurched backward as the guilt skewered her. She'd convinced herself that the whistle outside had been a mixture of the wind and her imagination.

"Tonight?" she asked, hoping he'd witnessed some other—any other—scene.

"I came to tell you I finally found Padma. I saw Adam bring you here. I saw you kiss him in the lobby. What happened to the week you were supposed to give me, Haven? Why didn't you stay away from him like you promised?"

"What are you talking about? I would have waited if Phoebe had let me!"

"Phoebe?" Iain repeated, his brow furrowed with confusion. Then his eyes rose to the ceiling, and he nodded as if an answer had been sent from above. "I get it now. Phoebe wanted to get me out of her hair, so she agreed to let me look for Padma. She swore she'd put her own plan on hold. But she didn't, did she?"

"No," said Haven. "She told me that we had to go ahead with both plans." Iain was right—they'd been double-crossed. And Haven had allowed it to happen when she'd shown up late for the meeting with the Horae. She had given Phoebe the perfect opportunity to drive them apart and get Iain out of the way.

"Well," Iain sighed. "That explains why you were with Adam tonight. But why did you have to *kiss* him, Haven? And how many times have you had to?"

He had every right to ask, but the question still felt like a slap to the face. "That was the first and the *last* time, Iain! So don't treat me like I'm some kind of traitor. I've been honest with you. Which is more than you can say. Why didn't you tell me that Mia Michalski is your ex-girlfriend?"

"What? Who told you *that*?"

"Does it matter?" Haven shot back. It was much easier to live with what she'd done when she imagined that Iain might not be innocent, either.

"Whoever it was needs to have his head checked. But in case you're concerned, Haven, I haven't seen Mia in days. She's been busy searching for Beau, and I've been looking for Padma. We've both been doing what we can to help *you*."

Haven saw the pain written on Iain's face, and she was shocked to think that she was responsible. That horrible girl must still be lurking somewhere inside her. Beatrice was doing her best to push Iain away, but Haven couldn't let her succeed. She had sworn she wouldn't let anything come between her and the person she'd fought so hard to find.

"I'm sorry," Haven said, pressing her forehead against Iain's slumped shoulder. Her tears were a skin-searing mixture of guilt, shame, and misery. "For everything. I shouldn't have kissed Adam. And I should *never* have questioned your loyalty. I know how hard you've been working to help me. If I went too far with Adam, it was because I just want this all to be over. I want to save Beau and grab the first flight to Rome. I'd give anything to be sitting on our balcony right now, listening to a story about one of our lives."

"Me too," Iain said. "That's why I came here. I thought you'd be happy to hear that we might be a little bit closer to getting back home."

"Because you found Padma?" Haven wiped her tears on the bedsheet. Forty-eight hours earlier, she would have been thrilled by the news.

"Yeah. I spent the last few days staking out some of the locations she used for interrogations back when she was president. Yesterday afternoon, I caught her coming out of a horrible rat hole on the Lower East Side."

"And? Did she agree to help you destroy the Society?" Haven asked.

"No, but she's open to talking, as long as there's something in it for her."

"So you guys haven't actually made any moves yet?" Haven probed.

"What are you getting at, Haven?" Iain asked, suddenly suspicious.

"I've been thinking, Iain. What if the Society *shouldn't* be destroyed?"

Iain watched Haven as if he expected her to start speaking in tongues. "You can't be serious. The Ouroboros Society is rotten to the core."

"That's what I thought too, but I'm not so convinced anymore." Haven edged closer to him, hoping her enthusiasm might be contagious. "I've met some people who could turn the OS into the organization Dr. Strickland meant it to be. There's this one guy, Owen Bell—"

"What about Adam?" Iain asked bluntly. "Have you changed your mind about him as well?"

Haven bit her lip, trying to decide whether he could handle the truth.

"I think Adam is different now," she admitted, "and I don't want to help the Horae lock him away. I'll betray him if it means keeping you and Beau safe. But I'm going to try to find another solution."

"See?! This is *exactly* what I didn't want to happen," Iain interrupted her. "This is why I asked for a week."

"I don't understand."

"You're in too deep, Haven. It's only been a few days, and Adam's got you just where he wants you."

Haven bristled. She was tired of being treated like a naive little girl. "Because I think the Society can be salvaged? Is that really so stupid? You're starting to sound like Phoebe. If you'd just let me introduce you to Owen—"

"I don't have time to meet anyone. We need to leave New York before you can get yourself into any more trouble. Mia can keep looking for Beau. She told me she's hacked into all his accounts. It won't be long before—"

Haven didn't hesitate. "No."

"No?"

"I mean it, Iain. I know you think I'm crazy, but sometimes you're wrong. Remember what happened in Spain when I was the Emir of Cordoba's daughter? Phoebe told me you wouldn't listen to anyone else, and you ended up getting us both killed! Maybe you should try being a little less pigheaded."

Haven could see from his stunned reaction that Phoebe had been telling the truth. "How did Phoebe hear about Cordoba?" he asked.

"She was there," Haven sighed, sorry she'd used the knowledge against him. "If you'd just let me explain why I think the OS—"

"Don't waste your time, Haven," Iain cut her off. "Look, I'll be the first to admit I've made plenty of mistakes, but this is not one of them. If you had any idea what kind of trouble you're in, you'd *run* to the airport. All those people you've met at the Society—they may not be monsters but they're all Adam's pawns. I saw the paparazzi pictures of you with Alex Harbridge and Calum Daniels. You think those two are your friends? Their loyalties lie with the *Society*, Haven. And how do you know the OS should be saved, anyway? You've only been allowed to see a small part of Adam's operations. Have you been invited to any of the secret meetings he holds at that mansion near the Society's headquarters? Have you taken the train up to Halcyon Hall? Have you figured out what's happening to the children Adam's recruited?"

"Actually, I do know a few things about Halcyon Hall," Haven interjected. "I don't think anyone's harming those kids. I've met a few of them, and they seem perfectly happy to me. Adam is wonderful with them."

Iain laughed as though the idea were too foolish to merit any other response. "He's *wonderful*, is he? It's taken less than a week for Adam to transform from the devil himself to a friend of all the little children. No wonder you two go around holding hands and kissing. You sound like you're in love with him."

"That's not fair!" Haven exclaimed, her face burning.

"You're sure? Not even a little?" Iain asked.

"I chose you over him! I've *always* chosen you over him!"

"But you feel something for Adam now, don't you?"

"Yes. I feel *sorry* for him." The statement was only half true. Haven remembered the kiss. She had felt far more than pity. Now she felt only guilt. She took Iain's hand, hoping to console him. He lifted her fingers into the light.

"Where's the ring I gave you?" he asked.

The ring. She hadn't thought about it in days. "I had to take it off. Adam noticed it. That ring could have gotten us both in big trouble."

"That wasn't my question. Where's your ring, Haven?"

"It's in my purse." She jumped off the bed and returned to Iain with one hand rummaging around at the bottom of her handbag.

"Never mind," Iain muttered.

Haven knew what he was thinking, and she silently cursed herself. "Please don't be mad! I haven't lost it. It's still in there." She set the bag aside and sat down on his lap. When she pressed her lips to his, Iain turned his head away.

"Will you leave here with me tonight?" he demanded.

"No."

"Fine." Iain rose from the bed with Haven in his arms. She thought he might carry her through the door and out of the hotel. Instead he set her right back on the bed and marched across the room.

"Where are you going?" she called.

"To find a way to save you."

"Iain!"

The door slammed behind him.

When it became clear that Iain wasn't coming back, Haven hurried to the window, hoping for one last glimpse of him. The streets below were deserted, but the park was not. A solitary figure walked the winding paths. The last thing Haven saw before she was blinded by tears was the figure passing from one shadow to the next.

CHAPTER TWENTY-NINE

Beatrice gazed down in horror at the empty plaza below her window, where a body lay facedown on the paving stones. She had watched the man stumble and fall. Not a single soul had come to his aid. Everyone in the square had fled the scene like cockroaches scuttling back into the gutters. They were the diseased ones, Beatrice thought. Then a figure in black emerged from a side street. Beatrice had sent a servant to summon a priest. But when the man stopped beside the body and glanced up at Beatrice, it was clear he was not the priest she'd requested. He'd hidden his face behind one of the hideous white masks with long, curving beaks. Using the tip of his cane, he roughly prodded the dead man's flank. A horse-drawn cart rumbled into view. Two men climbed down and picked the body off the ground. They swung the corpse back and forth, then tossed it into the back of their cart, on top of a pile of jumbled limbs, heads, and torsos.

HAVEN SLURPED BURNT black coffee from a paper cup as she waited on an underground platform at Grand Central Station. The train pulled in at eight thirty, and Haven found herself surrounded by a swarm of grim-faced men and women in black business attire, all arriving from well-heeled suburbs outside the city. Like automatons performing some preprogrammed task, they marched toward the exit, donning their coats without missing a step. Once the train had emptied, Haven boarded, trying not to slip on all the discarded copies of the *Wall Street Journal* that littered the aisle. As far as she could tell, she was the only passenger heading north.

Haven drained the last of her coffee and hoped it would be enough to keep her alert. She had barely slept after Iain left. Every time she closed her eyes, she heard him say, *You're in too deep.* Was she? Haven wondered. Had she really fallen for Adam—been taken in by his lies? Iain seemed to think it was the only explanation for her change of heart. Maybe he was right, but Haven's gut kept insisting that he had to be wrong. She felt something for Adam. And when she let her thoughts wander, they almost always ended up at the scene of their kiss. In Adam's presence, she felt more than mortal. And she was flattered by the lengths to which he'd gone to win her heart. But Adam hadn't bedazzled her. Haven was still capable of thinking clearly.

That was what she would have to prove if she intended to save her relationship. Iain needed to know that Haven's sudden desire to spare the Society had nothing to do with the feelings she felt for the man in charge of it. Haven had been given a glimpse of the wonders the OS might accomplish with people like Owen working behind the scenes. If she could just show Iain, he might understand. And maybe then he'd see that her love for him hadn't dimmed or died—even if her heart had found room for another.

Finally, at three o'clock in the morning, Haven found a way to put her convictions to the test. The Horae claimed terrible things were happening at Halcyon Hall. Iain seemed convinced as well. But it was time for them to stop taking Phoebe at her word. Even if it meant taking her focus off Beau for a day, Haven needed to see the school with her own eyes. What she found might help her decide whom to believe—all the people who said she was a confused little girl, or the voice that was telling her to trust herself.

HALCYON HALL SAT on the outskirts of a tiny town on the eastern side of the Hudson River. As she approached the village, Haven could see a rambling stone and wood structure from the window of the taxi that had picked her up at the Poughkeepsie train station. With its fanciful arches, balconies, and turrets, the building resembled a luxurious ski lodge. It wasn't the bleak, gray institution Haven had been anticipating.

"You're *sure* that's Halcyon Hall?" Haven asked.

"Yup," said the taxi driver.

"Do you know much about it? I hear it's a little . . . *unusual.*"

"It's just a school," the man said, making it clear that he was in no mood to chat. "Nothing unusual about it far as I know. Must have cost a mint to fix up that building, though. Used to be a hotel. Then a fancy girls' school. But it was empty for ages. Until Halcyon Hall opened up ten years back, people round here thought the place was an eyesore."

The driver's eyes disappeared from the rearview mirror as he focused on the task in front of him. Another violent storm had swept through the area the previous evening. Tree branches encased in ice drooped across the road, scraping against the taxi's roof. The plows had already been through, piling five feet of snow along either side of the road, but the asphalt was still slick, and turns could be treacherous. Finally, the car slid into the private drive that led to the school, and Haven waited to encounter some evidence of the security Phoebe had described. The cabbie steered through an open gate and past an empty guard-post by the side of the road. Maybe there had once been a security force at Halcyon Hall, but now the only creatures patrolling the grounds seemed to be a pair of large ravens strutting in circles across the pristine snow. When the taxi pulled up to the main building, no one appeared on the steps to order it to move along.

"Would you mind waiting here?" Haven asked the driver, still expecting to be chased off the property at any moment.

"You mind paying?" he responded.

"No."

"Then I don't mind waiting." He let his seat drop back, pulled his cap down over his eyes, and drifted off to the lullaby of his ticking meter.

THE GRAND RECEPTION hall was warm, almost cozy. Chandeliers hung from the exposed wooden beams that crisscrossed the ceiling. Two fires crackled at either end of the massive room. The leather sofas and lounge chairs stationed throughout the hall looked as though they might once have been filled with happy families on holiday. A framed photo on one of the rustic stone mantels showed groups of little girls in pristine white dresses playing croquet on the school's front lawn.

"May I help you?" A friendly young man with his tie tucked into a sweater-vest stuck his head out of the school's front office.

"Yes," Haven started to say as she took off her hat.

"Oh, hello, Miss Moore. I almost failed to recognize you." The man hurried out to greet her.

"Do we know each other?" Haven tried to camouflage her distress with a smile.

"Yes, but I wouldn't expect you to remember me. We met at the Society a while back. I was working as a receptionist at the time."

"I'm sorry—"

"Don't be! The OS uniforms aren't designed to make us memorable. My name is Albert Sinclaire. I'm the headmaster's assistant." He held out a hand, and Haven hesitated briefly before taking it.

"It's nice to see you again," she said, attempting to shrug off her awkwardness as she shook the man's hand.

"So what can I do for you, Miss Moore?"

"I took the train up to visit some friends this afternoon. I've heard so much about the school, I thought I'd drop by and have a look around. See what all the fuss is about. It's a lovely building—and so large! How many students do you have here?"

"Just short of two hundred at the moment," Albert Sinclaire said proudly. "Although we may be accepting a larger number than usual next fall. The program has been a remarkable success. You must have heard that our first class will be moving on to college this year. All of our graduates have been accepted at Ivy League schools—without any intervention from Society members, I might add."

"Very impressive," Haven said, playing along. How long would it be before he showed her the door?

A phone began to ring, and the young man winced. He seemed torn for a moment, but on the second ring, he started backing toward the office.

"I'm terribly sorry, Miss Moore. I'd love to give you a tour of our school, but I'm quite busy at the moment. The headmaster is away on business, you see, and I'm the only one manning the fort. Would you mind if I let you have a look around on your own?"

Halcyon Hall was certainly full of surprises. "Is that allowed?" Haven asked.

"Well, *no*, not usually. But since you're a friend of the Society, I'm sure no one will mind. We're a school, after all, not a prison. The classrooms used by grades four through eight are on the second floor. High school classes are on the third floor, and living quarters are on the fourth. Feel free to wander around, listen in if you like. But please don't interrupt any lectures. If you have questions, I'll be right here in the front office."

"Thank you," Haven called as he bolted for the phone.

THE SECOND-FLOOR HALLS were decorated with student artwork. Haven remembered that her own grade school in Tennessee had tacked finger paintings and self-portraits to a giant bulletin board next to the principal's office. Haven's drawings had never been posted. They made the others' art look bad, a teacher had informed her. At Halcyon Hall, however, student art was framed behind glass, and with very good reason. Most of the works could have found a home in any New York City art gallery. Haven bent to examine a small white card beside a painting of an electrical storm passing over the Hudson Valley. The lightning illuminated a strange scene in the foreground, where two men in a cemetery were either digging a grave or exhuming a body. *Jillian Thomas, grade four*, the card read.

As she continued down the hall, Haven's ears detected the soft sound of a violin playing a Mozart sonata. Peeking through the little glass window set into one of the classroom doors, she saw a small boy with the instrument tucked under his chin. When the music ended, he blushed and took a bow while his classmates and teacher applauded with gusto. In another classroom across the hall, a girl of about the same age was drawing a series of complex molecules on a blackboard with multicolored chalk. It took Haven a minute to realize that the girl wasn't solving a problem posed by a teacher. She was actually instructing the class.

This was the nightmare academy Phoebe had described? The sinister school where terrible things happened to small, helpless children? A bell rang and suddenly rowdy kids rushed from their classrooms, barely acknowledging Haven's existence as they weaved around her. They were giggling, joking, tugging on each other's backpacks, whispering with their friends. They weren't even wearing uniforms, Haven noticed. Just their own jeans, sneakers, and sweaters.

"You lost, good-looking?" The high-pitched voice belonged to a little boy.

Haven looked down to find a short child with dark, curly hair. When he winked at her, she couldn't help but laugh. "No," she said. "I'm having a look around. Do you always flirt with older women?"

"Just the sexy ones," said the boy. A couple of his friends waiting across the hall giggled. He was putting on a show for them. "Are you somebody's mother or something?"

"What?" Haven feigned outrage. "I'm not old enough to be anyone's mother. What's your name, anyway?"

"Jorge," said the boy.

"I'm Haven. So, do you like going to school here, Jorge?"

"Yeah, it's great," the boy said. "Everyone's smart, and we get to study all the things that we like. It's a whole lot better than P.S. 20. That place always smelled like poop."

"Don't you ever miss your parents?" Haven asked.

"Why would I miss *them*?" The boy put on a tough face. "They drive up from the Bronx every weekend. I told them to stop. All the other parents come once a month, but my mom and dad won't leave me alone. They're *really* starting to cramp my style."

"Well, they're probably just proud of you," Haven said.

"Sure they are. I'm going to be someone very important when I grow up. Everyone here is."

"Do you know what you want to do?" Haven asked.

"First I'm going to be a male model," said the boy.

"Of course." Haven barely managed to keep a straight face. "That makes perfect sense."

"Yeah, and then when I'm older, I'm going to go into politics. That's what I did the last time around. And Mr. Adam says it would be a shame to let this personality go to waste."

"He's certainly right about that," Haven agreed. "What about your two friends over there?"

Jorge pointed at the first boy. "Inventor," he said. Then he gestured toward the second boy. "Alcoholic."

"Hey!" the second boy whined. "That was two whole lives ago!"

"I'm kidding, you old drunk," Jorge laughed. "He was some kind of famous writer or something. You wanna come have lunch with us, Miss Haven? It's hamburger day."

"Thanks," Haven said, "but I should probably be getting back to the city soon."

"Well, next time you're in town, why don't you look me up?"

"Sure thing, Jorge," Haven told him. "I definitely will."

"See?" she heard Jorge tell his friends as the trio sauntered toward the cafeteria. "I *told* you I've always had a way with the ladies."

HAD SHE MISSED something? Haven wondered. Was there a secret dungeon under her feet, or a frigid attic where ill-behaved students lived on a diet of stale bread and murky water? Every child she passed on her way upstairs to the high school classrooms seemed as normal and happy as Jorge. The teachers and other adults she encountered in the halls either smiled or politely nodded in her direction. Nothing seemed out of the ordinary. Except.

A locker door swung closed, and Haven found herself face-to-face with Milo Elliot. He wore a navy blazer with brass buttons over a crisp oxford shirt. His blond hair defied the laws of gravity, and his blue eyes were blank. Haven had encountered toasters with more personality. Where was the charismatic young man from the fundraiser? Was there a switch or a button somewhere on his back that brought the android to life?

"Pardon me," Milo said, stepping around Haven. He gave no indication that he'd recognized her. Three books were tucked under his arm. She tried to read the titles, but all she could see was the name of one author, Edward Bernays.

Milo opened a door in the hall and joined a class already in progress. Relieved, Haven continued her tour, strolling by a room filled with teenagers just a few years younger than herself. A swatch of bright silk caught Haven's eye as she passed, and she quickly doubled back.

At the front of the class there stood a plain girl in a dazzling dress—a *robe à la française* grand enough for Napoleon's wedding.

The girl spun slowly as a boy pointed out details of the costume she wore. He was a slender bottle-blond with features prettier and more delicate than those of his female classmates. He had created the dress, Haven could see, and it was nothing short of a masterpiece. The boy's skills with a needle rivaled her own. And his sense of color and proportion were every bit as good as Beau's.

Haven's head jerked toward the other students. They were quietly taking notes. A boy at the back, a burly athletic type, raised his hand and posed a thoughtful question about the stitching on the gown's bodice. There were none of the snickers or jibes Beau had been forced to endure back in Snope City, Tennessee. No one inquired where the boy kept all the dresses he made for himself. Or asked him what kind of panties he wore under his jeans. Here the boy was accepted as an artist, and his talents were given the praise they deserved.

Haven turned away from the scene, a sob lodged in her throat. She wondered if the boy had any idea just how lucky he was. If only Beau could have found a place like Halcyon Hall—a place where he didn't have to throw punches or footballs just to earn a little grudging respect. It had taken every ounce of Beau's strength to survive in Snope City, and the wounds he'd suffered might never heal.

Who knew what Adam's motives had been when he first founded Halcyon Hall? Haven no longer cared. In the end he'd created a school where kids like Beau had a chance to become the people they were meant to be. Maybe Adam had once planned to turn them into mindless drones like Milo Elliot. But there were two things Haven now knew for certain. The Halcyon Hall kids weren't all little robots. And the Ouroboros Society had to be saved.

CHAPTER THIRTY

The café door flew open with a bang. Owen Bell stood on the threshold and let his eyes scan the room. Haven, Alex, and Calum sat at a table in the center of the empty restaurant while an anxious waiter lurked behind the counter. Haven had asked Alex for Owen's number, hoping she could meet him alone for coffee, but Alex had insisted on organizing a get-together.

"Alex! Did you make them shut down this whole place just for us?" Owen asked as he shrugged off his coat. "Don't you think that's a *little* obnoxious?"

"Is it?" Alex sounded genuinely surprised. "But I'm paying the owner handsomely."

"I believe Mr. Bell was thinking of the other customers, my dear," Calum explained as though translating from another language. "He's always so considerate."

Owen gave Haven's shoulder a friendly squeeze. "You know, I've been to your house, Alex. You have a ten-thousand-dollar espresso machine sitting in your kitchen and a maid who actually knows how to use it. Why did you feel the need to boot everyone out of a café at eleven o'clock on a Thursday morning?"

"Owen loves to lecture me like this," Alex said, rolling her eyes as she turned to Haven. "He thinks I don't remember what it's like to be a real human being."

"It's not *you*," Calum said. "Owen's turning into a robot. He doesn't know how to have fun anymore. I bet he's not even going to the party tonight."

"Party?" Haven asked.

"One of the fashion people is throwing it," Alex explained. "You must come! There will be tons of members who'll be thrilled to meet you."

"Forget networking, this party's going to be a throwback to the good old days," Calum said. "Booze, drugs, and pretty boys and girls who haven't learned how to balance their accounts."

"My three favorite things," Owen noted mirthlessly. "Too bad I have to work tonight."

"He means he needs to hang out with his best friend, Milo," Calum said.

"Milo doesn't have any *friends*," Owen countered. "He has *contacts*. He collects people who can help make him president."

"President of the OS?" Haven asked.

"President of the *U.S.*," Owen corrected.

"Owen, I know I've said it a thousand times, but you're the one who should have a future in politics," Alex remarked.

"And I've told you a thousand times—I'm a behind-the-scenes guy," Owen said. "I don't need the limelight like the two of you do. I prefer to write the speeches, not give them."

"Oh, but you'd look so good in the limelight!" Alex said before appealing to Haven. "Can't you just see him in one of his navy suits standing in front of an American flag? He'd look so handsome and trustworthy. He could be our first gay president."

Haven tried not to show her surprise. It had never occurred to her that Owen Bell might be gay. It had never occurred to her that he might have a sex life of any sort.

"You don't get it, do you, Alex?" said Calum, leaning across the table. Haven could see he was about to explode. Whatever was about to be unleashed must have been building inside him for quite some time. "Owen stays behind the scenes because he doesn't want anyone to know he's a big old poof."

Owen refused to take the bait. "I value my privacy. I don't want people poking their noses into my business."

Calum wasn't buying it. He seemed personally offended. "You sure that's the reason? You're not in the Middle Ages anymore, Owen. Being gay isn't a capital offense here in the twenty-first century. There are plenty of people like us in public office."

"There's no one like *you* in public office," Owen tried to joke. Calum didn't laugh.

"You know, if someone asked *me* to go into politics or take over the Society, you can bet your ass *I* wouldn't be afraid."

"Calum!" Alex said, looking shocked. "We're supposed to be having fun. Haven doesn't need to hear you two bickering."

"Well, I'm sick to death of listening to everyone ramble on and on about what a fantastic leader Owen would make. How can he inspire people if he's ashamed of who he is?" He locked eyes with Owen. "What would lover boy think if he knew you'd become such a wuss?"

"Calum!" Alex grabbed the young man by the back of his shirt and pulled him up out of his chair. "That's enough. You come with me *right* now!" She dragged him over to the café's counter and forced him to look at the pastry display with her while he cooled off.

"Wow," Haven said. "That was intense. I didn't know Calum had it in him."

"You didn't?" Owen asked. "You were under the impression that Calum Daniels is a sweet, gentle soul?"

"No, but I didn't think he could be so judgmental."

"It's easy for Calum to judge me," Owen said. "He spent his childhood being coddled by the Society. I spent mine with two otherwise decent people who think homosexuality is a moral disease. I left home a year ago, and it may take a few more years to recover from that particular experience. And believe it or not, Haven, this has been one of my easiest lives. I've told Calum a little bit about my previous existences, but he'll still never understand how it feels to be betrayed, disinherited, thrown in jail, or murdered—just for being gay. I've had nightmares almost every single night since I was a kid. So *that's* why I'm not eager to publicize my preferences. But, for the record, I don't hide them, either. Calum says I'm being archaic. Maybe he's right."

"Even if he is, it doesn't give him an excuse to be mean," Haven said angrily. "Why in the hell are you friends with him, anyway?"

"Calum decided to be friends with *me*," Owen said, setting her straight. "I've never had much of a say in the matter."

"Well, I know someone you might get along with a little bit better," Haven said, rushing to complete her secret mission before Alex and Calum returned to the table. Owen, she'd decided, was the one person who might stand a chance of convincing Iain to spare the Society. "He used to be a member of the OS, but he left because it was so corrupt. I've been trying to tell him that it's going to be a whole new place soon. I haven't been very successful. I think he needs to talk to someone like you."

Owen shook his head. "I hate to disappoint you, Haven, but even without the drug dealing and prostitution, the OS is almost the same as it was when I joined."

"What do you mean?" Haven asked, her enthusiasm trickling away.

"Look around." Owen gestured to the empty restaurant. "Is *this* how points are meant to be used? To let some nineteen-year-old movie star empty out an entire café on a Thursday morning? I'm not insulting

Alex. She's a sweet girl, and she doesn't know any better. But I'm fairly sure this is not what August Strickland had in mind when he devised the OS points system."

"Dr. Strickland didn't invent the system," Haven said. "There were no points while he was alive. They were introduced after he died."

Owen grinned. "That's right! Alex told me that you were one of the original members of the Society. So there were no points back then, huh?"

"Nope."

"So how did people keep track of the favors they performed?"

"They *didn't*," Haven said. "Dr. Strickland taught that doing good should be its own reward."

"Interesting theory," Owen mused.

"You know, I *really* think you should meet my friend," Haven repeated just as the door opened, and two men entered the café. They were both dressed in Dockers and white button-down shirts. They looked nothing alike, and yet they could have been twins.

"We're closed," Alex snipped from the other side of the room. "There's another café just down the street."

"Miss Moore," said one of the men. "Will you please come with us?"

Haven rose from her seat to face the gray men. Only one person could have sent the pair. "Why?" she asked. "Do you know what Adam wants?"

"No, Miss Moore. We were only told to find you."

"Do you need help?" Owen whispered to Haven. Across the room, Calum and Alex stood watching the scene, their jaws agape. But they didn't dare make a move.

"You need to come with us to the Society," stated the second gray man.

"Haven?" Owen whispered again, this time with more urgency. "Do you want me to deal with this?"

"It's okay," Haven assured him, though she was certain it wasn't. Adam would never have her hauled away unless Haven was about to be punished. If there hadn't been witnesses on the scene, she might have collapsed under the weight of her fear. But somehow Haven managed to keep her knees from buckling, and she hid her hands in her pockets so no one could see how much they were shaking.

"Let's go," said the second man, taking Haven by the elbow and leading her out of the café.

"How did they know where to find her?" Haven heard Calum casually inquire before the door slammed behind her.

CHAPTER THIRTY-ONE

The two gray men deposited Haven on the front stairs of the Ouroboros Society.

"Wait inside," one of them instructed her. They remained stationed on the sidewalk in front of the building, but they didn't follow
her up the steps.

Beyond the front door, it was business as usual, and several members were milling about the lobby.

"Hello, Miss Moore," the receptionist said pleasantly. "Adam will
be with you in a moment. Would you like to take a seat in the waiting
area?"

Haven walked in slow circles around the room but didn't settle into a
chair. She was trying very hard to appear calm while she secretly fought
the urge to vomit. Something had gone terribly wrong. A door opened
on the other side of the lobby, and a group of children emerged. Haven recognized them as the birthday kids she'd seen bird-watching
with Adam. They walked, almost single file, past Haven and toward

the front door. The last person in line was Flora, who stopped to zip up her coat.

"Hello, Miss Moore," she said when she spotted Haven.

Haven cleared her throat. "Hi, Flora. How are you? Did you have a good birthday?"

"Yes, it was wonderful," Flora said. "But I'm looking forward to getting back to school." There was something so odd about the kid, Haven thought once again. Flora had changed so much since their first meeting. Then, all at once, Haven figured it out. The politeness, the slightly stilted language—even the oddly penetrating stare. Flora was mimicking Adam Rosier. "I heard you were there yesterday. What did you think?"

"How do you know I was at Halcyon Hall?" Haven asked, feeling suddenly exposed.

Flora frowned. "Everyone knows. We don't have many visitors. Did you like it?"

"Of course I did!" Haven tried to laugh and nearly choked instead. Was this why she'd been dragged to the OS? Was Adam furious that she'd visited Halcyon Hall without his permission? "It's *so* much better than the school I attended. All the classes seem so interesting! What are you studying there?" Haven babbled.

"The same subjects as everyone else."

"But don't you have a special gift? Weren't you an epidemiologist in your last life? Shouldn't you be studying biology or medicine?"

"I don't *need* to study those things," Flora informed her politely. "I already know everything I need to know about medicine. There are many more subjects I'll need to master if I'm going to be ready for the future. Adam says we all have a great responsibility on our shoulders."

"Flora." It was the receptionist. "Please don't dillydally. The car is waiting for you outside."

"Bye, Miss Moore," Flora said. "I hope I see you soon."

"Yes," Haven said. "I hope so too."

Haven felt someone watching her. Adam was standing in the door of the room on the other side of the reception area. Haven hurried over.

"What's going on?" she asked. "Why am I here? Is this about Halcyon Hall?"

"I apologize for dragging you away from your friends," Adam said. "But I needed to speak with you at once."

"Is this about Beau?" she tried again.

"No. And it's not a subject we should discuss in public. Come with me, Haven."

Adam led the way up the stairs toward his office on the second floor. Inside, he pointed to a chair. Haven sat down while he closed the door. He paced the small room a few times, then came to rest three feet away from her. He leaned back against his desk and said nothing. His fingers gripped the edge of the wood with such force that Haven expected chunks to snap off in his hands.

"Adam?"

Suddenly his black eyes were on her. "I know Iain Morrow is alive."

Haven could feel the red-hot flush creeping across her chest and scaling her neck. "What?" she managed to croak.

"I've known for months. You were spotted together in Rome. My people tell me that Marta Vega is alive as well. I doubt that comes as a surprise to you." It wasn't an accusation—merely a statement of fact.

"You knew all of this and you didn't—"

"I promised you this life to lead as you chose, and I will keep my promise no matter what happens."

That was one possible explanation, Haven thought, her mind racing. Unfortunately it wasn't the only one. Months had passed since Adam had discovered the truth about Iain. If Adam had set his sights on revenge, he'd had more than enough time to put together a plan. Haven shuddered at the thought—and prayed that Adam would prove true to his word.

"I wouldn't have said a thing," Adam continued, "but Iain approached one of my men this morning. He asked to meet with me."

"He did?" Haven said, genuinely shocked. She had never known Iain to be so reckless. What was he trying to accomplish? What was he trying to prove to her? Phoebe had been right to warn her. If Haven wasn't careful, Iain might get them both killed.

Adam remained motionless—so still that he couldn't possibly be breathing. "May I ask what the state of your relationship is at this moment?" He looked down. "I wouldn't dare inquire if it weren't for the other night."

"Our relationship?" She could barely hear her own words over the pounding in her chest.

"Are you and Iain together?"

Adam had caught her off guard. She should have had a response prepared, but Haven had never expected the question to be posed so bluntly. What would happen if she said yes? At the very best Adam might call off the search for Beau. She didn't want to imagine the worst he might do. Everything now depended on her answer.

"We came back to New York when Beau disappeared," Haven explained. "I thought the Pythia could help me uncover the clues I needed to save him. Iain wanted to hire a private investigator. He didn't want me anywhere near the Ouroboros Society. Anywhere near *you*. He made clear from the beginning that he didn't trust me. When he heard that I'd seen you at the spa, he went crazy. I could tell that he didn't really give a damn about Beau. So I asked for your help instead. Iain and I haven't been together since. As far as I'm concerned, it's over. He didn't trust me, and he wasn't there for me when I needed him."

She lifted herself slowly from her chair, approaching Adam as cautiously as she would a wounded beast. When she was close enough, she took one of his icy hands. Her touch seemed to reassure him.

"Why did Iain want to meet with you?" Haven asked again. "Did he say?"

"Yes," Adam said. "He wants you back. And for the first and last time, he has my sympathy."

"It doesn't matter what Iain wants anymore," Haven declared.

"How can you be certain that you won't forgive him? You've for-given *me*, haven't you?" There was such sadness in Adam's question that Haven's heart hurt. "You don't need to answer. But you should know that Iain won't give you up easily. I believe he asked me to meet him with the hope of imprisoning me."

"What makes you think that?" Haven asked, forcing herself to speak.

Adam must have mistaken the grimace on her face for confusion. "Iain suggested we meet at an address in Harlem. He said it was neutral ground. I sent one of my men to do some reconnaissance. It was a store-front on a block slated for demolition. There wasn't much to see at the location in question, but my man discovered an abandoned bank vault in the basement of the building next door. I suspect that's where I might have found myself had I agreed to the meeting."

Adam paused to study Haven's response, and she prayed he would misread her horror. She now knew what Iain had been trying to accomplish. Phoebe had told them both where the Horae planned to confine the magos. Iain had substituted himself as bait. Had he believed he could lock Adam away on his own? Or had Iain planned to sacrifice himself just to prove that Adam was evil? Whatever the case, it was pure insanity.

"I doubt the vault was Iain's idea," Adam continued. "The modus operandi leads me to believe that he's been in touch with a group called the Horae. Have you heard of them?"

"No," Haven lied, hoping Adam didn't know more than he was letting on. "Who are they?"

"You might say they're my enemies. The Horae devote themselves to hindering my work. Once or twice a millenium they convince some gullible soul to assist them with their schemes. They spin a tragic story about how they were once sisters who met a terrible end because of something I did."

"The story isn't true?" Haven asked, her mind reeling. She had come so close to being that gullible soul.

"It could be. As you know, I've unleashed horrible things on the world. But in this case the accusations against me are false. The Horae were never innocent girls."

"What are they?"

"The world is full of forces that humans don't understand, Haven. I bring chaos. The Horae do their best to restore order. There are others at work, as well. We aren't the only ones."

"I don't understand."

"It's much like the weather," Adam explained. "Most people think of the weather as sun or rain. Heat or cold. But there are countless invisible forces forever battling to bring about one or the other. The battle itself is the most important part. It can't be allowed to end. If one force ever prevailed, there would be drought. If another won, the whole world would wash away."

"And the Horae are trying to end the battle by locking you up in a bank vault?" It sickened Haven to think that she'd almost helped them.

"They want their day in the sun. And they'll get it any way they can. They're as ruthless as I've ever been. You must realize that order is no better than chaos. Ask anyone who lived under Joseph Stalin— or the other tyrants and dictators who've been friendly with the head of the Horae. Remember, I told you I don't know what could happen to me now. I may be evolving, but the Horae are not."

"If you change, does that mean the Horae could win?" Haven asked. "What happens if there's no chaos left to battle their order?"

"I have no intention of letting them win," Adam assured her. "I'm simply testing a new approach. Chaos doesn't always demand death and destruction. You saw Halcyon Hall yesterday?"

"Yes, I'm sorry I didn't—"

"There's no need to apologize. Now you know what I have planned for the Ouroboros Society. Imagine each of those young people sent out into the world. They've never been told what to think. They've never had their creativity stifled by ridiculous rules or petty little minds. They will have all the resources they'll need at their disposal. Think of how they might shake up society. They have the power to create a new brand of chaos."

It would have sounded wonderful if there hadn't been one little fact still nagging at Haven. "You founded Halcyon Hall ten years ago, Adam. You were different back then. What did you originally have in mind for the students?"

Adam's eyes dropped from Haven's face to the floor. "I must admit that I had other intentions in those days. I set out to find the most gifted souls—the ones who possessed incredible power. I believed that by recruiting them as children, I could make them loyal to me. When the time came, I would manipulate their power however I chose."

It took every ounce of Haven's courage to ask the next question. "How did you make all those kids loyal to you?"

"I supported them. Educated them. Gave them my time and attention."

"That's it?" She found it hard to believe.

"You were imagining something slightly more sinister? Brainwashing, perhaps? You've been to Halcyon Hall. Did the children appear to be brainwashed?"

"No," Haven said, thinking back to Jorge, the little boy she'd met.

"I've never needed to employ such heavy-handed techniques," Adam explained. "Power is neither good nor bad. With the right inspiration, it can easily be nudged in either direction. Now the students at Halcyon Hall will be encouraged to improve the world. And they have been given the education to do so. Did you like what you saw during your visit to the school?"

"I was impressed," Haven admitted. "It really seemed like a wonderful place."

"I'm glad you thought so. Perhaps someday we can expand the program—start more schools around the world. But first . . . first we need to take care of the problem in front of us."

"You mean Iain?" Haven fell back into the present with an unpleasant thud. "What are you going to do to him?"

"That depends," Adam replied. "What would you like me to do?"

"You're asking *me*?"

"Why not? You know him better than anyone."

Haven had never faced a more terrible test. If Adam was still a monster, then the wrong answer—whatever it was—would risk three lives. If he wasn't, she needed to stay close to him. He was still her best hope of saving Beau. She was out on a limb, and there was no going back.

"You're the one who came to my rescue, Adam. My loyalties lie with you now. You should do what you think is necessary," Haven said, knowing full well that the Adam of the past would never have allowed a dangerous rival to live.

"You say that to please me, but I know you wouldn't want to see anyone harmed," Adam replied. "So I will do my best to ignore Iain Morrow for now. But there is one thing I must ask of you in return."

"Anything," Haven said, hiding her relief. She'd trusted her instincts and saved Iain's life.

"There's a gathering at the Ouroboros Society tonight. Nothing terribly important, but a few of our highest-ranking members will be there. Will you come?"

"Of course."

"As my date?"

"Yes."

"Do you realize what that means?" Adam asked. "People will know who you are. It will be our first appearance together as a couple."

"I know," Haven said.

"Things will change," Adam said. "In ways you might not expect."

"I know," Haven said.

CHAPTER THIRTY-TWO

The sound of ringing took Haven by surprise. Voice mail picked up, and Iain's voice on the message made her heart do a somersault before she remembered how furious she was with him. How could she still love someone whose recklessness had come so close to destroying them both?

"What in the hell were you trying to do, Iain?" she hissed into the phone. She was standing by the service entrance of an apartment building on Nineteenth Street. There wasn't a soul in sight, but Haven couldn't shake the feeling that someone might be listening. "Did you really think Adam would take the bait and come after you? Were you hoping to show me how stupid I've been? Well, you know what? Turns out I was right all along. Adam *is* different now. But I would never have risked our lives to prove it. You thought you had everything figured, out didn't you? Well, all you managed to do was make me get closer to him. Tonight Adam's going to introduce me at the Society as his girlfriend. Do you have any idea what that means? Do you—"

There was a loud beep in her ear.

"Your message has reached the maximum length," said a cheerful automated voice.

"Aaarrrrghh!" Haven screamed into the phone, no longer afraid of who might hear her. She kicked the wall and considered giving it a punch for good measure. Instead she stood with her forehead pressed to the concrete, breathing deeply and trying to recapture some calm. She was squeezing the phone in her hand like a stress ball when an e-mail arrived from Beau Decker's address.

There was no message, just an attachment. A single photo of Beau's face. One of his eyes was closed, already swelling, and the other glared up at his photographer with helpless rage. He'd been knocked to the ground, and blood poured from fresh gashes on his right temple and lower lip. Another trickle left a crimson trail from his nose to his ear. It had been bad enough to know that Beau might have been injured. But seeing him suffer was far worse than Haven had ever imagined.

The world went quiet, and she saw nothing but the picture on the screen. Adam and Iain were forgotten. Haven had no other worries, no other concerns. The terror coursing through her system had washed them all away. There were only two things that mattered. Finding Beau. And punishing the people who'd hurt him.

The photo disappeared, and Leah Frizzell's name appeared in glowing letters on the phone's screen. Haven answered the call.

"They hurt him again." She didn't have time to waste on hello.

"I know," Leah said. "Whoever took the picture sent it to everyone in Beau's address book. But he's alive, Haven . . ."

"I gotta go," Haven announced, her voice flat and emotionless. "I'm going to find the person who did this."

"And I'm gonna help," Leah called out before Haven could hang up. "Listen to me, Haven. You're in shock. Don't do anything until I see you."

"There's not enough time for you to get on a plane."

"I'm already here! I got a flight out of Raleigh last night. My uncle Earl let me use his credit card. I was going to call you this morning."

"You flew in last night? Where did you sleep?"

"On a bench in a park called Union Square. Matter of fact, I just woke up when my phone started beeping."

A jolt of annoyance brought Haven back to the world. "You slept on a park bench, Leah? Do you know how dangerous that is? This isn't Snope City. It's not even *Durham*. There are people here who hunt tourists for sport. I've already got one friend in trouble—I can't save you too!"

"Save that anger for the kidnappers, Haven. We both know no-body's gonna bother *me*."

"Well, stay where you are," Haven ordered. She had already started jogging west. "I'm coming to get you. How'd you end up in Union Square, anyway?"

"This is the place I've been seeing in my visions," Leah said. "I found the round subway entrance shaped like a temple. In fact, I found the man I've been looking for too. He was right here waiting for me when I showed up at five thirty this morning. I was so tired that I almost started talking to him before I figured out he's just a statue of Gandhi. You know the one?"

"Yeah," Haven panted. She'd seen the statue a hundred times. "Go stand next to Gandhi. I'll be there in two minutes."

THE PARK WAS PACKED with people braving the cold to forage for lunch, but, as always, Leah Frizzell was impossible to miss. An orange and black hunting cap sat on top of her head, and stringy red hair stuck out from beneath it. She was wearing an old army-issue coat with the name FRIZZELL stitched above the pocket, and a pair of battered black combat boots. Above the boots and below the hem of her skirt, four inches of bright white flesh could be seen. Pedestrians gawked at the odd-looking, underdressed girl and walked well out of their way to avoid her. She held up a hand as soon as she caught sight of Haven running in her direction.

"Jesus, Leah! Didn't you pack some tights or leggings or something?" Haven asked between gulps of air. Even Gandhi had an icicle hanging from the tip of his nose, and Leah Frizzell was walking around with bare legs. Haven almost wished she hadn't answered Leah's call. The last thing she needed was a bumpkin to babysit.

Leah seemed to read her thoughts. "Don't think you need to take care of me, Haven Moore. I may be a hillbilly, but I ain't stupid."

"You just flew a thousand miles to meet a statue," Haven noted.

"Yeah, and I reckon it was worth it. I found out what was causing that terrible smell in my visions." Leah pointed down at the sidewalk. "I had another one this morning, and I saw a bunch of bodies lying right here."

Suddenly Leah didn't seem quite so silly. "Dead bodies? Who were they?"

"Dunno. But from the smell, they'd been lying there long enough to get nice and ripe. Didn't look so pretty, either."

"What are you going to do?" Haven asked.

"Wait for another vision. You can't rush these things, you know." Leah always seemed so unflappable, as if someone were whispering instructions into her ear.

"A few days ago you said something terrible was about to happen. Now you're having visions of bodies lying in the streets. And you're just going to *wait*?"

"I've got some time," Leah replied, still as calm as ever. "The dead people were all wearing short sleeves, so I'm guessing I've got till summer to fix whatever needs fixing. I think Beau's problems are probably a little more urgent. So let's get started."

"First I have to call Adam and let him know what's happened."

"Excuse me?" Leah asked. "Adam *Rosier*?"

"He's been helping me look for Beau," Haven said, dialing the OS main number.

"Put the phone down for a second," Leah ordered. The girl hadn't raised her voice or changed her tone, but somehow Haven knew it wasn't just a request. She slid her hands back into her pockets. "Why didn't you tell me any of this?"

"I don't know," Haven admitted. "A lot has happened in the past few days." Why was she standing in the cold answering questions when Beau was seriously hurt?

"Well, I'm listening now," Leah said.

Haven sighed. "Remember the woman you saw surrounded by smoke?" Leah nodded. "Her name is Phoebe. She's the head of a group called the Horae. There are twelve of them, and they have human bodies. But they're not really human. They're Adam's enemies. They bring order while he brings chaos." Haven stopped to make sure Leah was following.

"Okay," Leah said, as if Haven hadn't said anything out of the ordinary.

"Phoebe told me that she would only help me identify the person who kidnapped Beau if I helped her lock Adam Rosier away. The Horae think Adam has been recruiting children into the OS to form some sort of army, and they want to stop him."

"How are you supposed to help the Horae lock him away?"

"By pretending to fall for Adam and luring him into a trap."

Leah blinked. "Sounds awful risky. I'm surprised you agreed."

"I was willing to do anything to save Beau. But when I started spending time with Adam, I realized he's not the same person he used to be. He's trying to clean up the Ouroboros Society. And he has the police commissioner and the FBI searching for Beau. I don't want to work with the Horae anymore. I don't want to betray Adam. . . ." She clutched her phone. "Please let me just call him. We've got to act fast if we're going to save Beau!"

"Hold on, Haven. I have a couple more questions. Where's Iain been this whole time?"

"It's a long story. But I'll tell you where he is right now: in the way. He thinks I'm crazy for believing Adam could change. He thinks I've fallen for him. So he's been trying to lock Adam away all by himself."

Leah lifted an eyebrow. "*Have* you fallen for Adam?"

Haven stood stunned. Leah's blunt question had hit her with the force of a medieval mace. She wanted to laugh or make light of it all. But Leah wasn't the sort to imagine things that weren't really there.

"I don't know," Haven admitted. "I still love Iain as much as ever. I just—"

"Do you think Adam loves you? You're sure it's not just some sick obsession?"

Haven's response didn't seem to come quickly enough for Leah. "Don't *think* about it, Haven. Just answer the question."

"He loves me," Haven replied. "I'm positive of that."

"And you really believe that he's changed?"

"Yes. Do you think I'm crazy too?"

Leah didn't pause to ponder the possibility. "No," she said, sounding completely certain. "I wouldn't have guessed Adam was able to love *anyone*. But if he does, we should probably rethink a few things."

Haven shook her head. She didn't want to think about Adam or Iain. She wanted her focus back. Beau was the only person she could care about now.

"It doesn't matter what Adam feels," Haven said. "The only thing that matters is *this*." She hit a key on her phone and held up the picture.

"The police already have the photo," Leah said. "I forwarded it to them while I was waiting for you. Half the people on the mailing list probably did the same thing. So you don't need to call Adam if that's all he can do."

That wasn't all he could do. Haven had twenty OS points sitting in the account Lucy Fredericks had opened for her. If fifteen points could purchase a party on the top of the Empire State Building, twenty could buy the services of a thug or two. When the cops found the people who'd beaten Beau, Haven wanted to make them suffer. Adam would know the perfect man for the job, and he wouldn't ask any questions. He'd understand why it was necessary. But Leah Frizzell never would.

"Then tell me what you think *I* should do!" Haven nearly shouted at Leah.

"Remember when I called you in Florence? I told you the clue you needed to find might be in your memories. I wasn't just making small talk. I think we should pay a visit to this Phoebe character. I wouldn't mind having a word with her myself."

"You want to talk to *Phoebe*? After everything I just told you?"

"I'm starting to think this is all connected somehow," Leah said, her eyes scanning Union Square as though the answers she needed might be hiding behind one of the trees. "Beau's disappearance. The dead people here in this park. These creatures who've been blackmailing you. You falling for Adam Rosier."

"I never said—"

"Okay, okay," Leah said. "You know how to find Phoebe?"

"She won't help me unless I betray Adam."

Leah shrugged. "So let her think you will. If she's been lying to you, why do you reckon you owe *her* the truth?"

"You're right. Phoebe has a house up near Harlem. But I'm not supposed to go there by myself. The Horae are afraid I'll be followed."

Leah looked around. "I don't see anyone watching us, do you?"

"No," Haven admitted.

"Then come on, let's get cracking."

CHAPTER THIRTY-THREE

Haven banged on the door of the little yellow house on the corner of Sylvan Terrace. Blue-haired Vera answered, and her eyes bulged.

"Haven! What are you doing?" the young woman whispered, looking around nervously. "You shouldn't have brought someone with you. Please go before Phoebe finds out. You'll make trouble for all of us."

"No one followed us," Leah stated, her tone polite yet firm. "But if you don't let us in soon, everyone in town's gonna know where we are."

"Is that Haven at the door?" Vera cringed at the sound of her leader's voice. Stepping away from the entrance, she gave Phoebe a full view of their unexpected guests.

The old woman smiled until she caught sight of Leah. "Who is *that*?" she screeched. "No one said you were allowed to bring friends, Haven! Get inside before anyone sees you. How dare you risk our plans like this?"

Haven didn't answer. She was watching Vera, who had anticipated Phoebe's outburst. The calm, composed head of the Horae must have been just an act.

"It's my fault, ma'am," Leah explained once they were inside the circular room with the spiral staircase. She wasn't at all intimidated. "You see, I'm the one who told Haven she needed to find you. Now that I'm in New York for a visit, I thought I'd drop by and say hi. So don't blame Haven. I made her bring me up here."

Phoebe trained her wrath on the redheaded girl. "Just who do you think . . ." Her words trailed off, and her anger drained away. "Did you say that *you* told Haven to see me? *You're* the reason she came to the spa?"

"I saw you in a vision," Leah explained. "You were sitting in a cloud of smoke with a towel on your head."

"A vision of the future?" Phoebe asked in an awestruck whisper. "Is it you?"

"Is it *who*?" Haven asked.

Phoebe ignored the question. "Why have you come here?" she asked Leah. "What have you seen?"

Leah grinned at the woman, playing dumb like a pro. But the power in the room had shifted with a single sentence. Leah was in charge now. "My name is Leah Frizzell. I'm a friend of Haven's from Snope City, Tennessee. I'm here to see what y'all can do to help us find our friend Beau."

"We are already doing all we can."

"Are you?" Leah inquired. "Haven's not so sure about that. I think it's time we all had a chat, don't you?"

"We should do as she asks." Vera stepped forward and put a hand on Phoebe's arm. "If she's the one . . ."

Phoebe clearly didn't appreciate the advice, and she pushed the younger woman back into place.

"Our sisters will want—" Vera tried again.

"*Enough!*" Phoebe shouted. "All of you. Follow me to the council room."

THE CHALK-COLORED CHAMBER was perfectly round and empty but for a blazing fireplace and twelve regal chairs arranged in a circle. There were no windows to distract the eye. No interior design to admire. Only the ceiling was decorated. Haven gazed up at the map of the heavens painted in gold on the plaster. For a moment, she could have sworn she'd seen it move. Then her attention was drawn to the small group of women who were wandering in through the room's open door. Vera and Cleo were there, as was the blonde girl from Florence. None of them spoke, but Haven realized they'd come to see Leah.

Phoebe opened her mouth to speak, but Leah interrupted. "Haven's got a few things she'd like to get off her chest first. I think you better sit down." She pulled one of the chairs out of the circle and gestured for Phoebe to take a seat.

Phoebe's mouth clamped shut, and she did as she was told. Six other Horae came to stand behind her chair. Haven's eyes rested on Leah. She was just a scrawny nineteen-year-old girl with a few extra servings of pluck. Why would the Horae obey her commands?

"Haven?" Leah asked. "You wanna get us started?"

"I know who the Horae really are," Haven announced. "I know the story about the twelve murdered sisters isn't true."

"The magos told you that, didn't he? How dare you speak of us to him! How dare you believe his lies!"

"Ah, ah, ah," Leah chided Phoebe. "You'll get your turn. Haven's talking now."

"Lies?" Haven continued. "Let's talk about lies. You double-crossed Iain, and you've been lying about Halcyon Hall this whole time. I took the train up there yesterday. There wasn't any 'impenetrable security.' They aren't brainwashing the kids or abusing them in any way. Adam may have had other plans when he opened Halcyon Hall, but now it's just a *school*, Phoebe."

Phoebe's smirk questioned Haven's convictions. "You're certain of that, are you?"

"I just know what I saw, Phoebe. And after I got back, I swore I wasn't going to have anything to do with you witches. I'm only here because I have to find Beau as quickly as possible. But unless you help me see Naddo, I'm never setting foot on Sylvan Terrace again. Which would be a real shame, since I've got Adam right where you need him."

"Do you?" Phoebe leaned forward on her chair like a pit bull straining against its chain. "You think I don't know everything that goes on at the Ouroboros Society? I heard you were hauled in against your will to see the magos this morning. Maybe he's not as convinced of your love as you think."

"He wanted to tell me that he knows Iain is alive. He's known for months. I managed to convince him that I couldn't care less. I'm making my public debut as Adam's girlfriend tonight. There's a party at the Society."

The women standing behind Phoebe exchanged loaded looks.

"If this is true, it could be excellent news," their leader offered cautiously.

"But there is one little problem. Adam knows about the bank vault."

"*How*?"

"Iain. He asked Adam to meet him at the address on Lenox Avenue. Adam had the place checked out, and his men found the vault in the basement. I don't think I can ever convince him to follow me there."

"That *imbecile*!" Phoebe turned on the women gathered behind her as though they were to blame. "I told you we should have gotten Iain out of the way years ago! This is what we get for protecting people's *feelings*."

"Stop!" Haven barked. "Iain may have made a mistake, but I have a solution. I know where you can put Adam."

"Where? It took us *decades* to find an ideal spot."

"No!" Leah interrupted just as Haven was about to speak. "*First* Phoebe's gonna help us find the answers we need, and *then* we'll decide whether we want to help her."

Phoebe rose and stood with her face just inches from Leah's. The girl didn't flinch, but the rest of the Horae watched the confrontation with a mixture of fascination and horror. "If you insist," the old woman snarled. "Haven, follow me to the roof. The rest of you make *Miss Frizzell* comfortable."

"If you don't mind, I think I'd like to tag along with Haven and see how all this works," Leah said.

"Absolutely not." Phoebe refused to budge on the matter. "You may have brought Haven to us, but she must face the past on her own. When she's done, we'll find out if she has the courage to tell her *friends* what she's seen."

BEATRICE WAS STROLLING *along the banks of the Arno River, a young man by her side. Ahead, the bridge that the water once washed away had been rebuilt. Four doctors dressed in long dark coats and terrible, birdlike masks stopped to knock at the door of a building on the other side of the street. A frantic woman ushered them inside.*

"The sickness is spreading," Beatrice stated. Her mother had warned her to stay at home, but nowadays Beatrice did as she liked.

"Yes," the young man confirmed with no emotion in his voice. Beatrice glanced over at him. He was handsome—all of her friends thought so. Tall and dark with a resonant voice that told the world he was someone to be reckoned with. But his eyes could be cold. They had little of Ettore's warmth. She liked him—even trusted him—but she didn't love Adam the way she'd once loved Ettore.

"Piero told me that the pestilence arrived on your ships," Beatrice said. "He almost suggested that you brought it here." It couldn't be true, she reminded herself once more. Piero let his passions rule him.

He didn't always see things rationally.

"Your brother is jealous," the young man said, "because he can never have what we have."

Beatrice bit her lip with such force that she almost drew blood. "I shouldn't have told you," she said. "I know you don't care who Piero loves, but it wasn't a secret I was meant to share."

"We're to be married. There can be no secrets between us. Which is why I must speak with you now. It concerns your brother."

"Yes?"

"When was the last time you saw Piero?"

"We had an argument three days ago. He's been avoiding me since then. My mother says he hasn't been home. He's with Naddo, I suppose."

"He is with Naddo. But I'm afraid they're no longer in Florence."

"Where did they go?"

"I do not know. No one does, and that is a very good thing."

"Why?" Beatrice asked cautiously, not certain she wanted to hear the truth.

Adam turned to her. His icy fingers gripped her bare hands. "They were going to be arrested, Beatrice. The city's leaders know about their relationship. Piero fled Florence with Naddo. He asked me to say good-bye to you."

A stabbing pain made Beatrice jerk a hand free and clutch her stomach. "You spoke to him?" she managed to ask.

"I went to see him. I wanted to end the animosity between us. He agreed, and he shared his secret with me."

"But how will they survive?" Beatrice moaned.

"They have everything they need," the young man assured his fiancée. "I gave them more money than they can spend in a year. Your brother is very resourceful, and Naddo will always ensure that he says the right thing."

Beatrice watched the murky waters flow away from the city toward the sea. She knew she would never see her brother again.

"The men who have done this to my brother must pay," she said. "I want you to make them suffer."

"They will," he told her. "And very soon indeed."

"THAT *WASN'T* WHAT I wanted to see!" Haven blurted out before she was fully awake. "It's what you wanted to show me. You're trying to make me doubt myself! I already know Adam and Beatrice were engaged. I've known from the very beginning. I need to see Naddo, not *Adam!*"

Phoebe peeled off her mask. "Tell me about your vision."

"Adam told Beatrice that her brother and Naddo had fled the city."

"You're right," Phoebe agreed flatly. "That doesn't sound like the vision you need to have."

"I'm sick of all this!" Haven raged. "You obviously don't care whether I find Naddo or not. What is it that you want me to see, Phoebe?"

"If I knew, I would tell you," Phoebe responded. "Beatrice never explained why she decided not to sell her soul."

A snippet from a recent dream began playing in Haven's head. A small blonde girl screaming at Beatrice. A child who masqueraded as the daughter of a servant. "Wait a second. You were there too, weren't you, Phoebe? In Florence. I've dreamed about you. You were just a little girl back then."

Phoebe regarded Haven with something close to respect. "Yes. I was there, as were my sisters. We were the ones who led the magos to Beatrice. All you had to do was follow our instructions, and human-kind would have been free of him. But you betrayed us. The magos gave you everything you wanted, and you refused to listen to our warnings. But then something happened. Your brother disappeared with his lover. We don't know exactly what took place in the days that followed Piero's death, but we do know that you witnessed something that turned you against the magos. Whatever it was, you need to see it again."

"Why?" Haven demanded. "I've already agreed to help you."

The respect on Phoebe's face was replaced by a look of distaste. "We've been seeking your assistance for centuries, Haven. You never made it easy for us. You would betray us again in a heartbeat if we gave you the chance."

Haven's face began to burn. She couldn't let Phoebe see she was right. "I can prove that I'm willing to help. You need a new place to put Adam. Well, I've found one. It's in Green-Wood Cemetery in Brooklyn."

"I wish that were an option, but we can't kill the magos."

"That's not what I mean. Adam used to keep six bodies in that mansion near the Ouroboros Society. *My* bodies. Now he's decided to lay them to rest. He had a mausoleum constructed in Green-Wood Cemetery. It's built into the side of a hill, not far from a lake. It wouldn't take much to convince him to give me a tour of the place. And while we were there, you could lock him inside."

Phoebe considered the proposition. "I will send Chandra and Cleo to look for your tomb in the morning," she said. "Tonight I shall attend the Society's gathering. Like you, I am only prepared to believe what I see with my own two eyes. You tell me the magos is convinced of your love? If you have completed the task we set, I will know."

"Spy on me all you like, Phoebe. Show me whatever horrible thing you want me to see. But I'm not going to help you imprison Adam until I have the vision that will help me find Beau."

"Yes, you and your friend have made that perfectly clear. Now tell me: How do you know the girl you brought here today?"

"I grew up with her," Haven said. "She went to school with me and Beau."

"She sees the future, doesn't she?"

"You should ask Leah yourself," Haven said.

"I'm asking *you*, Haven."

"And I'm not saying anything."

"These games must stop!" The water tower shook with the force of Phoebe's fury. "If Leah is the one, you've been brought together for a reason. This is a development that I never anticipated."

"Like I said, Phoebe, you'll just have to ask Leah."

Phoebe rose and opened the tower door. "So let's find her," she snarled.

Inside the council room, Leah was still wearing her winter coat. The chamber was scorching hot, but the girl hadn't broken a sweat. Haven suddenly remembered seeing ten-year-old Leah climb off a school bus in the middle of a snowstorm wearing only a T-shirt and skirt. And one summer, she'd arrived at the Snope City public pool in a woolly sweater that would have fit a grown man. A gang of swim-suited boys had gathered to harass the strange girl. Beau stepped in to defend her, and a fight ensued. But Leah just sat in the sun, paying less attention to the scuffle than she had to the weather.

Haven thought back to the night Adam had left his coat behind when they went for a walk. The way Phoebe bore the swelter inside the water tower. They didn't feel heat or cold the way others did. Now Haven understood why the Horae took Leah so seriously. She couldn't be fully human. She had to be one of them.

"You see what you wanted to see?" Leah asked Haven.

"No, not yet," Haven said, looking at the girl through new eyes.

"Then I guess we'll be on our way," Leah told Phoebe. "It sure was nice to meet y'all."

"Wait!" Phoebe barked, then softened her tone. "Wait. *Please.*"

"Yeah?" Leah inquired.

"Do you have any idea who you are?" the old woman asked.

"Who?" Leah asked, though she didn't seem to care.

"In each generation, there is a single woman who can see the future. Others may glimpse it from time to time, but there's only one person able to give true prophecy. She comes to us in times of great trouble. For the past two millennia, we have called her the snake goddess."

"Well, if there's only one person who can see the future, I guess that would have to be me," Leah said with a shrug. "But I'm no goddess. My abilities are a gift from the Lord."

"What have you seen?" Phoebe demanded, her suspicion confirmed. "Something brought you here. What is it?"

Vera stepped forward. "We will do whatever you ask of us. But please tell us why your visions have led you here."

"I'll think about it and get back to ya'll," Leah told the Horae.

"*When?*" Phoebe asked.

"As soon as I've decided whether you really need to know. We'll see you when it's time for Haven's next vision."

No one dared stop them as they walked out of the house.

CHAPTER THIRTY-FOUR

"You have a lot of nerve showing up here after what you did to Iain the other night," Frances Whitman growled at Haven. Then she offered Leah an apologetic smile. "I'm sorry, you've found us in the middle of a family spat. My name is Frances."

"Leah," said the girl as she shook hands with the older woman.

"A pleasure to meet you, Leah," Frances said. "Please come in and make yourself at home in the living room. If you don't mind, I'd like to have a quick chat with Haven."

Frances's eyes narrowed as Leah slipped down the hall.

"How do you know about the other night?" Haven asked, though it was the last thing she wanted to discuss. Beau was hurt. She hadn't uncovered a single clue that might save him. And in a few short hours, she would be making her official debut as Adam Rosier's girlfriend.

"Who do you think smuggled Iain into the hotel see you? He told me what he saw."

"I can explain—" Haven started to say.

"And I'm just dying to hear what excuse you've cooked up."

"But I can't explain *now*, Frances. Just believe me when I tell you that it's not what you think."

"Oh, really? So you're saying you *didn't* kiss some man in the lobby of the Gramercy Gardens Hotel?"

Haven could feel her frustration growing. "Everything I've done, I've done to save Beau, Frances," she said, though she knew that wasn't strictly true. "Is Iain here? Can you tell him I'd like to talk to him? It's important. Something's happened to Beau."

"Here?" Frances snorted. "No, Iain's not *here*. I have no idea where he is, but if I were you, I'd warn that guy you were kissing to watch his back. Who is he, anyway?"

"Just a friend."

"Yeah, I know all about *friends*," Frances said. "My last ex-husband had quite a few of them. It's just sad. I would give anything to have someone who looked at me the way Iain looks at you—like you're the only other person in the universe."

The sudden stab of guilt caught Haven unprepared. It was tempting to dismiss Frances's words, but this time the hopeless romantic was right. Haven was Iain's whole universe. But Haven's universe now had a population of two. "I'm sorry, Frances. I never meant to disappoint you."

"Don't worry about *me*. Worry about Iain. Now who's this girl you've brought to my house?"

"Her name is Leah Frizzell," Haven said. "She's an old friend of mine from Tennessee, and she needs a place to stay."

"Is she . . . is she *homeless*?" The last word was whispered.

"She's a physics major at Duke. She just dresses like she's homeless."

Frances looked around the entryway. "Did she bring a suitcase?"

"No," Haven said. "She came up here in a hurry and slept in Union Square last night." It wasn't the best thing to tell Frances. "Look, if you're worried, Iain could vouch for her too."

"I'm not *worried*," Frances said just as a large crash came from the living room.

Haven and Frances rushed to find Leah on the floor in front of the large window that looked out over the apartment's terrace, her hands covering her eyes. Her fall had knocked a silver tea tray off a side table. Puddles of milk and half-brewed Earl Grey tea were seeping into an Oriental rug.

"Leah! What happened?" Haven yelped.

The girl slowly slid her hands from her eyes. Her face was as white as the milk on the floor. Haven had never seen Leah Frizzell frightened before. The girl's terror was infectious.

"The bird," she sputtered, pointing out the window. "Is it gone? I can't look."

Frances hurried over to peer outside. "I don't see any birds," she said.

"Is there anything . . ." Leah grimaced. "Is there anything out there on the terrace?"

"Like what?" Frances asked, watching the girl with a wary expression.

"You'd know what I'm talking about if it was still out there. I must have had a vision just now."

"A vision?" Frances demanded.

"I saw a bird swoop down out of the sky. It was big, some sort of bird of prey. Like one of those hawks you see in the mountains. It had something in its mouth. Something green and rotten. It dropped it on the balcony outside the window. At first I thought it was a dead snake, but it wasn't the right shape. So I looked closer, and I saw it was a hand. A lady's hand."

"A hand!" Frances exclaimed. The look she gave Haven said she was more scared of Leah than the scene the girl had just described.

"Then the bird came back. It landed beside the hand, and it started . . ."

Frances pulled Haven aside. "We need to call this girl an ambulance. She's having some kind of hallucination. Do you think she's on drugs?"

"Leah's not high," Haven said reluctantly. "She's just seen the future."

CHAPTER THIRTY-FIVE

Adam had come to collect her from the Gramercy Gardens Hotel. Haven paused by the elevator bank, smoothed her dress, and tried to calm her frazzled nerves. Only twenty minutes earlier, she'd leaped out of a taxi and sprinted up to her room. What she had expected to be a brief pit stop at Andorra apartments had ended up lasting too long. Haven had been forced to slip out, leaving too many of Frances Whitman's questions unanswered.

Now she was watching Adam from a distance as he checked his reflection in a mirror in the hotel lobby. He straightened his bow tie and plucked imaginary lint from the sleeve of his tuxedo. He looked anxious, she thought, like any young man picking up a girl for a date. Haven waited for a wave of anxiety to pass before she commanded her feet to lead her across the lobby. Adam spun around to greet her, his black eyes gleaming. He didn't speak, but his expression said everything.

"Hello, Adam." Haven was wearing the red dress that had turned heads in the restaurant back in Florence. But tonight no one looked at her. It was as though they'd all been instructed to see nothing. As soon as she was close enough, Adam reached for her hand and delivered a soft kiss to her knuckles. The blood beneath Haven's skin turned to ice. The sensation wasn't entirely unpleasant.

"I didn't know if I would have the pleasure of your company tonight," Adam said with the somber, reassuring manner of an undertaker. "I'm not sure if you've heard, but there's been a rather unfortunate turn of events."

"I saw the photo." The statement sounded flat. She still hadn't cried.

Adam seemed to sense the despair buried deep inside her. "Commissioner Williams has assigned every officer the city can spare to the manhunt. I promised to triple his reward if Beau is located in the next twenty-four hours."

"I knew you would take care of things," Haven said, her voice growing hoarse. "I knew I wouldn't need to ask."

"I was worried when I didn't hear from you, Haven. I can't imagine how you must have felt when you saw that image."

Tears filled Haven's eyes for the first time that day. Most were for Beau, but a few fell for herself. "I felt helpless. I just wish there was something that I could do. I spent all day searching my few memories for clues. The man who hurt Beau is somewhere inside my own head, but I can't find him no matter how hard I look."

"I will find him for you," Adam pledged.

"When you do, I don't just want him arrested." Haven paused to study Adam's response, but his face showed no sign of disapproval. "I have twenty Society points. I want to hire someone to hurt him the way he hurt Beau."

"There's no need for you to use your points," Adam responded, his meaning clear.

"Yes, there is. I want to be responsible. I want his blood on my hands, not yours."

"Then I shall make a few calls on your behalf. Beau's assailant will pay dearly for what he's done."

The words conjured the last scene in Florence that Haven had witnessed. She wiped her eyes. "You said something similar a long time ago. I had a vision of one of my past lives this afternoon. I saw the two of us together in another life. You and me."

Adam stiffened, as if bracing himself for bad news. "I hope you weren't frightened by what you saw. The past . . ."

Haven took his hand again and squeezed it gently. "I trusted you then, and I trust you now. And as soon as we save Beau, maybe I won't need to think about the past anymore." Did she really mean it? she wondered.

"I promise that day will come soon," Adam said, using Haven's hand to pull her even closer. "I will take care of everything." She could feel his cool breath on the nape of her neck. His skin smelled of delicate white flowers that grow in the shade. They were all Haven had ever remembered of her very first life on the island of Crete.

Haven carefully eased him back. "There's one more favor I'd like to ask."

"Anything," Adam said. "From this moment on, you shall have anything you desire."

"After we find Beau, will you show me the mausoleum you built? I would like a chance to say goodbye to the past once and for all."

Adam blinked. "I think that would be a splendid idea. I'll take you there whenever you're ready. Just give me the word."

"Thank you, Adam." Haven forced her lips into a brave smile. "Now, I believe there's a party waiting for us?"

"Are you certain you're feeling well enough? After today's events, I would not be offended—"

"To be honest, I could use the distraction," Haven assured him.

Adam nodded. "Then it shall be my pleasure to provide it."

* * *

ACROSS THE PARK from the hotel, the windows of the Ouroboros Society were blazing. A line of black town cars crawled along Gramercy Park South, each braking in front of the mansion's steps to disgorge its fashionable passengers. As Haven and Adam strolled alongside the wrought-iron gate, the lights of a passing car briefly lit one corner of the park. Adam showed no sign that he'd seen the figure huddled by the trunk of a sycamore tree. But Haven was certain that the woman she'd glimpsed had been Padma Singh. When she tried to peer through the darkness, the specter melted into the shadows.

Haven clutched Adam's arm and refused to be rattled. Her performance at the party would have to be perfect. Leah was still convinced that Haven's memories held the clue that could save Beau. Haven desperately needed another vision, and that vision would only come at a price. Until she could identify Naddo, Haven would pretend to go along with Phoebe's horrible plan. The old woman would be at the party, and she would be looking for evidence that Adam was smitten.

When the front doors of the Society swung open to admit Haven and Adam, most of the crowd paid them no mind. They continued chatting or drinking or plucking hors d'oeuvres from the silver platters that floated on the waiters' fingertips. But the few heads that did turn wore stunned looks, and several sets of eyes followed the couple as they strolled through the party arm in arm. Only one woman dared approach them. She was dressed in a flowing white frock, and her hair was tucked into a turban. Haven barely recognized Phoebe. Gone was the woman in the chic beige dress. In her place was a mystic with kohl-lined eyes and lips the color of dried blood.

"Phoebe." Adam acknowledged the woman with a curt nod.

"Good evening, Adam. May I introduce myself to the lovely young woman you've brought with you tonight?"

"There's no need. You've already met."

Phoebe's eyes widened just a fraction. Adam had startled her.

"At the Morton Street spa," Haven added.

"Yes, of course." A streak of lipstick smeared across Phoebe's front teeth made her smile look demented. "I knew the moment I saw you that you were destined for Adam's side. The two of you have been married in many lives."

"Save your stories for the others," Adam replied. "I know better than anyone that they're nothing but lies."

"Perhaps, Adam, but lies are what most people prefer to hear," Phoebe pointed out.

"Is there something you need, Phoebe?" Adam asked coldly. "If not, there's one person here who would be thrilled to receive the attention you're wasting on me."

"Of course," said Phoebe, letting the insult slide. "Enjoy your evening."

"You really despise that woman," Haven remarked once Phoebe had been swallowed by the throng. She had almost enjoyed the terse exchange.

"Never trust anyone who betrays those who love them," Adam said.

"Who did Phoebe betray?" Haven asked.

"I'll share the story with you some other time. At the moment there appear to be two people by the bar who are desperately trying to get your attention. Perhaps you should say hello."

Across the room, Alex and Calum were waving cocktail napkins like miniature flags.

"Do you mind?" Haven asked.

"Not at all," Adam said, planting a kiss on her cheek. "You're here to forget about your troubles for a while."

Haven squeezed past a well-known rock star who was putting the moves on a trio of tipsy socialites and then slid between a flamboyant fashion designer and a man dressed in the pin-striped costume of an investment banker.

"Haven!" Alex gushed, grasping her in a hug. "You're okay! We were so worried!"

So worried that you didn't lift a finger to help me, Haven thought. Calum seemed to read her dark expression.

"Well, we didn't worry *that* much," he added quickly. "Everyone's hero, Owen Bell, followed you and your escorts back to the OS. He was in the reception area when you were released from custody, but he said you didn't look like you were in the mood to chat. So what *was* all of that in the café this morning? Some kind of lovers' spat?"

"It was just a misunderstanding," Haven explained.

"It must be over now if you're here together," Alex said. "By the way, you look absolutely ravishing tonight."

"Yes," Calum agreed, giving Haven a once-over. "Though I'd go for regal over ravishing. Marie Antoinette would seem like a filthy little peasant standing next to Miss Haven Moore."

"So how long have you been seeing Adam?" Alex whispered.

"A while, I guess," Haven said. "It almost feels like forever."

"You know what this means, don't you?" Calum said. "Everyone who's anyone is going to start kissing your ass. Just look over there. The mayor is trying to decide if now is a good time to come over and introduce himself. Go ahead. Be nice. Give the poor bastard a little wave."

"I'll pass," Haven said. "I don't want to talk to anyone but you guys."

"Awww," Calum said as he playfully pinched her cheek. "You should take up acting. That almost sounded sincere."

"Speaking of sincere," Haven said, "where is Owen Bell? I thought I might see him here."

"He's at home with Milo tonight," Calum said. "Remember? He *claims* they're prepping for a big speech tomorrow, but I suspect there might be some hanky-panky going on. Those boys sure do spend a lot of time together."

"Ewww! Calum!" Alex screeched. "Can you imagine? It would be like having sex with a mannequin."

"Oh, I've imagined it," Calum said. "Many times. And it would be so insulting if Owen chose Milo when he could have had yours truly. But he swears he's just making sure that robot boy says all the right things."

The phrase echoed around Haven's head.

"What was that?" she asked Calum.

"Owen swears he's not bumping uglies with Milo the automaton."

That wasn't the phrase she wanted to hear, but Haven didn't need the words repeated. Owen could make someone say "all the right things." It was exactly what Adam had said in her vision—about Naddo.

"So where does Owen live, anyway?" Haven asked, hoping the question would come off as casual.

"You know the old police headquarters—that fabulous building in Little Italy that they turned into condos a while back?" Alex asked. "Owen has the penthouse."

"The penthouse?"

"Owen has been good to the Society—and the Society has been very, very good to Owen Bell," Calum snipped.

"Haven?" Alex said. "Are you feeling all right? You look a little pale."

"Yeah," said Haven, forcing a smile. "I just need a drink. I'll be right back."

She started for the door, her anger building with each step. How could she have been so stupid? Beau's kidnapper was the one person she never suspected—the person she'd been told was incorruptible. Forget Adam's thugs, Haven thought. She was going to kill Owen Bell with her own two hands.

"There you are." Adam blocked her path. "I thought you might like to meet a few—"

He was interrupted by the sound of a scuffle at the entrance.

"Adam Rosier!" someone shouted. The voice belonged to Iain.

Silence spread throughout the party as guests craned their necks to catch a glimpse of the ghost marching across the room. Haven felt boiling hot blood rushing through her veins.

"Where is he?" Iain's voice demanded.

No one answered, but the crowd parted to let Iain pass. Haven could hear his footsteps cross the hushed room. When he reached Adam and Haven, she couldn't pull her eyes away from him. He was wearing a suit she had helped him choose from a store on the Via dei Condotti. Iain called it his James Bond costume. She'd tried to make the alterations herself, but he wouldn't stop shooting imaginary villains in the mirror. Haven had laughed so hard that she'd stuck him with a pin, and the tailor down the street from their apartment had been forced to finish her work. This was the first time Haven had laid eyes on the finished product. Iain had been saving it for a special occasion.

"Back from the dead, so soon Mr. Morrow?" Adam said glibly. "Perhaps you can teach the rest of us that trick."

"Why did you refuse to meet with me?" Iain demanded.

"I thought it was clear. I have nothing to discuss with you. Now if you'll excuse us . . ."

Adam reached for Haven's hand, and the gesture made Iain's fists clench. Two gray men grabbed Iain's arms before he could act on his impulse.

"No," Iain said. "You're not going anywhere, Adam. Now that I'm here, I have a few things to say."

"Go home, Mr. Morrow," Adam ordered in the same flat tone he'd use to dismiss an underling. "You are disturbing my guests, and you're making Haven uncomfortable. Is that what you want?"

"What I want?" Iain repeated with a sly grin. "I'll show you what I want." He broke free from the gray men, lunged forward, and threw a punch. There was a sickening crunch, and Adam's glasses flew across the room. Haven scrambled to retrieve them. By the time she held them out to their owner, the scuffle had ended. Adam looked none the worse for the wear.

Please don't hurt him, Haven silently pleaded. *Please, please don't hurt Iain.*

"Thank you, my dear." Adam tucked the cracked glasses into the breast pocket of his tuxedo. "Surely you see?" he asked Iain. "Haven has chosen me this time. A gentleman would accept that decision."

"I'm not here for her," Iain said. "I came to take away the thing you love best. And we both know it's not Haven."

Iain turned his back on Adam and addressed the crowd that had gathered around them. "Do you know who this is?" Iain shouted. "This is Adam Rosier. He's your *real* leader. Some of you know that. Most of you probably don't. But I bet you've all seen him, haven't you? You must be blind if you've missed him. He's been skulking around here since 1925. And while the rest of you grow old, he never will. Because he's not one of us. He's not even *human*."

Adam smiled indulgently, and someone in the crowd tittered. Haven's entire body was shaking. *Just leave,* she pleaded. *Now, before it's too late.*

"Go ahead and laugh," Iain continued. "You're the suckers here. He brought you all to New York and tricked you into selling your souls for Society points. He's kept you from fulfilling your destinies. He's taken people who were sent back to improve the world and turned them all into desperate, greedy addicts."

"Oh dear," Adam deadpanned. "Is it really necessary to be so rude?" This time several people laughed.

A woman stepped forward, a glass of champagne in her hand. She was slim and immaculately attired, with a sleek helmet of silver hair and cold blue eyes that radiated power. Only someone with an army of underlings could manage to present such an image of perfection. Haven instantly recognized her as Catherine Mason, the editor of Beau's favorite fashion magazine. She was the host of the party, and she wasn't pleased to see it being crashed.

"What on *earth* are you talking about, Mr. Morrow? Are you implying that we've all made deals with the devil?"

"That's one way of putting it," Iain confirmed.

"Then I think it's time you returned to the asylum. I assume that's where you've been hiding for the past year or so?"

"Call me crazy, Catherine, but you prove my point. You could use your magazine to help women, but you feed their insecurities instead. You hire perverted photographers who prey on your teenage models. You showcase designers whose overpriced clothes are sewn by children paid less than slave wages. You—"

"That's enough," a man snipped in a high-pitched, nasal voice. Haven recognized his freckled, feminine face as well. He often appeared on television beside well-known organized crime figures. He was a mob lawyer—the most successful in the city. "Do you honestly think we'll stand here and be insulted by someone who's wanted for the murder of one of our members? Unless you have some sort of proof, I don't think we need to hear any more of these ludicrous accusations." He pulled a phone from his pocket. "Charles, get in here, and bring Martin with you."

"No one touch him!" Adam ordered as the lawyer's two hulking bodyguards appeared at the edge of the crowd. "Mr. Morrow will leave this party on his own two feet. Good night, Iain."

Before Adam could turn away from the scene, Iain grabbed Catherine Mason's champagne flute and broke it against the heel of one shoe. Left in his hand was a long, jagged dagger of glass, which he plunged into Adam's chest. The crowd gasped. Haven screamed. Until that moment, she had prayed that the scene might end peacefully.

"You want proof? There's your proof!" Iain shouted.

Adam grabbed the base of the flute and yanked the spike out of his chest. The glass was perfectly clean, and there wasn't a drop of blood on the white shirt of Adam's tuxedo.

"You see! He's not human!" Iain shouted as the bodyguards tackled him and threw him to the ground.

"Give Mr. Morrow a tour of the Meadowlands," the lawyer instructed his men, referring to the dismal swamp just outside the city that served as the mob's favorite graveyard.

"No!" Adam's voice rippled over the crowd. "I forbid it. Iain Morrow is not to be harmed by any of you. Now or in the future."

Before the goons had a chance to release their captive, a woman shoved her way into the center of the crowd and helped Iain to his feet.

"You heard him! Call off your thugs, Bruce, you despicable little turd." The woman's cheeks were hollow, and there were dark circles under her feverish eyes. She looked ill, underfed—and oddly beautiful. It took Haven a moment to recognize Padma Singh.

"Everything Iain Morrow told you is true," she informed Adam's guests. "But I'm sure it won't make a difference to most of you. So. Here's a fact that none of you can ignore. Adam Rosier may run this place, but I was president of the Ouroboros Society for five long years. I personally monitored your accounts. I know who all of you are, and I know what each one of you has done."

Padma picked a plump, professorial man out of the crowd. He recoiled as she straightened his tie. "I know how *helpful* this gentleman is to all the young ladies here who need a few extra points. Is your wife aware of your philanthropy, Winthrop?" Padma moved along to the next guest, the host of a morning news show. "I know exactly how much cocaine it takes to get this upstanding citizen ready for work every morning." She glided over to the mob lawyer. "And I know Bruce here started life as a female. Nothing to be ashamed of, but I bet his gangster friends might be a little surprised. As for the rest of you, I know each and every one of your dirtiest secrets. I know which of you have sold your bodies for points. I know which of you cheat the IRS. I know which of you have literally gotten away with murder. I kept very good records during my time as president of the Society. And I still have them all."

"Yes, Padma, the account system was abused while you were in charge," Adam said. "But the Ouroboros Society will be a different place soon."

"Save it for someone more gullible, Adam." Padma stopped in front of Haven. "You and I both know how dirty things got around here. Quite a few of our members disappeared over the years—and I can tell the police where all the bodies are buried. There are still plenty of cops in New York who don't belong to your organization. And I doubt they'll be as forgiving your new girlfriend seems to be."

"Get away from her," Adam growled.

"Or what, Adam? If anything happens to me—if anything happens to Iain—or if I just decide I need some excitement in my life, all my files will be made public. And your little club will be over for good."

"What is it you want?"

"How about I send you an invoice?" Padma said with a smirk. Then she grabbed Iain by the sleeve of his suit and led him out the front door.

Haven's relief didn't last long. Iain was safe, but Beau wasn't. She turned to the figure beside her. "I'm so sorry, Adam. I have to leave."

"Now? With *Iain*?" Adam didn't seem to notice the high-ranking OS members gathering around him.

"Was Padma Singh telling the truth?" a man demanded. "Does she have files on all of us?"

"Why were she and Iain Morrow allowed to live?" a woman asked.

"What are you going to do about this, Adam?"

Adam wasn't listening. He was waiting for Haven's answer. "No, I'm not leaving with Iain. I found out who took Beau. I have to save him while I still have the chance."

"I'll come with you."

"You can't," Haven insisted. "You need to stay here and handle things before it's too late."

"Iain was wrong, Haven," he said. "I don't care about the OS. You're what I love. Please, let me help you."

"You need to stay here," Haven repeated. "You can't let Padma Singh destroy the Society. I'll be back when I'm done."

"You're disappearing now? After what Iain just did?" Phoebe caught up with Haven and tried to block her exit. "You'll ruin everything!"

"Go to hell, Phoebe," Haven said, shoving her to the side.

CHAPTER THIRTY-SIX

Leah Frizzell was standing in a doorway on Centre Street across from the old police headquarters. Haven might not have recognized her if not for the sight of the girl's bare, knobby knees. The rest of Leah's body was wrapped up in one of Frances's coats, and a scarf covered all of her face except her pale green eyes.

"You okay?" Leah scanned Haven from head to toe. "You look like you've seen a haint."

"I've seen worse than that. How did you get here so fast? I only called you ten minutes ago."

"Taxi," Leah said. "Maybe you should have taken one too. Some guy followed you."

Haven turned to see two gray men lurking near the end of the block.

"The other one was already here," Leah explained.

"Did he get a good look at you?" Haven asked.

"Naw, I think he figured I was homeless until you showed up. And I've kept my face hidden the whole time. But what about you?"

"I don't care if they've seen me," Haven said. "I've found Beau. He's in there." She pointed at the imposing structure across the street. Modeled after Europe's grand buildings, with a copper cupola and the statue of a goddess watching over its entrance, it was not the sort of edifice one expected to encounter in the shabby heart of Little Italy. And that was the point. When the police chose the site for their headquarters, the neighborhood had been little more than a slum. The magnificent palace sent a clear message to Manhattan's poor. *We have power,* it told them. *And you have none.*

"Pretty fancy for a kidnapper's hideout," the girl remarked. "You sure this is the right place?"

"You think I've lost it, don't you?" Haven asked.

"I think you waste too much time trying to read people's minds," Leah said.

A doorman greeted the pair in the building's lobby. He wore a simple gray suit with white piping. As dull as the uniform might have been, it was by far the most memorable thing about the man. Haven smiled, hoping a little charm could convince him to let them upstairs without being announced. He didn't smile back.

"Good evening, Miss Moore," the man droned. "May I help you?"

Haven winced. "How do you know my name?"

"I work for the Ouroboros Society, Miss Moore."

"Oh," Haven said, trying to decide if it was good or bad news. "Well, we're here to see Owen Bell."

"Mr. Bell isn't in at the moment. He left over an hour ago with Mr. Elliot. Would you like to wait upstairs in the penthouse for him?"

"You'll let us into Owen's apartment?" Haven asked warily.

"The penthouse belongs to the Ouroboros Society, Miss Moore. You've been granted unrestricted access. You may go wherever you like."

"Thank you," Haven replied, but as they made their way to the elevator, she couldn't stop checking over her shoulder to see if the doorman had changed his mind. Each time she looked, she found him in the same position, standing motionless in the lobby like a giant tin soldier.

"I'm really sorry if this turns out to be some sort of trap," Haven told Leah as soon as they were alone in the elevator.

"We're gonna be fine," Leah stated.

"You act like you just *know* these things," Haven said with a touch of annoyance.

"Maybe I do."

Before Haven could ask *how*, the elevator doors opened directly into Owen's penthouse.

"Not bad," Leah said as they stepped into the dark apartment. "We must be inside the cupola."

The massive windows that circled the room gave the impression that there weren't any walls. They could see the whole city. It was as if they were inside a bubble floating over Manhattan. One that might burst at any minute and send them plummeting down to earth. As her eyes adjusted to the gloom, Haven could make out the shapes of three modern chairs stationed around a coffee table, and a staircase that led to another floor. The living room was oddly empty, as though Owen didn't expect to stay for long. She could see no sign of Beau.

"You check around down here," Haven whispered. "I'm going up to the second floor."

She quietly made her way upstairs in the darkness. When she reached the top, she didn't need to turn on the lights to know there was nothing to see. Just a small chamber with an unmade bed. Stacks of books lined the walls. Haven got down on her knees and lifted the bedcovers, intending to have a peek under the box spring. She jerked her hand away and fell back on her butt. The sheets were still warm.

She scrambled to her feet and spun around. To her left was a closet, its door slightly ajar. The room on the right was the bathroom. She could see a sliver of white tiles. She lunged to the left and pushed the closet door open. Perfectly pressed suits were lined up in a row. There was nowhere to hide. She turned to face the bathroom. There had to be someone inside.

"Beau?" she whispered. "Are you in there? It's me!"

There was no answer. Haven gripped the doorknob. Then, with one quick twist of her wrist, she flung open the door. A bright light blinded her, and she stumbled backward. Then a thick arm caught her in a headlock.

"Who the hell are you?" Owen Bell growled. "What do you want?"

"Where is he?" Haven tried to demand, but only a few garbled sounds escaped from her throat.

The arm released her, and Haven fell to the floor with the bottom of her red dress puddled around her. She could hear Leah bounding up the stairs.

"Haven!" the girl yelled. "You okay?"

"Haven?" Owen asked. He was holding a shaving mirror in one hand. Its light cast a bright circle on the floor. "What's going on here? What are you doing? I could have hurt you just now!"

"Where is he?" Haven demanded once more, massaging her throat.

"*Who?*" Owen asked, turning on the overhead lights. He was wearing a pair of striped pajamas. The elevator's arrival must have woken him.

"Beau Decker! The guy you kidnapped. Where have you got him?"

Owen shook his head. "I have no idea what you're talking about, Haven. You're welcome to search the premises, but I swear I'm not hiding anyone. Would you mind telling me who this Beau is?"

"He's a friend of ours. I'm Leah Frizzell, by the way." The girl reached out for Owen's hand and shook it with enthusiasm. "Nice to meet you. I love your house."

"Owen Bell," he replied, looking even more confused than Haven felt. "What makes you two think *I* kidnapped your friend?"

"Beau flew up to the city from Tennessee to meet his soul mate," Leah explained before Haven had a chance to speak. "Some guy who called himself Roy Bradford got in touch with him online. He claimed they'd known each other in another life. Fourteenth-century Florence, I think. The guy supposedly gave details that proved it. But Beau disappeared the day he got to New York, and Roy Bradford doesn't seem to exist."

Owen froze. "Did you say Florence?"

"Oh, come on! Don't play dumb!" Haven snarled, stomping her foot with frustration. "The kidnapper said that his name back then was Naddo. Beau's name was Piero. I know you were Naddo, Owen. You have the same gift that he did. I just figured it out tonight. You can put the right words into other people's mouths."

"Do you mind if I sit down for a moment?" Owen mumbled. "I wasn't sure if it was real. I thought she might have drugged me."

"Who?" Haven asked.

"Phoebe. They call her the Pythia. She helps people see their past lives."

"I know all about the Pythia," Haven said. "You've met her?"

"Calum introduced us. We had a private session. She threw a bunch of plants on a fire and announced she was going to take me back in time. As soon as I inhaled the smoke, I saw something I'd never seen before. There was someone I loved. A beautiful blond boy who lived in a palazzo. The vision was incredibly vivid. I was sure the plants had made me hallucinate."

"Did you tell the Pythia what you saw?"

"No. She didn't seem interested," Owen said. "You're saying that it was *real*?"

"Yes," Haven confirmed with a sigh. Owen was far too astonished to be anything other than innocent. Haven could feel disappointment welling up inside her. "It was real."

"And this person you know. Beau. He's the one I loved?"

"Yes. He's my best friend," Haven said.

Owen grabbed a notebook off the bedside table and scribbled something. He handed the note to Haven with one finger pressed to his lips.

THE APARTMENT MAY BE BUGGED. PLAY ALONG AND FOLLOW ME.

Maybe she hadn't reached another dead end, Haven began to hope. Maybe Owen Bell knew something after all.

"Have you asked Adam for help?" he inquired.

"He has the police looking for Beau."

"Well, I wish you the best," Owen said, twirling a finger as if to say, *Wrap it up*. "If anyone can find Beau, Adam can."

"Thanks, Owen," Haven said. "I'm really sorry for barging in here like this. We'll let you get back to sleep."

"No problem. I'll show you out." He guided Haven and Leah downstairs to the front door. "It was nice to meet you, Leah. Haven, I'm sure I'll see you soon."

Owen stepped out into the hallway. There, he gestured for his guests to stay close behind him as he headed for the fire stairs.

Inside the stairwell, a motion-sensor switched on the lights. Owen leaned over the railing and checked to make sure that there was no one above or below them.

"Sorry about all of this," he said. "But I prefer my conversations stay private."

"Is your apartment really bugged?"

"I wouldn't be surprised. Maybe I'm paranoid, but sometimes I get the feeling that the doormen keep tabs on me."

"Then the one downstairs doesn't do a very good job," Leah said. "He told us you weren't home."

Owen grinned. "I do what I can to keep him guessing. Back when this building was still the police headquarters, some big shot built an underground passage that leads from the basement to the bar across the street. I keep expecting the doormen to catch on that I use it, but apparently they don't know I'm a history buff."

"Don't worry. Your secret is safe with us," Haven said.

"You know, it's strange, but I have a feeling it is," Owen said. "That's why I'm going to do something crazy and share an even bigger secret with you. One that could get me in a lot of trouble. Have Calum or Alex told you how I was invited to join the Society?"

"No," Haven said.

"My parents refused to pay for college unless I agreed to seek treatment for my unfortunate condition. So I borrowed a little money from my favorite aunt and came to New York to volunteer for my first political campaign. Late one night, I was sweeping up at the headquarters when I heard the chimes above the door ring. I was sure I'd locked it, so I ran out to see if we were being robbed. There was a man in the waiting area. He was young. Good-looking. Not terribly frightening. He asked if I was Owen Bell, and he said he'd been looking for me."

"It was Adam, wasn't it?" Leah asked.

"Yes, it was. He told me he'd been following my 'career,' which didn't make any sense since I'd just graduated from high school. Then he asked me if I knew why I could write stirring speeches or help people win debates. Why the perfect words always seemed to pop into my head. Before I could answer, he asked another question. He asked what I knew about reincarnation."

"I bet that got you thinking," Leah said with a snort.

"It did. I've had strange dreams since I was a kid. Nightmares, really. I've seen myself murdered. Beaten by people I've never met in this life. Kicked out of towns I've never set foot in. All because I was gay. Adam told me they weren't just dreams—they were memories. Things that had happened to me in previous lives. And he told me there were other people like me at the Ouroboros Society.

"Adam said I'd developed my gift for words as a way of defending myself. But with his help, I could use it to make the world a better place. At that point, I'd never even *heard* of the OS. Then Adam rattled off a list of the Society's members. That's when I knew I had to take him seriously.

"So I signed up with the Society. Calum tried to hit on me the very first day. Then Alex. She was the one who ended up convincing me that the OS really did need my help. There was drug dealing and prostitution—and members disappeared all the time. I started working with Adam to put an end to it all. He really seemed to value my opinion. Then one day Calum dragged me to visit the Pythia."

Owen took a deep breath. "What I told you back in the apartment was one hundred percent true. But I left something out. I saw Piero in my vision, but I also saw *Adam*. That's why I thought I'd been hallucinating. He looked exactly the same as he does today. *Exactly*. In my vision Adam was a powerful businessman who'd moved to Florence from Genoa. The city's leaders were certain he was planning to overthrow them. They were *terrified* of Adam. Some even claimed that he'd brought the black death to Italy. But I have no idea if Adam ever had his showdown with the leaders. Word got out that Piero and I were gay. My employer was one of the men who ran Florence. He had a few secrets of his own, and he couldn't afford a scandal—especially when the whole city was searching for a scapegoat. So he had us both assassinated."

"You saw all that?" Haven asked. "In one session with the Pythia?" Why had Phoebe made her wait so long?

"Yeah," Owen said. "I felt nauseous for about a week afterward. I don't think that smoke can be very good for you. So you're saying all of that really happened?"

"Yes," Haven said.

"Adam hasn't aged in seven hundred years?" When Haven shook her head, Owen paused to let the information sink in. "What is he? I've heard rumors, of course, but—"

"I have no idea," Haven admitted. "But he's been around for thousands of years. I've known him in other lives. Adam told me that he's met you before too."

The last sentence was barely out of her mouth when its full meaning slammed into her. Adam had been aware of Owen's gift before they spoke at the campaign office. Adam had mentioned to Haven that he'd known Owen in other lives. Haven knew from her last vision that Adam had met Naddo—and that he knew of Naddo's gift for words. Adam must have been aware all along that Naddo and Owen shared the very same soul.

A new horror began to creep over her. The man who had called himself Roy Bradford had known things that Haven assumed only Naddo could know. Maybe Adam had known them too.

"Alex told me you and Adam were a couple. Is it true?" Haven barely heard Owen's question, and it took her a moment to snap out of her trance.

"I'm only in New York to find Beau," she insisted. "By the way, did you ever tell Adam about your vision?"

"No, I couldn't trust him again after I visited the Pythia. In fact, I might have quit the OS if I hadn't met Milo. He's the reason I stayed. The kid scares the hell out of me."

Haven was thrown by the sudden shift in topic. "Why? He's just a robot."

"That's what Calum says because that's what Calum wants to believe. Milo's more like a puppet. The *perfect* puppet. Do you know how many points we raised at the fund-raiser the other night? Fifty *thousand*. I can't even tell you what that's worth in dollars. Millions. Many millions. People look at Milo, and somehow they see whatever they want to see. If he'd given a speech that urged them to donate points so that every kid in the U.S. could have his own Uzi, they'd have emptied their accounts just the same."

"Then it's a good thing Milo doesn't write his own speeches," Haven said.

"He *can't*. Milo's never had an idea of his own. But he's still convinced he's the chosen one. The speech I wrote for the fund-raiser was meant to say that the kids at Halcyon Hall thought it was their *duty* to lead the world. Milo changed it to *destiny*."

"Destiny?" The word seemed to mean something to Leah. "What's this Milo guy look like?"

"Like a Ken doll—blond and bland. But believe me, he's anything but harmless. I'm sticking around to make sure that someone plants the right ideas in Milo's empty little head—because otherwise we could all be in for a lot of trouble." Owen stopped himself. "I'm sorry. I'm venting. I know you didn't come here to talk about Milo. Is there anything else I can tell you that might help your friend Beau?"

"There is one more question I need to ask," Haven said. "You told us Naddo and Piero were murdered by the man you worked for in Florence. Adam didn't have anything to do with it?"

"I don't think so. At least I didn't think so back then. The only person in Florence who knew we were gay was Piero's little sister. I was pretty sure she was the one who let the secret slip."

CHAPTER THIRTY-SEVEN

"Just because Owen Bell believes it doesn't mean it's true," Leah said. "Haven Moore? You listening to me? He's a nice guy and all, but seeing pieces of the past is just like seeing parts of the future. One little part can't tell a whole story."

They had used the tunnel beneath Owen's building to evade Adam's gray men, and Leah had wrangled an off-duty cab like a native. Now they were traveling north along the river. Haven let her forehead rest against the window and watched the city race by, too distraught to cry. She'd had many lows over the years, but she'd never experienced anything quite like the soul-crushing sorrow she felt at that moment.

"It *is* true, Leah. I remember telling Adam that Piero and Naddo were gay. Who knows, maybe Beatrice told other people too. So there's no escaping the truth this time. I was the reason they died."

"Haven, it had to be a mistake. You would *never*—"

"Look, Leah, if you'd been at the Ouroboros Society tonight, you'd spare me the damn pep talk. This had already been the worst day of my life. Finding out I killed Piero and Naddo was just a bonus."

"What happened at the OS?" Leah asked.

Haven wasn't sure she had the strength left to relive the memory. "Iain showed up at the party while I was there with Adam. He told everyone there who Adam really is. And then he stabbed him."

"He did *what*?"

"He stabbed Adam with a piece of glass, but there wasn't any blood. Iain wanted the members to see that Adam isn't human. I guess he thought it would make a difference to them."

"And did it?"

"Are you kidding? They would have ripped Iain apart if Padma Singh hadn't shown up and saved his ass by threatening to expose them all."

"So Iain's okay?"

"Thanks to *Padma*." Haven sighed. "Then I figured out that Owen and Naddo were the same person—the one I've been trying to see in my visions. And it turns out I've been wasting my time. Owen's not the person who lured Beau to New York. It must have been *Adam*. He set a trap, and I walked right into it. Now I've lost Beau. I've lost Iain. I've lost everything."

"Is that what you really believe? That Adam's behind all this?"

"There's no other explanation!"

"That you've found," Leah said. "You're thinking too hard. Stop for a second and listen to your heart."

"You keep telling me to trust myself. What the hell do you suppose I've been doing? What do you think got me into this mess? Maybe I'm not the person you think I am, Leah. You never met Beatrice Vettori. You don't know what I was like in the past. Maybe my heart is the last thing I should be listening to."

With her head still leaning against the window, Haven could see the scrawny redheaded girl reflected in the glass. She looked no more than fifteen years old. Goddess or not, what did she know about the dark corners of Haven's heart?

"Iain's mother warned me, you know," Haven added. "She said I would do terrible things if the gods turned against me."

"What exactly have you done that's so terrible?"

Haven didn't respond, but the list of her crimes was forming inside her head. *Lied to Iain. Spied on Iain. Kissed Adam Rosier. Tried to hire a thug to beat up Beau's kidnapper. Broke Iain's heart. Proved his mother right.*

"Listen, I know it's been a bad day," Leah continued as the cab pulled up in front of the Andorra apartments. "But I'm not going to let you give up just yet. This story's more complicated than you think it is—and Haven Moore is starting to look like its heroine. You know that Milo kid you and Owen were just talking about? I think I saw him a while back."

"Where?"

"On television a few weeks ago. Talking some nonsense about 'destiny.' I thought it was just a weird dream at the time, but now I'm starting to wonder if it might have been the first vision I had about all of this."

"What do you think it means?"

"I'm guessing Milo could have something to do with the bodies in Union Square."

"Ladies, you getting out here or what?" the cabdriver barked.

"Come upstairs with me?" Leah asked. "Have a cup of coffee and help me save the world?"

It was Leah's idea of a joke, but Haven didn't feel like laughing.

"Where else do I have to go?" she said, sliding across the backseat.

WHEN THEY REACHED Frances Whitman's door, Leah pulled a key from her pocket and put a finger to her lips.

"She went to bed early," Leah explained in a hushed voice.

"I think we really blew her mind this afternoon. She could use a good rest."

"Can't say I blame her," Haven said as Leah opened the door. "Wait till she hears the rest of the story."

"*Whoops!*" Leah took half a step inside the apartment, turned around, and slammed the door shut with the key still in the lock. "I forgot. Frances said she ran out of coffee this morning. You know what? Why don't I just pop down to the supermarket and pick some up?"

"*Leah?*" Haven called as the girl hurried toward the elevator. "Do you even know where the supermarket *is*?"

"I'll be back in a few minutes," Leah shouted down the hall. "You just go on inside."

Haven pushed through the door to find Iain waiting in Frances's apartment. At first she stared at him, unable to sort through the relief, anger, and desire that were all vying for her heart. He met her eyes, but he didn't move. Haven felt herself being transported back two years in time, to a scene on a bridge in the middle of Rome. It was the day Iain had asked her to stay with him in Italy. The question had frightened her. She hadn't been ready to acknowledge who he was—the person she had always been meant to find. Now he seemed to be asking her to choose again. He didn't need to say the words. And Haven didn't need to search for an answer. Adam Rosier could never make her feel this way. She rushed into Iain's arms.

"Why would you do something so stupid?" she sobbed. "Were you trying to get yourself killed?"

"Haven, Haven," Iain whispered in her ear. "Don't cry. I was never in any danger."

"How can you say that?" Haven pulled back, leaving his shirt wet with tears. "What if Adam had agreed to meet you in Harlem? Do you really think you could have locked him in that vault all by yourself?"

"Believe it or not, I have learned a few things since Cordoba,

Haven. I had everything planned out this time. I never expected Adam to meet me. The whole point was to let him know I was alive—and let him think I was desperate to win you back. That way you'd be safe and above suspicion when I finally got a chance to confront him in front of you. I wanted you to see that he could still act like a monster. But that's not what happened, is it?"

"You just got lucky!" Haven exclaimed. "Some of those OS members would have murdered you on the spot!"

"Yes, but there was never any chance that they would. For two reasons. First, I'd arranged for Padma to show up as soon as it looked like I was in trouble. But the second reason is . . . well . . . I guess I've been wrong about everything."

"You've been wrong?" It was the very last thing Haven had expected to hear.

"And you've been right. Adam *is* different. Two years ago, he would have let those bodyguards beat me to death, but tonight he ordered them not to touch me. Because of you, Haven. As much as I hate to admit it, you *do* have some kind of power over him. And if you believe Adam is really trying to fix the OS, I'm going to take your word for it from now on. I know Padma scared a lot of people at the party, but her threats won't be enough to close down the Society. And all she wants is to be paid for her silence. So if you still think the Society should be saved, I'll do whatever I can to help you."

"I don't know what I believe anymore," Haven said, suddenly exhausted. The events of the evening had drained every last drop of the faith Haven had once had in herself. She felt hollow and empty.

Iain helped Haven to a chair and kneeled by her side.

"What's wrong? Did something happen after I left the party?" he asked.

"I found Naddo. His name now is Owen Bell. But he didn't take Beau. I think Adam might have. And if he did, then I'm just the idiot everyone thought I was."

"Are you sure Adam took Beau?"

"I'm not sure of anything," Haven admitted. "All I know is some-one kidnapped my best friend and beat him like a dog. Did you see the picture?"

"Yeah. It was e-mailed to me too." Iain drew in a deep breath and closed his eyes like a man preparing to take a plunge. "I can't believe I'm saying this, but I don't think Adam is behind Beau's disappearance. I don't think he would inflict that kind of pain on you. Not anymore."

"*Great.*" Haven threw herself back in the chair. "Now you trust Adam Rosier, and I can't even trust myself. I've done some horrible things in the past few days. I told myself that I had to do whatever it took to help Beau. But that was just an excuse. I've been pretty awful in all of my lives. That's who I am. Beatrice Vettori—the girl who betrayed her only brother and ended up getting him murdered."

"No," Iain stated, as if there were no other possible answer. "I don't know what you've seen in your visions, but if Beatrice betrayed Piero, it must have been a mistake. Don't forget, Haven, I knew you both. Beatrice would never have hurt her brother on purpose."

"That's what Leah said. I wish one of you knew for sure."

Iain's eyebrows rose at the mention of Leah's name. "I *thought* that was Leah who opened the door. What's she doing here?"

Haven's head throbbed. There were too many mysteries crammed inside it. "Leah's been having visions of the future. She sees dead bodies in Union Square. She's pretty sure something terrible is going to happen in New York. And now she thinks a kid named Milo from Halcyon Hall might be connected."

"How long have you known about this? Why didn't you tell me?" Iain asked.

"Leah asked me not to say anything. She said the future might change if other people got involved. She wanted a chance to fix things herself, and she thinks she's got time. Her visions all take place in the summertime."

"This coming summer?" Iain asked, and Haven shrugged helplessly.

"Well, that settles it. Leah's going to accept my help whether she wants it or not. As soon as we save Beau we'll get started saving New York."

"You're forgetting something, Iain," Haven tried to warn him. "You can't just go around saving anyone right now. The police must know you're alive, and there are a whole lot of people in high places who'd like to see you put away for murdering Jeremy Johns."

"The way I see it, that's the least of our worries," Iain said. "Let's just focus on finding Beau. I'll save myself later."

"But where am I supposed to start looking for Beau if my only suspect now is Adam Rosier?"

"Maybe you should start by finding out what Adam knows."

CHAPTER THIRTY-EIGHT

The lights of the Ouroboros Society looked as though they'd been out for hours. The building was completely still. Even the ivy appeared to have given up scaling the walls. A young man sat on the stoop in a tuxedo, contemplating the night. What he saw there held him spellbound, and he didn't seem to feel the world freezing around him. Haven could almost hear the ice forming on the trees of Gramercy Park. The sound of her heels on the cold concrete drew his attention. He watched her approach, his expression slightly befuddled, as if she might be a figment of his imagination.

"Did you rescue Beau?" Adam asked.

"No," Haven said, taking a seat by his side. "I'm sorry. I shouldn't have left when I did. Are you okay?"

"Yes, thank you. I survived the evening unscathed. I'm not so sure about the Society, however."

"What's going to happen now?"

"Some people will leave the OS," Adam said. "Most won't. But it may be the best who choose not to stay—the ones who might have made the Ouroboros Society a better place in the end."

Haven said nothing. Adam's eyes were on her, but she couldn't meet his gaze.

"Something is different," he said softly. "Did Iain manage to change your mind about me? I knew what I was risking when I allowed him to live. I'm willing to do whatever you ask of me, but I can't help what I am. I would give anything to have real blood in my veins."

"Do you know where I went tonight?" Haven asked.

"Yes. I sent a man after you to make sure you were safe. You went to see Owen Bell."

"I've wasted almost two weeks looking for the person Beau loved in Florence. You must have known who Naddo was all along. Why didn't you tell me?"

"Naddo? It didn't occur to me that you might be searching for *Naddo*," Adam argued. "You never mentioned which life held the clues you needed to find. Did you?"

Haven paused to search her memory. "No," she admitted. "I guess I didn't."

"And I was reluctant to pry. But if you had told me, I would have assured you that Owen couldn't be responsible for Beau's disappearance. Surely you must realize that now."

"I do. Which leaves me with a single suspect, Adam. Did *you* kidnap Beau so that I would have to come back to New York? Tell me the truth this time. *Please*."

"Haven!" Adam's shock seemed genuine. His hand rose to comfort her, then fell back into his lap. "I played no part in Beau's kidnapping. I've been doing everything in my power to find him, even though I know he will try to turn you against me."

Haven refused to be moved. She forced herself to stick to the facts. "The person who called himself Roy Bradford knew that Beau had once lived in fourteenth-century Florence. Whoever it was knew that Owen and I were there as well. You are the only one who shared the same life with the three of us. Are *you* Roy Bradford?"

"Haven, you must believe me. I *never* would have reminded you of our days together in Florence! And I had no desire to drag you back to New York in this lifetime. I needed to finish the improvements I've been planning—to myself and the Society. At this point, they're far from complete."

He was so persuasive. Haven could feel herself slipping back down the slope again.

"There's another thing, Adam. I've had visions of my life in Florence. I know that you and Beatrice were engaged."

"Yes," Adam said. "Those were some of the happiest days of my existence. I wish they had been as pleasant for you."

Haven felt a twinge of pity, but she pressed on. "I know that Piero didn't want us to marry. Did you start the rumors that he was gay? Did you arrange for him to be murdered?"

For a moment, under the moonlight, Adam's face was that of a very old being. "Florence was seven hundred years ago, Haven. I thought you wanted to let go of the past."

"Please, answer me."

"The truth is ugly," Adam told her. "I hid it from you then. I would prefer to keep it from you now."

"You don't have to protect me. I'm not as fragile as you think," Haven insisted. "I need to know what really happened."

"Your brother was going to stop our wedding. You weren't in love with me—even I knew that. But I'd given you the one thing you wanted in that lifetime—your freedom. You didn't want to be back under your mother's thumb. You and Piero argued, and you didn't watch your tongue as you should have. One of the servants must have been eavesdropping. Eventually Naddo's employer heard the rumors. He had your brother and his lover killed. Their bodies were dumped in the Arno River."

"No!" Haven whispered in horror.

"It was a tragic mistake, Haven. You never wanted Piero to be harmed. When you found out he was dead, you blamed me. I was the reason you were feuding with him in the first place. You turned against me, and then you helped the Horae imprison me."

"Even though you were innocent?"

"I've never been innocent. But I didn't kill Piero."

"Then why did I help the Horae?"

"I asked you that same question years later. You told me that it had been easier to believe that I was a villain rather than acknowledge your own role in Piero's death."

Beatrice had been selfish and reckless, but Haven had never imagined that she was capable of such cold-blooded cruelty. She wanted to reach inside herself and rip the girl out. "If what you've said is true, I don't know if I'll be able to live with myself."

Adam took her hand, and Haven didn't pull away. "Yes, you will," he promised. "You'll find a way to accept the past and do your best to avoid those mistakes in the present. Don't you see? That's what I'm trying to do now. The Ouroboros Society can make a difference in the world, but it will never repair all the damage I've done. It's a start, though. And if you're by my side, it could be a wonderful chance for both of us to make amends."

"You still want me to help you lead the Society?"

"I do," Adam insisted. "More than anything."

Haven turned to face him. "Then prove I can trust you. Find Beau. And get rid of Milo Elliot. Send him away from New York— somewhere he can't do any harm."

She had taken Adam by surprise. "What does Milo have to do with all of this?" he asked. "His only purpose now is to put Owen Bell's ideas into action."

But what was his *original* purpose? Haven wondered. "You know Milo is dangerous, don't you?" she asked instead.

"He doesn't need to be dangerous. I can control him. Milo is whatever I want him to be."

Haven couldn't help but shiver. "You've known Milo before?"

"Yes, we've worked together many times in the past. I've often thought of him as my secret weapon. I'm only able to tempt one person at a time, but Milo has the ability to inspire entire nations to follow him. I've used him in his other lives to lead the masses down perilous paths. Now I was hoping he could guide them in another direction."

Adam didn't seem to understand what he'd done. Milo could never be harmless. It was like using a loaded bazooka as a coat rack.

"You have to get rid of him, Adam. Something terrible is going to happen in New York, and Milo may be responsible."

"Are you saying you've seen the future?"

"No, but I know someone who has."

Adam stared into the dark garden in front of them. "My men told me there was a girl waiting for you when you went to see Owen Bell. Is she the one who sees the future? What has she told you?"

Haven didn't reply. She had already given too much away.

"Well then," Adam said. "It seems a wild card has been introduced to the game. Still, I'll do as you ask. My motives are pure. The snake goddess will confirm that I have nothing to hide."

CHAPTER THIRTY-NINE

"Here! Haven!" Calum jumped up and dragged a chair to the end of the table he was sharing with Alex. They had called Haven at ten in the morning and insisted she meet them at a diner down the street from her hotel. Haven had accepted the invitation, though the thought of food made her queasy. She was more interested in swapping information than sharing breakfast.

"You didn't pay the owner to empty the place?" Haven asked Alex. There were other customers inside the diner, a few of them sneaking peeks at the two teenage stars tucked into a booth. "Is there a reason you've deigned to dine with the great unwashed?"

"We're undercover," Alex explained. "This is where we come to get away from the Society. None of the members would ever set foot in a place like this. And after Owen gave me shit about buying out the café the other day—"

"Is he coming?" Haven interrupted.

"He got called in to the OS," Calum confided, leaning across an omelet that he hadn't touched. "The *merde* is hitting the fan at Gramercy Park. Owen told me thirty people resigned this morning. And Adam's just letting them go! If Padma were still president, she'd have them all picked off by snipers as they walked through the door. Speaking of which, Haven Moore, where did *you* go last night? You left in the middle of all the fun."

"It wasn't much fun for me," Haven said.

"You poor thing," Alex said, trying to commiserate. "Calum bet that you wouldn't be back. Looks like I won. Adam always gets what he wants."

"I have a feeling that may change someday soon," Calum remarked cheerfully. "Anyway, I was just rooting for Iain 'cause he's cuter. Adam's hot, but a little on the pasty side. Still, I'd be thrilled to see two guys fighting over me like that."

"Guys?" Alex queried with a mouth full of eggs. "*Guys* don't survive getting stabbed with champagne flutes."

"What are you two going to do now that you know the truth about Adam?" Haven asked. "Are you going to stay in the OS?"

"You're joking, right?" Calum asked. "We all suspected there was something strange about Adam. Besides, who knows how long he's going to stick around the Society, anyway? Speaking of which, did you hear about Milo?"

"Milo?" Haven asked.

Calum giggled. "It was announced this morning. As soon as Milo graduates from Halcyon Hall, he's being shipped off to Brazil. Adam wants to open another school down there, and Milo's going to oversee the plans. It's supposed to be an 'amazing opportunity,' but everyone knows Milo's been banished. Owen sounded as pleased as fruity punch when he told me. I can't imagine *why*—Mr. Bell must not realize that he doesn't have a job anymore."

Haven studied Calum. "You don't seem to be taking any of this very seriously. Shouldn't you be worried about the threats Padma made last night? Don't you have a skeleton or two in your closet?"

"In Calum's case, it's more like a mass grave." Alex said.

"Yeah? Don't act all prim and proper, Miss Harbridge. Everyone knows you must have done *something* wicked to keep your account in good standing."

"Think what you like," Alex snapped, though her face had turned as red as the ketchup on her plate.

"Anyhoo, Padma won't have time to embarrass any of us," Calum told Haven. "I bet she'll be recycled before noon."

"Recycled?" Haven said. "You think Adam is going to have her killed?"

Alex shook her head. "Adam doesn't do that sort of stuff, but I'd volunteer myself if I didn't have to catch a flight in two hours."

"That's right!" Calum exclaimed. "Oh, you must be so excited, Haven!"

"Excited?" Haven repeated, confused by the sudden shift in the conversation.

"It's the Oscars, darling! Alex is going to be wearing your dress tonight!"

"And just in time too," Alex said. "You could really use some good press."

"What do you mean?" Haven asked.

"You didn't see the papers this morning? They've got Iain Morrow all over them. You want my advice? Use those points Lucy Fredericks paid you to hire the Society's PR men. They can make you look like one of Iain's innocent victims. Otherwise people are going to think you've been hiding out with a murderer for the past eighteen months."

"And forging wills," Calum added. "You naughty girl."

Haven stood up, her chair scraping against the tile floor.

"Where are you going?" Calum asked. "You aren't running away *again* are you? We're just trying to help."

"I have to visit the ladies' room. I'll be back," Haven said, leaving her phone facedown on the table to prove it. "Order me some coffee, would you?"

She wove around the tables and charged down a set of stairs toward the bathrooms in the basement of the restaurant. Even when Calum and Alex were well out of sight, Haven tried to keep the shock from showing on her face. Once she was in the ladies' room, Haven turned on the sink's faucet and splashed her cheeks with icy water, hoping to rouse herself from the terrible dream in which she was trapped. When she looked up at the mirror, there were two violet eyes staring back at her.

"How the hell did *you* get in here?" Haven demanded.

"The back door," replied Padma Singh. Her dark wool dress could have used a good shearing, and a wide black belt had been wrapped twice around her emaciated waist. The rims of Padma's eyes were red, and it had been a while since her glossy black mane had been tamed by scissors. She looked like a beautiful, hungry beast. "I followed you from your hotel."

"You need to get out of here," Haven snapped. "The Ouroboros Society is out for your blood."

"So what? They'd be idiots to try anything," Padma said. "The moment I disappear, my files will end up on the desks of every reporter in town."

"What do you want from me, Padma? Does Iain know you're here?"

Padma leaned against the sink counter with an arrogant smirk and tried to impersonate her former self. "I couldn't believe you'd abandoned Iain until I saw you and Adam together last night. So you're really with the boss again. I guess it was only a matter of time. You sat back and judged the rest of us, but I knew you would join the party one day."

"Jesus, Padma, haven't you learned your lesson?" Haven asked. "Look in the mirror and see what happened the last time you messed with me. How's poverty treating you, anyway? Is it everything you hoped it would be?"

"I'm not going to be broke for long," Padma said. "I wasted too much time trying to win my way back into the Society. Now it's in trouble, and I have all the information I need to deliver the death knell. Tell Adam I want to be paid *well* for my silence."

"Tell him yourself," Haven snarled. "I'd rather cut off a finger than lift one to help *you*. I'm the only reason you're alive, Padma. I think I've done more than enough for you. Now get the hell away from me."

"Tell Adam, Haven, or the first people I'll take down are your two buddies upstairs. I have enough dirt on Alex Harbridge and Calum Daniels to keep them on the front page of the *National Enquirer* for the next twenty years."

"What do I care? Embarrass them while you can. Soon there won't be any more scandals to expose," Haven said. "The Ouroboros Society is going legit."

"I can't believe you bought Adam's BS," Padma snickered.

"What are you getting at?" Haven demanded.

Padma twirled a strand of hair around one finger. "Oh, I don't think I want to tell you. See, that's the thing about *adults*, they can be *so* difficult to persuade sometimes. *Children*, on the other hand, do what they're told."

"You're talking about the kids at Halcyon Hall?"

"That's his big project these days, isn't it? That's why Adam doesn't care if he has to clean up the Society to impress you. All the action's moved upstate."

"I've been to Halcyon Hall. I've seen it for myself. I know what Adam has planned for the children. So unless you've got some concrete information to share, I'm not interested in hearing any more half-baked theories."

"If you want the real scoop, just ask your friends. They know better than anyone what happens to kids at the Ouroboros Society. They were two of Adam's first experiments."

"Come on. Calum and Alex have never even *been* to Halcyon Hall," Haven said.

"You're right. But Calum was the first child Adam recruited. Alex was the second. They're his little lapdogs. They do whatever he tells them. If they're your friends, it's only because he made them play nice with you."

"I don't believe it."

"Believe what you want," Padma said with a shrug. "I don't give a damn about you or anyone's kids. Just make sure I get my money."

Padma left Haven standing at the bathroom sink, listening to the faucet drip into a pool of murky water that still hadn't drained from the sink's basin.

HER HEAD THROBBING, Haven charged upstairs to find a young man sitting in her chair at the end of Calum and Alex's booth. Haven could tell in an instant that he wasn't a member of the club. It might have been his overeager smile or his less than luxurious clothing. Calum looked thrilled to entertain the stranger, though Alex seemed bored out of her mind. She jumped up as soon as she caught sight of Haven and headed toward the stairs to the bathroom.

"Save yourself," Alex warned in a whisper. "Calum's getting his daily affirmation. Fanboy over there is giving him a verbal blow job. It's about to get really revolting. I'd steer clear if I were you."

Heeding Alex's advice, Haven avoided Calum and went to stand at the diner's Formica counter, where she pretended to examine the day-old doughnuts inside a smudged cake dome. She could hear the conversation back at the table, and she might have laughed if her sense of humor hadn't been drowned in the bathroom.

" . . . and you were *so* fabulous in that cameo you did in *Promises, Promises.* Don't tell Alex I said so, but that Oscar should have been yours, not hers. You were such an amazing frat boy that I was almost convinced you were straight. Not that it would have made any difference to me. I've been dying to meet you since the first season of *The Glittering World*."

"God, I'm impressed!" Calum laughed. "I didn't think anyone watched the first season. I had to call in a million favors just to keep the show from being canceled."

"Well, *I* was watching. I even bought the DVD. My favorite episode is the one where your sister brings her boyfriend home from boarding school. You pretend to be some neighbor named Roy, get the guy nice and drunk, and then seduce him in your parents' bed. I had a *serious* crush on you after that. I still dream about that scene sometimes! I can't believe I'm finally getting a chance to meet you in person!"

Haven ducked around the counter and squatted out of sight. Roy? Roy Bradford. The movie star name. The name of the man Beau had come to New York to meet. Could it have been Calum? Haven stayed low and out of sight. A confused waiter stepped around her but didn't blow her cover. A phone rang once in the dining area. She heard Calum answer.

"*What?* That's not possible! . . . Okay, *fine*. I'll be right there. But make sure *she* knows this wasn't part of the deal," Calum snipped. Then his tone sweetened abruptly. "Look, I'm sorry, handsome, but I didn't catch your name."

"Gavin," Haven heard his fan say.

"Gavin, it's been great talking to you, but I'm late for an audition uptown. Why don't I give you a ride?"

"Thanks," Gavin gushed. "But I live just around the corner."

"So?" Calum asked, his meaning perfectly clear.

"Then sure," Gavin replied, his voice low and conspiratorial.

"Hey!" It was Alex. "Calum, you big whore. Were you about to leave while I was still in the bathroom?"

"Don't worry, I'll pay you back for the food," Calum said.

"That's what you *always* say. Where are you going?"

"On a pleasure cruise," Calum told her. "Tell Haven I said sayonara."

"Where *is* that girl?" Haven heard Alex ask. "She left her phone."

"Give it to me. I'll make sure that she gets it," Calum said.

CHAPTER FORTY

Haven made it out the back door of the restaurant and around the corner just in time to see Calum and his boy toy tumble into a cab. Haven jumped in the next available taxi. Her car followed Calum's for ten blocks before the first cab pulled over to the side of the road. Gavin stumbled out of the curbside door. The pitiful expression on his cherubic face made it clear that all his dreams had been crushed.

"Don't stop yet," Haven told her driver. "Looks like we have a bit farther to go."

The meter read $35.15 when the cab finally pulled up behind Calum's car on the corner of 114th Street and Frederick Douglass Boulevard.

"You getting out, lady?" the driver inquired.

"In a second," Haven said passing two twenties and a ten through the partition. "You can keep the change if you tell me which building that guy enters."

"Isn't that the TV star? You some sorta stalker?"

"You want the fifteen-dollar tip or what?"

"West side of the street, two doors down. Whoa!" the man suddenly yelped.

"What?" Haven demanded.

"Looks like your friend has a few unexpected guests." Haven peeked out the window. Five police officers had surrounded Calum with their guns drawn. Slowly, he sank to his knees and placed his hands behind his neck. The cops handcuffed Calum and dragged him back to his feet. His beautiful green pants were blackened with winter sludge. "Holy shit," said the cab driver, holding his phone out the window. "I gotta get a picture of this."

Haven jumped out of the car and sprinted toward the scene. Calum saw her heading for him and smirked. He didn't appear to be shocked or chagrined. The police were guiding him toward a patrol car when Haven finally reached him.

"Back up, miss," one of the cops ordered.

"It's okay," a voice said behind her. Haven didn't need to turn around. She recognized the Brooklyn accent. "Give the girl a second."

"Where's Beau, you asshole?" she growled. She wanted to punch him, kick him, break his pretty little nose.

Calum looked back at the house behind him. "Gone," he said, completely unruffled. "I guess you'll need to keep looking."

"Gone?" Haven asked. "What do you mean *gone*? If something's happened to him, I swear I'll—"

"You'll what? Have your boyfriend kill me? Just because I've been playing house with a big blond stud?"

"But *why*, Calum? Why would you do something like this?"

"Don't act like a poor little victim, Haven. No one is innocent here. Especially not you."

Haven was about to demand what he meant when inspiration struck. "I have twenty OS points. I can hire someone to beat the truth out of you. I'll have him do things that plastic surgery won't be able to fix."

"Isn't that sweet?" Calum cackled. "So willing to turn to the dark side to save her best friend. Go ahead and try, Haven. Soon, no one will dare take that job no matter how many points you offer."

"Don't worry, Miss Moore. They'll make Mr. Daniels talk at the station," Commissioner Williams assured her.

"Will there be a cavity search, Gordon?" Calum winked at the police chief. "I've always wanted to try one of those."

"Just get him in the damn car," Commissioner Williams growled at his men.

"How did you know it was Calum Daniels?" Haven asked the police chief once Calum was locked inside the police car.

"We got an anonymous tip an hour ago. The caller suggested we check out this building. We found belongings and identification belonging to Beau Decker in one of the apartments, but he was already gone. The super told us the apartment belongs to Calum Daniels. It's not his primary residence, just a crash pad."

"Where's Beau now?"

"We don't know, Miss Moore. But we'll find him. Calum Daniels won't last an hour under interrogation."

"Would it be okay if I took a look inside his apartment?"

Although he didn't appear too fond of the idea, Gordon Williams could hardly refuse. "Just wait until all my guys are gone and go up to the fourth floor," he said, barely moving his lips. "But don't touch *anything*, okay?"

Haven marched over to a stoop across the street and waited for the cops to vacate the scene. The crowd of civilians on the sidewalk had scattered after the handsome television actor had been dragged away in handcuffs. Haven stared at the building where Beau had passed the previous weeks, and tried to arrange the facts she'd gathered into some sort of order. If Calum Daniels had been holding Beau captive, why wasn't he still in there? Where had he gone?

"Mind if I join you?" Haven glanced up to find Mia Michalski, looking like she'd just stepped out of a shampoo ad. "I'm Mia. We never officially met."

"Oh!" Haven exclaimed, feeling awkward and exposed. "Right! Yeah, sure, have a seat," she said, making room for Mia and hoping the beautiful girl wouldn't attract too much attention from male passersby.

"Did they find Beau?"

"No. But he's been here. All his stuff is inside. I'm waiting to check out the apartment for myself."

"I'm sorry this took so long," Mia said. "I wish I'd found the address quicker."

"Wait—*you* were the one who called the police?" If she hadn't been sitting down, the news would have knocked Haven off her feet. Iain's girl detective had succeeded where everyone else had failed. The meetings with the Horae, the evenings with Adam—none of them had been necessary.

"My partner and I broke into Beau's accounts," Mia said. "E-mail, Facebook, all the rest. He'd deleted his conversations with Roy Bradford, but nothing ever really disappears online. We found what we were looking for early this morning."

"Why didn't the police think of that? Or the FBI?"

"The authorities have to play by certain rules. I don't. I'm part of the best hacking team in the business. If one of us can't do something, the other one usually can. But both of us are too young to work for the cops, and my partner prefers to be paid in sexual favors."

"*What?*" Haven blurted out.

Mia winked at her. "It's my girlfriend. She's a genius."

"Girlfriend?"

Mia seemed to enjoy Haven's bewilderment. "Ha! I think your head might implode any second now. Iain told me you asked if we'd ever hooked up. I had a good laugh about that, but I bet you didn't find the idea so funny. When I saw you here, I figured I should set a few things straight. So did Iain even tell you why I took this case? I mean, aside from the fact that he begs so sweetly?"

"No."

"I figured. He's like that. Getting himself into trouble just to protect a girl's honor. You see, a while back, I had a little, bitty drug problem. I snorted through all my OS points and found myself on Padma Singh's hit list. She told me to make my body available to high-ranking members, or I could face the gray men. I was seventeen years old. I didn't know what to do. I tried begging Adam for help, but he wouldn't give me the time of day. I didn't even know Iain back then. He heard about my problem from Padma, and he gave me the points I needed to survive. He told Padma they were payment for sex, but Iain only asked me to do two things—get off the drugs and promise I'd never set foot in the OS again. Believe it or not, I actually tried to argue. I was hooked on the Society's sick little game. So Iain took a chance and told me all about Adam and his club. He could have been executed if I'd ratted him out, but Iain knew the truth was what I needed to hear. To this day, I don't understand why he risked his life to help someone he barely knew."

"I understand why Iain did it," Haven said. "He just thought it was the right thing to do."

"Yeah, at first I thought he'd expect me to pay him back. But he didn't. He never asked for a single favor until now. And as far as I know, he never told another soul about my escape from the Society— not even you. I mean, let's face it: How many guys would give up a chance to make themselves look like Prince Charming?"

"Not many," Haven admitted.

And that was it, she realized at last. *That* was the difference between Adam and Iain—the one she'd felt but hadn't been able to pinpoint. Iain was always Iain—even when no one was watching. But Adam's benevolence was strictly for show. Every improvement he'd made at the OS had been made to please Haven. Every little kindness had been a step toward winning her heart. It flattered Haven to think she was responsible for Adam's transformation. But Adam was hoping to be rewarded for his efforts. There was nothing selfish about what Iain had done for Mia. He had kept Mia's secrets though they could have proven his own innocence. Iain had done the right thing without expecting anything in return. And that was why Haven's heart would always be drawn to him.

"Heads up." Mia pointed across the street. The last of the cop cars was pulling away from the curb. "Your friends are leaving. Have a look around, and let me know if there's anything more I can do."

"Thanks," Haven said. "You have no idea how much you've already helped me."

"There's no need to thank me," Mia told her. "I've been hoping I'd get a chance to repay the favor."

THE POLICE HAD left the apartment door unlocked. Haven ducked under a strip of crime scene tape and into another era. The shades had been pulled, and the living room was dark. As Haven fumbled her way toward a lamp in the corner, she tripped over something large lying in the middle of the floor. With the lights on, she could see it was a tiger-skin rug with amber glass eyes and polished fangs. The other furnishings—heavy chairs upholstered in velvet, leather-bound books stacked neatly on shelves, a pair of old boxing gloves hanging by the fireplace, crystal decanters half filled with scotch—looked as though they'd been stolen from a bachelor's apartment circa 1910.

A portrait hung above the mantel. It showed a debonair man in his early thirties, his hair slicked back and a rakish grin on his face. Nearby, a framed cover of *Motion Picture* magazine featured an illustration of the same fellow in a tweed jacket, a pipe in one hand and wisps of pale blue smoke issuing from his lips. Wallace Reid. The silent-film actor Calum claimed he'd once been. Haven suddenly realized that the apartment was decorated with a dead man's things. Calum had created a shrine to his former self.

Inside one of the two small bedrooms, Haven found Beau's suitcase open on the bed. It looked full, and he'd left his wallet behind. There was no sign of struggle, and the bedroom door lacked a lock.

"I'm sorry, Haven."

Haven wheeled around to find Adam behind her. In his timeless dark overcoat and charcoal scarf, he fit in well with the antique furnishings. He looked tired, and Haven wondered if he sensed what she felt—that the bond between them was weakening. Mia had opened Haven's eyes to the truth, just as Iain had once done for her. Haven could see that Adam's transformation was nothing but a performance for her benefit. And now that Haven had been given a glimpse behind the scenes, she knew the show would never be the same.

"Gordon Williams called me before they raided the apartment," he said. "I'm afraid the news took me by surprise. I never expected Calum to betray me this way."

Haven crossed her arms and watched him through narrowed eyes. "Did you have something to do with all of this, Adam? Padma told me that Calum Daniels is your little lapdog."

"When did you speak with Padma Singh?"

"She followed me to a diner this afternoon. She wants money to keep her mouth shut."

A murderous look passed over Adam's face. "I'll take care of Padma. I should have seen to it first thing this morning, but you were my most pressing concern. Padma knows enough to create plenty of trouble, but she doesn't know *everything*, Haven. And she knows absolutely nothing about Calum Daniels."

"Maybe you should tell *me* what there is to know."

Adam's eyes made a rapid tour of the apartment before he began to speak. "Calum's mother brought him to the Society ten years ago. Until then, I'd never considered inviting children to join the OS. But the woman wouldn't take no for an answer. She had concocted a dozen stories about past lives her son remembered. The boy had heard the lies so many times that he believed them himself. His mother desperately wanted Calum to be special. And he was—just not in the way that his mother had hoped. I could tell in an instant that he hadn't lived before."

"Calum wasn't Wallace Reid?" Calum's shrine suddenly seemed pathetic.

Adam regarded the illustration of the silent-film actor smoking a pipe. "No, although his mother made a prophetic choice. I knew Wallace Reid. He shared many of Calum's weaknesses."

"So Calum isn't an Eternal One. You took him in out of pity?"

"We both know I didn't possess many noble motives in those days. Calum was a charming child—and hungry for affection. He'd never known his father, and he lapped up whatever attention I gave him. I allowed Calum to become a member because I believed his blind devotion would prove useful one day. When he was old enough, I even let him act as my welcoming party. He greeted new Society members and helped them learn how to manipulate the points system. When you arrived, Calum was furious that I asked Alex Harbridge to show you the ropes instead."

"Alex was only friends with me because you asked her to be?" Haven asked, stung by the thought.

"I didn't ask Alex to befriend you. I simply requested she introduce you to Owen Bell. I knew you would trust him, and I thought he could convince you that my plans for the Society were sincere. When Calum asked if he could tag along with the three of you, I gave him permission. I thought it might placate him. That is why I must apologize to you now. I should never have allowed it. I've known for some time that Calum was disgruntled."

"Disgruntled? Why?"

Adam sat down in one of the room's velvet armchairs, as if the tale were too weighty to tell standing up. "The changes at the Society haven't been easy for Calum. He's seen other young people grow more prominent as his own role has diminished. Calum's never hidden his hatred for Milo. But over the past year, he's come to see Owen as his true rival. He knows Owen represents the future of the Society while he represents its past. I thought his loyalty to me would prevent Calum from doing anything rash. Now I see I was wrong."

"I still don't understand, Adam. Where does Beau fit into all of this?"

"Calum must have discovered that Owen and Beau were soul mates. Perhaps he thought seducing Beau was the best way to get his revenge."

"Hold on." Haven's head was spinning. "So Calum went online and pretended to be Owen in order to lure Beau to New York. I guess I can buy that. But if this is Calum's first life, how did he know all that stuff about fourteenth-century Florence?"

"I suspect Owen shared a few of his memories with Calum. I wish I'd warned him to be more discreet. I wondered if Calum might be looking for information to use against Owen when I heard he'd dragged the poor boy to visit the Pythia. It was a desperate move. Calum hadn't spoken with Phoebe in years."

There was a big piece missing from the puzzle, thought Haven. Even if Owen had told Calum about his vision—even if he'd described the boy he'd once loved in Florence—how had Calum known that Owen's soul mate had returned to earth as *Beau*? Neither Calum nor Owen had ever met Beau Decker. Which meant someone else had to be involved. Someone who could have made the connection between a college student in twenty-first-century Tennessee and a merchant's son in fourteenth-century Florence.

Haven could feel her stomach beginning to churn. Who could have known that Beau had once been Piero Vettori? Who could have met him in both lives? Iain. Adam. And the Horae. They'd been in

Florence along with Piero. And Chandra had met Beau the day she hid Haven from the gray men.

"You said Calum hadn't spoken with Phoebe in years," Haven said. *"Why?"*

"Everyone assumed Calum had joined the OS on his own. The fact is, his mother joined with him. But she insisted their connection remain secret, and she abandoned him as soon as they both became members. His mother had a reputation to uphold—one that demanded she appear otherworldly. There's nothing more worldly than a child."

"Phoebe is Calum's mother?" Haven whispered in horror.

"Yes," Adam said.

"Do me one favor while Calum's still in jail," Haven begged.

"Certainly. I would be happy to arrange for a suitable punishment. How many points would you like to spend?"

"No—don't have him hurt. That's not what I want," Haven insisted. The fantasy had comforted her, but the reality disgusted her.

"Then how can I help you?" Adam asked.

"Don't let Calum post bail."

CHAPTER FORTY-ONE

"Haven!" Frances Whitman screamed just as the girl stepped off the elevator. "Hurry up! Get in here!"

"What's wrong?" Haven rushed down the hall toward Frances's apartment.

"Your friend is sick again! Didn't you get any of our messages?"

"No," Haven said. She'd left her phone on the table at the diner. Calum had swiped it before racing uptown. "What happened?"

"I woke up late this morning and found Leah lying outside on the terrace in her T-shirt and underwear. I don't know how long she'd been out there, but her skin felt like ice. Iain carried her inside. She's been praying and speaking in tongues ever since. The only thing she seems to understand is the word *doctor*, and when she hears it, she goes nuts. She keeps mumbling something about talking to you."

"Where is Leah now?" Haven demanded.

"In the living room."

Haven dropped her bag and ran. She discovered Leah lying

on Frances's silk sofa, swaddled in a half dozen blankets. Iain was crouched beside the girl, holding her limp hand. Haven dropped down beside him. Up close, Leah looked like a corpse. Her eyes were closed and her skin waxy white. The only sign of life was the twitching of her lips, as though she were speaking to someone she could see on the back of her eyelids.

"She doesn't need the blankets," Haven said, peeling a few away so the girl might be able to move. "The cold never bothers Leah. That's not what's making her sick."

Leah's eyes flew open at the sound of Haven's voice. "Haven! Something's gone wrong! We have to stop it!"

"What? What's gone wrong?"

"The visions. They're worse. The first one came when I was watching the news last night. They started talking about a terrorist attack. I know the date too. Five years from now on the Fourth of July. There was footage from a security camera at Union Square—you could see that subway entrance and the statue of Gandhi. And there were bodies everywhere. Hundreds of them. Maybe thousands. They said that was where it had been released."

"What had been released?"

"Some sort of disease that killed everyone. I was so shook up I had to go lie down. Then, this morning I woke up feeling terrible. Like my lungs were on fire. I went outside for a breath of fresh air, and when I looked down at the park, I had another vision. There were cars abandoned all over the roads and fires burning in half the buildings. The only things moving were helicopters filled with men in hazmat suits. And the birds eating the bodies on the ground. The whole city was dead."

"Oh my God," Frances gasped.

"What happened last night, Haven?" Leah asked. "Something pushed us closer to that future. That's why the visions are getting clearer!"

"I don't know!" Haven racked her brain. "I thought I'd stopped it. I made Adam promise to send Milo Elliot away."

"I guess I could have been wrong about Milo. I saw a girl this time." Leah struggled to sit up. "Maybe sixteen? Seventeen? She was on the news. There was a snippet of a press conference with her. She said she'd engineered the disease."

"A girl? Then it's got to be one of the Horae," Haven said.

"The *Horae*?" Iain repeated in disbelief. "I know Phoebe's a bitch, but—"

"They've got Beau. I just found out this morning. Phoebe had her son trick Beau into flying to New York so that I'd follow. She knew she'd never get rid of Adam without using me."

"Phoebe has a kid?" Somehow that was the part that seemed to surprise Iain most.

"Yeah. *Calum Daniels*. He's in police custody right now. Adam will make sure he stays there for a while. Long enough for me to visit the Horae and trade Calum's life for Beau's."

"I'll go with you. You can't see them alone, Haven."

"But I *can't* take you, Iain," Haven tried to explain. "Phoebe has to believe that I'd really have her son killed. I don't think I can convince her that I've gone totally rogue if you're there holding my hand."

"Take *me*," Leah insisted. "If the Horae are responsible for the things I'm seeing, I need to talk to them right away."

"You can barely stand up!" Iain argued. "Are you expecting Haven to *carry* you?"

"I'll go with them," Frances said. "Haven and I can help Leah into a cab."

"No. I don't want you involved," Haven told Frances. "It's too dangerous."

"Too dangerous! According to Leah, everyone in New York is about to die. Don't I deserve a chance to save my own life?"

"Okay!" Iain broke in. "Time out! Haven, may I speak to you for a moment in private?" He took her by the hand and led her into the adjoining room. "Have you really thought this through?" he asked once they were alone. "You're willing to face these creatures with no one to protect you but a half-frozen psychic and a daffy heiress?"

"I'd do it alone if I had to," Haven said.

"The Horae are nothing like Adam, you know. You have no power over them. If they think you're going to stand in their way, they'll destroy you."

"I'm not going to let them."

"Sometimes I really wish you weren't so brave," Iain said.

"I'm brave? How many times have you risked your life to help me? And I know I'm not the only one you've rescued. I heard about Mia Michalski."

"How do you know about Mia?" Iain asked.

"She was the one who traced Beau to Calum Daniels's apartment. After Calum was arrested, I ran into Mia on the street. She told me what you did for her. Why didn't you say anything?"

"It wasn't my story to tell," Iain answered.

In all their lifetimes together, Haven had never loved him more than she did then. "That's what I thought you'd say. I have a hunch there are a lot of stories I've never heard. And that's why I'm not going to let you go."

Iain grinned, but his eyes remained sad. "Feel like listening to one of my stories now?"

"There's nothing I'd rather do," Haven said.

"Okay, here goes. When I was a little kid—three or four years old—I used to search for you whenever I left my house. I would run up to any girl I saw on the street and ask her if she knew someone named Constance. Every time a girl said no, it almost broke my heart. I could have gone crazy if I'd known how long it would take to find you. Nineteen years feels like forever when you're living without the person who makes life *worth* living. And sometimes I've had to wait much longer than that. I don't like to think about the lifetimes I spent wandering the world on my own, but there have been far more than you know. So please, Haven—do what you need to do to help Beau. But promise you'll come back to me in *this* life."

"I swear," she said. "Nothing on earth could keep me away."

CHAPTER FORTY-TWO

"We've been expecting you," Phoebe said. "Come inside."

She led Haven, Leah, and Frances into the council room. A blazing fire made the chamber unbearably hot. The twelve regal chairs that Haven had last seen arranged in a circle now formed two straight lines like the rows in a jury box. Only one of the chairs was empty. The rest were filled with women and girls in identical white robes sewn from the finest linen. Phoebe took her place in the center of the group. There were new faces among the Horae—ones Haven hadn't seen before at the house on Sylvan Terrace. She spotted the elegant woman from the restaurant in Florence. Her finger no longer bore an ouroboros ring. There was the hotel manager who'd declined Haven's credit cards. And seated to Phoebe's right was Virginia Morrow.

"What the hell is *she* doing here?" Haven demanded. "Either she leaves or I do!"

"She is one of us," Phoebe said. "It has been many years since we've all been together, but Virginia has reunited with her sisters at last."

"I don't give a damn about your family reunion. I want her out of here now!"

"I would have thought you'd be more charitable toward one of Adam's victims."

"Excuse me?" Haven snarled. "What exactly did Adam ever do to *her*?"

"You'll know everything soon enough," Phoebe said. "Miss Frizzell appears to be ill. She may rest on the floor by the fire. Your other friend will stay with her."

"Perhaps I should bring a chair for the snake goddess?" Vera offered.

"You'll stay here," Phoebe commanded. "And Haven will come forward to face us."

"I think I'll be issuing the orders today," Haven snapped as Frances helped Leah lie down and placed her rolled-up coat beneath the girl's head.

"No, you will not," Phoebe said. "We have Beau Decker, and we can keep him as long as we like. Or we can put him to death. You saw what Chandra and Cleo did to his face. I believe they quite enjoyed themselves."

"You so much as *touch* Beau again, and I'll have Adam kill your son."

Phoebe didn't flinch. "That's a sacrifice I'm prepared to make," she said.

The other Horae shifted uncomfortably in their seats. Virginia Morrow stared at her sister with undisguised shock.

"Phoebe?" Vera whispered, only to be ignored.

"You're *disgusting*," Haven sneered.

"I'm a realist. One can't battle chaos with daisies and sunshine. So tell me. What has Miss Frizzell seen that has left her so ill?"

"She's seen your plan come to fruition. But we're here to stop you."

"Our plan?" Phoebe rose and walked to the spot by the fire where Leah was lying. "Tell me about your visions," she said.

"There's a horrible sickness. Something bad is in the air. Everyone dies. The whole city is dead," Leah told her.

"When?" Phoebe asked.

"Five years from now."

Phoebe spun around to face Haven. "And you think *we* will be responsible? This is what we've been working to prevent, you fool. The magos has spread sickness before. It's one of the tricks he employs when he wants to seize power. Seven hundred years ago, he brought the Black Death to Europe from the steppes of Asia. We tried to stop him. But we needed Beatrice's help, and you betrayed us. You fell for the magos's lies and succumbed to temptation. Because of you, most of Florence died. Because of you, half of *Europe* perished."

Haven remembered the corpses littering the streets of Beatrice's city. Could a single being have been responsible for such destruction? "Even if Adam did bring the plague to Europe, he isn't responsible for the disease that will hit New York," Haven argued. "Leah sees a girl in her visions."

"The magos is behind it somehow. I can assure you of that."

"And I'm supposed to trust *you*?" Haven spat.

"You're the one who shouldn't be trusted," Phoebe stated flatly. "*You* are the reason we were forced to kidnap your friend. We needed your cooperation to rid the world of the magos. You're the only creature for whom he'll let down his guard. But I knew that in the time it took you to win his confidence, the magos would be able to win your heart. We took Beau so you would have no choice but to pay us one final visit."

"Well, it's over," Haven said. "I'm not going to help you. Maybe you don't give a damn about Calum, but you're going to release Beau or I'll tell Adam exactly where to find you. And I'll tell him to do whatever he pleases."

"You'll *tell* him? You pathetic little creature. Do you honestly think the magos obeys your commands?"

"Adam will do anything to please me. He believes I was sent to earth to humble him. He told me himself—I'm his only weakness. You know it's true or you wouldn't be so desperate for my help."

"You are his weakness, Haven. But the magos knows *you* have a weakness as well. The Greeks called it hubris. He flatters you, strokes your ego, tells you how very *special* you are. He lets you imagine that you're in control. That he'd turn himself into a saint just to be by your side. And all the while, the magos goes about his business as usual. But you're too blinded by your own pride to see it."

Was it true? Haven wondered. Had Adam been up to his old tricks while she wasn't watching? Haven had to admit it was possible. But she wasn't about to admit it to Phoebe.

"I don't have to listen to this," she announced. "Let Beau go or be prepared to suffer the consequences."

"We will release your friend as soon as your work is done. Now the time has come for you to see the truth about the creature you call Adam. There's one more vision you must have. Beatrice was also convinced that she alone could command the magos. You need to know what happened to her." Phoebe took a mask from the pocket of her dress and strapped it over her nose and mouth. The other Horae followed suit.

"No," Haven said. "There won't be any more visions. Let's go," she said to Leah and Frances. But before she could reach the door, she was overcome by the odor of death.

ONE OF THE CARTS *laden with bodies rumbled through the square in front of Beatrice's house. Throughout Florence, the sweet stench of rotting flesh was growing unbearable. There were too many corpses littering the streets to be collected each morning. Only the very rich could afford a proper burial. No one received last rites anymore.*

The Vettori palazzo buzzed with activity. Most of the furniture had been carted away to the family's country estate. Trunks filled with cloth-

ing and other prized possessions were stacked in the courtyard, waiting to be collected. Grim-faced servants packed the rest, knowing only they themselves would be left behind.

Like the rest of the city's wealthy citizens, Beatrice's parents were fleeing. She had begged them to stay. If Piero and Naddo were to return to Florence, they would need a safe haven. Her father demanded she abandon these fantasies and prepare to leave for the countryside. But Beatrice refused to comply. She still held out hope that she'd see Piero again, and that hope was all that kept her alive.

The answer had arrived on a slip of paper shoved under her bedroom door. "Go see Adam," it said. Beatrice never paused to wonder which soul had taken pity on her. She fled her family's palazzo immediately, racing across the city to Adam's house. If they married at once, she could stay in Florence. She knew Adam would never refuse her.

When she arrived, she saw two men in a corpse-filled cart pull up outside her fiancé's house. Too horror-stricken to speak or move, she watched one of the men pound on the door. A servant answered, and Beatrice expected to see Adam's body hauled out into the street. But the men had come to make a delivery instead.

They slid two bodies off the pile in the back of their cart and laid them out on the stones. Adam's servant handed the men a few coins, and the cart rumbled off, arms and legs flopping over its sides. Beatrice rushed forward. Their clothes were wet and their bodies bloated, but she recognized the dead men in an instant. Piero's skin was free of the ugly black sores that marked all who had died of the plague, but a bloodless wound stretched across his neck. Before Adam's servant could stop her, Beatrice fell to her knees and placed her cheek to her dead brother's chest. She couldn't hear the inhuman scream that issued from her very own throat.

HAVEN WOKE ON the floor. Adam's men had killed Piero. And he had let Haven believe that she was responsible. Neither deed could ever be forgiven. Haven gagged and would have vomited had there been anything at all in her stomach. The room was thick with smoke, and through the haze, she could barely discern thirteen figures huddled together on one side of the room. Someone in the center of the circle was speaking in rapid-fire words that made no sense to Haven.

"What's in this smoke?" Haven heard Frances demand. "We have to get them both to the hospital."

"Quiet!" Phoebe ordered. "I must hear the prophecy."

"Leah's sick. She speaking gibberish!" Frances exclaimed.

"It isn't gibberish. It's the language of ancient Crete," one of the Horae informed her. "It hasn't been spoken in more than two thousand years."

"She has seen a young woman with an old name," Phoebe began to translate. "She created the sickness in a laboratory, and she was not working alone. She is part of a much larger group. Its members were told they would lead the world, but they were abandoned by their patron. Now they want the power they were promised, and they're convinced that they must take it by force. They believe the end they envision will justify their means. Their destiny is America's destiny."

The room went silent. Haven pulled herself up and staggered toward the circle of women. Her own vision had taken a terrible toll, but Leah's had been far more devastating. The girl's eyes were closed and her lips motionless. Frances put a hand on Leah's chest to check for movement.

"Oh my God, she's stopped breathing!" Frances screamed.

"Quickly. Get my bag," Phoebe ordered one of the Horae. "She needs to finish the prophecy."

The woman returned in an instant with a black leather doctor's bag. Phoebe pulled out a small vial of colorless liquid and filled a syringe with it.

"What are you giving her?" Haven demanded.

"Snake venom."

"You'll kill her!"

"I will revive her," Phoebe sneered. "She is not one of you."

The venom entered Leah's veins. She opened her mouth and drew in a long, desperate breath.

"Flora." The name seemed to come from deep within her. "The girl's name is Flora."

"No!" Haven gasped.

"You know the person who designed this disease?" Phoebe asked. "Where can we find her? She must die before the prophesy can be fulfilled."

"You can't kill Flora!" Haven said. "She's only a little girl. She hasn't done anything to anyone."

"She's a child?" Phoebe asked.

"She's one of the kids Adam recruited," Haven said. "She's a member of the Ouroboros Society. She goes to school at Halcyon Hall."

"They all did." Leah was speaking again, this time in English. "Everyone involved in releasing the disease once went to Halcyon Hall. Milo Elliot is their leader."

Leah's eyes fluttered shut.

"At last we know the magos's plan," Phoebe said, turning on Haven. "You thought his school was above reproach? *This* is what he's been working to achieve. If the magos is not stopped, we will have no choice but to kill all of the children."

Haven gawked at Phoebe, unable to speak. The old woman grabbed her by the arm and pulled her up the stairs and into the sunroom where they had first met.

"*Now* do you understand why you must do as we ask?"

"Yes," Haven said weakly.

"And your own vision. Did you see what I needed you to see?"

The horrible memory would never leave her for as long as she lived. The sight of the brother she'd loved so much, murdered by the man she had trusted. The man she'd thought she could control. She would make Adam suffer for his crimes.

"Yes," Haven said. "I know why Beatrice decided to betray Adam. I will help you lock him away."

"This is *your* destiny, Haven. I helped you face it, but you could not have avoided it." Phoebe sat down in one of the chairs, her energy spent. "Over the centuries, each of my sisters has tried to cheat destiny. Virginia was the latest to do so. She infiltrated the Society as a young woman, and Adam sensed her weakness immediately. She wanted a family of her own. He made her famous and introduced her to Jerome Morrow. Soon after they were married, Iain was born, and Virginia almost forgot her true mission. I couldn't allow that to happen, so I had Jerome give me a son as well."

"You seduced your sister's husband?"

Phoebe shrugged. "I did what I had to do. But even that wasn't enough to bring Virginia to her senses. It wasn't until Iain began to speak of his previous lives—and it became clear who he was—that Virginia lost her mind completely. She'd tried so hard to escape from us, only to have her own son be one of the souls we needed to find. It took a twenty-year sentence in that hovel in Tuscany for my sister to realize that she couldn't escape her fate. You've had to learn the same lesson far more quickly."

"I have no intention of running from my destiny."

"I can see that now," Phoebe said. "Until today, you've been searching for a way to betray us. The snake goddess has shown you what will happen if you do."

"Tell me what you want, Phoebe."

"Cleo and Chandra have visited the mausoleum in Green-Wood Cemetery. They say it will suit our purposes. There's an anteroom with a fountain. Beyond it lies a larger room with seven doors. Six of the chambers contain a sarcophagus. The seventh is empty. It's deep underground, and all the doors have locks. We've had a key made for the seventh door that will allow you to secure it. This is the room where the magos will spend eternity. I must say, it's much nicer than some of the other options we've considered. He'll be more comfortable than he deserves."

"You're sure the mausoleum will hold him?"

"Yes," Phoebe said. "Not even the magos could escape from it."

"Then I will call Adam and ask him to meet me there tomorrow morning at ten," Haven said. "Tonight, I'm going to destroy the Ouroboros Society."

CHAPTER FORTY-THREE

"And here comes Alex Harbridge, wearing what fashionistas are already calling the dress of the evening!"

"Good evening, Jack." Alex sauntered up to the handsome reporter standing at the side of the red carpet with a microphone in his hand. She looked stunning in her glittering green gown, her long red hair worn loose and wild. She might have been a young goddess who had risen from the sea.

"Alex, you don't enjoy a reputation as a fashion maven—"

"And I'll forgive you for saying so, *Jack*, since I know you don't have much experience flattering young *ladies*," Alex's laughter had a razor-sharp edge, and it didn't take a trained eye to catch the daggers her eyes shot in his direction.

"What I meant to say is that you seem more focused on your craft than on the superficial sides of the business. And yet here you are tonight in one of the most remarkable gowns ever seen on the Oscars' red carpet."

"Thank you. It was made by a young designer I discovered myself. Her name is Haven Moore."

Jack cocked his head. "Where have I heard that name?"

"She designed Lucy Frederick's dress as well."

"Ah, that must be it," Jack said. "Well, I imagine her name will be on everyone's lips tomorrow morning. Now that you're with us, Alex, I know the folks back at home would love to hear your thoughts on some of the things that have happened in the past few days."

Alex frowned. "I'm just here to—"

"Your friend, television actor Calum Daniels, was arrested this morning on kidnapping charges. What can you tell us about this strange turn of events?"

"It's all a terrible mistake. I expect the charges to be dropped any minute now."

"And what do you have to say about the recent reappearance of Iain Morrow?" Jack added quickly before Alex had time to make her escape. "You two were an item back in the day. How does it feel to hear he's returned from the dead?"

"I wish Iain nothing but the best."

"So you don't believe he was responsible for the murder of the musician Jeremy Johns two years ago?"

"This is America, Jack. Last I heard, we're all innocent until proven guilty," Alex said with an angry smile.

"Turn the television off," Haven demanded, and Alex's pretty face faded to black.

"Sorry," Frances said. "I thought it might take your mind off tomorrow. I didn't know—"

"It's okay," Haven assured her. She hadn't meant to snap, but the sight of Alex Harbridge had ripped open a wound she was trying to ignore just long enough to do what needed to be done. "I'm going to lie down now."

"Are you sure you want to go to sleep?" Frances asked. "Iain should be back soon."

"I didn't say I was going to sleep," Haven said. She doubted she'd ever be able to sleep again.

Instead Haven lay on the bed in Constance Whitman's room, staring at the ceiling and thinking of Beau. Even as a boy, he couldn't stand to see Haven unhappy. Whenever he discovered her looking miserable, he'd stop at nothing to make Haven laugh. Once, when Haven's grandmother was making life unbearable, Beau had stayed up all night sewing a giant replica of one of the old lady's dresses. He'd appeared beneath Haven's window the very next morning to deliver a lecture on the importance of shunning homosexual football players. The performance had made Haven's grandmother despise Beau with a passion, but it had sent Haven sprinting to the bathroom before she peed her pants laughing.

This time Beau could do nothing to lift Haven's spirits. He was still in the Horae's hands, and it was all Haven's fault.

The bedroom door opened, and Iain entered.

"Did you find Padma?" Haven asked.

"She was back at that rat hole on the Lower East Side. She thinks I'm the only one who knows she's there, and I really hope she's right."

"Did she agree to release the files?"

"She did."

"How much did she want?"

"All of it."

"All of it?" Haven's heart sank a little.

"Every last cent of the Morrow family fortune—the second we're able to give it."

Haven nodded solemnly. "It's worth it."

"I know," Iain said.

"So what's going to happen now?"

"Padma will speak to the newspapers tonight. She'll be on a plane tomorrow. The story will break the next day. We'll wire the money to a Swiss account once we have it."

"And then?"

Iain sat down beside her. "And then no one will go near the Ouroboros Society again. With no leader left and a scandal hanging over the club, the doors should be sealed for good. There won't be any money to fund Adam's school. Flora will grow up to be an ordinary doctor. Leah's prophecy won't be fulfilled."

"Thank God," Haven said.

"There's more. Padma says she'll admit to the papers that she ordered Jeremy Johns's murder. And she'll give the police the name of the gray man who did it. We'll finally be free to go wherever we want."

"We?" Haven asked miserably, no longer able to hold back all the horrible thoughts that had been multiplying in her head. "Are you sure you want me to go with you? I mean, think about it, Iain! I'm cursed! Adam and the Horae will follow me wherever I go. I'll ruin all your lives. As long as you're with me, you'll never be free of them."

"You've got it backward, Haven," Iain insisted. "I don't give a damn about Adam or the Horae. My lives would be ruined if you *weren't* with me."

"No, listen! There's something I have to tell you," Haven said. "I found out why your childhood was so miserable. I know why your mother despised you. She's one of the Horae and—"

"My *mother* is one of the Horae? Virginia *Morrow*? That's not—"

"*Please*. Just let me finish. She was there today when I went to see them at Sylvan Terrace. Phoebe told me that your mother spent decades trying to escape from her sisters. She wanted her own life, and she was desperate for a child—someone who would belong to *her*. Then she found out that you were one of the souls her sisters wanted to locate. Her heart must have broken the moment you told her you were looking for *me*."

The revelation had only stunned him for an instant. "You are *not* responsible for my mother's actions," Iain persisted. "Horae or not, I would have loved her too, if she had given me a chance."

"There's more. Phoebe seduced your father. Calum Daniels is your half brother."

"Whoa." Iain looked as though he'd been whacked in the gut with a baseball bat. "I could use a drink now too."

"Don't you see?" Haven cried. "None of this would have happened if it wasn't for me. I'm like your personal bad-luck charm. Every horrible force in the universe is drawn to me."

"I'm drawn to you too. So is Beau. So is Leah."

"And today I saw what can happen to the people who love me," Haven said. The horror show in Florence hadn't stopped playing in her head. "I saw Piero's body. He'd been murdered, his throat slit, all because I trusted the wrong person."

"I know what you saw was terrible, but you can't take responsibility for someone else's deeds."

"You don't understand. It *was* my fault that Piero died. The Horae were the ones who brought Adam to Florence and introduced him to me. I was supposed to help lock him away, but I betrayed them. I was so dazzled by the freedom Adam promised me that I acted too late. Piero died, and Adam's ships brought the Black Death to Europe. And to think—I almost let the same thing happen twice. I almost let a plague wipe out New York City."

"But you're going to stop the plague this time, Haven. That's all that counts. You're the reason Leah is here. You're the one who knew Flora. Without you, none of us would have figured out what Adam had planned for the kids at Halcyon Hall. And without you, we would never be able to imprison him tomorrow."

Haven felt a terror unlike anything she'd ever known spreading through her body. But she had to tell Iain everything. Even if it meant losing him.

"You don't understand, Iain. I'm not who you think I am. I'm not even sure you can trust me. There's still something I need to confess. I made a dress for one of the OS members, and she opened an account in my name. She paid me twenty points, and I was going to use them to have Beau's kidnapper punished. I wanted him to be beaten like Beau was."

"Did you actually spend the points?" Iain asked.

"No," Haven told him. "I could have, but I chickened out."

"So you think you should be punished for having evil thoughts?"

"It wasn't just an evil thought, Iain. I almost became one of them. I swear, I was *this close*."

"But you *didn't*. You're human, Haven. Terrible ideas are going to enter your brain from time to time. All that counts is whether you act on them. And in this case, you haven't done a single thing wrong."

"I kissed Adam."

"Okay, maybe you did *one* thing wrong," he joked. "But Haven?"

She looked up at him. He was so good, she thought. She couldn't believe she'd risked what they had—and would have to risk it all over again.

"I have faith in you," he told her. "If you've made mistakes, you still have a chance to fix them."

"I'm scared," Haven said.

"So am I." Iain lay down beside her, and she felt his warm hands sneak beneath the covers and find her warm skin.

CHAPTER FORTY-FOUR

"Haven, Iain, get out of bed!" Frances shouted through the bedroom door.

"What time is it? Am I late?" Haven mumbled.

It was still dark. Haven blindly groped for Iain's cell phone on the bedside table. When the light came on, the clock read 5:35 a.m.

"Haven, Iain, get out here!" Frances shrieked again. "Something's happened."

Iain pulled on a pair of jeans and was the first to the door. "Is Leah okay?" he asked. "What's wrong?"

"Leah's asleep. Come to the living room. There's something you need to see." Once they were there, Frances pointed at the television. "It's on most of the channels now."

The New York Post *is reporting that the former president of an elite Manhattan social club has come forward with some stunning allegations. Padma Singh claims that the Ouroboros Society,*

*located in Gramercy Park, has been functioning as an orga-
nized crime ring for decades. During her tenure as president,
Singh kept detailed notes on the illegal activities of the OS
club's members. In her files, she accuses some of the best-known
names in Manhattan of crimes ranging from prostitution and
drug dealing to arson and murder. Ms. Singh has even . . .*

"Those lying bastards," Iain growled. "The *Post* ran the story a day
early." He rushed back to the bedroom and returned moments later
in his coat and shoes.

"What does this mean?" Frances asked.

"It means I have to find Padma before the OS does," Iain said.
"She wasn't supposed to leave the city until tomorrow."

"No!" Haven shouted. "They'll be looking for you too!"

"Which is why I have to go right now." He planted a quick kiss on
her forehead. "I'll be back before you leave to see Adam."

"Iain!" Haven yelled again as he ran out the door. "Be careful!"
she added, but he could no longer hear her.

Iain didn't return in time to see Haven off. She tried calling, only
to hear his phone ring down the hall in Frances's apartment. In his
rush to save Padma, he'd left it lying on the bedside table. Haven
showered, dressed, and waited for word from him. At nine thirty, Leah
found her still sitting on the unmade bed, the ring Iain had given her
now back on her finger. She was gazing at the glass jewel set in gold
and praying it would bring her the luck she needed.

"The car is here for you," Leah said. "Frances says if you're going,
you need to go soon."

"Am I doing the right thing?" Haven asked Leah.

The scrawny girl shook her head. "You're the only one who knows
that. But I wouldn't be here if I didn't trust you."

Haven held out Iain's phone. "Will you keep this with you? Iain
might try to get in touch while I'm gone."

"You're not going to take it?"

"If Iain needs help, I won't be in any position to give it. I need you to watch out for him. If something happens to him, I won't survive."

"What *about* you?" Leah asked. "What if *you* need help?"

"If I need help, I'm not sure there's much you can do."

HAVEN'S CAR CAME to a halt outside the tall gothic gatehouse of Green-Wood Cemetery. Beyond the brown spires lay another realm—a silent, still, and perfectly white world. The snow that had long since turned to slush on the city's streets had yet to be sullied within the cemetery's walls. Only a few narrow paths were cleared, and they wound like black ribbons around the graves. The scene took Haven back to the day they buried Beau's mother. There had been snow on the ground then too. Haven had held Beau's hand as they stood at the edge of a hole carved out of the frozen earth. She took a silent oath by that grave—to give Beau everything he'd lost when his mother died. Haven promised him her protection, encouragement, and unconditional love. But it had only taken a few short years before she'd failed Beau once again.

Haven checked her watch. It was exactly ten o'clock, and aside from a solitary guard sipping coffee inside the gatehouse, she was completely alone. As the minutes ticked past, she began to worry. Adam was never late. Had the events of the morning kept him away?

"You waiting for someone? You want to come sit inside?" the guard addressed her from the door of his booth.

"A friend was supposed to meet me here," Haven said. "He must be running late."

"You talking about a tall guy in a dark overcoat?"

"Yes," Haven said. "That's him."

"He got here a while back. Aside from a couple of ladies, he's the only visitor we've had today."

"Did you see which way he went?"

367

"Up the hill to the left," the guard said. "Where he went after that, I couldn't tell you."

"Thanks," Haven said.

The city vanished, and silence enveloped her. A cold wind blew at her back, pushing Haven gently along the path. Everywhere she looked, angels refused to meet her gaze, their heads either lifted toward heaven or bowed down to the earth below. When she reached the top of the hill, Haven took one last glance at the gates and the guardhouse and then plunged into the woods. She had never felt so alone.

From the summit, the path wound down the other side toward a little lake set in a valley. At the base of the hill was a single door—the entrance to a tomb cut into the rock. The style was ancient, but the marble was freshly chiseled. The white of the stone blended in with the snow that concealed the land. On either side of the door sat two statues, a man and a woman. Haven recognized the hand of Matteo Salvadore in the sculptures' graceful curves. The figures wore long robes with hoods that cast dark shadows over their faces. Most visitors might have mistaken them for mourners, but the look in the eyes that peered out was not grief-stricken but proud. They were the only ones in this cemetery who'd come willingly. They were there to rule over it.

Seated on a bench near the pond, a figure in black watched the frozen water.

"It's lovely here," Haven said. She wished she could hold his head under the surface of the pond and let him experience the pain and panic that Piero must have felt.

Adam was so still he could have been part of the scenery. "Yes. And calm. I've never understood why some of you choose to return to this world. If I had a choice, I would stay in the land of the dead."

"Why didn't you wait for me outside the gates?" Haven asked him.

"I was almost hoping you wouldn't come."

"Why wouldn't I come?"

"Surely you saw the news," Adam said.

"Yes."

"Then you must realize that the Ouroboros Society will never survive. I have nothing to offer you now. But I want you to know that I did try. I tried to give you the one thing no one else could possibly give you. There were simply too many forces working against me. I wanted to evolve, but the world wouldn't let me."

"Adam . . ."

He stood up and took a golden key from his pocket. "Since you've made the trip, would you like to see the tomb's interior? It's a work of unimaginable beauty." Adam waded through the snow to the entrance of the mausoleum. The door was a slab of marble over twelve inches thick, yet he pushed it open as if it were Styrofoam.

The anteroom was small, with an arched ceiling. A stone fountain stood in the center, water bubbling from the mouth of a brilliant blue bird molded out of clay. A fine mist seemed to hang in the air, and the walls were decorated with scenes from a lovely garden filled with flowering fruit trees and fluttering creatures.

"It's beautiful," Haven remarked coldly.

"There's more." Adam removed a gas lantern that was hanging from a hook on the wall and made sure the flame burned brightly before he opened another door.

The inner space was much larger than Haven could have imagined, an empty room with seven stone doors. On the floor, tiny shards of glass and precious stones formed a stunning mosaic. A god on a golden chariot pulled by two black horses held a struggling maiden. A hole had opened up in a flowering field, and the horses raced toward the chasm, eager to return to the dark world that lay beneath. Haven knew the scene well.

"You brought it all the way here? The mosaic from our home in Crete?" Haven asked, her voice echoing around the chamber.

"No, this is merely a replica. Your feet never touched these tiles. It's the image itself that holds great meaning for me. From the moment I first saw you in your father's garden, I knew I could never deserve you. I was convinced that the only way to have you was to steal you as Hades did in the myth and trick you into staying with me. I bought this mosaic in Rome to remind me of the errors I've made. Each of the women inside this crypt was only mine for a season. Then, like flowers, they all wilted and died. I was hoping to end that cycle. This time, I wanted you to choose me of your own free will. If you did, I would never need to fear losing you. Now it seems my efforts have been in vain. When did you choose to side with the Horae, Haven?"

The walls of the tomb seemed to close in on her as she tried to figure out what it all meant. "You know about the Horae?"

"I had my suspicions. I thought they might be confirmed when you invited me here today. And yet I still hoped . . ."

He couldn't continue.

"You hoped?" Haven prompted.

"I hoped you would appreciate the changes I've made—to myself and the Society. I hoped you would decide to leave Iain to be with me—not just for a season, but forever. But somehow the Horae have turned you against me once more. What did they tell you this time?"

"They say you brought the black death to Italy in the fourteenth century, and that you will bring a new plague to New York."

"I did bring the black death to Italy; that is true," Adam admitted, much to Haven's surprise. "I had spent too much time in other lands, and the Horae had come to dominate Europe. There's a reason those centuries were known as the Dark Ages. The people were locked into an order they could not escape. Those who were born peasants died peasants. The very idea of learning was stifled. All power lay in the hands of a tiny minority. I found a way to break the system apart. After the plague there was chaos, but that chaos was preferable to the order that preceded it."

"Your solution killed millions and millions of people."

"Yes, but their descendants led better lives. Which option would you have chosen for the people of Europe? Death or hopelessness?"

"Is that why you've planned another plague? To shake up the system again?"

"I haven't planned another plague," Adam said. "Ask the snake goddess, Haven. She's the only one you can trust. She's the only one without a motive to lie."

"She's had visions of the future, Adam. There *will* be a plague."

"And I'm the only possible explanation?"

Haven didn't have an answer.

"I can sense your uncertainty. You know in your heart that I'm innocent, but there's still something else," Adam continued. "What more have the Horae told you?"

"It's not what they've told me, Adam. It's what I've seen for myself. I had a vision of Piero and Naddo's bodies being delivered to your house. Their throats had been cut."

"Yes, I had their bodies fished out of the river. I heard they had been murdered, and I wanted you to be able to give them a proper burial."

Haven shook her head furiously, as though trying to keep his lies from taking root in her mind. "You killed my brother, and you let me think I was responsible!"

"No, Haven. Once again I'm innocent of your charges. You've chosen not to see the truth. Parts of a life can not tell a whole story."

Those were the very words Leah had once used. And Leah Frizzell never lied. Haven felt her rage dissolving. She couldn't condemn him for crimes she had no proof he'd committed.

"Would you like to know how the tale ended?" Adam asked.

"You already told me. I helped the Horae lock you away."

"That wasn't the end, Haven. You locked me away. But thirty years later, you had a change of heart. You were the one who set me free."

"I did?" Haven asked.

Just then, they heard stone sliding across stone and iron hinges groaning under great strain. Haven rushed for the anteroom to see the pale winter sunlight shut out of the crypt. The entrance was closed. There was the faintest sound of a key rattling inside the lock. Then the silence was absolute.

"Stop!" Haven screamed, banging on the door with her fists. "I'm still inside! Stop!"

"No one can hear you," Adam said behind her. "The walls are more than a foot thick."

Haven spun around. The lamplight hollowed out Adam's eyes, and his pale skin shone like alabaster. The shadow he threw against the wall was that of a giant. Adam's human disguise was flickering, failing. She was trapped underground with something more—or less—than a man. An immortal being who now knew that she had betrayed him.

"It seems you've been double-crossed," Adam observed. "The Horae didn't think they could trust you."

For a moment, Haven couldn't find her voice. It remained lodged somewhere deep in her throat, choking her. "What are you going to do to me?" she asked, finally forcing the words out into the air.

"That depends," Adam said reasonably. His calmness frightened Haven even more than a rage possibly could. "Would you mind telling me what you know of the Horae's plan?"

Haven hesitated.

"You needn't tell me now. It looks as though we may have all eternity to discuss such matters."

"They came to see the mausoleum. They made a key to the seventh room—the one without a coffin. They wanted me to lock you inside and leave you there."

"A worthy scheme," Adam said. "If that door had a lock. May I see the key you were given?"

Haven dug into her pocket and handed him the key.

Adam barely glanced at it. "Useless," he pronounced, tossing it across the room. The metallic ping echoed four times around the chamber. "They never intended to let you go free." He came toward her, his steps slow and steady. She let her head drop, unable to face him. She could feel his cold breath stir her hair.

"Now that you've heard the truth, could you have done as the Horae asked?"

"I don't think so," Haven replied honestly. There was no longer any reason to lie. "I wouldn't have gotten involved with the Horae at all if they hadn't deceived me. They were the ones who kidnapped Beau—and they told me I needed their help to find him. You were the price I had to pay. I'm sorry I ever agreed. I still don't know if you're lying to me about the plague—or about Piero and Naddo. I go crazy every time I remember their bodies lying on the street in front of your house. But I couldn't lock you away unless I was absolutely certain you had something to do with their murders."

"So the Horae have Beau?" Adam asked.

"Phoebe is their leader. That's why Beau was at Calum's apartment."

Adam's laughter ricocheted off the marble walls. "Of course! How brilliant! She would have known about the improvements being made at the Society. She needed to bring you back to New York before they were complete. She knew that in time I might have made you an offer too good to refuse. If I won your heart, Phoebe would lose her only weapon against me."

"More time wouldn't have helped you win my heart," Haven said, trying not to be cruel. "Everything you've done was meant to impress *me*. And I've realized that isn't what I want. I want someone who does the right thing even when no one is watching. But let's be honest, Adam. You would never have made those improvements if you knew I'd never see them. You wouldn't have acted on your own. You were just manipulating me, and I was silly enough to feel flattered. It was wonderful to think that I might have inspired someone so powerful to do good things. But eventually I would have figured out that none of it was real."

"The improvements weren't real—because they were made for your sake?" Adam argued, though his face said he knew that he'd already lost. "All the wonderful things the OS might have accomplished would have been worthless? You're right, Haven. I don't have much of a moral compass. It makes no difference to me how chaos is spread. A plague or a school—it's all the same in the end. That's why I recruited Owen Bell. He could have compensated for my failings. It's a pity the Society will be destroyed. We both know Owen could have made the OS everything you ever wanted it to be."

"Does it have to be destroyed?" Haven asked.

"I'm not sure we can do much to save it from inside this tomb," Adam said.

"We won't be in here forever," Haven said with a surge of hope. "There are people who know where I am. They'll rescue us both."

"Anyone you told about the mausoleum won't have long to live." Adam broke the news to her gently. "The Horae didn't hesitate to lock you inside a tomb with me. They won't think twice about killing your friends."

"You really think so?" Haven gasped.

"It's what I would have done," Adam admitted. "And even if you were to escape, the Horae would make your life unbearable if you set me free. There are twelve of them, as you may recall. They can be everywhere at once."

Haven paced around the fountain in the anteroom, her panic building. The air in the tomb seemed too thin.

"There is *one* solution," Adam said softly.

"What is it?" Haven asked.

"You escape now and rescue your friends. But you must leave me behind."

"Please don't tease me. I can't escape on my own."

"Oh, but you can," Adam said. "Do you know why there were seven rooms built to house six bodies? The seventh room was always meant to be mine. I told you I avoided the mausoleum to give you your privacy. But I always planned to return. The stillness and silence here is the closest thing to sleep I've ever experienced. It gives me peace. I had the mausoleum constructed so that I could come and go as I pleased." Like a magician conjuring a coin, Adam flicked his wrist and a golden key appeared between his fingers. "The Horae never realized that the same key can open the door from *within* the tomb too. Here, Haven. It is yours."

"But there isn't a keyhole," Haven argued.

"Matteo Salvadore considered this tomb his masterpiece. He was particularly proud of the mural in this room. He wanted it to appear perfectly seamless, so he camouflaged the interior keyhole." Adam walked to the exit and pried a sliver of stone from the door. "You're free to go, Haven."

"What about you?" she asked.

Adam smiled sadly. "I'd like to stay here for a while. I could use a rest. The past century has been quite challenging, even for a creature like me."

"How will you get out? Do you have a key of your own?"

"No," Adam told her. "That's the only one I brought with me."

Haven studied him for signs of uncertainty. "You want me to lock you inside and leave you?"

"It's the only way I can make good on my promise to let you live this life as you choose. And if you go now, you'll be able to save the people with whom you'll want to spend it. Including the young man who gave you the ring you're wearing."

Haven hadn't removed her gloves. There was no way for Adam to have seen the ring she had on her finger.

"You know?"

"You've made your choice," Adam said. "And as a gentleman, I accept it. I only ask for two things in return. First, please deliver the key to the snake goddess. She'll know when the time has come to release me."

"Are you sure?" Haven asked. "Leah thinks you're the next closest thing to the devil."

"The snake goddess knows that even the devil should have his day."

"And your second request?"

"Kiss me again," Adam said. "Let me imagine for a moment that you belong to me. The memory will keep me company in my solitude."

It was a terrible deal, Haven thought. A single kiss in exchange for her life. He deserved much more than that. So without saying a word, she gave him a small piece of her heart as well. Iain could keep the rest, but Haven needed Adam to take something in return for the sacrifice he was making.

Haven stepped toward him and closed her eyes. Adam's lips were cold, his fingers ice. The kiss they shared felt different. In the lobby of the Gramercy Gardens Hotel, Haven had embraced a young man. Now she was wrapped in the arms of an immortal being. She could feel Adam draining the warmth from her body. Her heartbeat slowed. Death was dragging her into the chasm, and she couldn't find the strength to struggle. Her very last thought was of Iain.

CHAPTER FORTY-FIVE

Snowflakes floated down from the heavens and settled among the graves. The cemetery paths had vanished, and Haven wove around marble monuments in the darkness with the golden key burning like ice in her hand. A tiny angel blocked her path. Its hands were pressed together in prayer, and its eyes pleaded with her to stay. Haven tried to step around it and felt her knees buckle. It was so cold, and she desperately needed to sleep. A raised grave beckoned her with a plush, white bed.

How long had she been in the tomb? It was morning when they had been locked inside, and now it was already dark. She remembered Adam pressing his lips to hers, but after that her memories were a blizzardlike blur.

She lay down in the soft snow, her face turned to the sky. The flakes didn't melt when they met her skin. Haven closed her eyes and felt them burying her, one tiny crystal at a time. Then a warmth spread through her body, and she found herself standing on the balcony of her apartment in Rome. The sun was shining, and in the square below, someone was whistling an ancient tune.

With the melody still dancing inside her head, Haven opened her eyes, determined to forge on. She saw three bright circles of light appear on the hill above her. They bounced downward, expanding into radiant orbs as they drew closer.

"It's her! Haven!" yelled a voice.

She squinted into the lights that now held her in place. The pain that streaked through her body was that of a frozen finger dipped under a hot tap. Her eyelids flickered then shut. She felt herself fall again and sink into the snow.

BEATRICE COULD FEEL her bones creak as she made her way down the stairs. She wasn't yet old, but she was no longer young. Thirty years spent praying on the hard floor of the cathedral had destroyed her knees while the guilt had eaten away at her soul. Her loose lips had doomed her beloved brother. And she had allowed another to be incarcerated for a crime she wasn't convinced he'd committed.

At the bottom of the staircase stood the door to his cell. She listened at the keyhole and heard nothing. Then, one by one, she removed the wood planks with which the door had been barricaded. She drew in a breath, prepared at last to face her punishment, and dragged the door open. What would Adam say to her after all of these years?

"SHE'S FINE," HAVEN heard a man say. "No frostbite, and her temperature is back up to normal. When was the last time she ate?"

Haven moved her hand to her belly. It felt concave. She hadn't filled it in days.

"She just moved!" It was Leah's voice.

"Haven?" Now Iain. "Haven, are you awake?"

Haven opened her eyes and saw water-stained ceiling tiles and an IV stand. "Iain?" A shadow passed over her, and she felt his lips.

They were warm. She could taste the whole world in his kiss. Haven reached up and dragged him closer. She slid one hand under his sweater, just to prove he was real.

"Did you do it?" Iain asked, pulling back just enough to see her face.

Haven nodded, tears filling her eyes. "He *let* me."

"He *let* you?"

"The Horae double-crossed me. They locked us both inside the tomb. They must have been worried that I'd set him free someday."

The statement seemed to knock Iain senseless. She could tell he was imagining a hundred other outcomes, each more horrific than the last. He stared into space until he found the power to speak. "I should have known! Why wasn't I at the cemetery with you instead of looking for Padma? I could have lost you forever, and it would have been my fault!"

"How did you escape?" Leah asked.

"Adam had a key that opened the door from the inside. He gave it to me, and he stayed behind. He saved my life."

"And I didn't," Iain muttered.

"You're the reason I wanted to live," Haven told him, smiling for the first time in days.

"Is this what Adam gave you?" Leah asked, twirling the golden key between her thumb and forefinger. "You were carrying it when we found you." She tried to hand it to Haven.

"No. It's yours now," Haven told her, refusing to touch it. "Adam wanted you to keep it."

"*Me?*" Leah asked.

"He said you would know when to use it."

"The Horae *really* locked you inside?" Iain asked. He still couldn't seem to believe it. "Didn't they know we'd rescue you?"

"Adam said they probably planned to kill you guys, too" Haven explained.

Iain seemed to be playing back the previous twelve hours in his head. "Maybe they tried, but we were with the police most of the day.

I had to call them when I found Padma's body."

"Oh my God!" Haven exclaimed, sitting bolt upright on the hospital bed. "Padma's dead? What happened?"

Iain closed his eyes and took a deep breath. "It was horrible, Haven. I found her hanging from a tree in Gramercy Park this morning. Adam made an example of her."

"No! Adam didn't kill her. He couldn't have!"

"We don't know who did it," Leah admitted. "The police aren't exactly short on suspects."

"Well, whoever it was must have saved Leah and me from the Horae," Iain said. "I spent all morning being interrogated. Leah heard about the murder on the news and came down to the station. She was still there at three o'clock when the police made me answer questions for a bunch of reporters."

"That New York news channel was running a clip from the press conference a little while ago," Leah said. "I saw some nurses watching it when I went looking for the bathroom."

"See if it's on again," Haven urged.

Iain turned on the television that was mounted on the wall and flipped through the channels. When he found the twenty-four-hour news station, Haven took the remote from his hand and turned up the volume. It was the second time she'd seen Iain Morrow on television. Almost two years had passed since she'd discovered his handsome face staring out from her grandmother's TV screen.

Haven felt a surge of pride at the sight of the young man standing beside a grizzled old captain from the NYPD. Iain looked harried and uncomfortable. He clearly didn't enjoy being grilled by a roomful of rabid reporters. But there wasn't an ounce of fear in his eyes.

"Mr. Morrow. You're the one who discovered Padma Singh's body early this morning, is that correct?" A reporter asked.

"Yes," Iain confirmed, blinking as fifty cameras seemed to flash at once.

"Can you describe the condition of the corpse for us?"

Iain grimaced, as if nauseated by the memory, and the police captain patted him on the back. "I arrived at Gramercy Park around six thirty this morning. I saw Padma Singh's body hanging from a tree across from the Ouroboros Society headquarters. She was naked. The word *traitor* had been carved into her skin."

"Why were you at Gramercy Park so early in the morning?" It sounded more like an accusation than a question. Haven could tell the reporters were eager to make Iain the story's villain.

"I was searching for Ms. Singh. The *New York Post* had released the contents of her files on the Ouroboros Society a day earlier than agreed, and I wanted to help her get out of town before she came to any harm."

Another reporter jumped in. "Captain Fahey, would you care to explain why Mr. Morrow is not a suspect in Ms. Singh's murder?"

The tall police captain bent down to speak into the microphone. "Mr. Morrow has a solid alibi for the time of Padma Singh's death. And he had no motive for killing her. Ms. Singh accused many Ouroboros Society members of crimes, but Mr. Morrow is the only person she exonerated."

Another reporter popped up out of his seat. "Mr. Morrow, how *does* it feel to no longer be the prime suspect in the murder of Jeremy Johns?"

"Good. I look forward to being able to walk down the street without having to watch over my shoulder."

"Can you tell us where you've been for the last eighteen months?"

"I couldn't stay in New York," Iain said. "I'd been framed for a murder I didn't commit. When everyone assumed I'd died in the fire, I decided to lie low in Europe for a while."

"Where in Europe? Can you be more specific?"

"No, I can't." Iain glowered.

"And what do you have to say about the suit your mother has brought against Haven Moore, the young woman who inherited your fortune?"

"I'd rather not answer any more personal questions. But I think it's clear that my mother no longer has much of a case. My will was not forged. Haven Moore will keep the money."

"You were a member of the Ouroboros Society. Do you have any firsthand knowledge of the crimes Ms. Singh described?" Watching this scene from the hospital, Haven could no longer tell who was speaking. The reporters were like a pack of wild dogs fighting over the same scrap of meat.

"I will let Padma Singh's files speak for themselves." Iain was clearly growing frustrated.

"Captain Fahey, how do you respond to reports that Chief Gordon Williams belongs to the Ouroboros Society and has been known to perform favors for high-ranking members?"

Captain Fahey huffed. "It's ridiculous," he said. "Next?"

"There's one name that appears repeatedly in Padma Singh's files. Adam Rosier. To my knowledge, no one has been able to locate a man by that name. Captain Fahey, do you have any idea where Mr. Rosier might be found?"

As the captain began to address the question, Iain stole a look back at Leah, who was seated behind him. She held two phones up in the air and shook her head, her face grim. Iain tapped the police captain on the shoulder and whispered in the man's ear.

"I'm sorry, ladies and gentlemen, but we're going to have to cut this conference short," Captain Fahey announced. The camera followed Iain and Leah as they hurried out of the room. Standing at the edge of the crowd were Chandra and Cleo.

CHAPTER FORTY-SIX

"Are you sure you're feeling strong enough for this?" Iain asked as their taxi turned north onto the West Side Highway.

"You heard the doctor. I just needed to eat. Are there any more energy bars?" Haven asked, her mouth still full. Leah handed her another dirt-flavored treat.

"And you're convinced this is the smart thing to do?" Iain asked. "Even Adam thought the Horae would kill us."

"Are they going to kill us?" Haven asked Leah as she bit into her second energy bar.

"No," Leah said.

"How do you know?" Iain asked her. "Have you had a vision?"

"Nope. But this ain't how I'm going out," Leah said. "The Lord has other plans for me."

"You keep talking about the Lord, but the Horae always call you the snake goddess," Haven teased her. "Adam does too."

"They can call me whatever they want," Leah replied. "I know *exactly* who I am."

"And who exactly *are* you?" Iain asked.

"A girl with a gift."

"What about Adam?" Haven asked. "You still think he's the devil?"

Leah raised an eyebrow. "Maybe the devil isn't the best name for him, but I wouldn't trust Adam for a second. He ain't in love with *me*."

Their cab stopped at the foot of a staircase on St. Nicholas Avenue. On the hill above sat Sylvan Terrace. The quaint yellow houses were all dark but for one at the end of the lane. Leah led the way, bounding up the stoop and pounding on the door. Chandra answered.

"Hey," Leah said, pushing past her. "We're here to get Beau."

Chandra almost licked her lips, like a fox that's just had a rabbit hop right into its den. Then she caught sight of Haven. Her jaw dropped, and she rushed back inside the house.

"Phoebe!" Chandra shouted as she sprinted toward the council room where the Horae held their meetings. Haven, Iain, and Leah followed. All of the Horae were there. Haven counted twelve females in white robes and one brightly dressed young man. Calum Daniels was with them. He stumbled backward, almost falling onto the logs that were burning in the fireplace. Virginia Morrow caught sight of her son and swooned. One of her sisters helped her into a chair.

"Haven!" Even Phoebe's face was ashen. "What are you doing here? Where is the magos?"

"He's back at the cemetery," Haven said. "He said to tell you hello. He'll be catching up with you later."

"I don't understand," Phoebe said. "How did you escape from the mausoleum?"

"Adam had a key that opened the door from the inside," Haven told her. "He let me leave, and he stayed behind."

The Horae's whispers filled the room with a soft hissing, like steam from a kettle that's just begun to boil.

"The magos sacrificed himself for you?" Vera asked. "And you allowed him to do so?"

"Yes, but Leah can set him free whenever she likes," Haven said. "And if she does, Adam knows exactly where to find you. I told him everything."

Phoebe's nostrils flared, and her lips curled back from her teeth. "How could you let this happen?" she shrieked at Chandra. "You were supposed to make sure that the tomb could never be opened. All three of them should be dead!"

"We'll take care of them now," Cleo answered for Chandra. "They're all here. They've made it easy for us. We can cremate the bodies in the furnace."

"You can do *what*?" Virginia Morrow demanded, pushing past two of her sisters to reach Phoebe. Haven recognized the rage on the woman's face. Phoebe was lucky there weren't any Parma hams within reach.

The other Horae were whispering once more.

"Kill the snake goddess?"

"We'd be cursed!"

"They've lost their minds!"

"Our guests cannot be allowed to live," Phoebe said, ignoring the whispers while she tried to reason with Virginia. "Any one of them could set the magos free. I know this is painful for you, sister, but we must all sacrifice for the cause."

Leah sidled up to the warring women as if she were joining two friends at a cocktail party. "You know what they say about sacrificing, don't you, Phoebe? It's so much more fun when other people get to do it." Then she addressed Virginia Morrow. "You knew all along that the Horae would have to kill Haven, didn't you?"

"No!" Virginia insisted. "We never intended to kill *anyone*! We planned to lock the magos in a bank vault and destroy the buildings above. Haven could never have set him free—so there was no reason to harm her. But Iain made it impossible to use the vault—and the tomb could be opened at any time. None of us wanted Haven to die, but Phoebe said it was necessary in order to keep the magos imprisoned."

Leah shook her head in disgust. "And you didn't realize that your decision would have consequences? You thought Phoebe could get rid of Haven without killing Iain too? And what did you think she was going to do with me after I showed up?"

"Is this true, Phoebe? How long have you been planning to murder *my son*?" The volume of Virginia's voice was steadily rising. "That was *never* part of our arrangement!"

"I promised you the Morrow fortune in exchange for your help," Phoebe countered. "You didn't seem to care which means I used to procure it. You should have told me you wouldn't want to see Iain harmed."

"Some things don't need to be said!" Virginia screamed with such force that Haven nearly covered her ears.

"Aunt Virginia." Calum Daniels edged Leah out of the way and stepped between the two old women before they could come to blows. "I'm afraid Mother is right. We must all do what's necessary for the greater good."

"We are not responsible for the greater good," Virginia said, as though she were teaching a small child a lesson. "That is the snake goddess's purview. Do you think we should kill her as well, Calum? Do you have any idea what might happen if we were to commit such a crime?"

"We must do whatever is necessary," Calum repeated solemnly.

"Your mother would be the first to agree with you," Haven told him. "She was willing to sacrifice *you* as well, Calum. You see, I came here after you were arrested. I threatened to have Adam kill you if Beau wasn't returned. Phoebe told me to go ahead and order your murder. She didn't even blink."

"You're lying!" Calum appealed to his mother. "Tell me she's lying!"

"Haven is speaking the truth," Virginia said somberly as Phoebe grasped for an excuse. "We were all here in this room when your mother made the decision to let you die. She's never known how lucky she is to have you. She was given the gift of guiding you through your first incarnation, but she has badly abused that privilege."

"My first incarnation?" Calum sputtered. "But . . ."

"Phoebe has misled you since the day you were born. This is your first life, Calum."

"Mother?" Calum said, the last of his confidence crumbling.

Haven had to look away. No matter what Calum had done, she could only pity him now. Haven remembered how proud he'd been of his previous lives. Calum's whole identity had been built out of lies, and his world had imploded with a single sentence. Haven couldn't condemn someone who had never had a chance to know who he was.

"Don't listen to Virginia, Calum, she's always half drunk," Phoebe said, finally launching her own defense. "She's been jealous of us since—"

"That's enough!" Vera seemed to grow as Phoebe shriveled. "Virginia hasn't had a drink since she arrived in New York. Every word she's uttered is true, Calum. My sisters and I agree that it's time you should know." Haven noticed that seven of the Horae were now standing behind Vera. A new order was forming before her eyes.

Calum sniffed, trying his best to maintain his dignity. "I never did any of this for *her*, anyway. It was a business arrangement. If I helped Mother with her little plot, I would get to run the Ouroboros Society once Adam was gone."

"No, Calum," Vera corrected him. "Phoebe never intended to let a nineteen-year-old boy lead the Society. That was yet another lie."

Calum turned on his mother. "You *promised*," he whined. "You would never have known about Owen if I hadn't dragged him to see you! And it was my idea to use him to bring Haven's friend to New York! She wouldn't be here if it wasn't for me! I did everything you asked me to do! I let Beau stay at my house! When the cops showed up, I even let them arrest me just so you could keep him hidden!"

"You *failed*, Calum," Phoebe sneered. "You were too weak to see the plan through."

"Blame yourself, not your son," Vera said. "There was never a chance that your scheme would succeed. Chandra and Cleo may do whatever you tell them, but the rest of us wouldn't have allowed you to murder Iain or the snake goddess."

"Don't you see?!" Phoebe yelled in desperation. "This is all his doing! The magos is winning! He's driving us apart! This is what he wanted all along! He's planned all of this from the very beginning."

"The magos is locked up in a mausoleum in Brooklyn," Vera pointed out.

"If you're not careful, you'll join him," Leah warned. "The way I see it, Phoebe, you're worse than Adam is. At the very least, I think it's time you ladies looked for another leader."

"The snake goddess has spoken," Vera announced. "Now that the magos is locked away, we should take the opportunity to reorganize. Unless there are objections, I will assume leadership of the Horae. From this day forward, we will not stoop to employ the tactics of our enemies. Phoebe, Chandra, and Cleo, your rights are suspended. You may rejoin us in your next incarnations."

"You can't do this, Vera! You've always been too fainthearted to lead! You'll let them set the magos free!" Phoebe raged. "You can't trust any of them!"

"I trust the snake goddess. She never chooses sides," Vera stated. "You may leave whenever you like," she told her guests.

"But what about Beau?" Haven demanded.

"Where is the boy?" Vera asked Phoebe.

"You won't find him," Phoebe said with a nasty smirk. She still had one last trick up her sleeve. "He'll be dead before sunrise. If he isn't already."

"He's in the bank vault under Lenox Avenue," Calum Daniels announced. "They had to hide him after the police raided my building. You'll need to get there fast. The combination is . . ."

CHAPTER FORTY-SEVEN

If Iain hadn't grabbed Haven and thrown her into the back of a cab, she would have run the whole way to Lenox Avenue. She cursed herself for not checking the vault earlier. It had been prepared for Adam, who needed neither water nor air. Haven rested her head on her knees and prayed that they'd make it to the vault in time. No one in the taxi spoke. It was as if they were saving both their breath and their energy for Beau.

The neon sign in the middle of the block was still flashing its red-and-white warning, but the buildings had all been prepared for demolition. Next to the storefront church sat the sad remains of a neighborhood bank, with ads showing smiling, satisfied customers taped to its door. Leah was still staring up at the neon sign when Iain kicked in a sheet of graffiti-covered plywood that covered a broken window. Haven squeezed in through the opening and searched for the stairs.

There were none—just a hole in the floor with a rope dangling inside. She slid down to the building's basement without waiting for her friends. At the bottom of the hole, she found an enormous vault with a circular door.

"You here to see the boy?" a voice asked, and Haven nearly jumped out of her skin. Two women had been sleeping in a corner of the room. One had woken up and was rubbing her eyes.

"You know?"

"He showed up yesterday with two people. They left him inside there."

"Was he okay?"

"A bit beat up, I guess, but other than that he seemed fine."

"You knew that someone's been in this vault for a whole day, and you didn't call the cops?" Haven demanded, amazed that the woman could be so blasé.

"It wasn't like he was fighting when they put him in there. And those two ladies said that if I didn't mind my own business they wouldn't let me and my friend sleep down here when it snows," the woman said. "Sorry, but I have bigger worries than some dumb Southern boy who likes to hide in old bank vaults."

"Did these *ladies* happen to tell you that this building is about to be demolished?" Haven asked. "Did they tell you that you need to find somewhere else to stay or you'll be buried in a mound of rubble?"

The woman stared at Haven for a moment. "They neglected to mention that. So how are you going to get him out, anyway?" She seemed curious, now, nothing more.

"I have the combination."

"Hell, that's only *half* the battle," the woman announced as she dragged herself up off the floor. "If you want, I can show you how they opened it. Didn't look all that easy."

Just then, Iain and Leah slid down the rope.

"Who's she?" Iain asked.

"Who're *they*?" the woman responded, gazing at Leah, who looked otherworldly in the glow of the flashlights.

"These are my friends, Iain and Leah. This nice lady . . ." She paused for the name.

"Ramona," the woman offered reluctantly.

"Ramona is going to help me open the vault," Haven said.

"Will Ramona be getting compensated for her efforts?" Ramona asked.

"I'll give you my last twenty bucks," Leah said, rustling in her pocket for a wadded-up bill.

"It's got to be around midnight," Ramona said, checking an imaginary watch. "That means this is overtime. I get time and a half."

Iain dug into his coat. "All I have is a five."

"Then you owe me five more," Ramona said, snatching the bill from his fingers. "You look like you're good for it. Let's get to work."

She showed Haven how to enter the combination and which wheels to turn. When they pulled the door open, a whoosh of hot air escaped the vault.

"Good *God*, it smells nasty in there!" Ramona noted. "Sorry," she added unconvincingly when Leah shot her a look. "Well, at least he was warm! I'm lucky to still have my toes!"

Inside, Beau was lying on his side, his face to a metal wall and his curly blond hair wet with sweat. A reeking slop bucket sat in the opposite corner, surrounded by candy bar wrappers. An empty bottle of water was the only other object in the cramped little room.

"Beau!" Haven screamed as she slid across the metal floor and knelt with a hand on his back. She could feel his chest rising and falling. "Beau," she said, giving him a shake. "Beau, please wake up!"

"What the hell?" Beau mumbled. He rolled over and shielded his bruised eyes from the glare of the flashlights. "Haven? Is that you?"

"Beau!" Haven nearly collapsed with relief. "Are you all right?"

"Haven." Beau blinked furiously, still blinded by the light. "God, I was just having the worst dream. There was this evil goddamned little girl and she . . . Wait. Is he here? Did you bring him?"

"Iain's right outside," Haven assured him. "Leah, too. They're going to help me get you out of here."

Iain stepped inside the vault. "I'm here, Beau," he said.

"No, not *Iain*." Beau seemed confused. "*Adam*."

"Why would Adam be with me?" Haven wiped her tears on her coat sleeve.

"You told me to wait inside! You said I needed to hide and surprise him so you could lock him up in the vault. You think I'd sweat my ass off in some metal box if I thought it would all be for nothing?"

"*I* told you to wait inside?" Haven looked up at Iain. He shook his head in confusion. "When did I say that?"

"Yesterday, goddammit! Have you lost your mind, Haven?"

"Beau," Haven said gently. "I haven't spoken to you in weeks. I've been searching all over for you. I came back from Italy to find you."

"Of course we haven't *spoken*. Adam's got all the phones bugged. You *e-mailed* me."

"He's hallucinating," Haven whispered to Iain. "We need to—"

"Goddammit, I am *not* hallucinating!" Beau barked.

"Hey, you guys?" Ramona was standing in the doorway to the vault, her eyes wide. "You better come out. Something's wrong with that redheaded girl."

"Who's *she*? And what the hell is *Leah* doing here?" Beau croaked. "Hey!"

HAVEN AND IAIN were already outside in the basement. Leah lay on the floor, her limbs twitching uncontrollably. Her eyes had rolled back so far that only the whites were visible. Her lips spelled out silent words.

"What's happening to her?" Ramona asked. "Is she sick? You want me to run and fetch a doctor?"

"No," Haven said, reaching down for Leah's hand. "A doctor won't help. She's seeing the future."

"That child's giving prophecy?" Ramona asked, awestruck.

"Yes," Haven told her. Ramona dropped to her knees, her head bowed and her fingers laced in prayer. Her friend woke and shuffled over to join her. They waited, scarcely moving, until Leah was still and her lips sealed.

"Leah," Haven whispered. "Are you back? What did you see?"

Leah's eyes popped open, and her lungs filled with air. "It ain't over," she said.

"What in *the hell* is going on?" Haven looked up to find Beau watching over the scene.

"The plague is still coming," Leah continued. "We haven't stopped it. We've only made it more certain."

"But *how*?" Haven groaned. "I've done everything I could. Adam is locked away in the mausoleum. You're the only one with a key."

"What?" Beau interjected. "But I thought . . ."

Iain put a hand on Beau's broad shoulder. "We'll hear your story next," he promised him. "Just listen for now."

"I was sure we'd put an end to it all," Haven continued. "The Ouroboros Society will be shut down. Halcyon Hall will have to close. The kids will all go home."

"I think that may be the problem," Leah said. "They can't go back to their ordinary lives. They know who they are now, and they know what they can do. But they're still so young. They need to be taught that their power can be used as a force for good."

"You're saying Halcyon Hall has to stay open?"

"The closer this future comes to being certain, the more I can see of it. Now that Adam's gone, Milo won't have to leave New York. And we're not the only ones who know about him. Pretty soon, someone's going to start putting the wrong ideas in his head. She'll have Milo convince the Halcyon Hall kids that they need to seize power by any means necessary."

"*She*? Other than us, who knows about Milo?"

"I recognized a woman in this vision. I'm pretty sure it was that girl Chandra."

"Chand—" Beau started to exclaim before Iain gave him another reassuring pat on the shoulder.

"I get it now," Haven said. "Chandra knows exactly what the Halcyon Hall kids can do. She heard the prophecy too, which means we've even given her a plan. She's going to use Milo to seize control—of the Horae and the whole city. The only way to stop her is to save the Society and Halcyon Hall."

"But how?" Iain asked. "Have you seen the papers today? The Ouroboros Society is dead. No one will want to be associated with it. You really think we can save it at this point?"

"We're not the ones who can save it," Haven said. "I should have figured that out a long time ago. But I think I know someone who might be right for the job."

"You mean?" Leah asked.

"Yep." Haven held out a hand and helped Leah to her feet. "You feeling good to go?"

"I am now," Leah said.

"What in the *hell* are they talking about?" Beau asked Iain.

"No idea," Iain replied.

"Hold up, Haven," Beau said. "Will you *please* tell me what's going on? Where are we going?"

"We're going to introduce you to your soul mate," Haven said with a grin.

"You're joking," Beau said.

"Nope," Haven told him. "I'm so serious that I'm even going to insist you take a shower."

"Who *are* you people?" Haven turned to see Ramona and her friend staring at them. She'd forgotten they were still there.

"I'll be back soon with the money we owe you, Ramona," Leah said. "I appreciate you praying with me. I never forget a good turn."

CHAPTER FORTY-EIGHT

"I got off the plane and took a cab to the address on 114th Street that I'd been given," Beau told his rapt audience in the back of the taxi. "Course the driver dropped me off on the wrong corner, and it took me a while to find the right building. So I finally get there, and I walk up the stairs and ring the buzzer. And Chandra answers the door. What was she doing in Leah's visions, anyway?"

"We'll explain later," Haven told him. "We want to hear your side of the story. Just assume we know nothing."

Beau took in a deep breath. "If you say so, but for the record, this all really couldn't get any weirder."

"No kidding," Haven replied.

"Okay, so Chandra answers the door at the apartment where Roy Bradford was supposed to live. I don't recognize her at first, and I'm not expecting to see some *girl*—much less a girl who lives in an apartment that looks like it's right out of another century. So I tell her I'm sorry to bother her. But she insists I'm at the right place and tells me to come inside and have a beer. I'm sitting there thinking 'I know this chick from somewhere.' Then I figure out *where*. She was the one who saved our butts in that Indian grocery. And that really started to mess with my head."

"Were you scared?"

"Of Chandra? Hell no! The girl's what, five feet tall? I've eaten sandwiches bigger than her. But that was when I started to realize the whole trip was going to be about *you* again, Haven. No offense, but I was a *little* disappointed."

"Sorry," Haven said. "I swear I'll make it up to you soon. What did Chandra tell you?"

"She said she belongs to a group called the Horae. Their job is to watch over you."

"Watch over *me*?" When Haven started to snicker, Iain and Leah joined in.

"Am I supposed to ignore the fact that I'm not in on your little joke?" Beau growled. "I just spent the night in a bank vault for you."

"Sorry," Haven said. She squeezed his muscular arm. "I won't laugh again."

"Anyway," Beau reluctantly continued. "Chandra reminded me of the time she saved us, and that seemed like proof enough of what she was saying. She told me that you were in trouble again. Adam had found you guys in Italy. Chandra said that the Horae were trying to figure out a plan to save you, and they needed my help. I had to convince you to fly back to New York."

"Wait—what happened to Roy Bradford?"

"Roy Bradford doesn't exist. He was just a play to get me to come up here."

"So how did Chandra know about our previous life in Florence?"

Beau looked at Haven as if she were crazy. "She was there too!"

"Interesting. But if my good friends the Horae wanted me back in New York, why didn't they just ask me to come?" Haven asked.

"Because Adam would get suspicious if you flew back for no reason. It needed to look like there was some kind of emergency."

"I see." Haven nodded. "Continue."

"I don't like this game," Beau said.

"It will be over soon," Haven assured him.

"Chandra asked me to send you a message that would make you think I was in trouble—one only the two of us would understand. She said it would be more convincing if you really thought I'd been kidnapped or something."

"So you texted pan-pan," Haven said.

"Exactly. See, you *know* all this, Haven!"

"*Please*, Beau," Haven begged. "Just humor me."

"Chandra swore they told you the truth when you got to New York. But I couldn't be sure 'cause they wouldn't let me talk to you, and I didn't want you worrying about me on top of everything else. So one day when we went out to do some grocery shopping, I slipped away and called you from a pay phone. Chandra was *pissed*. She said that Adam might have the phones bugged and that I could have gotten you killed."

"Is that when they beat you up?"

"What? They didn't beat me up. I was *mugged*. Why do you think I had to call you from a pay phone? The day after I got here, I went out for a soda, and two kids in masks jumped me from behind. Took all my money and my phone. Chandra wouldn't let me leave the house without an escort after that. So I just started staying inside. Then Adam found the apartment and sent the cops to raid it, so they hustled me up to the roof and across to another building. I was almost on the verge of walking out the door when they showed me that e-mail you sent." He paused and searched Haven's face for any signs of recognition.

"*Please*. What did the e-mail say?"

"That it was time to go ahead with the plan. You'd found a way to lure Adam down to that vault. But you weren't strong enough to trap him all by yourself. You needed me to wait inside and surprise him."

"How did you know the e-mail was from me?"

"Because the message came from your e-mail address. You're telling me that you didn't write it?"

Haven shook her head.

"Then who did?" Beau asked.

"It must have been Calum Daniels. He stole my phone yesterday."

"Wait. You guys know Calum too?"

"You could say that," Iain said.

"Hmmm," Beau said. The notion that a television star might have been impersonating his best friend didn't seem to shock Beau as much as it should have. "I'm guessing I've been wrong about a lot of stuff. But to tell you the truth, Calum was the only part of this whole thing that felt totally off. The first night I got here, he showed up with a bottle of champagne. Chandra said he was friends with the Horae, even though she didn't seem to like him very much. I guess she couldn't really do anything to keep him away, since it was his apartment and all. By the way, have you seen that place, with the tiger-skin rug and the furniture that looks like it's right out of some old granny's house?"

"Yeah," Haven said.

"Goddamm creepy, ain't it?" he asked with a shudder.

"Oh yeah," Haven agreed.

"Anyway, Calum started putting the moves on me right away. Kept promising he'd introduce me to Alex Harbridge. At first I was a little starstruck, and I kinda found it flattering. But then it just got weird. He didn't want to know anything about me. Didn't even ask where I went to school. I got the sense that he was using me for something, though I still don't understand what it could have been. Finally, I just came out and told the little weasel that he wasn't my type, and that about drove him batshit insane. I've never seen anybody so mad. Not that it worried me. If Chandra hadn't sent him packing, I would have made sure his face wasn't fit for television anymore."

"You may still get your chance," Haven said.

"Really?" Beau asked eagerly.

"As long as you let me get a punch or two in," Iain said. "He's *my* little brother, after all."

"*Excuse me?*" Beau interjected. "Okay, I've had just about enough. Who here is going to explain why Iain's *brother* was so desperate to get into my pants? Or why I just spent twenty-four hours in a bank vault? And what's all this crap about a 'soul mate'?"

"Which question would you like me to answer first?" Haven teased.

"Start with the soul mate!" Leah insisted. "That's the best part."

IT WAS TWO in the morning by the time they reached the Andorra apartments. Across the street from the building, ten lawn chairs were lined up against the rock wall of Central Park. Each was filled with a dark, amorphous blob. Haven saw one of the shapeless creatures move and a glint of light reflected off a camera lens. The chairs, she suddenly realized, held men tucked into all-weather sleeping bags.

"Paparazzi," Haven said. They were staking out the Andorra apartments. "They're looking for us, aren't they? How do you suppose they knew to come *here*?"

"It's probably my fault." Iain sighed. "I told the police I've been staying at the Andorra. Someone must have leaked it to the press."

"Hey, y'all? Is there anywhere else we can go?" Beau asked, massaging his temples. "After everything that's happened, I'm not really in the mood to pose for pictures." He was still trying to absorb the outlandish story they'd told him, and he looked as if his brain might explode at any second.

"I'll run inside," Leah said. "Those guys don't want any photos of *me*."

"You're going inside?" Haven asked.

"Frances will kill us if I don't tell her what's going on! And I figure I can get some money for the cab and a fresh change of clothes for Beau. He smells like a slop bucket. You mind if he borrows some of yours?" she asked Iain.

"Not at all," Iain replied with a lopsided grin. Leah clearly couldn't wait to introduce Owen to Beau.

"I see Leah's still crazier than hell," Beau remarked once the girl had slammed the car door behind her. "Nice to know some things don't change. But I just can't get over the stuff y'all just told me on the ride over here. You really think *Leah Frizzell* is supposed to save everyone in New York City from a plague?"

"I think that's why we're *all* here," Haven said.

"So you've gotten me involved in some sort of cosmic conspiracy?"

"Isn't that what friends are for?" Haven asked.

"Jesus," Beau muttered. "I guess I need to start spending more time on my own."

"I bet you don't feel that way when the night's over," Haven joked.

"You know what? I'm getting pretty tired of you screwing with my head, Haven Moore. In fact I think I'll take this opportunity to spend some time with my thoughts. At least I know *they're* sane." Beau closed his eyes, and Haven pressed her face to Iain's chest, trying to muffle the sound of her giggling.

"I can hear you!" Beau barked.

A few minutes later, Leah slid back into the cab. "Boy, that woman's got a one-track mind," she said. "The first thing Frances asked was if we're all going to die. The second thing she wanted to know was if Haven and Iain are still working things out."

"Technically, that's a two-track mind," Iain said.

"So, I got the clothes. What's our plan now?" Leah wanted to know.

Haven leaned forward and rapped on the Plexiglas barrier that separated the driver from the back seat of his cab. "Gramercy Gardens Hotel," she ordered.

*   *   *

THE HOTEL'S LOBBY was virtually deserted, and Haven breathed a sigh of relief. The clerk at the reception desk nodded at the party of four and returned to surfing the Internet. Now that Adam was gone, it seemed a spell had been broken, and Haven was blissfully anonymous once more.

"Iain?" Virginia Morrow was sitting in one of the lobby's love seats. She glided toward them like a ghost. Still dressed in a white linen dress, she wore neither coat nor stockings.

"You guys go on upstairs. Room 2024." Haven gave Leah and Beau her room key. Without thinking, she stepped in front of Iain as if to protect him.

"May I speak to my son alone, please?" Virginia asked.

The changeling? Haven wanted to say. *The boy you tortured because he couldn't be yours alone?*

"Haven is my family," Iain said, his tone matter-of-fact. "She can hear whatever you have to say."

"Fine. I want you to know that I'm leaving New York," Virginia said. "I'm returning to my villa tomorrow, and I won't be back. I thought we could speak just once before I go. Alone, if possible."

"Haven stays," Iain insisted. Haven took his hand. His grip was too strong; she could feel her bones beginning to crack. She bore the pain without complaint.

Virginia nodded. "You must have many questions to ask me," she said.

"No. Not anymore," Iain told his mother. "I know what you are. I know about you and Phoebe and Calum."

"So Haven told you. You're lucky you found her again," Virginia said. "I know how terrible it is to be alone in the world."

"Alone?" Iain's temper was rising. "You were never alone. What about all your sisters? What about *me*?"

"*Sisters* is just a word we use. The Horae are related in name only. I wanted a child so I could finally have a real family. I dreamed of a child who would look at me with nothing but love. Someone I could devote my life to. You won't remember, of course, but when you were a baby, I smothered you with affection. I wouldn't even allow your father to hire a nanny. I wanted you all to myself. And then—"

"And then I learned how to talk," Iain said.

"Yes. That's when I discovered that you weren't mine at all. You belonged to Haven."

"I could have belonged to you too," Iain said.

"Perhaps. But the disappointment was devastating. Then your father had his affair with Phoebe. She paraded her son in front of me. It was clear from the beginning that this was Calum's first time on earth. I was so jealous. My hideous sister had been given a pure soul."

"And look how Calum turned out," Haven said. "He's not so pure anymore."

"Yes," Virginia replied. "The poor child never had a mother to guide him."

"Neither did I," Iain noted.

"You didn't need me. You had *Haven*. Calum is the one who was left all alone. He's the one who deserves my pity. That's why I've asked him to return to Tuscany with me. There's nothing left for him here. If Calum stays, he'll only end up in jail."

"I still don't understand why you came to New York in the first place, Mother. If you hate Phoebe so much, why on earth would you help her?" Iain asked.

"Because there was no more money. That and scotch were the only two things that seemed to dull my pain. I knew the day would come when I would have to do without both. I was terrified. It had been almost twenty years since I'd seen the world through sober eyes."

"I would have given you anything you'd asked for," Iain said. "I could have found help for you too."

"I didn't want your help," Virginia stated. "It would have made it impossible for me to hate you. I needed that hate. It was the only thing keeping me alive."

A silence settled over the group. Haven prayed for the strength to keep herself from strangling Iain's mother.

"Things have changed now," Virginia said at last. "You're the only one I can turn to. Calum and I must have money if we're to survive."

"Why should I give you more money?" Iain asked. "You'll only spend it on scotch. God only knows what Calum will buy."

"It's been two weeks since my last drink," Virginia said. "I don't expect you to have any faith in me, Iain. I know I can't salvage our relationship, but perhaps I *can* help your brother."

"What about the Horae?" Haven asked. "Don't they want you to stay with them?"

"My sisters and I have elected to go our separate ways. Now that the magos has been imprisoned, we deserve to live our own lives for a while. If the snake goddess chooses to release him, we will reconvene. But Phoebe will never be allowed to lead us again. Vera has taken charge."

"Make sure she keeps an eye on Chandra and Cleo too," Haven said. "They're every bit as bad as Phoebe."

"Possibly," Virginia said. "But don't judge them too quickly. We're *all* capable of terrible things."

"So I've been told," Haven quipped.

"You're referring to our conversation at the villa?" Virginia asked. "Have you stopped to wonder what might have happened if I hadn't warned you about yourself? I did you a favor, Haven. You should *thank* me."

Iain must have sensed an argument brewing. "Haven," he said before she could respond, "why don't you go ahead to the room while I show my mother to the door?"

Haven gritted her teeth and nodded. She headed toward the elevator bank but didn't go upstairs. She watched the pair from around the corner. A half hour later, they were still chatting, but even if they'd talked for the rest of the night, Haven wouldn't have left Iain alone with his mother.

"Engaged in a little espionage?"

Beau and Leah stepped out of an elevator. Haven spun around to shush them, but she couldn't help but smile at the sight of the freshly scrubbed boy with sandy blond hair. Even the fading bruises around his eyes couldn't ruin his looks.

"Cleans up real nice, don't he?" Leah joked.

"You sure I look okay?" Beau asked. "Iain's jeans feel a bit tight on me."

"They look pretty darn good to me," Leah said.

"It might help if you told me where we were going at two o'clock in the morning," Beau said. "Then I'd know if skintight pants were appropriate attire."

"We're going to wake up a friend of ours," Haven said. "Right after Iain says goodbye to his mom."

"So that's his evil old mama?" Beau said, peeking around the corner. "You know, that dress isn't doing her any favors. Most women with a figure like hers would want to show it off a little. If I made her a formfitting Cruella de Vil number, she'd be the hottest villainess this side of Disneyland."

A memory flitted through Haven's mind, leaving behind a wide smile on her face. "Oh boy. Have I got a surprise for you," she told Beau.

"Save it for later. My surprise reflex is dead at the moment. Anyway, looks like Cruella's just hit the road."

Haven saw Iain standing alone in the lobby. It took less than a second to reach the boy and wrap him up in her arms. She didn't need to ask what answer he had given his mother. Whatever his decision had been, Haven knew it had been the right one.

CHAPTER FORTY-NINE

"*This* is where my supposed soul mate resides? I don't know if I could get used to such luxury," Beau joked, but Haven could tell he was nervous. The four of them stood in the grand lobby of the old police headquarters, waiting for the doorman to materialize.

"Yeah, it'd be a real struggle," Leah said, gazing up at the gilded ceiling. "He's got the penthouse too."

"*You've* seen my soul mate's apartment?" Beau asked her.

"Weren't you listening in the back of that cab? I'm the snake goddess—all knowing, all seeing."

"Save your bragging for people who didn't go to kindergarten with you," Beau said. "What's old Earl going to say about all that, anyway? D'your uncle always know he was in the presence of a goddess?"

"He does now. I called him the other night and told him all about it. He didn't stop laughing till I hung up the phone."

"You should have one of your snakes give him a nice little nip the next time he's preaching. That ought to teach him."

Leah's brow furrowed. "I don't control Earl's snakes any more than I control my visions. You know I was just joking, right?"

Beau mussed the girl's hair with his knuckles. "Yeah, Leah. I know you were joking."

"ARE YOU HERE to see someone?" The doorman appeared holding a cup of coffee and a microwaved burrito.

Haven stepped toward the front desk. "I'd like to see Owen Bell. Please tell him Haven Moore is here."

"You leave your watch at home, sweetie? It's almost three o'clock in the morning. You sure Mr. Bell will want visitors?" He clearly wasn't with the Ouroboros Society.

"Why don't we ask him?" Haven said, almost regretting the sudden loss of her VIP status.

"Okay," the doorman agreed reluctantly. "What are your friends' names?"

"I'm going up alone first." She glanced back at Beau. "Business before pleasure."

"If you say so," the doorman said. He rang Owen's apartment. It took forever before anyone answered. "I'm really sorry to bother you, Mr. Bell. I have a Haven Moore here to see you. Mmm-hmm. Will do." The man hung up and pointed toward the elevator. "Go right on up, Miss Moore."

"HAVEN." OWEN WAS in his boxers and a T-shirt. "I've been trying to reach you at your hotel for the past two days. I heard Calum had something to do with your friend's disappearance. Is that why you're here? I *swear* I wasn't involved."

"I know," Haven told him. "I found Beau. He's downstairs right now. He wants to meet you."

Owen looked down at his outfit. "I suppose I should get dressed, then."

"No rush," Haven told him. "I was hoping I could have a word with you first. About the Ouroboros Society."

"What's there to talk about?" said Owen, leading Haven to the seating area in the middle of the large round room. "It's over. Have you read the papers?"

"I know what happened, but I've been a little preoccupied for the last twenty-four hours. How bad is it?"

"It couldn't get any worse. Padma Singh destroyed hundreds of careers. Some of the stuff these people did . . . I can't even imagine. Calum Daniels was one of the worst. Even the *mayor*. Did you know about his little *fetish*?"

Haven shook her head.

"I didn't either. But I guess there were a lot of things that I conveniently overlooked. I feel sick that I ever had anything to do with Adam Rosier. I had to take a shower after I read the *Post* this morning. I suppose he'll get away with it all. But to think that I helped . . ."

"Adam was going to reform the Society," Haven told Owen. "I really believe that he was."

"How can you be so sure?" Owen asked her.

"Because he hired *you*. But you don't need to worry about Adam anymore. He can't cause any harm where he is."

"Where is he?" Owen asked.

"Probably best if you don't know."

"You're right," Owen agreed.

Haven sat back in her chair. "So you said Padma destroyed hundreds of careers. But there must be a thousand members of the Ouroboros Society."

"Twelve hundred if you include the kids at Halcyon Hall."

"Then only a small percentage of the people at the club were corrupt."

"No, we were all corrupt," Owen said. "But only some of us were criminals. Most of us were just like Alex Harbridge, trading points for nose jobs and Oscars votes. Then again, poor Alex doesn't really deserve the embarrassment she's going to suffer."

"What do you mean?'

"It's one of the things the press picked up on in Padma's report. A while back, Alex let her account get low. She went to Padma to beg for help, and Padma decided to humiliate her. For about a year, every time some bigwig's kid had a birthday, Alex was the entertainment. She only got paid about five points per party, but it got her out of debt in the end."

"That doesn't sound *too* bad," Haven said.

"Oh, it gets better. You know how sensitive Alex is about her weight. Well, Padma made her dress in a pig costume and serve cupcakes to the kiddies. I guess the guests never figured out who she was. But Padma kept pictures from the parties in her files."

"Damn," Haven said, trying not to laugh. "That's cruel. But your story proves the point I'm going to make."

"Which is?"

"Cupcake-serving pig wasn't the first job Alex was offered. Padma asked her to deliver drugs to an OS member who was vacationing in France. Alex turned the job down. She didn't tell me what Padma made her do instead. I'd never have guessed if you hadn't just told me. But I suppose Alex chose to be humiliated rather than do something she knew was illegal."

"But still, she hung around with Calum."

"Yeah, but so did we. And just so you know, Calum's gone too. He's going to be taking an extended vacation."

Owen sat back and crossed his arms. "What exactly are you trying to tell me, Haven?"

"I'm trying to say that the Ouroboros Society isn't quite as rotten as everyone thinks. There may be people in the organization who were led astray, but I remember the speech you wrote for Milo. You said

OS members had the 'money, talent, and brainpower to change the course of history.' That's as true as it ever was. With the right leader, they could do a lot of good."

"Who do you have in mind? Wait. Hold on. You're talking about *me*?" Owen asked. The suggestion seemed to scare him. "You know why I can't say yes to that, Haven. I'm not one for the limelight. As much as I'd like to help you, I can't."

"I don't want you to do it for me," Haven said. "I want you to do it for the kids at Halcyon Hall."

"Halcyon Hall?" Owen looked confused. "I thought they were all little robots."

"And who told you that? *Calum*?"

Owen nodded. Haven could see that her message was starting to get through.

"I went up there. Spied on a few classes and talked to some of the kids. I've never been more jealous in my entire life. When Beau and I were in school, everyone knew we were different, and they made life pretty hellish for us. Especially for Beau. You know that old cliché, 'What doesn't kill you makes you stronger'?"

"Sure."

"Well, in Beau's case that's been true. But most people couldn't have survived the first eighteen years of his life. They'd have ended up dead. Or dead on the inside. I can't help but think that's what could happen to the kids Adam recruited. I watched this boy up there who had created one of the most beautiful dresses I've ever seen. None of the other students poked fun at him or called him names or threatened to beat him up. They just appreciated his talent. So think of what Halcyon Hall means to that kid. And think of what it might mean for him to see someone like you at the head of the Ouroboros Society."

"That's a pretty big responsibility, Haven. I never set out to be anyone's role model."

"I know, but consider this: If there's no one around to inspire those kids to use their talents and skills to improve the world, we could all be in for a whole lot of trouble. You said the same thing about Milo, and you were right. He's incredibly dangerous. And there are people waiting for their chance to whisper in his ear. People much worse than Adam. That's why you need to stick around. Someone's got to guide Milo and his classmates down the right path."

"Wow," Owen said. "And you *really* think I'm the one who should take charge of the OS?"

"There's no doubt in my mind, Owen. I think I knew it from the moment I met you. Even Adam said you were incorruptible. Just out of curiosity, how many points do you have in your OS account? Three thousand? Four?"

"Something like that, I guess," Owen said with a shrug.

"And how many have you spent?"

"God, Haven, I wasn't expecting such a hard sell. Can I have some time to think about all this? Maybe when I'm wearing pants?"

"Sure," Haven agreed. "Why don't you go ahead and get dressed? I'll go downstairs and send Beau up."

"HE'S GOING TO think about it," Haven told the others who had been waiting downstairs. "He's still a little wary of all the attention. But I think I know someone who can convince him to go public. You ready, Beau?"

"I guess so," the boy said.

"Then go on up to the top floor."

"By myself?" Beau asked.

"Why can't we go too?" Leah complained. "I've been looking forward to this all night!"

"Because Beau's going to look back on this day, and when he does, he's going to be glad none of us were watching from the sidelines."

"She's right," Iain said. "No offense, but I'm glad neither of you were around when Haven found me."

"Are you sure about this?" Beau asked. "I can't take another disappointment just now."

"You're not going to be disappointed," Haven told him. "I promise."

CHAPTER FIFTY

An e-mail had gone out to all of the members of the Ouroboros Society. Not just the famous and distinguished. The workers and the gray men too. A meeting had been set for nine in the morning on March tenth. Attendance was not mandatory.

"Do you think anyone will come?" Haven asked Iain as they strolled up Irving Place hand in hand. Even Leah wasn't going to be there. She had stayed in New York to make sure her visions were over. But she was done with the Ouroboros Society, she'd told Haven that morning. She was going to the Bronx Zoo instead.

"I don't know," Iain said. "A lot of these people have had a pretty tough time. Let's just hope *Owen* shows up. Did you talk to Beau?"

"I called him, but he wasn't all that interested in chatting. I can't even imagine what kind of sordid things have been going on in that penthouse."

"Yes, you can," Iain said with a laugh.

"Yeah, I guess I can. But it's been a *week*! You'd think they'd have gotten sick of each other by now."

"You're just jealous because you have to share your best friend with someone else. No wonder you've been in a funk."

Haven narrowed her eyes at him. Beau's absence wasn't the only reason she hadn't been herself. Something else was gnawing at her.

"You know I'm right," Iain said. "You also know that Owen needed this week to get ready."

"Well, let's just hope he knows what to say today," Haven grumbled, though there was no doubt in her mind that he would.

They turned on to Gramercy Park South. Haven checked the time on her phone. It was only eight fifty-five, but the sidewalk outside the Ouroboros Society headquarters was packed. The doors to the building appeared to be locked, and the mob was growing restless. As Haven and Iain approached, a woman at the edge of the crowd pointed in their direction.

"It's *him*," she shouted, and hundreds of heads swiveled at once.

Iain and Haven both froze and checked over their shoulders. It was clear the woman was talking about Iain.

"This is all your fault," the woman snarled. "You've destroyed the Society. You and Padma Singh sold us out to the press. Now everyone thinks we're all drug dealers and prostitutes. I write *children's* books. I'll be the first to admit that I've gotten a lot of help from the Society, but I've never sold my body to *anyone*."

"She's right," a man added angrily. "My ex-wife's been raking me over the coals for a week. She's convinced that everyone at the OS is a pervert. She told my kids not to talk to me."

The crowd was marching forward toward Haven and Iain, refusing to let them defend themselves. An image suddenly flashed through Haven's mind. The painting Iain had hidden away in their closet back in Rome. The one Marta Vega had sent as a housewarming present. It had shown an angry mob converging on Haven and Iain. Was this the way their story was meant to end?

"STOP!" THE FAMILIAR voice was so forceful, Haven was certain Owen had brought a bullhorn. But his hands were empty. With all eyes on him, Owen gave Beau's arm a quick squeeze, then pushed his way through the mob to the steps of the Ouroboros Society. Seeing Owen face his fellow Society members, Haven suddenly knew. Marta Vega's painting hadn't foretold a future disaster. It had predicted a triumph.

"I'm Owen Bell," the young man announced. "I'm the one who suggested we meet here today."

"We know who you are!" someone shouted. "Are you going to open the doors or what?"

"No," Owen replied, and the crowd began to buzz once more. "Too much at the Society has taken place behind closed doors. From this point forward, all our business will be conducted in the open."

"Where's Adam?" another person shouted.

"Adam Rosier is gone. I am assuming temporary command of the Ouroboros Society until an election can be scheduled. In the meantime, I intend to make a few changes. Anyone who disagrees with these changes is welcome to resign from the OS or run against me in the first election."

"What sort of changes are you talking about?" The latest voice was less angry than curious.

"First, any member who is convicted of a felony will have his or her membership revoked immediately. Second, our membership rolls will be made public. And last of all, the Society's points system will be completely abolished. As of this moment, all debts have been expunged."

The crowd reacted with stunned silence.

"But the points system encourages us to help each other," a man finally said. "Don't good deeds deserve a reward?"

"There is a reward. Some people call it *karma*," Owen said. "And in addition, you'll have the satisfaction of belonging to an organization that's devoted to changing the world for the better. That's what our founder, August Strickland, intended the Ouroboros Society to be—a powerful force for good. It might take years to put this scandal completely behind us, but I believe we have the resources to start improving the Society's image and the lives of our members this very day.

"In fact, the two people you were about to string up a few minutes ago have been the first to take action. Iain Morrow and Haven Moore just donated fifty million dollars to Halcyon Hall. Without their generosity, the school would have been forced to close by the end of the month. Neither one of them has received a single point in return."

While Iain watched Owen save the day, Beau threw a muscular arm around Haven's shoulders. "*Damn*, I have great taste in men," he said.

Owen had started taking questions from the crowd. He had an answer for everything—and it was always the right one. No one would have guessed for a moment that he was a reluctant leader.

"Yeah," Haven replied. "Hot and righteous. The very best combination."

"Thank you," Beau said. He stopped her before she could make another joke. "No. Seriously. Thank you for this, Haven."

"It's the least I could do," she told him.

"Hell, I'd have spent a month in that vault if I'd known this would be waiting for me. Consider us more than even."

"That's not what I'm saying. My whole life you've been there for me. I wish I had done more to deserve it. Maybe now I'm getting close."

Beau's face twisted with confusion. "You wish you had deserved it? Are we thinking about the same life? You remember that time you fixed my Barbie lunch box after I got into that fight with those kids in fourth grade? Or the time you punched Dewey Jones in the head 'cause he asked me if I was wearing a bra? Or how about when you boycotted Mr. Goodman's class after he said homosexuality was a psychological disorder?"

"Yeah, but there were other times—"

"Other times? So goddamm what? I got news for you, Haven: You've never been perfect, and I'm the last person who'd expect you to be. But all I had to do was send you a text that said 'pan-pan,' and you were on a plane to New York in a heartbeat. Could you ask any more of a person?"

"I didn't get on a plane right away. I stayed in Florence to try to see more of our past life together. I was hoping to find a clue that would lead me to the person who took you. By the way, I know a few things about that life that I should probably tell you."

"Oh hell, here we go," Beau muttered.

"Listen, Beau. You need to know that I was the one who got you and Naddo killed back in Florence. I didn't keep your secret. I told Adam you were gay. I may have told other people too. I don't know who killed you, but I do know it was my fault."

"No, it wasn't," Beau said. "It was that little bitch whose mother worked in our house."

"*What*?"

"That night in the vault, I had a nightmare. At least that's what I thought until I mentioned it to Owen, and he told me it must have been a memory. In the dream Naddo and I were in a stable, getting ready to leave town when a bunch of men showed up. They caught us kissing, and, well, things got ugly from there. But I remember seeing that little blonde-haired demon who was always snooping around our house. She was the one who'd led them to us."

"Oh my God, it was *Phoebe*! She tricked me into betraying Adam back then too!" Suddenly Haven could see everything clearly. "I've been wondering how Phoebe knew exactly what vision she wanted me to have. The only reason she was able to take me back to just the right moment was because she was *there*. Phoebe must have been the one who suggested Beatrice go to Adam's house the day her parents were fleeing the city. She arranged for Beatrice to get there just as the bodies were being delivered!"

"That blonde kid was Phoebe? Jesus. She gets around, doesn't she? So you see, you've been going around feeling guilty for nothing."

No. Not for nothing, Haven thought.

"Haven?" It was Alex Harbridge.

Beau glanced over at the young woman who'd just joined them and did a double take. "Holy shit," he mumbled under his breath.

"Alex," Haven said, "this is my friend Beau. He's your biggest fan."

"Beau Decker?" Alex grinned. "*The* Beau Decker? The one Owen Bell won't shut up about?" She gave Beau a once-over. "Well, now I know why. I'd let a big, juicy Southern boy like you drag *me* out of the deepest, darkest closet on earth."

Beau looked over at Haven. "Did Alex Harbridge just call me a big, juicy Southern boy? This is the single greatest day of my life."

"It's about to get even better," Haven said. "Alex, this is the person who designed the dress you wore to the Oscars."

"What?" Beau yelped.

Haven rolled her eyes. "Were you and Owen so *busy* that you didn't bother to turn on the TV? Alex asked me to make her a dress. I used your design. All I did was sew it together."

"The slinky green one?" Beau asked. "The one I made for Barbie? Alex Harbridge wore that to the *Oscars*?"

"Yep," Haven confirmed. "People said it was the best gown of the whole evening."

"You know, that dress might be the only thing that gets me past this whole cupcake scandal," Alex said. "The tabloids have been running the pictures side by side. The 'before' photo may be horrible, but the 'after' couldn't be better."

"What's this about a cupcake scandal?" Beau asked.

"Damn, Beau, you've even stopped following celebrity gossip? What exactly has Owen Bell done to you?"

Alex laughed. "Well, I was going to ask Haven, but since you're the real genius here, you want to make me a few more dresses?"

Beau was speechless.

Haven poked him in the side. "Say yes, you doofus."

"What about school?" Beau asked.

"Are you in such a hurry to go back? Last I heard you were failing out."

"Aw, Jesus. You heard about that?" Beau groaned.

Haven rolled over and kissed the boy sleeping beside her. Their farewell party had lasted late into the night, and Frances Whitman's guests were only now beginning to rise. Haven had heard Leah's door creak and soft footsteps padding down the hall. She slid out from between the blankets, careful not to wake Iain, and followed Leah into the kitchen.

She found Frances dressed in flannel pajamas pouring coffee for the girl, who was wearing a fancy silk and lace nightie.

"Oooh. *Sexy.* Where'd you get *that*?" Haven laughed.

"It was a present from one of my husbands," Frances explained. "To another woman. He had the store send it here by accident. I've been keeping it as a souvenir, but I think I'll let Leah take it home with her."

"When's your flight?" Haven asked Leah.

"Noon," Leah answered. "When's yours again?"

"Not till nine this evening."

"I can't believe everyone's leaving me," Frances moaned.

"Beau and Owen are staying in New York," Haven said.

"But they're both going to be so busy," Frances said. "I'll have to commission a dress next time I want to see Beau."

"Well, you're always welcome to come and visit Iain and me in Rome."

"Or stop by Duke," Leah said. "You know, it'd probably do you a world of good to get out of this apartment and go a few places."

"Why? Do you know something?" Frances demanded. "Have you seen a big, strapping North Carolina man in my future?"

"I don't know if he's from North Carolina," Leah said, chomping on a pastry. "But he ain't the cable guy, and that's the only man you're going to meet sitting here."

"What?" Frances squealed. "Are you teasing me? Is there really a man somewhere waiting for me?"

"Maybe, maybe not," said Leah.

"Oh, come on!" Frances pleaded. "Can't you be more specific? You told that woman in Harlem she'd make a fortune off that neon sign. And she didn't even give you a gorgeous silk nightie!"

"Ramona?" Leah asked. "That was just a onetime deal. Didn't have anything to do with seeing the future. I just figured an old sign that said SIN WILL FIND YOU OUT might be worth a buck or two. And to think they were going to tear it down along with the rest of the block."

"Haven!" Frances begged. "Make her tell me!"

"You guys are going to have to settle this on your own," Haven said. "I have to go get dressed. There's an errand I gotta run this morning. Leah, give me a hug. I'll see you when school's out."

The two girls embraced.

"Be careful today," Leah whispered in Haven's ear.

"Don't worry," Haven told her.

* * *

IAIN WOKE AS Haven was wriggling into her jeans.

"Still going?" he asked.

"Yep," Haven told him.

"Wear your new snow boots."

"Planning to."

"And give me a kiss."

Haven crawled across the bed toward the beautiful boy with a sheet wrapped around his waist. She didn't need Leah's gift to know that her future belonged to him. At least for one lifetime, she had all she desired.

THE GUARD AT Green-Wood Cemetery recognized Haven and came out of the booth tucked inside the gatehouse.

"You know where you're going this time?" he asked.

"I do," Haven said.

"The paths are clear today," he said. "You shouldn't get lost again. But if you aren't back in an hour or so, I'm gonna come looking for you. Deal?"

"Deal," Haven agreed. "I appreciate it."

The snow was thawing in the bright sunlight. Her body grew warm as she walked, and Haven stopped to take off her coat. There was still a chill, but the air was beginning to smell like spring. When she reached the little lake, she walked along its shore. The trees that circled the water were filled with birds—cardinals and blue jays and countless tiny feathered creatures that Haven couldn't identify. She paused to listen to them sing before she continued toward her destination.

Haven had come to say goodbye to Adam. She'd spent a whole week hashing over the decision. It made no sense to anyone, but it felt right to Haven. If Adam had sacrificed his freedom to save her, it was the very least she could do.

The entrance to the mausoleum gleamed in the sunlight. The two hooded figures on either side of the door still hid their faces in the shadows. Haven peeked under the woman's hood and saw her own face looking back at her. A shiver shook her body, but the sun on her back soothed her nerves. She took out the golden key that Adam had told her to give to the snake goddess. It would be FedExed to Duke as soon as Haven returned from the cemetery. The door was heavy. It took all her strength to push it open.

"Adam?" she called into the darkness.

There wasn't an answer. The tomb was empty.